A FAE DESTINY

A KINGDOM OF WITCHES AND WANDERERS

LESLIE O'SULLIVAN

A KINGDOM OF WITCHES AND WANDERERS
Fae Destiny, Book 3

CITY OWL PRESS
www.cityowlpress.com

Cover Design by MiblArt. All stock photos licensed appropriately.

Page Edges by Painted Wings Publishing Services.

Edited by Lisa Green.

For information on subsidiary rights, please contact the publisher at info@cityowlpress.com.

Paperback Edition ISBN: 978-1-64898-522-5

Hardback Edition ISBN: 978-1-64898-523-2

Digital Edition ISBN: 978-1-64898-521-8

Printed in the United States of America

ALSO BY LESLIE O'SULLIVAN

Fae Destiny:

A Kingdom of Souls and Shadows

A Kingdom of Deceit and Desire

A Kingdom of Witches and Wanderers

***

Rockin Fairy Tales:

Pink Guitars and Falling Stars

Gilded Butterfly

Wild Azure Waves

Crimson Melodies

Emerald Spire

***

Behind the Scenes:

Hot Set

Press Release

Not to Scale

PRAISE FOR LESLIE O'SULLIVAN

"O'Sullivan wraps up her *Fae Destiny* series with this spellbinding standalone romantasy... With inventive magic, emotional stakes, and some high-heat love scenes, this sends the series out on a high note." — *Publisher's Weekly*

"Romantic and magical, O'Sullivan whisks you away to an Ireland you could only dream of... Except it could very well be real." — *Evelyn Skye, New York Times Bestselling author of Damsel*

"O'Sullivan's writing is rich with metaphors. The story from reality to the secret Veil is so seamless, you believe it's truly possible. *A Kingdom of Souls and Shadows* is full of charming characters, intriguing Celtic folklore, and a delicious slow-burn romance. A perfect introduction to the romantasy genre." — *Dana Elmendorf, author of In the Hour of Crows, a GMA Buzz Pick*

"Full of surprises, lots of surprises, and secrets, lots of secrets that left me speechless. Everything Eala learns makes her question her life and who she really is. The book ends with a question which I can't wait to be answered in the next book in the series. I highly recommend. 5 Stars."— *Paranormal Romance Guild*

"*A Kingdom of Souls and Shadows* was a great read. I loved Eala and Sion both as individual characters and as a couple. They both felt very real and relatable (yes, the 200-year-old man felt relatable to a modern woman). O'Sullivan takes Irish folklore and moves it forward into the next century in a fun and exciting way." — *Cosmic Circus*

"*Pink Guitars and Falling Stars* is an interesting take on the story of Rapunzel... O'Sullivan has definitely nailed the initial animosity between Justin and Zeli. As they become closer, the relationship jumps off the page and morphs beautifully. There are awesome love scenes with a lot of description which pull the reader right in and keep a tight grip... A fascinating remix of a popular fairy tale with some very sexy differences. One to add to the e-reader and to be read list!" — *InD'tale*

"*Hot Set*, by Leslie O'Sullivan, is a contemporary love story that creatively infuses modern concerns with the nostalgia generated by a period television show. The Irish setting was fantastically romantic, and I thought the cast of characters was refreshingly practical for a group involved in show business." — *Reader's Favorite 5-star review*

"*Pink Guitars and Falling Stars* is a fast paced and very engaging read, with a constantly evolving main character and a colorful cast. The adventure wraps up nicely, and ends with a hint of what is next in the Rockin' Fairy Tales series. This is a great read if you are looking for an action-packed modern fairy tale with aspiring rock stars who fall from the sky." — *Paranormal Romance Guild*

"*Gilded Butterfly* is a unique and magical mashup of fairy tales, Shakespeare, and lore, unlike anything I've read before. At its heart, is a beautiful story about family, the destructive power of chasing fame and money, and the healing power of love. The twists, turns, and magic sprinkled throughout create an engaging story that brings a new kind of fairy tale to modern Hollywood." — *Megan Van Dyke, author of Second Star to the Left*

"Submerging readers into a fantastical world, *Wild Azure Waves* is a love story swimming with music, mysticism, and magic... Villains deliver with evil schemes and diabolical characteristics that readers will hear their sinister chuckle every time they are on the page. Leslie O'Sullivan's whimsical fantasy tale is an interesting take on sorrow, second chances, and soulmates." — *InD'tale*

"With wickedly clever wordplay, fresh and lovable characters, and an utterly unique take on a classic fairytale, *Pink Guitars and Falling Stars* is one of the swooniest romances I've ever read. You'll be cheering for B.A.S.E. jumper Justin to help Zeli escape her tower in the heart of Hollywood's twisted music industry and fall equally hard for their chosen family on the Boulevard. A romantic, heart-in-your-throat read!" — *Sarah Skilton, author of Fame Adjacent*

For Lisa, Sarah, and Julie who've been there since the beginning.

To Ireland, the land of beauty, magic, and stories, that made the people who made me.

To Felicity and Tim who made this series come alive.

CHAPTER 1

THE THREE NOTES OF A SOULSONG

EALA

Inside the Veil, Sionnach's cries of despair surround me like the decaying notes of a lament. I cling to the music of his voice as it deteriorates into a faraway echo…until it's gone.

The Veil is silent, no soothing notes of violin or gentle chime of bells.

I'm alone.

The poetic notion of a heart hardening to stone feels frighteningly real as I claw at my chest.

Sionnach, my soulmate, my *anamchara*, my fox, the deepest love I've ever known has been ripped away. The very situation we fought with our hearts, bodies, and souls to prevent is now a reality—and it's my fault.

If I'm entitled to breathe, I *must breathe.*

The Veil wavers, then pauses in an uncharacteristic stasis around me. Its scent of lemongrass and spearmint is faint. It waits for my intention to define the place I wish to be whisked off to. My spirit bleeds to be at Sionnach's side, but the Veil doesn't move.

Finnbheara, the very real King of the Connacht Fae lived up to his cruel and callous reputation. Only moments ago, he attempted to expel Máthair, my beloved grandmother, out of Tír na nÓg and into what he named the merciless void of consequence. Naïve me. I thought she'd already been gifted an eternal home in the Faerie kingdom. I was wrong.

Per our bargain, I earned the right for two people to live forever among the Faeries by solving Finnbheara's impossible riddle. My spontaneous choice to leave Tír na nÓg, granted those slots to Sionnach and Máthair. In the heat of the moment, I convinced myself my ties to the king afforded me the best shot at finding a way back into the Fae realm.

On this side of that impulsive rationale, the decision feels as absurd as my never-changing wish on birthday candles that my mysterious birth parents would suddenly appear. I swore the Faeries stole me away from them. Of course, I blamed Faeries for my abandonment after listening to a lifetime of my grandmother's Irish folktales.

I puff a bitter gust from my lips. I'd been right all along. Faeries, Finnbheara in particular, have always been the source of my troubles. Thanks to the Fae king and his magical *beads of being*, my origin story is reduced to a Faerie science experiment.

I shake off the self-deprecating definition. My soulmate's love proves I am a real person.

Here in the motionless Veil, the people I love most are literally a world away.

"Sion-nach…Sion-nach…Sion-nach," I whimper, thumping a fist to my breast with each heartbeat. A wave of unbearable pain hits. Both my Fae and human essences dwindle into an inky pool of regret and defeat. My Veil sprites, the luminous beings coursing through my Faerie spirit, are drowned from any attempt at overcoming the darkness. My muscles groan and bones quiver, threatening to transform into powder.

How can I survive this loss?

I'm a being devoid of form or spirit, but one made of agony alone. Where have I gone? Where is Sionnach's Eala *bán*, the white swan who banished the shadow from the land?

Now, I'm the shadow.

For two hundred years, Sion didn't give up on the soulfall. In two hundred heartbeats, I'm on the verge of defeat.

I failed him by leaving him behind. He would never let our separation stand if the reverse were true. He'd fight his way back to me.

I owe him my strength.

I push through the pain. Sion's Eala *bán* would not accept this as the end of our story. I must find her. I must be her.

"I'm coming for you, Sionnach." I close my eyes and will my swan wings to unfurl.

Beat.

Beat.

Beat.

With each stroke, my swan's confident spirit surges through me as I change from flesh to feather. We rise above the greedy darkness grasping for my soul. The Veil sprites rekindle and incandesce within me. I command the Veil to take us back to Tír na nÓg.

A silent breeze propels me through this mystical passage. My wingtips sketch ripples through the prismatic walls surrounding me. Up ahead, a circle of blazing brilliance marks the entrance to Finnbheara's front door. I'll demand to be admitted back into the Faerie kingdom and refute his hot-headed, royal edict of banishment.

I pray my abrupt exit shocked the king enough that he will accept he acted like an unfair bastard. Impulsive choices do not have to be endings.

My wingbeats falter from the weight of what I must overcome. Sion, Máthair, and I aren't the only victims of the Fae catastrophe. My lifelong friend, my sister of the heart, Colleen, has also been swept into this morass. To strike at me, Robber Bright, Fae thief and villain, enchanted Colleen and stole her away into the Oweynagat hellmouth. I shudder at the thought of her in Aodh's underworld kingdom, a hellscape so often painted with flaming pits and agonized wails of the dead.

Colleen is in danger and needs my help as much as my soulmate and my grandmother.

A fresh wave of panic wrecks the rhythm of my flight. I rebound off the shimmery Veil wall. Pausing in midair, I right my swan body and gather my thoughts.

As mercurial as Finnbheara is, I'm hoping I still have some value as *Finnbheara's Treasure,* the fraught and oppressive title he foisted on me. Even though admitting it sours my stomach, the king and I are irrevocably connected. I am one of his Connacht Fae. I've balked at fully accepting that truth too many times because my human life is precious to me. But going full Fae may be my last hope to rejoin my soulmate.

With a mighty stroke of my wings, I'm off again toward the gleaming circle. As I close in on my target, the burning white light intensifies. Its edges pulse with a golden corona made of dozens of fiery whips tipped in emerald barbs. They stretch then recoil with sizzling snaps.

My retinas throb. It's as if the sun itself leapt inside the Veil to block my way into Tír na nÓg.

"Finnbheara," I scream at the blaze. "Let me in."

The sparking tendrils shoot out to wrap around my wings in hot, thorny vines. They squeeze, mashing my feathers, threatening to snap my hollow bones beneath. Unaware of how damage to my swan translates to my human body, I transform. If I can't protect myself, how can I save the people I love? Fierce Faerie whips snake around my arms, torso, and waist. The cursed bindings threaten to singe whatever skin they touch.

With a teeth-cracking jolt, I'm yanked toward the inferno. Is Finnbheara dragging me back into Tír na nÓg or killing me? Raging heat burns my throat and lungs. Suddenly, like a boulder flung from a catapult, my body rockets away from the scorching light until I crash onto the Veil's forgiving floor. My arms are covered in thin, stinging, bright green welts. An electric shock crackles through my body then dissipates.

Is this yet another of Finnbheara's tests? Do I need to prove I will not be deterred from smashing my fist against the gates of Tír na nÓg? I stumble to my feet and run in the direction of the villainous light.

Before I've gone more than a few steps, the roiling blaze implodes with a deafening roar, knocking me backward and leaving only the wall of the Veil behind.

"Finnbheara, I'm coming in," I shout, pressing forward again. My hands reach for a door, a gate, an opening in the portal that isn't there.

My mind screams. *Take me to Tír na nÓg.*

The Veil walls shudder then still.

I repeat the command aloud. "Take me to Tír na nÓg."

Breaking the Veil's silence, three melancholy notes of a violin repeat over and over without ceasing. Is the Veil singing to me?

A more crushing thought takes hold. I lay both hands over my heart.

"Sion, is that you?"

Is my soulmate singing his soulsong to me as a farewell? There are three notes in a soulsong, the melody a soul plays in the Glade of Chimes to open the path to their chosen eternity.

"No, Sionnach. No." Tears finally destroy the barrier of my strength and fall in a ceaseless trail. They drip onto the Veil floor then rise as spectral haze. As each misty teardrop touches the silky elegance of the Veil wall, the bead solidifies, changing into a crystal that floats around me. Every gem shines with the multitude of hues born inside a rainbow.

As I weep, supplying more chromatic droplets, the Veil transforms around me into a shimmering chamber. It gathers my tears, reflecting them to me with a vibrancy that validates my sorrow.

These are worthy tears.

The Veil is home. We are kindred spirits.

Home.

The Veil may be my ethereal home, but Sion is my true home.

A swirling transparent circle appears in the Veil's wall. Beyond it, I see the Loho cottage with its whitewashed walls, thatched roof, red trimmed windows, and a door to match.

Home.

I burst out of the magic portal and run to the door. When my heart cried out for Sion and home, the Veil brought me here. This is where I belong.

Where we belong.

I pound on the red-painted wood. "Sionnach."

There's no answer. With a shaky hand, I retrieve the key hidden among flowers in the window box and let myself in.

I face an empty room. A minute ago, I belonged in the kingdom of Tír na nÓg. A minute ago, I had a *péist síoda*, a silk dragon. A minute ago, my soulmate was by my side for eternity.

What do I have now?

Sunlight bullies its way past swatches of gray clouds to shine through the rain-spotted windows of the cottage. The path of golden light encourages me to leave the refuge of the doorway and take a tentative step inside. Entering the home Sion and I shared ever so briefly without him feels like a betrayal.

The fragrance of the lady's bedstraw that fills the mattress of the king-sized bed in a nook off to the right makes my breath hitch. I stare at the place Sion and I made love first as soulmates then as husband and wife.

I see him in the two empty whiskey glasses we toasted our marriage with, in the stack of books next to his desk, in the landline phone on the kitchen counter he used to keep in the cupboard.

He's everywhere and nowhere.

It feels as if I've been away from the cottage for months. I expect a layer of dust to cover the simple wooden table then shake my head. It's only been one night…possibly. I need to see the phase of the moon to tell how much time has passed in the mortal world while we were in Tír na nÓg.

The passage of time used to be a steady barometer in my life. Not anymore. How much time will drip away before I see my beloved *anamchara* again? Will Finnbheara delight in robbing us of days or years this time?

Struggling to pluck a coherent thought from the chaos in my mind, I breathe in and close my eyes, calling on my Fae essence to awaken. It's healed Sion and me before. I hope it'll reset me now.

The sparkling energy flows through me, lightening my heart and clearing my head. I allow it to bathe my emotional bruises as well as heal the emerald stings on my skin from Finnbheara's strike. After a few more peaceful moments, I open my eyes and refocus on a single thought.

Get Sion out of Tír na nÓg.

Almost as soon as the thought becomes my beacon, rings of doubt hover around it. How in the deepest hell am I going to do that alone? I tried to return to Tír na nÓg, and Finnbheara attacked me then locked his gates. The Veil can't take me there. If I'm blocked from getting to Sion, how can I free him?

And Máthair?

"Oh, shit, Colleen."

The enormity of it all dizzies me again. I take wobbly steps to a chair at the kitchen table. Right where Sion and I left them are the scribbled notes we used to solve Finnbheara's narcissistic riddle. The one falsely promising to grant us an eternity together.

Atop the table, in the center of a splash of sunlight, glowing like the grin of an evil cat, is a gold ring.

Robber Bright's ring.

A key to unlock one pathway back to the Fae.

CHAPTER 2
THE FURY

SIONNACH

The king is a statue of glass engulfed in a wreath of flames. Inside his transparent form, one color flashes then gives way to another and another, cycling through a hundred shades faster than his ever-changing eyes. This spectacle of his rage doesn't burn or melt. The Fae menace is no phoenix who will turn to ash and regenerate into an improved version of himself. He's a devil as sure as I'm standing here, clinging to my ma like a child at her skirts.

Ma breathes in my ear, "Patience."

I answer through gritted teeth. "Patience, Ma? Over what? That I'm not going to be the next one consumed in his hellfire?"

My gaze locks on hers, and again I'm knocked sideways by her ageless appearance and storybook getup, pearls woven into her hair. If there were a crown upon her brow, I'd believe her to be the queen of the Faeries. This version of Martha Loho has barely left girlhood behind. Disgust seizes me, and my lips twist into a snarl. This must be the way she was when Finnbheara first caught her in his despicable net.

"He's gone into private torment," says Ma. "It's a rare thing for him to show himself in such a state in front of others." She nods at the Fae soldiers, proving her point.

A storm cloud of suspicion rolls through me. "But you've seen him do it?"

Ma sets her jaw, staring me down. "I have."

Her unapologetic look raises bile in my throat. It implies intimacy between my mother and the king. I raise a hand, signaling her not to go on.

"Trust me, Sionnach, *a stor*." She gently strokes my hair. "Patience is your best weapon at present."

My shoulders wilt like a vase of flowers left too long without water. Patience has never been my most plentiful commodity. What will patience grant me? Finnbheara not ending me? Facing an eternity without Eala?

I love my mother, but we've had two hundred years to accept our inevitable parting. Ma being forced from Tír na nÓg to face what lay beyond the gates was not a cruelty any of us suspected, but she would go willingly to sacrifice her life for my future, for Eala's.

Eala making such a sacrifice shreds the skin from my bones. If not for Ma's hold on my arm with its soothing touch, I might be tempted to join Finnbheara's flames and burn away the anguish in my breast over Eala's selfless madness.

I pull away from Ma, ducking my face in my hands as the last agonizing moments batter my mind. After Eala threw herself out of the gleaming gates, I gripped those bars tight enough to bend, trying to wrench them open and follow her. One of the soldiers clamped a hand on the back of my neck. His fingers wrapped around my throat, nearly choking the life from me, before the man peeled me off the gate and flung me to the ground at Ma's feet.

Moments later, the gates rattled with such a racket they about struck me deaf. Finnbheara doubled in size, his preferred power play, and charged toward them. With a forward thrust of his arms, he conjured dozens of golden serpents, each with multi-faceted emerald eyes. The gleaming streaks of searing gold and green light soared over the swooping top of the gate to plunge into the swirling cyclone of an agitated Veil.

There's no doubt in my heart or mind Eala was at the center of that maelstrom, trying to return to me. Her essence reached for mine as if to seize me clean off Finn's doorstep. She was beaten away by those slithering manifestations of the king's wrath until every sense of my *anamchara* faded.

Once the Veil left us, Finnbheara lost his fecking Faerie mind, shifting between giant and man. He stomped across the ground before the gates, raising a dozen steaming whirlwinds that ripped up his green and silver grass along with the sod beneath. Ma, the soldiers, and I covered our faces as best we could to keep from being pelted with his tantrum's debris. He cursed in a language bearing the sound of ancient Irish. I could only make out the names of Eala, Aodh, and Robálaí Geal in his rants.

Ma understood him plainly enough. She marched straight up to the king. When her approach prompted him to settle into a reasonable size, my mother struck Finnbheara across the face.

The king grasped both her wrists, yanking her close so their faces were inches apart. They both wore expressions of such ferocity, I didn't know which of the two chilled my bones more. Fae soldiers surrounded her with unnatural speed.

Finnbheara jerked his head to the side, and his Folk faded back into line.

My ma showed her teeth to the king. "You've done unspeakable harm. A thousand curses are too good for ya."

The bite in her words rattled ole Finn, and he dropped her hands. She squared her shoulders and looked as if she was set to take another run at him when he backed away, waving his hand up the length of his body to turn himself into the tower of glass and flame now blazing before us.

Ma eases my hands away from my face and speaks to me in a low, soothing voice. "It's a mercy the king's wrapped himself up for a bit." She takes my chin in her hand, examining my face. "And what of you, *Mac*? Are you able to stand tall and keep faith with Eala no matter what Finnbheara throws at you?"

"Faith, is it?" I step away from her and the fiery king. "Faith in what? Faith your king won't end me? Faith I can survive in this place where I've no say in my future or a single drop of power?" I fling an arm toward the royal pyre. "Faith Eala has any chance against that flaming bastard?"

The next thought raises a fever in me. What if Finn's onslaught of golden serpents harmed Eala? She's alone somewhere when I should be at her side.

I'm captive in my own glass case of deep-seated fear. The fight drains from me like water from a bucket with a hole in the bottom. "Ma, without the protection of Tír na nÓg, what dangers wait for Eala? Aodh? Or some new devilry breaching the Veil from more of Finnbheara's enemies?"

As soon as the question leaves my lips, Finn bursts into a conflagration.

Sparks shoot high out of sight. The transformation melts his glass casing into swirling, liquid diamonds that disappear into the grass.

He roars, and hot wind stings my face. "It is you as you have always been, spawn of Loho, not I, who is the cause of any danger Eala Duir faces."

This Fae fucker has no right. "King or not, you, Finnbheara, are a venomous, power-drunk donkey's ass." I raise both fists, undecided if they'll be needed to ward off a blow or deliver one. I'm a man who's been stripped of everything that matters in the world. Feeling the crack of a royal cheekbone beneath my knuckles would count as a satisfying final act.

The king's Faerie elegance contorts into a countenance terrible to behold. His changeable eyes snap to full black, not a speck of white to be seen. The sword that appears in his hand makes it clear I don't have a fool's chance to win this fight. As much as I'd enjoy having a go at his perfect nose, I choose to surrender and drop to my knees before him.

Staring at the ground, I muffle my words, hoping to look weak and not worth killing. "I can fight you no more. You've been waiting two hundred years to be rid of me. Swing your sword and be done with it, but don't leave Eala out there alone."

I squeeze my eyes and pray there's no blow heading my way. When I can't stand the wait anymore, I raise my head to take the slice looking.

There is indeed a sword poised for a good chop, but the anger on Finnbheara's face has been replaced with a flicker of pain as deep as my own. His gaze is unfocused. The color of his eyes flares with the white-hot flame of a star then slowly fades into the deep hue of a purple iris. His voice is as quiet as faraway birdsong carried on a breeze.

"Eala out there alone," he repeats my words into the ever-present Faerie mist.

Ma tugs at my collar, encouraging me to stand. The king stabs his sword into the grass, and she eases us away.

Well, if that wasn't the mother of all Faerie mood swings.

Finnbheara's eyes flash again, turning as reddish-brown as a drop of dried blood. "I do not abandon those dear to me. If they are gone, it is by their choice."

His mood keeps swinging like a pendulum, and he's on me again, lifting me by the front of my shirt. The ground falls farther and farther beneath me as his figure grows to godlike proportions.

"It's not his doing, Finnbheara," Máthair says, reaching for the king.

He flicks his gaze to her and then to me. "There's mercy in your mother's eyes you do not deserve, spawn of Loho. You stole Eala, my treasure, and are the cause of Aodh and his agents blighting my Veil and threatening war. You do not deserve a soulsong or the peace of my kingdom."

Finnbheara's huffing breath wraps us in a thick fog. The haze hides Ma, the gates of Tír na nÓg, and the soldiers. In a move worthy of a supreme eejit, I grab a fistful of Finnbheara's tunic. Its metallic fabric crackles beneath my fingers.

"Then why aren't you taking the head from my shoulders?" Our gazes sear into one another.

Without twitch or blink, Finnbheara utters a single word. "Eala."

Well, there's a right shock. Despite his piss and flames, the ole boyo has at least a pinprick of something decent left in his worthless Faerie soul if his reason for not killing me is to spare Eala pain.

I squeeze his fancy tunic tighter, the metal filigree cutting into my palm. "Tell me your flying vermin didn't hurt her." If they did, I'll drive a fist between his eyes.

"She's unharmed," he says in a voice so low I question if the sound even passed his lips or if I willed the answer into my head.

There's not a drab of emotion on the king's face. Relief steals the fight from me, and I release my hold on him.

Eala is alive. That's gift enough to keep a fragile flame of hope burning in my chest.

The king continues to wear a face of stone, but the way he twists my shirt tighter in his grip, threatening to cut off my air, is a deadly hint as to his rising anger. "Eala wears the taint of the traitor Robálaí Geal."

My last encounter with Robber Bright snaps into focus. Silk dragons with their menacing riders who wore bloody red armor with a triple flame crest upon their chest nearly caused me to soil myself. I'd hardly had the time to register the goings on before the bastard, Bright, switched me back and forth between human and fox forms, wickedly twisting and stretching bone and muscle.

My heart stutters in my chest.

The triple flame crest.

Hellfire.

Another Faerie devil is surely in play here—Aodh.

I wear a sneer to match the king's. "And your traitor is sharing a pint with Aodh."

Finn's shake drives my teeth together hard enough to crack. "What do you know of this? Speak," he roars.

Fate handed me a weapon. True, it's a bitty knife next to Finnbheara's mighty sword, but at least it's got a sharp point.

I jut my chin toward the ground, remembering how he dropped me from an unforgiving height the first time I scampered through his gates as a fox. "Once my feet stop dangling in the air, you'll have the truth of it."

We drop so abruptly, my guts fly to my throat. The king releases his hold on me. I roll across the clumps of silver and green grass that Finn's trampling tore up and land in a heap at Ma's feet. His sword is once again uncomfortably close to my throat. "What do you know of Robálaí Geal?"

I rise to face him, pushing Ma behind me. His sword follows my neck, its proximity ever poised to end my life. "When Eala and I were breathing sense into your lunatic riddle…"

Ma clears her throat behind me, warning me to choose my words with care.

"We were stripped from the Hill of Tara into a mockery of the Veil made of charred branches with fire burning within them."

The tip of Finn's sword touches my skin. "How is this relevant to Robálaí Geal?"

"Your man was there as it happened and waiting for us when we returned."

The kiss of steel or whatever shite Faerie blades are made of sends a trickle of warm blood down my throat. "Do not delay your point, fox, or you will feel mine even deeper."

I swallow, causing the blade to slide near places I'd rather leave unsliced. "And while we're speaking of devils, Robber Bright and his Host came to devil Eala and me on our doorstep. The lot of them wore a sigil of triple flame on a field of black."

For a blazing second, I swear my admission will send Finnbheara's sword clean through my neck. Instead, thank Ma's blessed saints, or at least the ones I used to think she prayed to before I knew of her Faerie inclinations, ole Finn takes a trio of steps away from me.

"Aodh has once again thrown wide his gates to challenge me," he growls.

So much for my dramatic build-up to finger-point at the Irish God of the Underworld. Finnbheara's not surprised, just livid.

The king whips around to face the visible line of soldiers. "Be off to alert every cadre and host. We prepare for war."

His armored minions bow and back away into the mist surrounding them. Finn waves an arm. The gold and glass gates of the kingdom disappear. The grass beneath our feet transforms into planes of white metal stamped with the branch and leaf pattern I'm beginning to realize is Finnbheara's chosen motif. Instead of walls, we're ringed with trees made of glass and gemstone leaves. Silver fire within each trunk shines bright enough to bring shimmering daylight to the great room where we stand.

I scan the space, looking for a door to slip out of while the king is distracted. There's no telling if we're inside or outside. I wonder if there is such a thing as inside here in Tír na nÓg. Does ole Finn keep a castle bedchamber with a mattress filled with flowers, or do the Folk live freely among trees, playing lutes and lyres to pass the time when they're not making trouble for those of us who live under sunshine instead of crystal Faerie light?

I've not a spare minute to go on with my wonderings before a massive glass table blinks into view near the center of the space. It's set upon legs made of gray stacked stones like the fence Da and I built around Loho land.

A mizzle of metallic rain blinking with bursts of silver, dark gold, dozens of green tones, and as many blues as the sea drifts down from opal leaves to settle on the tabletop. My jaw feels unhinged as I gape at the glistening pools forming across the surface. Mountain ranges with silver flecks christening their peaks to give the impression of snow sprout around the map from coppery colored puddles. Woodlands rise in patchwork patterns of the darkest forest green to a pastel emerald like sun catching the night's kiss of dew off fields of grass. Villages crop up from other puddles in shades of muted pewter. Bordering all sides of Finn's mystical sculpture is a miniature raging sea. Cresting waves bearing edges sharp enough to slice skin stand frozen ready to strike.

I'm seeing a Faerie model of Tír na nÓg. I'd always pictured Finnbheara's kingdom as endless, stretching beyond horizons born of dawn and dusk. Standing here, seeing his realm laid out, I see the truth of it. Ireland is an island, and the tales do say the Folk dwell beneath its blessed earth. There's sense to the Fae's home being a mirror of the land above.

Finn strides to the table, plucking at his chin with his long, willowy fingers. A circle of Fae covered in armor decked out with pointy knives, arrows, and spears, flow to the table from between trees. Ah, this is the king's war room. I put more distance between the Folk council and myself.

I take advantage of Finn's focus shifting off me to gather my thoughts. There's no peace in reflection. My spine turns to rubber, and it's nearly impossible to stand up straight. The loss of Eala removed a scoop from my insides. Here I am sucked into another Faerie maze without her.

A groan equal parts despair and frustration rattles deep in my chest. I played the Aodh card, which should have thrown the round to me. What did I gain for sharing that bit of information about Robber Bright? Nothing but Finnbheara showing me his back.

Before I'm aware of his movement, the king is in front of me again, his hand clamped around my throat. I hear Ma's low grunt of disapproval.

"My commanders are all in agreement. You, spawn of Loho, brought the cry of war upon my lands when your actions drew Aodh's agent into my Veil to seek revenge on your miserable soul. The eventual demise of the servant ignited the wrath of the master."

I clutch at Finn's viselike fingers. "What happened to Olk was a case of kill or be killed. What else would you have had me do?" I pray my next words hold sway with the man choking me. "The fiend chased us both. It follows that Aodh was after Eala as well."

The heat of Finn's stare causes my skin to feel as if it might melt from my bones. His gaze switches to Ma as she approaches the king and lays a hand on the Fae's royal arm. His fingers still grip my neck.

"Finnbheara, is not Sionnach's love for Eala, a soul you also cherish, a testament of his worth? Let him be."

The thought of Finnbheara cherishing Eala in any way sickens me enough to want to kill the Faerie king.

Finn hurls me to the ground. "Have you more to say of Aodh's desire for Eala Duir, Fox?"

Rubbing my throat, I stand to face the king. My hand comes away damp with my blood, but I avoid taking stock of just how much.

"Aodh showed himself to us in the rocks of Howth Head. I think the bugger would have snapped us between his teeth if he could get to us. The Veil kept us from him."

Finnbheara stands in absolute stillness, unblinking midnight blue eyes lit with bursts like endless falling stars. The sight is as chilling as his blade.

He's confessed Eala is alive. As long as she draws breath, my swan will not give up on me. I'd best not be a bleeding eejit and finish my days as a kabob on the end of a Faerie sword for my runaway mouth.

I yearn for more detail. Is she still *fánaí*, a Veil traveler, or did he rob her of that gift to keep her from reentering his gates? Wherever she is, can Robber Bright and Aodh get to her?

The king skewers me with gleaming silver eyes. "I will allow you to see the next sunrise, Fox." His words are a dismissal. The royal ass turns back to his enchanted map.

Fisting both hands, my body leans forward, poised to storm after him and demand more answers about Eala. I never get the chance. Ma grabs a handful of my shirt and drags me into a fecking tree.

CHAPTER 3
THE CAVE OF CATS

ROBBER BRIGHT

An acrid smell of ash and burnt things plagues my nose. The Host of a Thousand Wings and I pass through the cave mouth of Oweynagat, the Cave of Cats, into the serpentine tunnel leading to the gates of Bráchthine, the realm of Aodh. I spit to rid myself of the vile char coating my tongue. Aillil, my *péist síoda*, hisses steam to accomplish the same.

Fires in Tír na nÓg produce no ash. Feast flames dance, illuminating bough and trunk as they coax delectable juices from roasting game, filling the air with the sweetness of honey and the tang of peppercorns. This place offers no such comfort. No matter how unappealing we consider the realm we will soon call home, Aodh now holds the reins of our allegiance. The *péist síoda* will adapt. We must all adapt.

Acacia, my trusted second in command, pulls her dragon, Eachna, alongside Aillil. The passageway is wide enough to accommodate side-by-side riders, but we travel in a single line to avoid outcroppings that may pose hazards.

Our two mated dragons huff a greeting to one another, relishing their closeness.

"Commander, assure me the entirety of the underworld does not hold this loathsome air. We may well suffocate from the stench before we reach Aodh's gates," Acacia says with a frown.

In the luminous light emanating from our dragons' eyes, I fix her with an inscrutable stare.

She flips a thick braid over her shoulder. I glimpse the woven kaleidoscope of earthy tones I once delighted in running my fingers through. Her hair harmonizes with Acacia's deep bronze skin, echoing colors of the rich, bountiful land we left behind in Tír na nÓg.

"I *assure* you," I say, parroting her word, "What I have seen of Bráchthine does not share such..." I search for terms neither complimentary nor uncomplimentary. "...redolence."

Acacia scoffs, followed by an answering snort from Eachna. My second clicks her tongue. "I suppose nectar of lacewing and daffodil cake are also not to be expected at Aodh's table."

I have no room among my own conflicted thoughts to entertain hers. "Time for doubt has passed, lieutenant. We will take what is given from Bráchthine in both elevation of our status and local bounty."

"The baggage sharing your saddle..." Acacia says, indicating the human woman bobbing against my chest, "...is in for a greater surprise than the rest of us combined."

Colleen's slumbering breaths warm the underside of my jaw. Copper strands peeking through her chestnut hair dance in the dragonwing-made breeze, tickling my neck. I tighten my hold and resist the temptation to rest my weary head atop hers.

A jolt of despair sears through my essence like a heated blade. I instantly recognize its source.

Eala.

Something dire has happened. Tír na nÓg no longer sings in her blood. She lives, but her soul is cleaved in two. It is the fox she mourns. I push harder into our dwindling connection. It is not his death she laments. She cries out desperate to reach him, but he cannot hear. A great chasm lies between them.

I smell not the ambrosia of Finnbheara's kingdom in her essence, but the earthy snap of the human realm. Eala's spirit floats away from me like a feather in a storm. Try as I might to hold fast, the contact is broken.

It is she who must summon me with the only bridge remaining between us

—the ring I left in her keeping. I pray to the ancient gods and goddesses her call will not be long in coming.

Acacia's voice cuts sharply through the air. "Robálaí?"

My attention has drifted from without to within. I return my focus to my second. "I ponder the way ahead."

Acacia hesitates, then gives her words free rein. "I acknowledge the seemingly unending oppression and devaluation you have suffered at the hands of Finnbheara."

"This is not the time—"

She cuts me off. "You did no wrong in ordering the final charge in the war between Tír na nÓg and Bráchthine. Had you not given the command, it would have come swiftly from Finnbheara's lips. It is an injustice he blames you for the tragic outcome and relentlessly punishes you for it."

I need no reminder of the king's animosity. "It is well known Finnbheara does not suffer disobedience." I meet her obstinate stare. "From anyone."

She does not back down, one of the qualities that earned her the place as my second.

"Like you, I foresee no end to the king's mistreatment, but it is not a new thing. We follow you into Aodh's service willingly, but why now, Robálaí? What weighed your scales in the Dark Prince's favor?"

Weariness threads through my bones. I have repeatedly provided a plausible answer if not the fullness of truth to this inquiry about the purpose laid before us. Still, she mines for deeper layers. My shadow truth must remain protected in my soul, even from my most trusted.

"Must I point out the rhetorical nature of your question?"

She sputters, then swipes at her lips as a new coat of residue settles on them. "Yes, yes. War. Always a war." Her voice is bitter. "The ever-looming war with Aodh that Finnbheara has threatened since the hour the last one ended. Is it any more imminent now?" She snorts. "The scales of our lives tip from the bluster of greedy kings."

"Careful. Wherever our allegiance lies, words such as those bear the color of treason."

She tosses her head, treating me to her haughtiest expression. "I know when to hold my tongue, Commander Geal."

I chuckle. "Fall back, Acacia. The way ahead narrows."

Acacia follows orders. I do not have the luxury of misgivings from myself or those who follow me. The Host has come of their own free will. I promised all greater respect in the Kingdom of Aodh than what they were shown in Finnbheara's realm. Aodh remains Fae Folk, as do I. He may have chosen to be a god of the land beneath the land, but we still share the blood of kin. We will play this out.

I squint into the shadows ahead. Even though I have traversed this dour route before, it feels as if its length has tripled. Perhaps the growing knot of foreboding beneath my breastbone affects my impeccable sense of time and distance. I must show no sign of unease. It will weave its way through the Host as a bitter vine. They trust me, and I led them here. When my cadre looks to me, they must see only strength.

I focus on the path. There is beauty in the Cave of Cats, this tunnel to the underworld. Its walls are wrought of faceted black stone with minuscule licks of fire embedded in intervals along its surface. A thousand pinpoint reflections of ripe persimmon flame dance across the highly polished rock but offer scant illumination. If not for the added glow of our silk dragons' eyes, the Host would surely scrape wing and hide against unforgiving edges of the cut stone.

A sudden longing for the baked persimmons my mother insisted upon for Faerie feast days drones in my chest.

Colleen shivers, cuddling closer. A drowsy yawn precedes her hand stretching to cradle the side of my face. "Quit hogging the covers, Robin."

Her palm is soft against my skin. This woman I am spiriting away to Bráchthine believes us to be bound in her mortal world. I showered her with my influence to create a fiction I have yet to erase. As the warmth of Colleen's skin seeps into mine, I sense the narrowed eye of judgment upon me. I sweep admonition aside as I often do.

An ethical being would have left this woman, so dear to Eala, at the mouth of Oweynagat to find her way back to the mortal world. I have never been called ethical, nor am I ignorant. Colleen is a lure in my plan to deliver Eala to Aodh. A true fisherman does not set aside the rod until the fish is landed.

I allow myself to linger in Colleen's touch and nuzzle my cheek against her hand for a moment before planting a kiss on her palm where her lifeline meets her heartline. The action is intended to assure her slumbering spirit that all is well.

The moment my lips meet her smooth skin, there is a surge of heat like passing a finger through candleflame. I swiftly draw back, dabbing fingers to my mouth. My lips are tender from the brief meeting with Colleen's flesh. I have taken pleasure with many a mortal maid but never have I been stung. In fact, as theatrics for Eala's benefit, I kissed this very woman in my arms, feeling nothing but the fleeting indulgence offered by any kiss. What mischief is in play within the walls of Aodh's passage?

"Peace, Robálaí," I chide. There is no magic sent to taunt us. The prick of heat between us was naught but an errant spark from the fires burning along the gleaming black walls. It simply alighted on this mortal's palm ahead of my kiss. Nothing more.

I glance down to find Colleen staring at the place on her hand that held my brief kiss. Her face tilts to meet my gaze, eyes wide with confusion. In a voice laden with shivers, she speaks. "Robin, why is your hair glowing orange?" She twists her head to take in the tunnel. "Where are we?"

Curse my wandering mind. She reads the reflection of firelight on the pale strands of my hair. With tumbling thoughts of the new life before me, I have neglected to fortify my charm over the mortal. I must not let her clarity of thought gain purchase.

Before her awareness grows, I lower my forehead to meet hers and pour my influence into her ragged consciousness. "It is merely a trick of the light. Return to your dreams, my sweet," I rumble in a purr laced with honey using the timbre of Robin Bright, the man she believes herself in love with from the human realm. With the intent to soothe, I run the tip of my nose along the silky skin on the side of her neck.

My action has the opposite effect on me. Temptation winds its way through my body. Inhaling deeply, I revel in this human's scent of peppered apple and lose count if I have stroked her skin once or a hundred times as we ride.

My hold slackens, and she lists precariously to the side. Aillil unleashes an angry trill as our balance is thrown too far right.

I string an arm more firmly around her waist and clutch her to my chest, resettling us solidly on the dragon's back. My heartbeats fly faster than Aillil's forward progress. I press my lips to Colleen's hair. It is thick and smooth, and as soft as riverside moss. "I am sorry, sweet one."

Abruptly, I withdraw from her. There is no call for tenderness here. Thankfully, she has returned to the drifting unconsciousness of my enchantment, ignorant of the tension and foreboding around her. I chide myself for allowing the distraction. Colleen is a pawn in my game. I will dole out only the minimal comforts necessary to assuage her spirit's turmoil. She must remain my docile doe.

Fatigue threatens to dull my judgement. I must remain a vigilant blade in Aodh's company. Plunging teeth into my bottom lip, I bring forth a welling of blood. The pain revives me. I suck in the salty liquid mixed with ash, allowing its revolting taste to remind me of the potential peril for my Host that awaits if I falter in my dealings with the God of the Underworld.

I raise my hand holding Aillil's reins, signaling the Host to stop. We have reached a branch in the tunnel. It is a place of reckoning where those approaching are either granted permission to move onto the gates or delivered into Aodh's dungeons for trespassing.

Acacia positions her dragon at my flank. The hides of our two bonded creatures slide together with ease. I turn to meet her gaze, shoring up energy for another challenge.

Her voice is softer and pitched low for my hearing alone. "I never thought I would once again linger in this place of poisoned memory."

I give a curt nod, acknowledging the melancholy we share in returning to the threshold of Bráchthine. "We shall pass swiftly. You have my oath."

The clawed feet of silk dragons crunch on the gravel beneath our feet. This rocky carpet was first created from the skeletons of great oceanic leviathans. The beasts sank to the bottom of the sea and then were leached down into the underworld to be used by Aodh's road builders. It is the later addition of metal from shattered weapons and the crushed bones of fallen soldiers that sickens me. I've ventured through this graveyard of the long-ago Fae battle between the forces of Finnbheara and Aodh, but never allowed Aillil's feet to touch the remains of his kin and mine. On forays to treat with Aodh, we always hovered while I spoke the words of admittance.

We have no such luxury now with a unit of this size. The buzz of a thousand wings would drown out my request.

"In your negotiations, did you see her, speak to her?" asks Acacia.

My heart lurches at the reference to our queen, Nuala. It was her sacrifice that ended the war, saving legions of Fae after I gave the command to charge into the final doomed battle. I picture her still, choosing to leave Finnbheara's side, and sparing the lives of her Folk when she accepted Aodh's terms. Nuala reigns now as a queen of hellfire instead of the light of our crystal sun. Finnbheara and their seventeen sons wept and mourned for an age before my king emerged with a heart banished to an eternity of sorrow. Malevolence shadowed his spirit since that day, the bulk of it launched in my direction.

What should have been the end of conflict ushered in a millennium of fresh hatred between Tír na nÓg and Bráchthine. It simmers still. I am excruciatingly aware my defection may act as the final catalyst for cataclysm. If that dreaded day arrives, I shall fight.

I manage a tight smile for Acacia. "I have not had the honor of being in Nuala's sphere. Thus far, my business with Aodh has been brief and clandestine. Perhaps we shall be rewarded with the sight of our lost queen once we dwell in his realm."

My second is fierce, but I do not miss the tremble in her voice or the hands clutching her dragon's reins. She was at my side when we fought the forces of Aodh. The persimmon flames embedded in these cave walls are the shades and spirits of those lost on that fated day. I will not chide nor begrudge her this moment of dark anticipation. Fear is the whetstone that sharpens the blade. "Faith, Acacia."

"In you, Commander—always."

She rests her hand on my arm. Acacia's gaze runs deep, flickering with the wish biding in her heart—the dream of a bond-promise between us. Such a union can never be. The scar slashed across my chest was not the sole punishment Finnbheara delivered for my disobedience to him.

For my part in driving Nuala to sacrifice herself, the king shackled me with a parting blow in the form of the geas uttered from his royal lips, ensuring I would face the endlessness of my life without a bond-promised, without a soulmate. The king proclaimed that words spoken by any who profess tender feelings for me would cause my desire to harden instead of opening to them. The geas obeyed Finnbheara, and when Acacia was first to make such a confession of love, a shroud of granite encased my heart, trapping my feelings for her in a stony prison.

In desperation to prove Finnbheara's geas false or breakable, I lay with Acacia. The sensual pleasure did not pluck even a single string of my emotions. Our intimacy set her stubborn will to hold to the possibility that I would share not just my body but my soul with her one day.

It cannot be so. The geas steals the chance for me to make a home, a life with someone who can wake my useless heart. I am unfit to love or welcome the love of another.

Acacia believes I remain untethered due to conceit and prizing myself above all others. It is the costume I have worn for centuries. She waits for the day I see her as more than a sworn sword. Granting her heart's wish would create nothing but an empty bond. We would share an existence but the mockery of a home. Any offspring would only know a father with a frigid pulp where a heart should beat. A loveless eternity is not what this woman, whom I hold in highest esteem, deserves.

Gently, I lift her hand from my arm and will my eyes to reveal the depth of regret pulsing within me. "I am sorry, Acacia."

The set of her jaw relays the toll my ongoing rejection takes on her. With no further response, she bows in the saddle and trains her stare on the way ahead, fading behind me to rejoin the line. My gaze remains fixed on the space she vacated.

Once again, I embody the title of heartless scoundrel many have labeled me. If only they knew I call myself much worse.

The energy of anticipation rises from the Host and prickles against my skin. Their loyalty is truly a gift. They have not wavered in their oaths and followed me here. I must honor that commitment by forging ahead at this crossroads.

Turning back to face the branching paths, I clear ash residue from my throat and speak.

"My fire may burn for good or ill,
When flames do meet their prize.
On thresholds black beneath the world,
Intentions court demise."

The right-hand corridor, a path promising torment and eternal night, begins to blur.

From deep in my gut, I summon a herald's tone. "Robálaí Geal has brought the Host of a Thousand Wings to serve Aodh, King of Bráchthine."

A muffled roar precedes the deluge of vermilion sparks from above. The flecks do not singe, only brush against armor and dragon scale. Our beasts trill and growl as the downpour shields our surroundings from sight.

In a blinding burst of flame, falling drops turn to red glass and scatter across the graveled ground. The tunnel vanishes to reveal the gates of Aodh's kingdom. I whip my head to check on the Folk at my back. An unwavering unit of Fae and dragons stands at the ready. The Host of warriors, their dragons, and the woman I clutch to my breast, prepare to enter the underworld.

I experienced this garish invitation to the Dark Prince's realm on my first foray into his lands. Once Bráchthine grants you entrance, you are not treated to such fanfare on subsequent visits.

Like Finnbheara's kingdom, mist permeates the air. While the thickened air in Tír na nÓg shines white and silver, Bráchthine's is a muted crimson bearing flakes of twinkling obsidian. The gates themselves are twisted blackened branches with gashes to reveal glowing embers within the boughs. This entrance to the Dark Prince's lands soars high, out of sight, perhaps to scrape the underside of the world above, a constant reminder to Finnbheara of what lies under the soles of his boots.

A creak as hideous as the wail of a dying beast rises as the smoldering gates swing outward at a glacial pace to admit us. Just beyond the entrance is a massive wall of blackened bones constructed from the Fae and *péist síoda* that have fallen on this threshold of Bráchthine. The barrier blocks Aodh's lands from view.

I raise a fist and give the command that will alter our destiny. "Forward." Behind me, Acacia repeats the order, which bounces down the line until the entire Host takes wing.

After passing through the gates, I turn sharply to the left. The Host streams behind me. We forge ahead through thinning mist. I halt before the wall of bones ends, waiting until the last of my company enters the underworld. As they do, a renewed deluge of sparks descends. When it clears, the gates have vanished from sight. There is no sign of the way in or out of Aodh's kingdom.

I do not give the Host time to fret. Instead, I pick up speed to clear the wall, knowing once my fellows do the same, many of their fears will be allayed.

"Behold the lands of Aodh," I cry and motion riders and mounts to break around me in a wave, joining them once the last dragon moves past the end of the wall of flame-blighted bones.

I am surrounded by gasps of surprise then the buzz of discourse as they take in the sight. Aillil releases a snort of superiority over the musings of the other *péist síoda*. This is not his first glimpse, and he chooses to adopt a haughty attitude. My mount's wonderment is not hidden from me as his scales thrum beneath the saddle. My lips curl into a half smile, remembering my dragon's thrill and the great clouds of mulberry steam Aillil blew when he first beheld these lands.

Acacia peels back to once again ride alongside me. "This is far from what I expected."

I smirk. "Are you disappointed at the lack of belching volcanoes and rivers bubbling with the blood of Aodh's enemies?"

"They lack the grace of Tír na nÓg, but I concede that Aodh's lands hold claim to savage beauty." Her gaze wanders to where my thumb strokes Colleen's shoulder.

The action had escaped my notice until Acacia's scrutiny uncovered it. I clear my throat. "The human stirred."

Acacia narrows her eyes but holds her tongue on the matter. Aillil nips at Eachna's haunch as my second skirts past us to rejoin the Host.

I slide a hand up the back of Colleen's neck. My breath hitches with an urge to wake her and show her the sky cascading around us in a gradient from amber to gold, lit from the rays of a blood-orange sun. In the distance, a row of mountain peaks shines with the gloss and richness of rubies. The plains stretching before us do not bear the verdant hues of Tír na nÓg's grasses, but they are splendid nonetheless with their coat of silty russet and cinnamon earth. It is as if Aodh painted his land in a warm palette with intentional contrast to the cool blues, greens, and violets of Finnbheara's kingdom.

In the center of the valley below, the great round fortress of the Underworld God seethes like a nest of smoldering coals. Four distinct towers curve outward from the main body at points north, south, east, and west. Each is topped with the carving of a great black swan. Outstretched wings of one touch the next at their tips, forming battlements.

The sight of the castle never fails to move me. The swans are a tribute to Aodh's siblings, the other three Children of Lir, who, along with the Dark Prince, were cursed to live as swans for centuries before being freed from torment. When his brothers and sister were restored to their humanity, they accepted death and blessed afterlives. Aodh alone festers in never-ending malice.

Once we settle in Bráchthine, perhaps I will bring Colleen to this hillside and rouse her just enough to enjoy the alien loveliness that exists beneath the world she knows. Again, guilt pricks my chest at the decision to bring her into the land ruled by a Dark Prince, a realm where the potency of my power is yet undefined.

I reprimand my skittish inclination toward compassion. "Enough of these delicate thoughts, Robálaí Geal." Commanding Aillil in the tongue of the *péist síoda*, we take our place at the head of the company and lead the Host of a Thousand Wings to what awaits us in the presence of Aodh.

CHAPTER 4
THE WISE WOMAN

EALA

When I snatch Robber Bright's ring off the table, heat seeps into my palm. Is this the Faerie's foul magic or metal warmed by the sun? Remembering the day I allowed his essence to mingle with mine is like biting into rotten fruit. The arrogant ass insisted that lust for him floated through my spirit.

I absolutely needed his help, his guidance, to understand how to deal with my emerging Faerie self. That was the sum total of his worth to me. He twisted my desire for knowledge into his fiction of a deep longing to fuck him.

I slam the ring onto the table, covering it with my hand to hide the cursed thing. Robber Bright is my enemy. He's taken my best friend to a place impossible for me to reach and aligned himself with a malevolent Fae underworld god. Why in the name of sanity would I consider using the ring to reconnect with him?

As if there's a single drop of sanity in this Faerie nightmare.

An urge to heave the damned ring into the fireplace thunders in my chest.

One distasteful fact remains. *Damned to Faerie hell* Robber Bright may be the only option to break through Finnbheara's locked door to Sion.

I press my palm down harder on the ring until I feel its imprint against my skin. Robber may be my enemy, but he's also the king's. I've always believed the *enemy of my enemy is my friend* adage to be full of holes, but if I choose to discount it in this case, I have nothing.

Reconnecting with Robber Bright could prove to be worse than nothing. As far as I'm concerned, anyone in cahoots with Aodh wears a flashing danger sign above their head. Memories of the nightmarish illustration of the Underworld God from my childhood book, combined with the vision of his hideous face in the rocky cliffs of Howth, sets off the sensation of an unseen insect crawling up the back of my neck.

I rip my hand away from the gold band. Robber wasn't specific about how the ring works. I don't want my mere touch coupled with thoughts of him to bring the bastard to my doorstep. He must be considered a threat, even if he turns out to be a necessary one.

I bump the side of my fist against my forehead. "Last resort, Eala." Picking up the ring again, I drop the gold band into one of the kitchen drawers and slam it shut.

A draft of cold air from the bedroom nook's window carries a mix of Sion's scent and lady's bedstraw across the room. I stagger toward the bed, longing to curl into a ball.

"No." I punch the mattress, then sit instead, arms crossed.

I have to come to grips with the fragments of me that are left. These miserable pieces must find a way to knit themselves back together. The flannel sleep pants Sion tucks under his pillow every morning catch my eye. I press my face into the fabric, inhaling deeply and snuggling it as a child would a beloved blanket.

Máthair kept a threadbare wool coat she claimed belonged to her husband, the man I now know as Timothy Loho, Sionnach's father. When I see her, and I will see my grandmother again, I'll tell her I finally understand how dear that single piece of clothing was.

I stand and address the empty room. "Day one: Eala gets her shit together." My back is stiff from tension, so I lean forward to touch my toes and stretch. The position gives me a clear view of the detritus stowed beneath the bed. A well-worn book catches my eye, and I slide it free.

Swiping my hand across the cover robbed of its dust jacket, I read the title. *"What Dreams May Come: A Guide to the Sleeping Mind."* I suppose Sionnach experienced many odd dreams while confined to this cottage and Loho land in the time from Beltane to Oestre for all those years when Finnbheara forbade Sion from attempting to free the soulfall. Another heartless restriction from the Fae king.

I notice page corners turned down throughout the book. Flipping to one of the dog-eared entries, I read, *"The silver-horned stag represents an invitation to the fantastic."* Next to the image analysis are notes scribbled in Sion's careless hand.

Make the creature beautiful and non-threatening. Eala's but a wee girl. Add a fanciful saddle for a playful nymph to ride.

All at once, I'm seven years old in Central Park in the midst of a dream flash, one of the magical daydreams that would spontaneously appear to me. The ones Máthair never questioned but always wanted me to describe in detail. As I got older, I kept a journal filled with as many as I could remember.

I slip my finger between the pages to open another of Sionnach's place markers and continue to read. *"The fox embodies intelligence, which can branch off to cunning. It is an apt guide when navigating situations where diplomacy is essential."*

I press a hand to calm my racing heart as I read Sion's notation.

Send the beastie across the hearth fire, dancing a jig. Make Eala laugh. Let her know she need not fear the fox.

A fox did indeed dance through the flames many a time as Máthair and I sat before the fire while she told me stories of Faeries, magic, and Irish folklore. Sionnach, my beloved fox, was always there with us. I devour every one of his notes, adoring him more with each scribble.

Crushing the book to my chest, I'm dizzy from a rush of love for my *anamchara*. Seeing proof of the meticulous care and consideration woven through every message he sent in dream flashes or stories in the fire, buoys my courage. Sionnach knew one day I'd be the key player in a grand tale of my own.

I've always adhered to a doable and safe life script. Falling in love with a Veil guide blew that to bits. If I was created to be the balance point in Sion's off-kilter reality, I embrace the role. He is indelibly etched on my spirit. My fox is my joy, my soulsong, and I will hear his music until the end of my days.

I set the dream book on Sion's sleep pants and stride into the kitchen. Pulling the rubbish bin next to the table, I sweep the notes we made to solve Finnbheara's riddle into it. Smacking both palms on the tabletop, I prepare to conquer a new Faerie challenge.

Thin shadows crisscross my knuckles. When I glance at the window to see what's making the pattern, my heart leaps.

"Alfie," I cry and run out the red front door.

I throw my arms around the white poplar's slender trunks. The pattern of green triangles adorning her bark announces to the world she is my *fánaí*, Veil traveler's, companion tree. Mine and Sion's. Two canvas bags holding the trove of period clothing we've used in our travels through time, nest inside the base of her curving trunks.

I rest my forehead against her. "Oh, Alfie, I've lost him."

Her comforting presence punches through my resolve, and fresh tears spill from my cheeks onto Alfie's trunk. Droplets trickle downward, skittering over the scratches in her bark. When they touch the highest green triangle, its outline begins to glow with a thin creamy, golden light akin to milk laced with whiskey. I pull back to watch as each piece of the triangle pattern lights up in sequence, then a thread of that brilliant whiskey gold bursts from the trunk to wrap around my wrist.

I'm suddenly adrift in a bower of swirling bladed poplar leaves and white bark, waltzing with the *fánaí* tree. The only sound is the breeze whispering through leaf-laden boughs. It's a lovely, unexpected peace amid my heart's turmoil.

The whispers form words that repeat in a delicate melody.

Crann na Beatha
Crann na Beatha
Crann na Beatha
The Tree of Life.

Once, I'd taken Máthair to visit a gorgeous grove of aspens near my apartment in Kennard Park back home in New York when she came to visit. She viewed the trees with adoration, murmuring *eadha* and *Crann na Beatha* to each as she laid her palm against their trunks. My grandmother insisted I'd found a holy grove of mystical trees connecting our world with other realms.

Since then, I'd catalogued aspens, *eadha*, as the Tree of Life, but here is Alfie, a white poplar, teaching me my view had been too narrow.

I'm weightless in this tranquil escape. My hair floats in soft, white-blonde strands around my head. The heaviness of despair lifts off me like dewdrops becoming mist as they rise to greet the morning sun.

Faintly, through spaces between the soft teeth of dense poplar leaves, I see my Sionnach. His smoky pumpkin curls sparkle as if bathed in crystal radiance. He holds his head in his hands, back bent, alone in the shadows of great trees.

When I cry out his name, I'm ripped from the vision. Alone, outside the cottage, my fingers grip one of Alfie's trunks hard enough to crush it. Her dark green triangles lay dull and flat against white bark.

I open my hands and step back, staring open-mouthed at the *fánaí* tree, part of the mystical *Crann na Beatha*.

Alfie found Sion.

Not Alfie alone. The Faerie essence swirling within me spreads, a wave made of fireflies, the silver mists of Tír na nÓg, and magic.

"I hear you," I say to the once foreign energy coursing through me that I'm only now beginning to understand.

Finnbheara may have shut me out, but the realm still calls to me, its daughter. I was right to make sure Máthair and Sion stayed behind. Neither has the claim on the *Sidhe* I possess.

I long to throw myself at the white poplar to reclaim even the faintest glimpse of my dearest love, but caution keeps me in check.

Think, Eala.

My professor brain screams to understand the vision before wasting any precious magic that allows me to see Sion again. How was the connection forged? Can it be repeated? My tears made the markings glow, thrusting me into an otherworldly bower, but then the sound of my voice ripped me away from the vision.

Research is my weapon. Legends of the Tree of Life may hold answers. I'll track them down and learn the rules.

As I stare at the sea cliffs in the near distance, ocean mist slides across my skin. There's no doubt in my soul Alfie showed me my *anamchara*. We three are connected by the sacred roots of *Crann na Beatha*. Sionnach looked as miserable as I am, but he's alive. The crystal light shining on him had the complexion of the Faerie sun I've experienced in Tír na nÓg.

He is somewhere in Tír na nÓg.

I dot a kiss against Alfie's bark. "We'll bring him home, I promise."

Walking into the cottage, shoots of dawning hope break through despair. I'm not alone. I have Alfie's magic to join with mine.

And Sionnach's love.

I am loved. That is its own brand of magic.

Magic.

I chew on a broken nail. If I'm going up against Finnbheara, magic is something I could use more of. I scan the books piled atop Sion's desk and on the floor next to it, looking for a title that might hold some insight into the Tree of Life myth. I land on something unexpected and free it from the haphazard stack. The embossed cover reads, *Wise Women You Dare Not Cross: Unforgettable Powerhouses from Ireland's Past.*

Wise women is one term that was used for witches, a more complimentary title than many other less favorable names like *hag* or *devil's bride.*

Women of magic.

I pat my chest in concert with the surge of adrenaline bubbling inside me. What a pessimist to believe I'm powerless in my task to free Sion. Veil sprites dance within me. Alfie's *fánaí* tree magic is bound to me.

And I can travel through time.

The Veil gives me access to a rich history of magic makers—wise women and witches. Maybe just maybe, I might be able to recruit one of them to help or advise me.

I grab a pad of paper and pen from Sion's desk and drop into a kitchen chair. Flipping to the table of contents, I run a finger down the names of candidates.

Alice Kyteler – The Witch of Kilkenny

Bridget Cleary – Ireland's Last Witch

Biddy Early – Keeper of the Blue Bottle

The Morrigan – A Pureblood Witch and Celtic Goddess

Ruling out potentially prickly if not outright dangerous deities such as The Morrigan, my curiosity leans in favor of Biddy Early. Máthair had several stories about Biddy and her famous blue bottle that allegedly contained potion with significant magic. The book states she was thought to be a friend of the Good Folk, the Fae, and possibly a liaison between Faeries and humans. As I read, I chew on the pen in my hand.

"Old pal of yours Máthair?" I say once I discover Bridget Ellen "Biddy"

Early, nee O'Connor, would have been a contemporary of my grandmother's in Máthair's first lifetime in Ireland. Both women are from County Clare. The coincidence acts like a magnet, drawing me to the woman. Biddy was known as a *bean feasa*, Irish for wise woman or seer. The book didn't offer an abundance of information, so I plug in my laptop and fire it up to search for more.

My deep dive piles more and more evidence that Biddy might be the type of person who wouldn't shy away from my mad predicament. She was a healer and herbalist, and there's a mountain of other supernatural doings attributed to her and her practice.

Then there's her blue bottle.

I remember the oversized perfume-shaped bottles with mushroom caps scattered across the Gem Kissed Forest, each filled with different colored elixirs.

Biddy's potions, Faerie elixirs, Friend to the Fae...

I sit up, crashing into the chair back hard enough to tip the front legs off the floor. Gripping the edge of the table to steady myself, my thoughts swim with possibilities. Could Biddy be Fae? Was her blue bottle filled with magic from Tír na nÓg? If she wasn't Fae, is there a chance her blue bottle and its contents were a gift from a Faerie lover?

Máthair had been the paramour of Finnbheara. Biddy hooking up with a Fae hottie isn't so out there. Damn, the woman had a parade of husbands. A Faerie tryst could have just been one more bullet point on her romantic to-do list.

I continue to scroll through all things Biddy as I pace the length of the living room, my resolve growing with every lap around the couch. I will Veil travel to meet the famous witch and pray to St. Brigid I can soften Ms. Early's heart enough to join me in my battle to save my soulmate.

Back at the table, I list potential moments in time to connect with my target. Scanning the possibilities, I rule them out one by one.

For Biddy to agree to join me, I'll need to offer her something in return. The best time to drop into her life is when she's vulnerable. She might be more amenable to bargain for the help I can offer to spring her from a sticky situation.

My finger taps the sheet of significant moments in the witch's life. "What do you think, Biddy?"

At my question, a sea breeze snaps through the boughs of the pair of yew trees growing near the back corners of the cottage. A piercing whine heralds the onset of a fiercer gust. The door rattles, then branches scrape against the cottage, woody fingernails trying to claw their way inside.

I shiver as robust drafts force their way into the room from under the door and secret pathways they find through the roof thatch. Wind is as much a part of this landscape as morning fog or the blooming patches of yellow archangel flower Sion once pointed out to me on the nearby hillside. But this rising blow possesses a much more intense and threatening vibe. When I walk over to the couch to grab the blanket hanging over its back, the whine escalates to a howl. Outside, bits of leaves and multi-colored flower petals stripped from their stalks fly by the windows like a band wrapping around the cottage.

This sucker is no natural wind. It swirls in ceaseless horizontal laps. I gawk at the parade of color. Is it meant to keep me in, or should I open the door to greet it?

Máthair used to accuse me of being a *tempest in a teapot* when I'd get belligerent. In an ironic juxtaposition, there's a literal otherworldly tempest brewing around me, and I'm the damn ceramic teapot about to shatter. As the cottage shakes with the vivid riot circling me, fear douses my insides in an icy wave far colder than the chilling wind. I know of only one abnormal wind that I dread to the depth of my soul, the *Gaoithe Sidhe*, that foul blow that precedes the Faerie hunt, the Host of a Thousand Wings.

The hunt that is now pledged to a dark god.

Is Robber Bright coming for me? I stare at the drawer holding his ring. I never should have touched the traitorous Fae's talisman. If Robber steals me away, how will I ever get to Sion?

I dare a glance out the window, expecting the tumbling cloud of gray fog that surrounds the approach of Robber Bright and his Host of a Thousand Wings. Beyond the screen of the circling wind and its debris, all I see are wildflowers matted to the earth like a rumpled blanket.

One of Alfie's trunks begins to pound against the window frame with an insistent *thump-thump-thump*. There's a low groan, then a split appears in the red wood trim. An finger of wind shoots through the breach, sending my witchy notes flying to the floor.

Sion would help me make sense of the bizarre, flowery cyclone. He'd hold me against his solid chest and whisper *whist whist* in my ear before dabbing it with a kiss.

I stoop to retrieve the pad of paper from the floor while I wrestle with my next move. Do I sit tight or walk out to confront an oddity that carries the markings of Faerie mischief?

The top sheet with my list of notable moments in Biddy Early's life is torn clean across the page. There above the tattered rip, as if underlined by the wind's antics, is a dark time for the *bean feasa*.

When I run my finger under the date and place, the rogue wind settles back into its usual afternoon exhale as if satisfied with my discovery. The swirling petals flutter to the ground to create a colorful carpet outside the cottage.

I shoot an accusatory glare at Alfie. "Did you churn up this breeze, Ms. *fánaí* tree, my *Crann na Beatha* friend?"

The white poplar is as still as a tree should be. A little too still, considering the now predictable breeze encourages shoulder-high wildflowers lining the path to the gate to sway in an elegant dance. Not a single leaf on Alfie's branches moves. If I've learned anything from my travels with Sionnach, our chats with ancient druids, visions, and folktales come to life, it's not to discount anything.

A Faerie tree summoning a scary wind peppered with shorn-off flower petals is mild compared to things I've come face to face with since I stepped into the Druid's Cave at Blarney Castle and into the life of my soulmate.

I tap my finger on the torn page and accept the otherworldly nudge.

"Okay, Alfie. Looks like we're headed to a witch trial."

CHAPTER 5
THE KING AND THE FOX

SIONNACH

Ma shoves me out of the golden-brown trunk of a rowan with bark twinkling like it's been dusted with flecks of glass. The crystal sun hanging low in the Glade of Chimes sends blinding streaks of fiery white light through the tangle of branches in the hovering canopy above. I stumble across the lush clover covering the ground until my foot catches on a sprawling root, and I thump onto my arse.

Light reflecting off the diamond film covering the lake behind Ma gives her the look of wearing an angel's halo. The vision is not consistent with the woman striding toward me with the wrath of a murderous goddess. "Get up, Sionnach Loho."

I scramble to my feet in a dead confusion over her rage. Ma is tall, but I'm a good head taller. That doesn't stop her from cracking a hand across my face harder than the whack she gave Finnbheara.

"Do you have naught but mutton stuffed between your ears, reckless son of mine?"

"Ma," I gasp and cup a hand over the sting on my cheek. My mother has cuffed my ear on occasion but never struck me. Taking one from the hand of this fecking Fae princess version of Ma is mind-addling.

My ears ring. I can't tell if it's from the force of her smack or the chiming of countless silver tubes hanging from branches of sacred trees in the glade.

"A single blow, Sionnach." Ma jabs a finger into the cleft in my chin. "That's all it would take for Finnbheara to cut you down."

We stare at each other. Our eyes wear matching lights of fury, until mine dull with remorse.

Ma kneads her temples. "I fear I've emptied my pot of favors from the king where you're concerned." Both her look and voice address my mulishness. "Stop provoking him."

I can see from the set of her shoulders that there's more coming.

"He's a king to be sure, but also a man bearing the weight of great sorrow."

My voice explodes through the glade. "He's no man at all. Finnbheara is a right Faerie villain undeserving of your sympathy." I fling my arms wide. "The bastard was on the verge of tossing you out of his gates into God knows what."

Her mouth is pressed so tightly that the skin around it blanches white. I know the look. She's carefully crafting her next words. "Sionnach, you and Finnbheara share the deep pain of lost love."

The notion I share anything with that monster guts me. "My love for Eala isn't in the same bucket as the king's twisted claim on her." Dropping hands to my knees, I hang my head. Each breath is a relentless squeeze. Separation from Eala suffocates me.

Ma's hand rests lightly on my heaving back. "I do not speak of our Eala, *Mac*."

Words stick in my throat, considering who she is speaking of. I can't bear to think about Ma being Finn's love, lost or otherwise.

"Sionnach, I can hear your thoughts like they're being shouted." My mother's warm fingers lift my chin. "I am not the source of the king's heart wound. 'Tis his lost queen, Nuala."

"Lost queen?" I'd assumed Finnbheara's missus was floating on Fae mists somewhere deep in Tír na nÓg, surrounded by Faerie music and an endless banquet of splendor. Nuala is known to me, of course. Now there is a woman of great patience given her husband's sport of collecting mortal lovers. Maybe the right regal gal dabbles in her own feast of human trysts, turning a blind eye to old Finn's roving cock.

I've no chance to question Ma before the ground beneath us begins to tremble. All the thin silver cylinders in the trees join in a single sharp note.

Ma scans the Glade of Chimes, worry lines showing deep in her flawless alabaster forehead. "The king. Mind your words and wit for Eala's sake if not for your own."

Before my eyes, Ma transforms into the glittering whirlwind her spirit has inhabited for two hundred years in this glade as she beckoned the dearly departed to choose a soulsong before they passed into their chosen afterlives. A slatted wooden door of a mighty tree on the banks of the striking blue lake yawns open. Even as Ma's twinkling mist slips inside, her voice floats toward me.

"Remember, *Mac*, life isn't served in a straight line. Mind the curves."

There's a *bang* as the door slams shut. I've traveled many times over my centuries as a Veil guide to face those familiar crooked slats, searching for solace and guidance from Ma. There's a stab of fresh loss in my weary heart. Will I ever meet her again as someone who can gather me into her arms and help me believe my fate is not bleak, or is she back to being only a wisp of wind?

I slump onto the polished amber stone cradled between trailing tree roots in front of Ma's tree. Martha O'Dwyer Loho, a woman who bears a core of grace and wisdom, begged for my patience. Finnbheara won't discover a man full of piss and fight, burning to confront him. I'll heed her advice and meet my Faerie foe with a façade of calm I don't truly feel.

At least, I'll begin there. There's no telling how long I'll be able to wear that set of clothes.

Hidden by the half-circle of blessed trees, Finnbheara's voice is no louder than the scratch of branch against bark. "If this is where your mother means to hide you, she failed." He steps into the clearing from behind a yew with bark wearing a coat of crushed gems the color of my fox's russet fur. "While countless souls may pass through this sacred glade, it is still under the purview of Tír na nÓg. Therefore, it's mine."

The king sucks in a quick breath through his clenched jaw.

"You, Fox, stand out in my kingdom as a diseased knot on an otherwise perfect trunk." Finn strokes a hand down the yew's shimmering bark. He saunters to the center of the clearing, then shifts into a wide stance, arms crossed over his chest. Corded muscles flex along his bare arms from shoulder to wrist. I can't tell if the bastard means to bait or intimidate me. Despite Ma's claims, this royal ass certainly doesn't outwardly wear the same stain of loss and despair shading my heart.

My gaze locks on the bladelike tip of his right ear that's defied its curtain of silver hair. It's a small blessing that particular Fae trait is not one Eala bears.

Thoughts of my *anamchara* grant me more incentive to keep this situation from turning into burnt gravy.

The king stands with the unnerving stillness of the Fae. His only movement is the narrowing of eyes with a color mirroring the deep teal of the lake. "I've prolonged your miserable existence well beyond what you deserve."

Staying true to Ma's wish, I lift my palms in a *then get on with it* gesture, as if I'm showing him my belly like a submissive hound.

Does disappointment flicker in his trick eyes? Ha. No doubt, the bastard was looking to provoke my brainless rage to justify a fist to my jaw.

Finnbheara tilts his head to one side, studying me before jerking a chin almost as pointed as his ear in my direction. "Do you not beg for my mercy, mangy fox?"

"Will it do me any good, your majesty?"

His eyes darken to the color of a midnight sky. Have I thrown the ass off by asking questions rather than swinging my fists?

"Only if you convince me your worth is anything besides cannon fodder in the approaching war with Aodh."

Och, so the snake is going to let Aodh do his dirty work. No surprise he doesn't let me answer before yammering on.

"For that is your sole value to me, spawn of Loho."

It takes massive effort not to explode at the demeaning title he takes pleasure tossing at me. The last marble of sense rolling around in my head warns me to keep acting undisturbed when in truth I'm a pot near to boiling over.

I rise and mask the aggression itching under my skin. "You should know this, sir. If Aodh's cannon takes me, it will destroy Eala with the same blow. Severing an *anamchara* bond by killing one of us is death to us both."

A single twitch of the eye betrays Finnbheara's unease at this revelation. My claim may not be true, but hopefully ole Finn's lack of understanding human bonds rankles him enough to believe it could be.

I shrug, choosing words to subtly push the pin in a bit deeper without showing the anger choking me. "I suppose Fae don't forge such deep loyalties."

Judging from the pinch marring his perfect royal face, my comeback may not have been as subtle as I intended. Royal fists curl at his sides and an angry flush darkens his majesty's pale skin. My accusation hit a Faerie nerve to be sure. The king's venomous glare feels like hot needles poking me from the inside. It takes everything I've got left in the strength department to endure the harrowing sensation and not let my temper rise.

Finn's irises pulse the color of a deep bruise, his tone ragged around the edges. "Your ignorance of our kind does not surprise me, spawn of Loho. A simple mind cannot comprehend such complexities as Fae bonds."

Is this unsettled Finnbheara my glimpse at the truth of what Ma revealed to me? Can a soulless creature weep for his lost queen?

"True, your highness." I tap a finger to the side of my head. "This simple mind does not understand why you allowed Eala to sacrifice her right to be in Tír na nÓg?"

Finnbheara's scowl deepens. "I allowed nothing she did not forfeit in favor of you."

He smacks an open palm to my chest, shoving hard enough to knock my feet out from under me. "You deserve nothing better than to wear your fox skin for the remainder of your days here." Finn's anger shifts into a royal smirk. "I'll even send a vixen to lift her tail for you. Mount the hapless beast and spread your vile kits across my kingdom. They'll make excellent sport for hunters."

I call on the last of my willpower not to lunge at the fucker after his vulgar portrait of my future in Tír na nÓg. Sliding away to add distance between us, I find my feet and face him.

"I'm going to decline your thoughtful offer to my fox." I straighten my clothing, striving for poise. I swear the ass stretches a few inches taller so he can look down at me from an even higher vantage point.

Not a blink from the fool. I'm speaking to a fecking wall of stone.

"As to the question of my worth to you, it lies in the bond Eala and I share. She will return. I believe there is fairness in your heart …" I hold back from insinuating he may not possess a heart. "…to honor the fair won bargain you made with her to let those dear to my *anamchara* dwell in your kingdom."

Finn rests his chin on a knuckle, mouth downturned. Royal anger is replaced with mischief in his twinkling eyes.

I look past the hammered silver band on his bicep to the tranquil lake beyond. "Until Eala comes for me, I'm happy to bide my time here with Ma in the Glade of Chimes and not bother you."

"You will bide your time, Sionnach Loho." He spits my name. I count the fact that he uses it at all as a small victory. "But not in this glade or with your mother." Finn nods at Ma's door in the tree. A malicious gleam brightens his deep emerald stare as he clasps his hands behind his back and saunters toward the shore. When he reaches the place where easy currents break and retreat under their crystal casing, he turns to me.

"You do indeed dwell in my lands at present, but you are not Fae." The king has the gall to chuckle. "Here, time is the enemy of a human mind. And yours, as is the way with others of your kind who linger in Tír na nÓg, will crumble and fade with madness."

My mind swims with stories of people returned from their visits with the Folk. A common thread between them being the alteration of who they once were. Some are said to grow dim of mind, others age at an unnatural rate, racing toward death, and many suffer unbearable sorrow at leaving the land of the Fae, where they lived in joy. Most never reclaim a solid footing in the mortal world. Then you have the fanciful yarns of departed humans who remain in Tír na nÓg, grow pointy ears and keep house in a storybook cottage with their Fae lover and generations of half-Faerie offspring. A pretty picture.

Finnbheara paints my future with the darker shades.

The king wears the smug expression of the upper hand. The smile stretching across his face is a frightful thing. "Eala may have bought your body an eternity in my kingdom, but your sanity was not in the bargain."

Finnbheara's truth isn't heading in a lovely direction for me. How long does it take a human to lose their mind in Finn's realm, where time trips along at a different pace? Instead of a husband, my swan may return to find a gibbering eejit.

"It's fair to presume the only way Eala'll walk back through your gates is if I'm waiting for her...untampered with." I clasp my hands together in supplication. "I'm just trying to reason with you here, man."

Finnbheara's laugh is a terrible thing. "Your audacity to presume my fate with Eala Duir is amusing. She will return because it is her true path. In the breadth of time, you'll be nothing more than a passing fancy to her." His laugh cuts off with bollocks-chilling speed. "I control your fate as I have since your mother first begged pity for your insignificant soul."

Oh, but he's a cold bastard.

"Once left alone with nothing but the fallacies of your thoughts for company, the path of your mortal mind's decay will be swift."

Damn this Faerie to his version of hell. He'll keep me here until he can get his filthy Fae hands on Eala. I'll be alive, but a raving shadow of the man she loves.

"You mean to drive me mad then? Ruin me for Eala so you can have her?"

The king raises an eyebrow. "I see your mother didn't raise an absolute imbecile for a son." His gaze darkens, brows slanting. Finnbheara shows me his teeth. "By the time my Eala returns, you will not possess enough mind to recognize her."

The last drop of restraint leaves my bones. "You soulless monster." Overlapping images of Ma in Finnbheara's embrace, Eala pounding on his gate, screaming my name, and me drooling like a mindless goat propel me at this Fae villain. Before my fists reach the underside of his jaw, the Fae king thrusts both arms forward, and a massive cyclone slurps me into its violent jaws.

CHAPTER 6
THE BOND-PROMISE

ROBBER BRIGHT

As we round the first sweeping curve of the walls of Aodh's fortress, *Caisleán Brón*, the Castle of Sorrows, I hear uneasy murmurs from the Host behind me.

"I fear touching those stones will burn my skin to the bone."

"Aye and melt those very bones along with it."

Snorts, trills, and growls tell me the *péist síoda* are on edge. A miasma of thick reddish-purple dragon steam hangs just above our heads. The Host's buzzing wingsong is deadened as it reverberates against the castle walls, adding sinister resonance to its usual high-spirited whir.

My Host is right to be on their guard. Each massive stone brick making up Aodh's castle is crafted of raw onyx, the single flame of a lost soul collected by Bráchthine enshrined within each one. The entire fortress gives off the appearance of a banked fire that would require but a puff of breath to encourage it into a raging conflagration.

Above us, the eyes of the first great swan high on the battlement follows our progress. I sense the fiery presence of Aodh's magic in the creature.

The Dark Prince watches.

I circle my fist in the air, giving the signal for silence. The Host of a

Thousand Wings' footing here is tenuous. We are unproven as of yet. I pledged our loyalty to Aodh, but the Underworld God is as untrusting as Finnbheara. Careless Fae kings do not keep their thrones. There will be tests, spoken or unspoken, and we must be vigilant.

My movement jostles Colleen, but she does not stir. I debate whether to give her into Acacia's keeping as I present the Host to our new master, but discard the notion. I brought the mortal here to bait Eala. This human's well-being is my burden.

The dragons retract their wings and march after me through the grand archway into the castle yard. Their clawed feet are no louder than a whisper against the silty ground. Obeying my command, the *péist síoda* cease all sounds and signs of discontent. We are a stoic unit as we form ranks throughout the courtyard before the formidable black steel doors of the castle.

My heartbeat ratchets when a company of Aodh's soldiers surrounds us. They wear heavy crimson armor, breastplates adorned with a black shield bearing the triple flame of Aodh's sigil. My Host is fitted with thin metallic tunics provided by the Dark Prince. I must see that soon, they too are given the studier battle armor of Aodh's legions.

The brawn and might of the Bráchthine soldiers may be a match for ours, but they bear the markings of Aodh's world—skin the color and texture of ash set to crumble off the end of a charred branch.

The biggest brute of all strides to the center of the top step. Unlike the other soldiers, the shield on his armor is outlined with three bands of gold, a sign of rank.

The man spins to face me, his movement practiced and officious. "Robálaí Geal, I am Dóite, First General to the King of Bráchthine. Your Host will dismount and stand beside their beasts. Only you and your high command are granted an audience with his majesty, Aodh."

I command the Host to follow the instructions of the Dark Prince's mouthpiece. Before I slide off Aillil's back, I press my lips close to Colleen's ear to alter the enchantment in which she lingers. Her current state of sleep must shift into tacit acceptance of the Fae company she keeps. "Within the castle, you will stir, and every action will endure. Have no question, doubt or fear, for Robin Bright is always near."

It is strange to speak the mortal version of my name I have used of late. To Eala, I am Robber Bright, a mere translation of my Fae name to her tongue.

Colleen only knows me as Robin Bright, a mockery of my true name. She perceives me to be human, an honorable member of the *Garda*, the police of her land. Shades and shadows of truth have I fed this woman, fabricating in her mind both an altered past and present for her to embrace. Human minds are so malleable. Under my continued influence, the mortal baggage should pose no hardship for me during our presentation to Aodh.

I hand Aillil's reins to the closest member of my Host and tuck Colleen's hand through my arm. Acacia, my second, and the trio of my most trusted fall in line behind me. Artos, the bear of a warrior with his mane of dark umber hair twisted into a single braid, positions himself at Acacia's side. Ciallmhar, my wisest strategist and a Fae witch of great power, and Nettle, the slightest and most underestimated soldier in my cadre, who delivers the swiftest sting with his blade, bring up the rear of our contingent.

We are led straight through a circular antechamber that could accommodate a hundred soldiers. At least twenty black stone hearths as tall as Artos and wide enough to fit a fully grown *péist síoda* drake blaze with roaring fires to light the great hall.

I flash a look at Colleen to see how my enchantment is faring. She takes in the surroundings with interest, but no distress. I pat her hand, and she smiles at me. The simple black damask frock with red beading around the cuffs and neckline I chose for her should demonstrate adequate respect for Aodh.

We cross beneath the arch farthest from the main entrance. It is framed with a glossy onyx trim bearing carvings of four swans in flight. Once inside the long hallway, the light dims as we travel deeper into the castle. The walls here are reminiscent of the tunnel in the Cave of Cats, all made of cut stone with intervals of small niches filled with finger-sized flames. I sense the rising tension of my companions. Perhaps I was remiss in my portrayal of what they were to expect in Aodh's palace. After all, I experienced similar trepidation the first time I traversed this route.

Turning my head, I strive to reassure my high command with words casual enough not to alert Dóite and the guards that both lead and follow our group of the concern I sense in my Folk. "We are close to entering Aodh's throne room. Its magnificence is worth a journey through shadow." I pick up the pace feigning eagerness to be in Aodh's presence.

Aodh

Dark Prince

King of Bráchthine
Underworld God

I release a low grunt at Aodh's collection of titles. The man likes to flaunt his importance. He could add *stealer of queens* and *grand master of grudges* to his monikers. I wipe any trace of judgment from my expression. Fae arrogance is expected, but any visible disrespect for Aodh's person could earn me a slice or two from his fiery onyx blade.

The black lacquered oak doors of the throne room suddenly appear as if conjured. Acacia stifles a gasp. I want to assure her the illusion is a trick of the dim light, but am loath to draw any attention to reactions signaling concern in my high command. Unease will not work in our favor.

Dóite takes hold of an iron ring the size of a platter fit for a roasted pig and pounds it against the door with four distinct blows. I am reminded that four is a sacred number to the God of the Underworld. Four, to symbolize the Children of Lir, Aodh's tragic legacy. It is no random happenstance I chose four of the Host to represent my high command. It is meant as a sign of acknowledgement and respect to Aodh's valued number.

The general stands aside as the massive doors creak open on their own, driven by Aodh's power. From the corner of my eye, I catch Colleen staring upward. She may search for the topmost portion of these doors but will not find them as they disappear in shadow.

Dóite clears his throat. "Our king awaits." Ah, so today Aodh chooses to be addressed as King of Bráchthine. Our escort widens his stance, waiting for us to move past him. When our contingent enters the room, the soldiers fan out across the opening behind us, blocking potential escape. It is one of many signs Aodh questions my shift in allegiance.

I did not speak falsely when I named this chamber magnificent. A circle of a thousand slender trees made of black glass comprises its walls. Each trunk rests perfectly against the next. Twisted branches reach upward then writhe across the ceiling to meet and intertwine with their fellows from the opposite side of the round room, forming a canopy overhead. Adornments of crimson crystal leaves are scattered over tangled boughs. These dark brethren mock the clear glass trees that illuminate Finnbheara's realm. Here each trunk houses a robust red scorch the height of a man instead of Tír na nÓg's delicate silver flames.

Heat licks the soles of my boots. Here is another detail I failed to prepare my Folk for. The floor of the chamber is made of thick black glass. Beneath it lies a bed of crushed obsidian mined from the volcanic park nestled among Aodh's faraway red mountains. The stone still bears the heat of its birthplace. Pinpoints of red mica glitter like bloody stars scattered throughout gleaming black silt.

I lift my gaze to the center of the chamber and the six-sided platform made of the same rough onyx as the outer castle walls. Atop it is a throne of brilliant black diamond fashioned in the likeness of a swan taking flight, its mighty wings outspread. Leaning back against the breast of the great bird is Himself, Aodh, God of the Underworld, Dark Prince, and King of Bráchthine.

Beside me, in a voice more breath than word Colleen says, *"Eala dubh."* Eala's name catches me off guard until I realize it is not the name of her friend the human utters, but the phrase *black swan* to voice her awe at Aodh's throne. She unexpectedly drops into a curtsy, prompting the rest of us to dip our heads in reverence.

"My king," I say in greeting as my companions maintain silent deferential poses.

Aodh slowly rises. Peering through my lashes I watch as he scrutinizes us. Even though I prepared the Host for the unnerving sight of our new master, nothing compares to being in his presence. Unease radiates off my company like the snap of winter frost.

The king releases a guttural chuckle at their attempt to mask discomfort. "I sense there is need for the Host of a Thousand Wings to redefine what is considered beauty."

His skin is a swirl of grays from dark to light, reminiscent of the ashen remains of a spent bonfire, but the king is anything but spent. A deep glow matching his blood-orange sun radiates from within him, bathing his skin with warmth that belies the barrenness of his charred exterior. Aodh's face is unnaturally long and gaunt, with faceted black diamond eyes so deeply set they live in shadow except for flickers of crimson irises that illuminate overlarge pupils.

Aodh's gaze continues to bore into us. "Here in Bráchthine, loveliness is not measured as it is in the gilded pages of Finnbheara's beloved tomes. You will come to appreciate the splendor of cinder, glass, and flame."

There is no possibility the king misses Artos's loud swallow. I do not begrudge my lieutenant his reaction, but wish it were at a lesser volume. The first time in Aodh's presence, near-disgust rose in me so palpably, I feared he would sense my aversion and refuse to treat with me. Forcing myself to accept the similarities between Finnbheara and this royal before me instead of their stark contrasts is what allowed me to maintain my poise on that fated day.

Both kings assume the form of a warrior, similar in stature. Similar to Fae and human alike, Aodh and the Folk of Bráchthine share the likeness of the ancient gods and goddesses that came before us. We do not bear tail, horn, or the over-sharp teeth of beasts. The fine taper of our ears forever points to the skies from whence all Fae were wrought of ageless stardust.

I sneak a glance at my fellows to see how they fare at their first glimpse of the god. They seem to have adjusted their initial surprise and found the wherewithal to perceive the Dark Prince as a fellow Fae, albeit in a foul wrapping.

Colleen releases a loud sigh beside me, and I tense. This mortal is untested against a being such as Aodh, who is dissonant to anything that exists in her world. I pray my influence over her holds true, and she does not treat him as a horror. Risking a glance in Ciallmhar's direction, I twitch a finger at my head, questioning in our well-practiced shorthand if he senses Aodh invading the human's thoughts. My Fae witch forms the word *no* with his lips.

Still, I hold my breath, awaiting Aodh's pronouncement of my name to release us from our posture of obeisance. Instead, he marches off his dais toward us. Each footfall of his black metal boots covered in ornate crisscrossed bands of red crystal reverberates in muffled thunder around the throne room. He moves to stand in front of Colleen.

"Rise, Finnbheara's Treasure," he commands.

Colleen does not stand. Her head flicks side to side, searching for the object of Aodh's attention. I taste the tang of her confusion on my tongue.

"Do not be coy. Your contributions shall be honored in Bráchthine. I will raise the statue of a white swan among my onyx ones to show my gratitude." The Dark Prince presses a knuckle to the underside of her chin and lifts, forcing her to look upon him. "You will answer the request of your new king, Eala Duir."

Heat radiates from him like kindling catching fire. Unblinking eyes narrow as he takes in every detail of Colleen's face. Aodh lowers his nose to the top of her head and inhales deeply. An ominous rumble sounds from his chest.

If I have any hope of preventing this meeting from devolving into something merciless, I must speak before he does. "A thousand pardons, your majesty. I am at fault for failing to present my companion, the Lady Colleen."

Aodh fists the front of my metal breastplate as if it is made of paper, pulling me to him. The Dark Prince roars. "Robálaí Geal, you dare to present this mortal instead of Finnbheara's Treasure? I smell nothing in her vapid human essence of the *beads of being* you vowed on your life and that of your Host to bring to me."

Beside me, Colleen whimpers at the fury in Aodh's voice as my companions draw closer. I wave them off and do not resist the king. "I assure you, she is a treasure of a different sort."

Aodh lets loose a hearty laugh, breaking the tension, and flings me backward. I smack into Artos's broad chest. The Dark Prince shakes a thick finger at me. "Aha, an offering to your king." The god palms his crotch, treating himself to a few quick strokes as he leers at Colleen. I restrain the urge to drive my sword into his evident arousal.

"You have brought me the first course of our banquet to celebrate your arrival in Bráchthine." He grabs Colleen's shoulders, holding her at arm's length while his lascivious gaze rakes down her body. His fingers thread into the auburn hair at her nape, which shines ruby in the reddish light of the chamber.

When he jerks her head back, dipping low to run a thick gray tongue along the length of her throat to the swell of her breasts, my blood turns to ice. It is a grievous error to bring a helpless, hapless friend of Eala's into the realm of a restless god as mercurial as Finnbheara without a drop of the scant mercy flowing through the King of the Connacht Fae's veins. My hands fist tightly enough for my fingernails to gouge flesh.

I force nonchalance into my voice and move closer to Colleen. "That is not my purpose in bringing this particular woman before you. Apologies for my lack of foresight. I should have procured a different human delicacy to present to you for flesh sport."

Aodh straightens and insinuates himself between Colleen and me. The flickering crimson flecks in his eyes multiply and frantically swim through his irises. His breath is hot enough against my skin to blister. The air grows thick with a scent of burning garbage. "I will give you two hundred words to explain why this human and not Eala Duir is in your company before you and your Host will suffer my wrath."

Nettle attempts to move closer to Colleen's side. Even with a royal, irate bulk in the way, I see her tremble. Without taking my gaze from Aodh, I strengthen my influence on her to rid the woman of any fear threatening to break through.

"This mortal plays many parts in our game, my king." I bow my head in renewed deference. "She shares a deep bond with Eala Duir." I hate myself for the stutter in my breath as the lie ripens on my tongue. "Eala Duir's ties to Finnbheara were stronger than I anticipated. The campaign to bring her before you will require a bit more finesse than my original plan."

Aodh stares at me, the stink of his malevolence spoiling the air.

"I revealed to Finnbheara's Treasure that the Lady Colleen left the world above to accompany me through Oweynagat. I swear by my oath of loyalty to you, great Aodh, Eala Duir will agree to journey here with me in search of her friend. You shall have the white swan in your thrall soon enough and fulfill your desire to uncover the mystery of the *beads of being*."

The Dark Prince's lips curl into a snarl, revealing ivory teeth veined in black. "These ramblings are an admission of your failure, Robálaí Geal."

Aodh stalks around me, showering me with evidence of his disgust in the form of floating ash that sticks in my nostrils and on my lips. In the corner of my vision, I see Nettle succeed in drawing Colleen aside.

The Underworld God's sneer sharpens cheekbones jutting above the crevices of his sunken face. His mask of menace is as repulsive as it is concerning. "You vowed your famed powers of seduction would be no match for a creature the likes of Eala Duir, who holds fast to her flimsy core of humanity." Those disgusting veined teeth sink into a bottom lip that resembles spoiled and cracked earth baked beneath a relentless sun. "Finnbheara's Treasure is the promised prize, yet you bring only a human lure before my throne." He pounds a fist onto his open palm. "This is an inauspicious beginning to our allegiance."

"Evidence of my loyalty lies in the act of defection from the Connacht king, avowed service to you, my liege lord, and the arrival of my Host and fifty *péist síoda* at the gates of your fortress." My two hundred words are nearly spent. Aodh is a literal hot head, but my turned coat alone marks me as an asset in the rising tension between Finnbheara and him.

A corner of Aodh's mouth twitches. "If the human is but a lure, you will not object if I burnish your lovely companion's womb with my hot seed?" The Dark Prince snaps his teeth together on the word *hot*.

The wise reaction is to pretend to appreciate Aodh's lewdness and show no interest in the bastard's desires to use Colleen as he will. In this instant, I am not wise.

"No." The unfortunate response has passed my lips before my wit can stop it. I am a fool. There is no sane reason for me to protect this woman. Her purpose is nothing more than to attract the true prize Aodh desires—Eala.

"No?" Aodh bellows, malignant anger swirling through his voice. "You refuse to extend such generosity to your king?"

My misstep raises a scorch of dread in my chest as torrid as the flames that pepper this kingdom. I must overturn my error before it ends in disaster for the Host of a Thousand Wings.

I paste a conspiratorial expression across my face to wrap my objection to the king's request to defile Colleen in the guise of a jibe. "As wondrous as it would be for any mortal to receive the gift of your royal cock, the experience for you would be lacking. Especially when the incomparable true queen, Nuala, attends to your pleasures." I top it off with a salacious wink.

Aodh answers with the unyielding stare of a true Fae. I am accustomed to the tactic as it is one of Finnbheara's as well. The arrogance of Faerie kings gives them a similar transparency. They thrive on constant strokes to their egos. I will give this tyrant the stroking of a lifetime to get what I need from him.

I tap a finger to my lip. "Then again, if you tire of Queen Nuala's bed, perhaps I shall fetch a fresh mortal beauty to invigorate your appetite." Aodh reveals nothing as to his current status with my former queen. My loyalty to her and what she sacrificed by forfeiting our realm for this place of strange, dismal beauty yearns for reassurance that Nuala has found some brand of peace here. Does she retain her vivacity and royal elegance, or has she faded to gray beneath rock and root?

The Dark Prince's eyes widen as he points an ashy finger at me. "I see you Robálaí Geal. You are bargaining with me." To my surprise, Aodh breaks into robust laughter before shaking his outstretched finger. "I appreciate a general that does not reveal all." His mirth shifts into unsettling seriousness as he nods toward Colleen. "You dance around this mortal's presence on your arm?"

Here is the test. If I claim she is nothing, he will take her from me. If I admit to a bond between us, I expose her as potential leverage he may use against me.

"Your hesitation does you no favor." Aodh approaches. His knuckles grind against my stingy breastplate. "You fail to bring me Finnbheara's Treasure. Your mention of Nuala reeks of hidden purpose. The truth of this mortal at your side remains elusive." He pulls away then punches me just below the throat, sending me stumbling backward.

I must not show weakness. Standing up to his doubts about me is essential. I do not back down. "I have laid the trap for Eala Duir. She possesses my ring, the key that will bring her to me. The mortal Colleen is sweet bait to call Finnbheara's Treasure to us. Does not nectar capture the prey better than the net?" I drop to a knee before the tyrant. "Sire, you shall soon possess the *beads of being*."

Aodh looms above me. "I must have unshakeable trust in those who serve Bráchthine. Your allegiance to Finnbheara withered when he failed to value and respect you. You ask of me what he failed to bestow. I acknowledge, Robálaí Geal, you are a fine warrior with the impressive Host at your back." He jerks his chin for me to stand then leans in close. "Value is earned. Until you have done so, I will pour this feminine nectar you bring to Bráchthine into my vessel."

The Dark Prince sweeps over to Colleen and takes her by the arm, turning his back on me to ferry her to the swan throne for nature knows what debasement.

I am dismissed.

Surrendering this woman as a hostage weakens my position with Aodh. All I gained in our negotiations will crack like ice in dawn light if he thinks I am so easily cowed. This is a test. I denied him my human, yet he grasps for her a second time. My purpose here and the safety of my Host may be in peril if I do not counter his affront to what I have claimed as mine.

There is but one declaration guaranteed to throw victory to me. Its cost will shake the foundation of trust with those I hold in sacred esteem, but I see no other path.

"I fear that would be unwise, sire. This woman who enters your realm by my side also willingly serves our combined purpose to call Eala Duir to Bráchthine...for Lady Colleen is my bond-promised."

From the corner of my eye, I see Acacia's hands snap into fists. What deity under the stars will ever forgive such an act of overt betrayal? None. And none should. Shame gouges the core of my soul, but I must not show it.

Crimson flames dance in Aodh's eyes. "I am to believe Robálaí Geal, great commander and general, bestowed the most precious of gifts a Fae has to share on this human, a lesser being?"

I must embrace my falsehood. The first of many prices I fear I will be asked to pay to gain Aodh's trust.

"There are some powers that overcome even the mightiest of us, my king." I stretch out a hand to bid Colleen to return to me. She curtsies to the Dark Prince and comes as I beckon. The clarity in her eyes is jarring. Something in her gaze as it locks on mine transcends the gauzy light of affection my influence creates. She threatens my composure, which cannot waver in front of the Underworld God. I force myself to focus on her hand as I touch my lips to her knuckles.

When I again face the king, I am met with a ghastly, calculating scowl. "Yet you did not present her as your bond-promised upon your arrival."

"I did not think it pertinent to our discourse."

The scowl on the Dark Prince's face reforms into an expression of satisfaction as if he has discovered the means to overturn my victory.

"If this claim of bond-promise is true, your king demands proof."

CHAPTER 7
THE HARE

EALA

I puff my cheeks in frustration as I stand inside the Veil and jab a finger for at least the tenth time into the account of Biddy's trial in Sion's book. Nothing happens. This beauty of prisms and possibilities around me remains still. How could I be any clearer about where I want to go?

A darker thought punches through my impatience. My grip slackens on the book, and it drops onto the cushy orbs of the Veil's floor. *Has Finnbheara rescinded my ability to travel?*

I stare at the book at my feet. If I can't travel to other times, how can I hope to consort with a witch from the past? The very witch who may have a connection to the Fae and knowledge of a way into Tír na nÓg.

Fighting panic, I flip through every instruction Sion ever gave me on Veil travel while I babble. "Biddy Early. Biddy Early. Biddy Early."

There are numerous myths and tales citing that a repetition of three will jar something loose in the ethereal and mystical.

I get nothing.

I've got to get hold of myself. In my rattled state, Biddy will meet a blithering mess. I retrieve the book. Sion always said calm intention was the best compass to guide Veil travel.

"Well, Alfie, let's try again," I say to the white poplar poised inside the Veil window. I made a few adjustments once I'd embraced my ability to move through the Veil. A preview window and Alfie travelling inside the portal give me more confidence when traipsing through time.

I grip one of her branches. Energy thrums against my palm, but no visions or answers pop into my head. I've got to think. Why didn't the Veil take me to Biddy's trial when I showed it the book?

"Oh, for god's sake, Eala." I'm tempted to knock the book against my head as the problem becomes clear. I was focusing on its pages, not the place or time. Dammit, Sion is so much better at this than I am.

The Veil will answer to you, Swan.

The memory of Sion's words encourages me. I close my eyes and let the location of Ennis, Ireland, instead of the book in my hand, overtake my thoughts. Picking at memories from my research, I picture a courtroom in the 1860s, Victorian times. For the last piece in my mental GPS, I allow two words to float above it all—*witch trial.*

The Veil moves forward like a reluctant puppy on a leash.

Renewed confidence fills me. I lay a hand on the portal's dazzling wall. "Thank you."

The response is a whoosh that would knock me over if Alfie weren't close enough for me to cling to for support. For a few uncertain moments, I'm caught in the crosswinds of time being bent and reshaped. Memories of how my first experiences of Veil travel turned my stomach come rushing back. That was before Sion taught me how beautiful the sensation of shifting time could be.

The Veil's window, a transparent vortex with a border of melted colors, spins in front of me. Off in the distance, I see an official looking building in the style of Greek architecture complete with pediment and columns framed by two massive trees. Even though I've arrived at night, there's a group of people milling at the bottom of the grand steps leading into what I'm hoping is the Ennis courthouse.

I chose a black Victorian dress with a snug buttoned bodice, long sleeves, and a full skirt from Alfie's bag of clothing. I look like a Civil War widow. Hopefully the outfit is simple enough not to stand out. The portal opens near a cluster of trees so I'm not too conspicuous as I leave the confines of my personal highway.

I approach the crowd, pretending to be searching for someone and keep my ears open for any snippets of why the bystanders are here. The sounds of a heated argument reach me. Sure enough, I hear the word *witch* being bandied around in the same sentence as Biddy Early. There seem to be two schools of thought, one raring for a good old-fashioned witch burning, and the counterpoint dismissing the concept of witchcraft as ludicrous and antiquated.

In my opinion this whole circus is ridiculous. According to Sion's book, Biddy is being tried on laws dating back to the 1500s. Charging her as a witch is as ignorant as believing donkeys have enchanted hair.

A raised voice catches my attention. "She consorts with Folk who do dark deeds for her."

The answer is every bit as vitriolic. "Until we see her turned to ash, she may yet call devils down on us all."

It would be gratifying to shut these idiots up by announcing Biddy will not be convicted. I rub my lips together to keep from laughing. I'd love to spook every narrow mind with a list of magical retaliations due to them for daring to bring a potential witch to trial.

Lantern light shines on the face of a tall man, giving him a ghoulish look. "Have they brought the witch to town?"

The answering voice makes no attempt to mask her anger. "If she's here, we should set flame to her in case the fools in court see fit to grant her freedom."

And people say Faeries are evil bastards.

Someone else in the throng chimes in. "I heard tell they're bringing her in at dawn."

I wonder what's going through Biddy's head on the eve of her trial. Is she frightened? Disgusted? Vindictive?

If Sion were here, he'd been using his wry and wicked sense of humor to rile these superstitious jerks, knowing full well Biddy will have the last laugh.

But Sion isn't here.

The jolt of missing him is so sudden and acute, I double over, clutching my stomach. I must have cried out because a man who looks far too refined to be part of these dim-witted pot stirrers rushes to my side.

He bends to look into my face. "Are you well, miss?"

My lip quivers as I straighten and meet his gaze. "It's missus—Mrs. Sionnach Loho."

I turn, attempting to leave.

"You do not look well." He sets a hand on my arm to keep me from running off. "May I send for your husband then?"

"You can't. He's, he's…" I can't say gone. I won't say dead. I answer this good Samaritan with tears welling in my eyes. I hate my lack of control.

The man takes notice of my black dress and uncomfortable awareness dawns across his face. "Och, my sympathies to you missus." His gaze rakes over the clusters of people gathered in buzzing conversations. "This bubbling pot is no place for a woman bearing your burden." He nods at a group of women at the edge of the crowd. "My wife is just there. Let her see you home." His hand clamps firmly on my upper arm, and I'm dragged closer to the mob.

Home.

Do I have a home anymore? The Loho cottage is nothing more than a shell without Sion's laughter, grumbles, and tender touches against my skin.

Crushing anxiety starts to set in as my impeding meltdown draws more attention. I can't let myself get tangled up in a past where I may very well stick out as *other*. With this rising witch fever, I might be suspected as another one of the devil's alleged brides. I'm an odd woman on the eve of a witch trial. I might as well have a black cat at my heel.

I pull from his grasp. "Thank you, but no." I'm off and running for the shelter of the trees where I can call the Veil. There's no point in lingering. Biddy is not here. Even if she was, it could be dangerous to try and get in contact surrounded by all this stupidity and suspicion as thick as custard on Máthair's Irish apple cake. In my desperation to feel as if I'm making any progress toward saving my *anamchara*, I didn't take time to consider the necessary nuances of my plan. I'm becoming as impulsive as Sionnach Loho.

I fall into the Veil, shaken and filled with shame at my inability to handle the task. How does falling apart at any reference to my husband help him? I can't do this, but I have to. I've left my *anamchara* vulnerable and powerless under what has to be an avalanche of Finnbheara's rage.

"Be strong, Eala. Be strong for Sion." I blow out through my mouth as if to expel the weakness clinging to my spirit. All around me the lights of the Veil dance, waiting for direction.

I'm seeking a woman rumored to be wise in the way of the Folk. If the history and accounts hold any truth, Biddy will be well-schooled in the art of Faerie bargains. Instead of pulling off an eleventh hour save before the trial, the better choice is to show up when its unknown conclusion poses a future threat to Biddy. Then, I can offer her a deal that if she lends me her magical expertise to get my husband out of Tír na nÓg, I will guarantee the outcome of this witch hunt ends in her favor. The true facts of history are my bargaining chip.

It's sneaky and has the stink of manipulation but it might work. I huff. Apparently, I'm more in touch with my Fae chops than I think.

Driving on Irish backroads is trial by fire. Thank goodness the borrowed car from Bobbo Corrigan and his husband, Dale, is a compact automatic. I'm going to owe them for a new paint job due to the numerous scrapes I've inflicted on the poor car from getting too close to wild hedgerows. These teeny roads have one lane with questionable pavement and only a strip of grass down the middle to navigate by.

I knead the tension cramp in my thigh when I pull off to let a tractor pass. Sion drives these roads without a care, even though he was born long before cars were a thing.

The heartache of missing him, coupled with guilt for leaving him, spikes for the thousandth time. I want him here next to me so badly, driving us to some new breathtaking spot in Ireland to enchant me. Maybe a hillside blanketed with blooming wild irises or a lake where dozens of wild swans glide through the water next to an ancient castle. I yearn for his kisses and the safety of his arms.

"Enough, Eala," I yell. It's time to stop losing myself in memories and daydreams. I must hold fast to faith that the real thing, my love, my *anamchara*, will be by my side soon.

Last night, I did what a rational college professor would have done in the first place and analyzed other possibilities of the Faerie wind's message. Focusing my attention on the immediacy of the witch trial blasted me into the middle of a dicey situation. Now, with my thoughts clearer, I'm convinced foretelling Biddy's legal predicament will be the leverage I need to clinch a bargain with her.

I hope traveling to meet the witch in her home will make her more at ease and amenable to listening to my situation. Since I can't go to her until sunset and the start of the half of the Celtic Day when I'm allowed to Veil travel, I've decided to visit the place she lived and see what else I can learn about her to bolster my case.

The houses here are spaced far apart, each set in the middle of its own sprawling fields. Around the next bend, the Feakle cemetery where Biddy Early is said to be buried comes into view. I head there first. My Faerie *sight* led me to Strongbow's true grave. Trusting in visions worked before. I'm counting on it to work again.

The small car park is empty except for a row of donation bins. I check the website on my phone, confirming the locator number of Biddy's grave then walk through the gate. The cramped cemetery is on a steep hillside without much space between headstones or monuments. I search the first few plots with names and dates chiseled into marble. None are marked with locator signs or tags.

This final resting place of Feakle's residents, past and present, is a mishmash. Some gravestones are polished and new, others are so old they're pitted from the weather and smeared with black, white, and brownish-red growths of lichen or moss. The names they once bore have long since washed away.

My legs burn as I trudge up and down the slope in a systematic pattern between the graves. I can only make out the dates carved into stone on one or two oldies from the 1800s. I scoured the Internet, and even though there are accounts of people finding Biddy's marker, they are vague and do me no good. At the bottom of the hill, I stare up at the collection of monuments and crosses, both shiny and dull, silhouetted against the watered-down blue sky. Using the concrete post next to an iron Gothic gate for support, I close my eyes and let my mind search for Biddy.

Come home.

My body stiffens, alert and on guard, uncertain if the words came to me from inside or outside my head. Did a restless soul beneath the earth try to hail me? Máthair's phrase about a goose walking over your grave sends a sharp chill through me. In this case, I'm the goose to the folks resting nearby. Thank heavens, a glance around the cemetery confirms I'm still alone. My

Faerie gifts are new to me. If they include striking up a conversation with every chatty ghost in the place, I'll pass.

A car pulls onto the gravel and parks near me. I hate to disturb people coming to pay respects to someone more recently passed than a long-dead witch.

A pair of elderly women chatter and laugh as they head for the gate. A sudden pang of longing for Colleen hits me. Would we have been like those two ladies years from now if I hadn't brought the Fae into her life? Is there any hope we can still find days of carefree laughter together?

"Hiya, dear," says an iron-haired woman in a bright floral floor-length skirt topped with a bulky oatmeal-colored sweater. The shorter of the two leans on a cane and nods at me.

"Good morning."

They stare at me as if waiting for more.

What the hell do they expect me to say? "Be careful. The grass is pretty mushy."

That sparks a laugh from them. Cane lady taps the rubber tip on the gravel. "Oh, we know all the treacherous spots, darlin'."

They don't give off the vibe of mourners. In fact, given their gaiety, I wouldn't be surprised if they were here to picnic.

She fans her cane across the cemetery. "Who are your people then?"

Possibilities tumble through my head. Should I say O'Dwyer, Máthair's maiden name, or Loho, or—

Biddy's name rushes out of me. "Bridget Ellen Early O'Connor."

Delight shines on their faces. "Well then," says the one with the overly bright skirt. "You're family. I'm Mary Bridget O'Connor, also from Biddy's line." She opens her arms wide. I'm afraid not accepting her embrace would be an insult, so I do.

I break away first, and the cane points in my direction. "You're American?"

"Yes." They wait for more, and I oblige. "But I've recently married a County Clare man and relocated."

They both nod. The hugger lays a hand on my shoulder. "Perfect. So many leave. It's lovely to know some hearts are coming back home."

Her kind welcome moves me. I push on. "I've heard Biddy's cottage is close by. Do you know where it is?"

This time, the cane points past the cemetery wall toward the rolling green countryside. "Over that way," says the cane's owner. "Go four or five minutes and you'll pass a farmhouse on the left. Keep a sharp eye out for a broken-down gate. It's an old one, wood, not metal. Don't go through it. Cross the road and find the elder tree by the hedgerow. There's a path waiting. The walk is short, but it's got plenty of nettles waiting to stick in your clothing. Once the way tilts up a bit, you'll see the old chimney and ivy swallowing what's left of the cottage."

Oh Lord. I'll never find it.

"Or," says the hugger, pointing up the road. "You can go to the pub just there and have Andrew drive you. He's the town historian and can fill you with lots of Biddy stories."

I thank them, then tootle off to find Andrew the historian, a cheery fellow in his sixties, seated in a corner of the pub on the main highway through Feakle. He's reading a newspaper, a real newspaper.

The man does not disappoint. He's friendly and larger than life as he gleefully regales me with details of Biddy's multiple marriages, including one to her stepson. He assures me with a wink that there was not as big an ick factor for that brand of coupling back then as there is now. I decline his offer to drive me to the spot where I'd find the path to Biddy's cottage and follow him there in my borrowed Corriganmobile instead. With a honk and a shouted invitation to rejoin him at the pub for more Biddy lore, he leaves me.

I'm glad I opted for my hiking boots as I make my way along the muddy path. It doesn't seem as though there's much foot traffic through here. Wild vines and robust ferns encroach as if to hide the trail. On this cloudless late afternoon, a finger of chill breeze stirs branches and leaves. The overgrowth makes the way shadowy, and while not ominous, it certainly isn't welcoming.

I wonder if lingering wisps of the witch's spirit don't appreciate people snooping around her home place. Remembering the hostile crowd from the courthouse last night, I suspect there were more than a few unfriendly visitors who followed this same path while Biddy was alive.

Rocks, roots, and other tripping hazards force me to keep my eyes locked on the ground. The energy here is unmistakable. Whether it's for protection or prevention, I can't tell. Andrew assured me the way would be less than ten or fifteen minutes. I glance at my watch. I've been walking for more than twenty.

"Shit." I'm lost.

My expletive disturbs a hare hiding under a scrubby bush. It darts out, running across the toes of my boots. The critter's movement is so swift and unexpected, I lose my balance and accidentally kick the poor thing. It rolls a little way in front of me, and I rush to crouch by its side to see if it's injured.

"Oh, sweetie. I'm sorry." I start to reach for it and stop. Touching it may scare the poor little thing to death. It's rapid breathing sets its sides fluttering. Long black tipped ears quiver as its round amber eyes lock onto mine then flick to my hand. I slowly move away, letting the creature know I'm not going to harm it.

The hare flips to its feet, but instead of running off, it faces me. I get a strange feeling the critter is trying to read my mind. Our standoff lasts only seconds before it wiggles its nose and hops right past me back the way I've come. I expect it to disappear into layers of overlapping ferns, but it stops, then turns to watch me.

I don't move, worried I'll spook it again. "Go on, bunny."

Can I call this wild hare a bunny without insulting it?

A shaft of light knives through the trees, and the animal's golden-brown fur takes on a luminous luster. Damn if my visitor doesn't give off an enchanted vibe.

Staring me down for a second, it turns, hops twice before it pauses again, then swivels to face me. I take two careful steps in its direction. Satisfied, it resumes hopping along the skinny trail surrounded by vegetation.

As long as I keep moving, so does the hare. I've seen enough weird things lately to believe I'm being led. So, I follow. We backtrack until I see the place where I veered off the broader path. Not much further on, there's a slight rise. As I round its curve, my hair begins to float, causing me to look up from the hare. The ivy-covered ruins of Biddy Early's cottage stand in front of me.

It's more intact than I would've guessed. Peering inside a window, I see vines clinging to the walls with blossoms here and there, decorating worn gray stone like natural wallpaper. The mucky floor is covered with a layer of loam and dark crimson leaves. Shadows play across stone punctuated with a splash of light, calling attention to the crumbling hearth. The place has the look of scenery on a stage waiting for actors to appear and begin the play.

All along the sill are offerings to the witch. Coins, crystals, and even a silver chalice with the name O'Connor etched into its tarnished surface crowd together. I move through the square opening where I imagine a red painted wooden door used to be like the one at Loho Cottage. Inside, there are more goodies tucked into corners, including dusty bottles of wine or whiskey. A rusting black iron cookpot, which I doubt is Biddy era accurate, has been shoved against the wall next to the hearth. I bend to study a wooden candlestick ornately carved with stars, pentagrams, and hexafoils—witch symbols.

In the sky above this quiet little wood, clouds arrive, blocking the sun. I wish I'd thought to bring a flashlight. When I reach for my phone, silvery-blue light fills the cottage.

"I could have done without your boot to my side."

I gasp, startled by the nearness of the voice. Warm breath moves through cool air.

There, not a foot away, rubbing a hand to her hip against the skirt of a simple homespun dress the same brownish-gold color as the fur of the hare, is a woman. She's rounder and taller than I, with twinkling sea blue eyes that stare over a long, almost bladelike nose. Her form wavers, not transparent but not substantial. She's outlined in the same shimmery light spilling into the cottage.

The ghostly gal points a warning finger at me. "If you've come to blame me for your cow's milk drying up or the catarrh rolling through the village, I'm not the cause."

I shake my head strongly enough to rattle my teeth. "No. I'm not here to accuse you of anything."

"On with it then. Tell me why you've come, lass." The corner of her wide lips curls as she cocks her head to the side, then raises a finger. "You needn't say. A yearning for love shines bright in your lonely green eyes." She nods then glances away from me around the cottage, looking for something. "It's a potion you'll be asking me for."

"You're the hare." Countless Irish tales of magic folk taking the form of hares support my theory.

The woman stiffens as she studies me through narrowed eyes. Whatever she finds on my face eases her wariness. With hands on hips, she flashes a mischievous smile.

"I'm the witch."

CHAPTER 8
THE GEM KISSED FOREST

SIONNACH

I fly backward through the Finn-whipped whirlwind and land with a thump on my back. It knocks half the breath from me, but not all. I've got enough wits to become aware of ear-piercing snaps and crashes all around.

The king stands above me. Violent swirls of slate gray haze pour off Finnbheara's body. He's the eye of a hurricane, generating whips of destruction in every direction. Colors of blood and blinding white explode in his eyes.

Well, Sionnach Loho, your runaway gob has finally done you in.

The king's roar piercing through this cacophony is more animal than man. "Let the misguided Host hate me and revile my name. They will perish long before I take my last breath. I curse this forest where once they dwelt."

Finn's sudden disappearance is as ominous as his tantrum.

Once I'm certain there's no more rubbish flying through the air to brain me, I sit up. The angry blow settles, letting me see my surroundings. The grassy ground beneath me is forgiving, or I'd surely have shattered bones from dropping in here. We're in a wood, but not the Glade of Chimes. Slender trunks shine like pearls while others shimmer with a golden sparkle. Colors here are bright, vibrant, and a click or two away from real. A green is not a green, but a glowing lime. There's moss that looks as if it were painted the dark purple-pink of a fuchsia flower. Blues reflect the aqua tint of the sea in hidden coves.

Off a way, down a narrow dirt path is a cottage with a collapsed roof that looks like it took a boulder from a trebuchet. Adding to the otherness of this place, I see fancy bottles scattered all over. They could be part of a fantasy giantess' collection of perfumes. Some are shattered, but others nestle in the trailing roots of these strange trees or tuck against boulders with surfaces so polished they reflect like mirrors. Most bottles appear intact even though a few wear wee chips in the glass.

A handful of tree trunks and the great rocks don't fare as well, bearing deep scratches and dings no doubt inflicted by the Finn storm that raged through here moments ago.

At first, I think the man himself abandoned me, but his voice rings out from behind, making me jump.

"Let the echoes of betrayal in this cursed place hasten your madness. A beautiful prison is still a prison, Sionnach Loho." Without another word, the king is gone. I keep still while the minutes tick, expecting the bugger to pop back and rekindle his taunting.

He doesn't.

I approach the closest pearlescent trunk and run a hand along its velvety lime moss. Resting in a clump of grass at its base is a broken bottle with a mushroom-shaped stopper. Eala told me of a woodland where Robber Bright took her for one of their Faerie lessons. She described it as having abstract colors and a magic forest feel, but it's the bottles that convince me this could be the same place. She called it the Gem Kissed Forest.

No sign of that Fae bastard or anyone else now. I glance around, but it's still as death here. "Hello?" Not even a fecking bird answers.

Before leaving me, Finnbheara spouted off over betrayal, more proof I've ended up in the traitor, Robber Bright's, neck of the woods. The pair of those damned Faeries brings the devil Aodh to mind. I wouldn't give a right damn about Fae feuds, but a flaming rock in my gut tells me Eala is somehow mixed into their chaos.

Eala.

First, I think her name, and then I holler it into the trees. "Eala. Eala. Eala. Can you hear me, love? Are you in the Veil? Eala, come to me, *anamchara*."

I'm on my knees with hands to the sky. Can she hear me or sense my longing for her? The tear that catches in the corner of my mouth tastes like the rot of despair.

Finnbheara called this my prison. If I can't break out of Fae confinement, can Eala's Faerie powers break her in? The king sealed the grand gates of Tír na nÓg against her, but is every door locked?

Finnbheara doesn't bend. Eala will never breach his barricade. I punch my thigh, welcoming the oncoming bruise from the force of my blow. "Stop, Sionnach. Don't you dare lose faith in your Eala *bán*." My white swan would not wish her fox to surrender, and so I shall not. I press a fist to my heart to fortify my hope.

Specks of light dapple the path, and patches of moss scatter across the ground. Looking up, I see a swarm of small bubbles that look to be made of glass floating out of the woods as if they were hiding from Finn and have now decided it's safe to go bobbing about. The sun's light reflects off the wee things to sprinkle dots all over the place. It's a lovely bright dusting.

Chittering in the treetops startles me. Something's up there. When I squint into the thick branches, they shake as if the hidden beastie looking down on me scampers from one tree to another.

I wave a hand at the boughs. "Och, nothing but a wee squirrel." As soon as the words leave my mouth, a flash of nerves runs through my middle. Are there squirrels in Tír na nÓg, or is my visitor something Fae with teeth aching to sink into my skin?

Ripples of fear seize me. "Think you fool, think." Then I think too clearly of Fae creatures or wandering Folk who'd likely stab their sword through my belly as ask for a cuppa tea. I've faced plenty of danger in my life, but at least I knew then what an enemy looked like.

I clench my fists and spin in a circle as if expecting an attack. It'd be just like Finn to plunk me in the middle of a battleground. I consider calling my fox and keeping hidden among the shrubs dotting the forest floor. Finnbheara's threat about his Folk hunting foxes puts a quick end to that notion.

When I catch sight of the battered cottage, I sprint for it. My lungs burn not from running, but from the panic nipping at me.

The door of the little house is carved with a serpent-like beast. It has a snaky snout and three tails twisting into a spiral. "Don't want to meet you any time soon." I tug at the handle with no luck. "I don't know any fecking magic Faerie words, so how's this…open up you piece of shite?"

The right side of the frame is tweaked. The pairing of a shoulder shove and a good solid kick wrenches the door open. Only when it closes behind me do I realize my error. Knocking first is what a thinking man would do. I'd assumed the place was empty. Surely even Finn wouldn't smash a house on top of his kin.

I'm in it now. "Hello to the house."

Nothing stirs, but that doesn't mean much when it comes to Fae. Those fuckers can stand as still as a weathered stone.

I still, one hand on the door in case I need to drag my careless arse out of here.

The inside of the cottage is dark. Its roof may look crushed, but it hasn't been breached. A loft above me prevented the thatch from falling in completely.

The fourth time I hold my breath long enough to see stars, I decide I'm alone. The windows are covered with wooden shutters, only letting in thin shafts of shaded forest light. I'm in no rush to throw them open. If the occupant of this place left it buttoned up, all the better for it to keep looking unoccupied to discourage anyone who comes a calling. I'll lay low in here while I get more familiar with what is or isn't out there.

The main room is half the size of my place in County Clare. A stone hearth is set in one wall, but I don't dare light it. Smoke would issue a foolish invitation for sharp teeth or ill intentions. Two chairs in front of the fireplace look to be made of woven reeds. My hip bumps a table large enough to accommodate at least ten people. Maybe it's a meeting house and not a home at all. In the center of the thick table planks is a fat candle resting on what looks to be a copper dish. I pat around the wooden top to try and find matches. Finding none, I snort at the candle.

"I've got no Faerie magic to pull out of my arse to light you."

Suppose I'd best get used to the dark. I brace my hands on the table and blow out a long exhale. To my surprise, the candle gutters to life as if my breath were flint and stone. Instead of the buttery candlelight I'm used to, the pillar is topped with a sparkling silver flame. It casts a metallic sheen around the room, but not a blaze. The glow isn't even bold enough to reflect off the window glass, but it does reveal platters on the table with abandoned hunks of bread and what looks to be dried fruits.

"You'll suit me fine," I say to the candle.

An archway with an open door near the corner of the room catches my attention. I grab the candle and its dish. When my finger brushes the honey brown pillar, I startle. It isn't smooth with the wax of a proper candle. I'd swear I was holding a wooden branch in my hand. Even its surface is a deep brown with grooves like bark. There are no drips or heat, only the silver flame.

"Never seen the likes of this," I mutter, continuing to examine the enchanted candle. When I huff, the silver flame burns brighter. My next experimental blow increases the intensity again. Curious, I suck in a breath near the wick, and sure enough, the glow dims.

Coaxing the flame up again, I'm able to see a bed through the archway. When I poke my head in the room, I'm met with a sight I didn't expect. In a corner of the space is a nest of straw, twigs, and flower petals large enough for a stag to settle into. Thin looping vines weep from the ceiling, touching the floor in many places. There's an odd scent of earthy ground mixed with what could be sweet cream. If I didn't see walls beyond the vines, I'd swear I left the cottage for the woods.

It's far from cold in the cottage, but a shudder runs through me when I think of the beastie carved on the door. Who or what dwells in this place, and are they fixing to come back? I search both rooms for another way out in case the resident returns while I'm holed up in here.

When a long, low howl weaves its way through the trees and straight through the stone walls of the cottage, I whirl to face the sound. My sharp intake of breath dowses the candle, and I'm plunged into near darkness.

In the days before my natural life began, wolves thrived in the temperate forests of Ireland. I've toyed with the idea of Veil traveling to a time past when I could behold these great beasts. From afar...extremely afar.

Do those magnificent creatures driven from the realm above continue to exist here? As the *Tuatha Dé Danann* were banished beneath the land, did ancient wolves accompany the Fae to Tír na nÓg as well?

How interested might those wolves be in a lone human wandering through their forest?

The howl sounds again, closer this time. I blow into the candle for light and begin to search the cottage for anything to use as a weapon in case an unnaturally large Fae wolf decides to chew down the door. There's nothing useful to speak of in the big room, so I return to the strange bedroom with its nest. Partially hidden by a vine, I find my first stroke of good luck. Three daggers of varying lengths are mounted on the wall in the shadows near the bottom of a stone column.

I snatch all three. After setting the candle on the long table, I stuff one blade into the thick rope belt around my waist and clutch the other two in my hands. I will my heart to stop ringing like a church bell as I slide over to one window and then the other, trying to spot shadows of wolves hunting through the forest. The shutters all but blind me to any goings on. Moving as silently as my cloddy feet allow, I sidle up to the door and press my ear to it.

Noises scrape along the ground, announcing the approach of God knows what. The beasts have caught my scent. How big are these monsters? Will they stand on hind legs and shove the door open with a single heave of their front paws?

I'll fight, Eala. I swear to you I'll fight even if claws rip me bloody and teeth scrape me to the bone. I'll not give up.

I take a fighting stance, swallow the rush of bile rising in my throat, and prepare to meet countless sets of yellow eyes.

"*Mac?* Are you there?"

The blades in my hands clatter to the slate floor. I throw the door open and fall into my mother's arms.

CHAPTER 9
THE ALLY

EALA

My stomach is jittery as I face the hare turned witch. "Are you Bridget Early?"

"Aye. I was she."

Was.

Chatting with the spirit of Biddy Early is not my end game. I must face the living, breathing woman in the time before the threat of a witch trial hung around her neck.

Need screams through my mind before bursting through my essence as a violent wind. Turbulence spins through the cottage, catching the mulchy leaves on the ground to whip them into a wicked cyclone that spirals up and out through the space left by the missing roof. Streaks of rainbow light crisscross the room then feverishly circle the walls, enveloping me and the ghost witch beside me.

A flash of terror rips through my mind, remembering a thrill ride, called Gravity-something, Colleen coerced me into joining her on at a traveling carnival in Kennard Park. The giant metal cylinder spun at an insane speed, sucking us helplessly against its walls.

Before falling to my knees with fright, I realize I'm to blame for this melee. I called on the Veil with ferocity to take me back in time, and it responds with equal fervor. I will the movement to slow and then calm, easing into the past.

Around us, vines recede, disappearing over the top of walls as a thatched roof settles into place. The hard-packed clay floor is clear of plant debris. Simple wooden chairs with woven straw seats tuck up to a small table. A butter churn sits beside a split double door with an open top half that lets in the night breeze. There's a fire in the hearth. A mouthwatering aroma of herbs rises from a cookpot hanging over the flames.

Backed against the wall opposite the door with hands covering her cheeks, and eyes wide with either fear or wonder, is the witch. This version of the wise woman is much younger than the silvery blue spirit I encountered back in real time who'd just swapped a rabbity form for human. Her posture is straight and strong. Freckles spill across the bridge of her nose onto broad cheekbones, and there's not a wrinkle to be found. She's fresher and prettier than the pictures from her later years that showed her with drooping jowls and a face lined with age.

"Bridget Early?"

"Aye, that I am."

Am—not was. I'm not with the ghost of Biddy Early. The woman in front of me is the living, breathing witch I need. She nods and rakes her gaze down my clothing.

I glance at my jeans and Sion's Mackinaw rain jacket. Flustered by the hare turned witch, I didn't spare any time to raid Alfie's wardrobe. The stream of air I blow ruffles my bangs. These clothes are the least of the truth bombs I'm about to drop on this poor woman.

After a quick breath, I dive in. "I'm sorry to barge into your home like this. I meant to be more subtle with my visit."

Biddy lowers her hands from her face but doesn't leave the wall. I watch her eyes dart to a clay pitcher on the table. She's probably calculating the possibility of grabbing it to knock me on the head.

I raise my hands and put a little more distance between us as if it'll erase some of her fear. "I've come to beg...I mean, bargain for your help."

This piques her interest.

"I know I must look and sound strange to you, but I mean you no ill will. Would you like to hear all my truth, or only the specifics of my proposal?"

She shifts her weight onto one foot, leaning back. "You've got a busy mouth on you, girl."

My face heats. I'm not projecting the confident deal-making personality I'd hoped to pull off.

Biddy circles a finger in the air as if drawing a circle around me. "You've come from Himself, haven't you?" She snorts. "His Folk that've come before you speak in roundabout ways or rhymes, but I've never heard one spouting gibberish before or wearing such clothing."

"Himself?"

She waves a hand at me. "Time's past to be coy. You know full well, I'm speaking of your king."

My king, not my queen. Biddy's home here in County Clare is technically in the province of Munster, where the Fae queen, Clídodhna, was said to rule. The closest "Himself" must be Finnbheara. I'm sure the king wouldn't hesitate to trespass in the royal territories of others.

"Och, Finnbheara's people have not called on me for quite some time. What's he wanting now?"

I'm not sure if I should be relieved or wary Biddy's been dealing with the Faerie king I'm about to ask her to work against.

"You think I'm Fae?"

Completely unafraid of me at this point, Biddy goes to stir her stew. "I don't think, I know." She turns to me, chewing on her lip. "I've never had one of you show up with the colorful lights and commotion before."

So, the stories of Biddy's connection with the Folk are not exaggerated.

She waves a wooden spoon at me. "Sit you down and say your piece."

"You are very accepting of me."

Biddy chuckles. "You did give me a bit of a stomach turn at first, but there's always some surprise with your kind." Her expression turns more serious. "I can't promise I'll be able to provide what Himself wants. There's trouble brewing for me. No one's got great love for a *bean feasa* unless they want a cure for sickness or a potion to make their crops bountiful."

"What if I told you I'm here to help you with that trouble?"

The ladle drops from her hand. "You know of it then?"

I nod. "I know a lot. I know you are a wise woman, and you've done good in this world."

She stoops to pick up the spoon then wipes it on her apron, never taking her eyes off me.

"I know there are many people who call you *witch* and blame you for their misfortunes."

As she returns to the hearth, firelight gives her blue eyes an amber sheen, reminding me of the hare's. Biddy sighs. "The need to blame can burn a hole in many a heart."

"I know you change into a hare."

Her head whips up at this. "You're speaking nonsense, girl."

I finally accept her offer to sit at the table. "Maybe you can't do it yet, but you will be able to one day."

A rumble of mistrust colors her voice. "And how will you be knowing this?"

I twine my fingers together and set them on top of the table, hoping I look more comfortable than I feel. She thinks I'm a Faerie, so self-assurance and arrogance are surely something she's used to from them. "Because as a hare, you led me here."

She starts to protest, but I'm on a roll. "Not in this time." Here comes the big leap. "In the future. Yes, I'm Fae. I'm also *fánaí*, a wanderer, a time traveler. The colors you saw brightening the walls of your cottage were the Veil itself. It answers to me."

Biddy's hands clutch her skirts, confirming my visit is unlike any other she's had from the Fae.

"I was raised human and only recently learned I'm of Finnbheara's Folk."

She's still for long moments, both of us gathering thoughts of what to say to the other.

"I may be of his kind, but the king and his kin betrayed me. They've taken my husband and my dearest friend as prisoners and locked me out of my rightful home of Tír na nÓg." Okay, more dramatic than I intended and lacking relevant details, but more or less accurate.

Biddy walks over to the table and pulls out the other chair. She sits and leans on her forearms, staring at me. "And what do you suppose I can do?"

I copy her position. "You are a witch, a *bean feasa*."

"Aye, I'm called such."

I swallow hard. "I believe you have true magic and have more knowledge where the Fae are concerned than you've let on to anyone. You seem like a person who sees beyond and through the thoughts and actions of others. Do you disagree? If you swear to me now you are powerless and all I presume about you is fantastic and wrong, I'll leave."

We stare at one another as the moments tick by. I've thrown down the first challenge.

Biddy presses her palms to the wooden tabletop and closes her eyes. The floor begins to vibrate, sending waves of heat through my boots and up my legs. The fire within the hearth spits and sizzles into a barely contained inferno. My hair crackles with electricity and sticks to my face.

When the witch claps her hands, the flames recede and the air stills. Her unblinking gaze holds me fast until she leans back in the chair and crosses her arms.

It's my move. Saying *I told you so* to a witch doesn't seem like the best idea. "I acknowledge your impressive magic." I hold her gaze. "Do you believe I am what I say I am?"

Biddy tucks a loose strand of her dark peach-colored hair into the bun on her head. Weariness seems to overtake her. "I've seen too much of what you call fantastic in my years to doubt a woman with both magic and desperation clinging to her bones."

I sag in relief. "Thank you, Biddy. Is it okay to call you Biddy?"

"Aye, as many do."

"You'll help me then?"

She pats my hand. "I don't know." She pauses. "What are you called, Faerie girl?"

"Eala. Eala Duir O'Dwyer Loho." It feels right to include Máthair's clan in my ever-growing name.

"Virtue Alone Ennobles." My confusion at her words raises a chuckle. "'Tis the O'Dwyer clan motto."

Virtue.

In this great game I've fallen into, Sion and I were brought together to restore missing virtues. It seems apt that the word is embedded in the name given to me by the woman who bargained with Finnbheara for my very existence.

"*From God, every help* is the motto of my da's people. I don't know what part the Lord plans to play in this Faerie business you're wanting me to meddle in, but it never hurts to have the big man on your side."

My side. Not our side. "Are you going to help me?"

She shakes her head. "As I said, I've got my own troubles." Biddy rises and heads toward the hearth. "Maybe after the bad business passes, you'll come and ask again."

I feel Biddy's interest slipping away. An unsettling thought occurs to me. Biddy was in her 60s at the witch trial. This woman looks to be my age. Maybe the troubles she's referring to are a general mistrust from the village. I imagine she's faced a lot of "bad business" from superstitious neighbors. She's yet to face the pinnacle of narrow minds at her witch trial in Ennis.

So often, a gloom and doom prophecy drives a good folktale. I'd better pull one out now to increase my odds. "There is a great trouble coming your way in the future, Biddy Early. Those who fear you will dredge up witch laws from the past and use them to try to destroy you with an unjust trial. If I promise to use my Fae power to guarantee you an innocent verdict in your witch trial, will you agree to help me?"

She's completely bewildered. It's time to dole out the rest of my lie while she's vulnerable. Acid churns in my stomach at the manipulation. Sion could handle this with much more confidence. "I'm sorry to say that if you turn me down, the outcome will be very grave for you."

Color drains from Biddy's face. Shit, I'm a horrible, horrible person.

This is for Sion. This is for Colleen.

She moves to the window and grips the sill, bowing her head. I wait, hating myself more with every passing second.

"They'll try to set the torch to me like those dark times past?" She releases a series of loud breaths. "And here I thought my worst troubles would be no one buying potions and charms or doing damage to my home place until their latest flood of misgivings pass."

So, her current bad business is just pissy villagers.

Biddy spins to face me. "You say you can spare me a witch's death in the trial you speak of?"

"I can." This shading of the truth slips out with unsettling ease. How very Fae.

She mutters to herself as she turns to stare into the dark wood. With a slap to the sill, she whirls away from the window. "Fine. I'll take your promise and give you mine in return." She swats the air. "No telling what use I'll be to you, but there it is."

I stand and face her. "I'll tell you everything as we go along, and I swear to keep you as far from danger as I'm able."

"May the goddess Bríd help us."

The goddess, not saint. Interesting. I'm more confident than ever before that I've come to the right person for help. "Are you ready to come with me through time?"

Reluctance sharpens her gaze. "We can't be fixing it all from here?"

"I want to take you to my home place near the sea. It's where I trust myself to be strong and make the best decisions." It's where I feel closest to Sionnach.

"I understand that well, girl." She fans an arm around the room. "Home is the heart of us. It's where we love the dearest. A place the people you're tied to share your joy and struggles. Home is sacred."

Tears well in my eyes. I ache to build a home with Sion. Why do Fae kings and fate deny me, deny us, such a simple dream?

"If I'm to be of any worth to you in these Faerie dealings, Eala. There's something I'll best be needing. My powers can be unfocused and unpredictable without it. I speak of my blue bottle."

Ah, the legendary blue bottle.

I turn in a circle to take in the cottage. "Yes. I know about it. Absolutely, you've got to bring it. Where is it?"

Her chest rises and falls with her next breath as if she's mustering the courage to answer. "Tír na nÓg."

CHAPTER 10
THE PROOF

ROBBER BRIGHT

Curse Aodh and curse my ill-timed proclamation. A Dark Prince does not maintain power without keen observation skills. Of course, he sensed Acacia's distress, no matter how fleeting, on the unthinkable truth that I, a warrior of Tír na nÓg, entered a bond-promise with a human. The lie would have been better executed if my high command had been prepared for it. That was an impossibility since I had no preconception of speaking such a falsehood.

This masquerade must be seen through to its conclusion.

Threading my arm around Colleen's waist, I pull her to my side. "What more proof do you require beyond the reality that I brought a human into your realm?"

Aodh tilts his head, his mouth curling in amusement. "Perhaps a declaration from your lovely bond-promised."

My mouth dries as if it is full of the floating ash from the Cave of Cats. Fuck this smoldering realm and its chief. Colleen has as little knowledge of the lie as my companions. Fate knows what words will pass her lips. With a gentle touch to her chin, I tip her face to mine and treat her to my most potent seductive smile. "Darling—"

Aodh's shadowed eyes now twinkle with clusters of flashing crimson sparks as he cuts off my words. "Stop. You are a sly one, Robálaí Geal. The human basks in your influence. Whatever she speaks will be no more than her puppet master's intention."

A Dark Prince, God of the Underworld he may be, but Aodh is still Fae. His sense of other Faerie charms is as sharp as the jagged edges of the obsidian shards decorating his forearms. He reaches out to slide a thick ashy finger past Colleen's slightly parted lips and into her mouth. My hand twitches with the urge to seize the knife in my boot and part him from his finger.

"You will bring me proof of the resonant cry that only blooms at a bond-promised's ultimate moment of ecstasy." He removes his foul digit from Colleen's mouth and slides it into his, smacking his lips as he tastes her. I suppress a shudder from the image of Aodh's charred touch against Colleen's wet tongue. The moment we leave the beast's presence, I will force Colleen to cleanse her mouth with sweet wine.

I am at the edge of a precipice of my own making. Aodh has sampled this woman. There will be no fooling him with another's howl of pleasure from my seduction.

"Despite your failure to bring me Eala Duir and your questionable truth telling, I will be satisfied with the legitimacy of our association once you present the proof I require." Aodh snaps his fingers and a black glass cube appears in his hand. On one side is a gold crank which he turns to open the lid. The Dark Prince extends his arm and the vessel floats to my outstretched palm. "I shall give you until the blood sun completes its nightly revolution around the mountains of glass to capture your bond-promised's howl of climax in this casket."

With that, our audience is at an end. Aodh flicks his wrist, summoning his guards. As he returns to the swan throne, soldiers form a line between us and their king to herd us out of the chamber. With the claim of my bond-promise to Colleen hanging in the air, I must act accordingly. I thread her hand through my elbow to keep her close as a bonded Fae man would be expected to do.

The brutish Dóite executes the same fancy swivel he used to greet us on the steps of the castle. "Your creatures have been settled in the dragon hold."

"What of my Host?"

He eyes me with condescension. "They bide in the barracks as do all common soldiers. You and your high command will occupy rooms in the castle proper, thanks to the generosity of our master. Follow me."

Ah, rooms where Aodh can easily fix his shadowy eye. I am not overjoyed to be separated from the Host, nor am I easy with the *péist síoda* housed apart from their riders. In the Gem Kissed Forest, dragons share our dwellings as revered family members. They are not cattle or swine. Since my clout with Aodh after my less-than-successful initial presentation is in question, there is no recourse but to hold my objections until the Dark Prince's doubts of my loyalty are subdued.

The silence from Artos, Ciallmhar, Nettle, and Acacia is a plague. The trek to our quarters would need to be a hundred leagues for me to have time enough to prepare an acceptable explanation for naming Colleen as my bond-promised.

I risked the tenuous safety of my Host to protect a human.

We travel the red marble halls of *Caisleán Brón* in silence save for the echo of our boots scraping against the charred stone floor. Black veining in the walls could be scratches from beastly claws. The polished obsidian cornice continues the quartet of swans pattern with intervals of waves between. The endless reminders of Aodh's tortured past are nothing short of unnerving. I suppose if my siblings and I had been cursed for 900 years, I too would dwell on such a history.

Dóite stops before a black steel door inlaid with a spikey flower design made of red tile. I hold my tongue to keep from exclaiming, "*No swan?*"

"Commander Geal," he says, with a curt bob of his head as he shoves the door open.

"General Geal," I correct.

"General Geal," he repeats in a bitter tone. "These are your rooms. Your fellows' quarters will be in the north tower. My lieutenant will escort them there now." His gaze lands on a stone-faced soldier in his detail.

I raise a hand. "First, I will meet with my high command here. Your lieutenant may wait at the end of the hall."

My current agreement with Aodh installed me as a general of his inner circle, a rank Finnbheara denies me. Even though I may have temporarily undermined my position, I will not carry myself as anything less.

The grayness of Doite's ashen skin assumes a darker reddish undertone as

I countermand his intention. He follows my instructions but storms to the end of the hall, his underlings in tow.

My four most trusted shove past me into the room. Heat from their anger engulfs me as sure as Aodh's flames. I nudge Colleen ahead of me before entering and shutting the door behind us.

The chamber is large and opulent. A fireplace as large as the ones in the castle antechamber takes up the entirety of one wall. A pair of luxuriant velvet sofas bear Aodh's crest as adornments on their four cushions. They flank the hearth, a low, smoked glass table poised between them with a decanter of wine and four glasses of cut black crystal. I set Aodh's box next to the goblets. Before a floor-to-ceiling leaded window with diamond-shaped panes, each outlined in burgundy, is a massive black oak table surrounded by four chairs. I see the Underworld God's obsession with four infuses all decor.

I let out a breath. These are quarters worthy of a general. Even though Aodh could strip these rooms from me on a whim, I am relieved to see his intention to honor our agreement remains in place.

My high command stands shoulder to shoulder, pinning me with matching glares. Acacia is the first to break as she spits on my boots. I would rather she struck me. I deserve the sting of her ire.

Artos gestures toward Colleen. "We would speak with you without your *bond-promised*."

Given his rancid tone, he might as well have named her dragon shit.

Colleen's gaze flits around the room like a sparrow searching for seeds in the grass. Her insipid movement is out of place given the palpable rage seething from my Folk.

I snatch her arm a bit too harshly, eliciting a whine of pain from her lips as I drag her into the adjoining bedchamber. This woman has become the bane of my reality. Wearing Colleen on my arm to provoke Eala was bothersome enough. Now this human threatens to destroy everything I have built with Aodh. She is the symbol of my current distress and that of my lieutenants.

"Sleep," I hiss in her ear, and Colleen falls limp against my body. Scooping her into my arms, I fling her onto a bed large enough to sleep my entire high command. Slamming the door behind me, I pound into the main room to wrestle with the consequences of my impulsivity.

I silence my four companions with a warning finger to my lips. Aodh is no green tyrant. There will be means of overhearing all that goes on in this chamber unless I use my magic to plug his ears. I circle my arm in an arc, igniting a wavering masking charm to cover the walls, then spread my arms wide to invite the judgment of my most trusted.

Nettle is first to the lists. "Is it true? Are you bond-promised with the human?"

Artos snorts loud enough to rival a bull. "It might as well be the truth since you left no other avenue to fix this damage you created."

Acacia pulls at her hair. "I warned you she is a liability. After flashing this baggage in front of Finnbheara's Treasure, it would have been better to leave your game piece chained to the walls of Oweynagat."

I scratch at my temples, honeyed strands coming loose in my fingers. "I blundered and thrust us all into jeopardy."

Acacia surges at me until our faces are inches apart. "You realize you cannot just fuck the human and present Aodh with a counterfeit scream of what your cock wrings from her cunt."

She pounds her fists against my chest. I make no effort to thwart her. My second could thrust a blade into my heart, and I would accept the cut.

Ciallmhar eases Acacia away from me and into his embrace. For a moment, I fear she will shove him into the black granite wall. She wilts but for a moment then steps free of his arms.

I inhale deeply as the initial wave of their fury dissipates and shake my head. "What I have done is done." I eye each of them in turn. "Folly or not, I saw no other avenue to spare the human desecration from Aodh. Did you?"

Artos strokes his chin and is the first to break the silence. "We could kill her in the guise of mercy."

A growl accompanies Acacia's contribution. "As I said, chain her to the walls of Oweynagat and be rid of the liability."

Nettle remains silent, pupils spinning as evidence of his deep thoughts.

Levelheaded Ciallmhar shakes his head. "She must live. This is a quandary of ifs. *If* you had not brought this woman from the land above, there would have been nothing to convince Aodh that a strategy to overcome your failure to him is in place. *If* you had not claimed Colleen, your mortal would become Aodh's toy. *If* that came to pass, Eala Duir may believe her friend is spoiled beyond saving. *If* so, you lose the bargaining power to coerce Finnbheara's Treasure into this realm. *If* you do not bring her here and grant Aodh his promised prize of the one who bears the secret of the *beads of being* at her core, I fear what may befall the Host of a Thousand Wings."

I appreciate that Ciallmhar's reasoning does not paint me a blatant ass.

My wise counsel's mouth dips into a frown. "However, Commander, there is no recourse now except to seal the bond-promise between you and the human."

I stagger back until my legs hit one of the couches. A groan slips from me. The very state I vowed never to accept with another is now what I must do to protect my Host.

And to a human.

I close my eyes for a long moment and swear I hear fate's laughter in my ear.

While it is preferable to hand a human my empty spirit rather than saddle one of my Fae kin with my hopeless heart, I abhor this solution. A life unburdened by the unrequited longings of another is one I have accepted.

My voice is laced with more desperation than I intend. Clasping my hands before me, I implore my dearest friends. "I beg you. Speak now if you see any other path."

I receive stares of pity from the three men and disgust from Acacia.

Ciallmhar covers my folded hands with his. "A final *if* for you, my... general. If there were more time than what passes for a single night in this land of the blood-orange sun, we might uncover another solution. But there is not. Fate imposes its iron fist even here in Aodh's underworld."

Our gazes meet and hold. I told a falsehood and now must create a truth to ensure the safety of my Host. Nodding my head, I pull my hands free and take a step away from my high command. "I thank you for your counsel. I seek your understanding but not your forgiveness." Pounding a fist to my chest, I say, "For the Host of A Thousand Wings."

They answer in kind. Artos opens the door to the chamber, and my four most trusted leave me to my duty. Acacia's stuttering sigh is the last sound I hear beyond the great door.

I sneer at the only other door in my new quarters, the one leading me to a future thrust upon me by my lack of forethought. The carefree swirls of red grain in black wood mock my anguish. Laying both palms against the door, I shut my eyes and bow my head. Grasping for any thread weaving through my thoughts that might lead me down a different path sets off nothing but pounding in my temples.

I snap my posture into one of strength, shaking my head. I will do this for my Folk, my Host. Returning to the low table in front of the hearth, I grab Aodh's box by its gold crank then push open the bedchamber door.

My gaze falls to the massive bed, but Colleen does not lie upon it where I tossed her as I would a piece of unwanted refuse. It takes but a moment to find her. To my horror, like a broken doll, her head twisting at a disturbing angle, Colleen lies beside the bed in a heap on the carpet.

CHAPTER 11
THE BLUE BOTTLE

EALA

I gape at Biddy. "Didn't you hear me? I'm banned from Tír na nÓg."

"I heard you fine. Even though that may be true, I'm sure you can call on one of your Folk to open a wee door for us?"

"No," I say with more volume than necessary. I hold my hands in supplication. "That's why I've come to you for help. I can't get into the Fae realm."

She lets out a prolonged *pfft*. "If I've learned nothing from my dealings with your kind, it's that what they say and the way things truly are walk different paths."

I'm tempted to grab her hands and shake them. "The only allies I have in Tír na nÓg have no power to let me in."

Biddy frowns at my desperation. "Sorry to say then that this bargain between us is folly. I thank you for wanting to relieve my burden, but without my bottle, there's no hope I can help you. Best you leave me to my own fate, dark as it may be."

Success is slipping through my fingers. No blue bottle, and the magic bearer who can help me is backing off. I've shared the bare minimum of my dilemma. It's time to open the floodgates. "Do you know what an *anamchara* is?"

Her eyes sparkle. "Aye, a soul bond. 'Tis a rare gift to find in another."

"Finnbheara holds my *anamchara* and my grandmother in his lands." The puzzled look on her face makes it clear I need to continue. "They are both human but tied to the Fae. Sionnach, my *anamchara,* is stuck in Tír na nÓg because of a bargain I struck with the king. Martha, my grandmother—" A surge of complicated emotions derail me.

Biddy raises an eyebrow, waiting for me to spit the rest out.

"She was Finnbheara's lover."

"Ah, there 'tis." She nods. "She'll take him to her bed, and you won't, so out the gates you go."

I wipe my hands through the air. "No. It's much more complicated." I take a quick breath. "I bargained with Finnbheara to allow two souls to stay in Tír na nÓg. It was supposed to be Sionnach and me, but the king was incensed when I bested him in our deal. In his anger, he altered the bargain and involved my grandmother." I imitate Sion's signature derisive grunt. "Stupid me thought she was safe, permitted to live in the Faerie kingdom, but Finnbheara tricked me."

She's nodding. "As they do."

"He threatened to shove my grandmother out of Tír na nÓg. I leapt through the gate in her place."

Confusion swims in her eyes as she tilts her head from side to side, attempting to make sense of my verbal vomit. "You left your *anamchara* behind?"

The gravity of my decision comes crashing down on me as cruelly as the moment I made it. "I decided if anyone had a chance to return to Finnbheara's kingdom, it would be me…because I'm Fae." I cover my eyes with shaky hands, imagining how insane this must sound to her. Digging deep for courage, I lower my hands and pin my gaze on her. "There's more."

Biddy's expression switches between skepticism and incredulity as I unleash my whole story—Máthair's affair with Finnbheara, the deal she made with the king to assign Sion to a soulfall to save her only son's soul, her plea to her former lover to create me to help Sion in that quest, Máthair's banishment to the Glade of Chimes, and the bargain I struck with Finnbheara to allow Sion and me to stay together forever in the land of the Fae.

"I couldn't separate Sionnach from his mother after all she'd sacrificed for him." I swipe the back of my hand across my sweaty forehead, waiting to see if she'll accept this or boot me out on my ass.

"Mothers are made to sacrifice for their children."

Her words wound me more than she could possibly know. My heart aches. I may never be given the chance to become a loving mother to Sion's child. Robber Bright said only Finnbheara's *beads of being* would allow such a miracle. I can't imagine a reality where the king shares that rare gift with me.

"Do you not see, even though the woman you call grandmother did not bear you, from the tale you've told me, she looks on you as her very own child?" She gives me a pitying look. "You stole the sacrifice she gave willingly when you took her place."

Shock rolls through me with this new perspective, and I barely make it to the chair.

Biddy worries her hands, sliding them over one another in rapid movement as she walks to the hearth, stares at me, then walks to the bed fitted into a corner of the cottage and sits. "You've given me a tale the likes of which I've not heard before."

I watch her try to work out this huge helping of bizarre.

She seems to come to a decision and slaps her hands on the bed. "I won't lie and say I grasp all the bits of it, but I hear truth in the telling." To my surprise, Biddy rises and comes to take both my hands in hers. "You've a good heart, Eala of the Fae." She squeezes. "Let's see what we can do to mend it."

I haven't lost her.

She purses her lips and lets go of my hands. "Without my bottle, I may be of little help to you."

Well, this is an unexpected stalemate. Sure, there were plenty of stories about Biddy's damned blue bottle and its magic properties, but I never took it as the main source of her powers. "I watched you douse your cottage with magic. Do you mean to tell me, without the blue bottle, all you can do are a few scary tricks?"

She stabs a finger at me. "Look here, girl. Those were no tricks. I called the forces of the earth, and they answered. I'll not have you insulting me in my home."

I pinch the bridge of my nose and try to regroup. Okay, she's got some magical chops without her talisman, but will they be enough to make a difference? "You do have some powers without the bottle?"

"Aye."

My legs feel steadier, so I start pacing. "Maybe with what you have... naturally and my Faerie, uh, gifts, we'll be able to figure something out." She grunts, which pisses me off. I came to this woman for help, and now everything's back on me. Is it even worth the trouble of trying to fit her into my world? If we can't get the blue bottle back, will she become another burden I've got to deal with?

I return to the table and drop my forehead onto my hands. None of the other magic-touched women in my research had as much potential as Biddy Early. My hunch has been proven now that I'm in her presence. She's not just the village wise woman with more knowledge of herbs and common sense than the rest of her contemporaries. There's true magic in her veins.

Her power reaches out to mine, like one animal sniffing another. It pushes toward me but can't quite connect. There's a barrier. Do I dare try to meld my essence with hers the way Robber Bright taught me?

My muscles tense. No, I'm not going to risk it. Finnbheara freaked when he sensed Robber Bright's influence still dripping through mine. I'm not going to risk adding in traces of a witch. Tales of wise women being accused of consorting with the devil shoot a fresh stream of dread up my insides. Does Biddy get house calls from Aodh, too?

I rub a thumb across my cheekbone. Am I becoming an evil eye-fearing Puritan fanatic?

Thoughts of Robber Bright and Aodh rev up my fear for Colleen. I can't go down that road right now. It's essential to stay focused on the witch.

If Biddy and I are going to break down whatever barrier is rising between us, I know in my gut we need her blue bottle. I press her for more, digging for anything I can use to strengthen my case to convince her to stick with me. "Biddy, how did your bottle come to you?"

The witch glowers at me. "'Tis a tale I've been asked to tell many a time, but none have I trusted to hear it. I won't be starting now."

"Has a Faerie ever asked you to tell the story?"

I can tell my query unsettles her by the way she gathers handfuls of her apron and twists it.

Her voice is sharp. "You're the first of your kind that's come nosing around on the subject."

"If you believe I have a good heart, as you said, then please believe I'm not asking about your bottle with any intention to take it or use it against you."

Biddy holds a hard line for a moment longer then she softens. "I suppose I could take your comin' as a sign it's time to speak of it." She sighs, and her hands relax against her skirts. "I've always been touched by powers most folks never know, but it wasn't until after I healed a wandering Fae who showed up half dead at my door that my magic partnered with Faerie kind. The wounded man was Finnbheara's son, you see, and the father himself arrived to collect him. Whether for payment or in gratitude, the king placed the blue bottle in my hands and told me if I joined with its magic, I'd become a twice-blessed wise woman."

In the Irish folktales I've devoted my life studying, there are magic coins, golden eggs, enchanted trees, but one of Biddy and Finnbheara doesn't exist. Generosity isn't a trait I'd ascribe to the King of the Connacht Fae, but in truth, I've experienced little of him and only in an adversarial capacity. He did give Máthair what she asked of him on more than one occasion. Hell, Finn and his *beads of being* are the reason I exist. This isn't the time for me to examine my complicated relationship with the king.

"How do you know your bottle is in Tír na nÓg now?"

Biddy scrunches her nose. "I put it there."

This meeting is getting weirder and weirder. "You went to the Fae realm?"

"No. I've not received an invitation." She smooths a strand of hair behind her ear. "As I said, village folk are coming soon to devil me. I didn't want the bottle to fall into the hands of those who would use it for ill. So, yesterday before the light, I went to the bitty *lough* up the way, the one with the hawthorn at one end and yew on the other—Faerie trees both. The water's an unusual color, a mix of bright blues and dazzling greens I've no name for. When the hint of dawn first glows over the horizon, a fine lustrous sheen like the thinnest pane of diamond glass spreads across the top of the water. Once the sun is fully up, the glistening layer sinks below the surface, dissolving into wee bits of shine that give the water a fine sparkle. The *lough* is a Faerie door, don't you see?"

Biddy could be describing the lake in the Glade of Chimes. Robber Bright took me into the Gem Kissed Forest through an incredibly sparkly *lough* as well. I have no doubt she's right about this *lough* being Fae.

"As I stood on the shore, the potion in my blue bottle began to swirl in harmony with the waters of the lake. I felt the one calling the other home."

"So, you threw it in?"

"Aye. And sure as I'm standing here, my bitty bottle melted right in without so much as a splash."

"You gave it up?"

Her eyes wear a coating of tears. "Better that than having it misused, don't you think?"

I tap a finger against my lips, pondering this. A subtle heat surrounds me, no doubt the source is the intensity of Biddy's stare. The witch leaks magic.

"Is it far to the *lough*?"

She nods. "A few hours by donkey."

"Biddy," I lock my gaze on hers. "I'm going to use my Fae magic, but I'll need you to make the *lough* clear in your thoughts to take us there. I hope together we can call your bottle back. Are you willing to do this with me?"

I expect fear. Instead, the witch looks delighted.

"I've learned in my day that there's more under sun and stars than this…" She taps the side of her head. "…can imagine. Show me your magic, girl."

I beckon Biddy closer. "Stand here with me and put your hand in mine. Don't let go."

She walks over and takes my hand.

"I'm going to call the Veil. You may believe the Veil is only a curtain between our world and others, but that doesn't begin to describe its magic. I'm asking for your trust. Do I have it?"

"Yes, Eala, you do."

At her word, I call the Veil. It's a joy to watch her expression as she takes in the dancing prismatic glory of the Faerie passageway. I give her a moment to enjoy it. Her gaze falls on Alfie. "You've a tree with you."

"This is Alfie, my *fánaí* tree. She travels with me."

"A familiar then?"

I've never thought of the white poplar as my familiar since I don't consider myself a witch. "A companion." The simple term shortchanges Alfie. I'll elaborate later for the witch on the *Crann na Beatha's* importance.

"It's time, Biddy. Close your eyes and picture the *lough*. You may feel something pushing on your mind. That'll be me. Please let me in. I need to borrow your thought to guide us."

Without an ounce of reluctance, she snaps her lids shut. I do the same and send an exploratory tendril of my essence to seek hers. What I discover is dazzling. Biddy's thoughts swim in a bright blue haze with sparks like gold glitter shot through it.

My Veil sprites begin to swoop through my body and pulse as if they're welcoming in Biddy's magic. When I wrap the energy of my Fae core around Biddy's power, an image of the *lough* shines brightly in the space we share.

Within moments, I see what I hope is our destination through the Veil window. Shadows of the yew and hawthorn trees stretch across the moonlit dappled surface of the *lough*.

"Open your eyes, Biddy. Is this the place?"

Hands fly to her mouth. "Aye. Isn't your Faerie carriage a wonder?"

A sense of pride fills me, even though I can't take credit for the Veil's splendor.

"Follow me out." I take a step toward the portal, then turn back. "Fair warning. As soon as we leave, the Veil disappears, but don't worry, I can call it back."

Biddy follows me through the opening like a trooper. I hear her intake of breath as the Veil and Alfie leave us. The squelch of our shoes against soggy ground breaks the silence. When the water laps at our toes, I snatch Biddy's hand again. I should confess I have no clue what I'm doing, but I don't want to shake her belief we can retrieve the bottle.

When I needed Finnbheara to end Jeremy Olk, my magic called him. When I needed to keep the Carrabuncle from killing the Viking on the shores of Lough Geal, my magic set his axe on fire. Both times, I was desperate like I am now. I pray it's enough to let my Faerie magic kick in.

"Show me your blue bottle, the way you did the *lough*."

My essence pours into Biddy's magic like it's found an old friend. The blue bottle is exquisite. It's the size of an orange with an elegantly tapered top. Intricate silver filigree in the familiar pattern of leaves and branches that adorn Finnbheara's tunics with a few extra curlicues circles the glass.

"Now I want you to picture the bottle floating under the water and see if you can imagine guiding it back up to the surface then into your hand."

Biddy tenses beside me, but she follows my directions. In her mind's eye, I see the deep blue cloud of her magic blending with the clear waters of the *lough*, searching.

"Try calling the bottle to you?"

The heat I felt rising from Biddy at the cottage now pours off her like a river of molten air as she struggles to reclaim her bottle. Nothing disturbs the sway of the *lough*. Did Finnbheara snatch his gift back? The damn thing is probably sitting in a fancy case in his royal trophy room.

My frustration breaks the connection with Biddy, and her shoulder slumps against mine. The temperature around us drops dramatically. Shit, I was making her do all the work. I was just watching and not helping.

I pat her arm. "Great start. Let's try again. I'm going to push a bit harder on your magic. Don't be afraid if it feels, uh—" I search for a word that doesn't sound threatening or frightening. "Uncomfortable."

She wipes her face with her apron. This time, without prompting, she releases her magic into the *lough*. I try to give my essence more intention. If Robber Bright hadn't been such a villainous dirtbag, I might have learned more about what my Fae gifts were capable of.

As I twine my magic firmly with Biddy's, the water begins to glow a brighter blue. Suddenly, her attention darts toward the bottom of the *lough*, and I see the source of the light. There, embedded in the silt, is Biddy's blue bottle. I push harder, sending our joined power down through the depths until it surrounds the bottle.

"Come on. Come on," I say to encourage the bottle, pouring more oomph into wrestling it free.

Biddy's breathing has become labored, too labored. Oh no. This could be bad. Is my magic hurting her? I break the connection and grasp her shoulders. "Are you alright?"

She looks shaken but not damaged. "I tugged with all my might, but it wouldn't budge." Biddy gazes out over the *lough*. "It's as if the earth itself was holding it fast."

"Let's take a minute. Maybe sit and rest before we try again."

Biddy shakes her head. "Eala, I've got no more strength than what I gave. Have you?"

My lungs constrict until it's painful to breathe. Is our weakness proof that even with our combined magic, we're useless?

She's panting. "The earth lent me its powers more than once, but its voice has gone quiet."

What do I do now? Go visit another witch, bring her here, and see if three bursts of power are better than two? The thought exhausts me. My soul is already overburdened with loss, fear, and growing hopelessness.

Tell me what to do, Sion. How did you find the will to keep pushing on alone?

A word sparks an idea.

Alone.

Sion wasn't alone. He had Alfie. My fingers tingle, remembering Alfie's energy running through me as I grasped her trunk and felt the whiskey gold threads that gifted me a vision of my Sionnach.

Connection.

Crann na Beatha.

The Tree of Life.

Alfie's magic travels deep into the earth and beyond. I call the Veil to bring me the *fánaí* tree. Within seconds, Alfie's glorious curving trunks are by my side.

I laugh like a madwoman as I touch my forehead to the snow-white bark covered in the green triangle pattern marking the tree as mine and Sion's. I voice a variation of my husband's explanation of Alfie's ability to stick with him over the centuries. "Al-find your sorry arse, Eala."

Biddy clears her throat. "Is this the same wee tree from your magic place?"

"She sure is." I drop a kiss on a low branch. I wave at Biddy to join us. "And she's going to help us get your blue bottle."

To say Biddy looks skeptical is an understatement.

"Take my hand and put your fingers around one of her trunks. We're going to do what we did before, but not alone. Trust me."

Beneath a trail of stars, on the quiet shores of a Faerie door, the witch, the *fánaí* tree, and I allow our magic to dance together. I see the blue bottle sunk into the bottom of the *lough*, but this time as Biddy calls to it and I wrap my powers around hers, Alfie's delicate golden threads plunge into the silt with us. The *Crann na Beatha's* glow lights a brilliant path to the surface. The bottle shudders as a cloud of lake bottom puffs up around the glass, and then the witch's treasure begins to rise.

The magic feels effortless. Not a struggle at all. Within moments, the gift to Biddy Early from the Faerie king bobs on the surface of the *lough*.

In an instant, Biddy dives into the water, swimming like an Olympian on their victory lap until she reaches her bottle. Hugging it to her breast, she laughs with unabashed glee.

Well, look at that. Witches do indeed float.

CHAPTER 12
THE TÊTE-À-TÊTE

ROBBER BRIGHT

I throw myself onto the carpet next to a lifeless Colleen, dropping my ear to her chest to check for a heartbeat. Thank the bounties of nature, I hear its steady rhythm. Gingerly, I lay my palm against her neck to sense the state of her weak human bones. Nothing is broken.

In my haste to answer to the high command for my rash actions before Aodh, I heaved the woman recklessly at the bed. My strength and her fragility might have ended in her death.

Fuck this haphazard being who inhabits my skin. Such an outcome could dismantle my plans with Aodh and the safety of my Host.

I catch sight of my hands resting on my thighs. They tremble from the terror of what might have been if I had killed Colleen. With more gentleness than I am usually inclined to show, I smooth down the skirt of her gown from where it is has ridden up to reveal red satin underthings. Her skin is the whitest of cream as if untouched by any sun, mortal or Fae. The flesh is so sleek, my fingertips tingle to explore further as they slide along her calves.

I jerk my hand away. Fate has decreed the delights of that skin will be mine, but not yet. There is a reckoning to be had first.

Slipping one hand beneath her knees and the other behind her shoulders, I lift her from the crimson carpet. I intend to lay her properly on the bed, but once she is in my arms, I cradle her against my chest.

"Forgive me, darling one."

When I press my lips to the cool skin of her temple, a jolt runs through me, and I nearly drop her. My legs quiver, and I fall with Colleen upon the bed. An intimate memory from the shores of a glacial lake overtakes my conscious thought.

My essence pools with Eala's. The expectation that mingling my spirit with one of an unschooled Fae will be simple is blown apart. This Faerie possesses strains of love so intense, so powerful for her fox, they threaten to shatter my reason.

Greed becomes my master, and I attempt to twist Eala's devotion away from her human mate so she will seek satisfaction with me. I am drunk on the fleeting ambrosia of her passion as the flame of her stolen desire races toward my Fae spirit—

Until she denies me.

My panting breaths ruffle Colleen's hair. I half collapse on top of her, pinning her body beneath me on the bed. Shifting so I do not crush her, I sink into the softness of the mattress to restore my wits. The coolness of a tear running down my cheek is as reviving as a slap, and I sit up.

I smear the moisture across my fingers and stare at its shine. Damn Finnbheara and his geas. For centuries, I forced myself to banish any yearning to love. The king never intended for me to meld my essence with Eala, but I took advantage of the opportunity. Instead of it damaging her, it has shredded my heart with the reminder of what will never be mine.

"Strip every star from Finnbheara's sky," I growl through gritted teeth. I hunger for what I have seen the swan feels for her fox. I would betray any king to take back my ability to love another.

I swipe sweat from my brow and refocus on my task. The geas binding my heart is not the priority. Aodh's proof is all-important.

I arrange Colleen on the bed, fanning her hair around her head like an auburn corona. The beauty of the Fae is indisputable, but this woman possesses a warmth our cool Folk seldom show. She believes she loves me as Robin Bright. In human parlance, she told Eala I was her "person" as Sionnach is to Finnbheara's Treasure. That will be my entre into enticing her to accept my bond-promise.

I stand and pace the room. But will the bond be truly sealed if she is under my influence? If we consummate under those conditions, will her cry of ecstasy bring the evidence Aodh insists on?

Growling, I thread fingers through my hair and pull tight enough to sting. "Robin?"

Fate, take me. I let my influence slip again. With a flick of my wrist, I douse every light in the bed chamber to a meager glow so she cannot perceive her surroundings.

To make our bond legitimate, I fear I must reveal realities that may damage her human mind. A stone of dread seats itself in my gut. There are levels and layers of truth to be finessed here. I have no choice but to proceed.

I rejoin Colleen on the bed. She pats my chest and arms. "There you are. I can't see you in the dark."

I stroke her wrists, up the soft skin of her arms, and across her delicate shoulders before cupping the sides of her face. I whisper using the flavor of language Robin Bright speaks, not my Faerie cadence. "Honey, I'm going to need you to trust that you're safe with me."

She leans her cheek into my palm. "Always with you, Robin."

My stomach twists. I am a fiend. How is Finnbheara's geas against me any worse than my enchantment to steal this woman's affections like a child sneaking a sweet from the feast table?

I rub my nose against hers. "Why do you believe that?"

She tries to kiss me, but I pull away. Her pouty lips rest against my jaw. "Why wouldn't I? When I was lost, you were the insightful friend who grounded me. That kind and caring person I needed. You've never pushed or taken advantage." I feel her smile against my skin. "I hope you know you wouldn't be taking advantage." She giggles. "Please take advantage, Robin. I'm ready for more. A year is a long time not to cross the finish line. Too damn long." Her hand slides down my side to wrap around my hip. My cock gives an appreciative twitch at the proximity of her fingers.

Her words shed the outer layer of my trepidation. Perhaps this will not be as difficult as I expected. Colleen believes Robin Bright to be a good man and that we have been building a slow and steady foundation. Even though we have not enjoyed physical pleasures, I infused lustful satisfaction through my influence over her. She believes we shared intimacies typical of a human couple on the threshold of consummation. I would speak falsely if I denied lying with her has not been a temptation since the first time I tasted her peppered apple lips. Given that she is a player in the drama involving Eala and Finnbheara, I counselled myself to resist.

"What if I told you I'm ready for more, too?" I dot a kiss to the silky stretch of skin in front of her ear.

She flings her leg over my hip so quickly that we rock to the side. Taking advantage of the imbalance, Colleen continues the slide until she is atop me.

My cock thickens from the enticing feminine invitation. Lust whispers in my ear that I could take her multiple times this night as long as at least one crescendo rises after we have given our bond-promise. Reason elbows lust aside, cautioning how very wrong things could go between us.

I grip her waist and lift her off me.

She coos. "It's okay, baby. You're already hard. Let's take advantage of this fluffy bed and pitch-black room. My imagination is already on fire."

When she tries to remount me, I hold her in place next to my body. "There are things to be said first, Colleen."

"You're very old-school for a hot, hunky Irishman."

Human phrasing escapes me as I struggle to find the right words. Asking if she will enter a bond-promise with me will make no sense to her.

She stills. "God, Robin. I'm not asking you to marry me. Just ravish me."

Marry her, yes. Marriage is her version of a bond-promise.

"I believe it's time for us to be married, sweetheart." Can she tell I am holding my breath or that my heart is beating at twice its rate? If she agrees, then this will be far simpler than I imagined it would be.

Colleen rolls back on top of me and starts peppering my face with kisses. "I swear I wasn't hinting, but yes, yes, yes, Robin Bright, I will marry you." As bountiful breasts with ripely hardened nipples mash against my chest, lust threatens to dictate my next action until our reality spears lust through the heart.

Robin Bright.

Fuck.

I am an imbecile. She agreed to bond-promise with a fiction. Aodh will demand that such an oath be with Robálaí Geal, the Fae, not Robin Bright, the fabrication of a human.

I wince as the erection inspired by Colleen's proximity and obvious desire for me painfully strains against my britches. Flipping our position, I pin her wrists to the bed with my hands.

"Stop, Colleen." It would have been wiser to continue using endearment to keep her calm, but my rational state unravels as each minute racing toward Aodh's deadline ticks by.

She tenses beneath me. "What's wrong?"

My grip on her is unnecessarily tight. I ease up to avoid causing her pain, but still hold fast, abandoning my attempts to use her human vernacular. "You must listen and heed my words. There are truths I will speak, and they will not be easy to bear."

She tries to pull free. "Robin, you're freaking me out."

There is no point in continuing the charade of Robin Bright. "I am going to restrain you further now but not harm you."

"Wait. Define restrain? Is tying me to this squishy bed in the dark your kink? I'm up for mystery, but I draw the line at straps or ropes or—"

Her hand flails in the darkness, reaching for me, but I have already moved to stand beside the bed as my magic wraps around her in a translucent, sparkling sheath.

Colleen thrashes against the confinement. She will not feel pain, but neither can she escape my cage.

"Not cool, Robin. What are you doing?"

I attempt to lay a hand on her cheek in a feeble attempt at reassurance, but she recoils from my touch. I should not care about a gesture of disdain from a human, but it unsettles me.

"Take whatever this thing is off me," she snaps.

"I shall bring back the light now and reveal all." I wave my arm to encase the bedchamber inside a second charm of silence to forbid Aodh and his ilk from being privy to what I am about to put this woman through. As if lifting the coverlet off a sleeping babe, I ease my influence from Colleen, then reawaken flames inside the sconces around the walls as well as the chandelier above the bed made of a swirling cascade of red glass leaves. The rose gold light sets Colleen's fair skin aglow.

For a moment, I stall in my purpose. This vision of Colleen, laid upon the crimson watermarked bedding with unruly waves of hair splayed around her head like crackling flames, paints her in brushstrokes I have not appreciated before. Yes, she entices me in the way Fae are often attracted to mortals as fleeting distractions, but I never paused to absorb the extent of beauty or the wildness surging close to the surface of her being. My constant influence has been subduing a fierce whirlwind.

She releases a prolonged whimper as her mind clears of the smudges I have left upon it.

Colleen bucks against her restraints as her mind once again becomes her own, and she takes in her surroundings. The glaze of Fae influence lifts from her eyes. "What the hell?"

Her glare pierces me like a fire-tipped arrow. "Who the fuck are you? Where have I seen you before?" She thrashes violently in her attempt to free herself, bellowing loud enough to cause ripples in the dousing magic I placed on the bedchamber. "Let me go."

Her second question is concerning. How can she hold any awareness she has *seen* me prior to this moment? I should only exist for her in the influence I just dissolved.

I stand motionless next to the bed, preparing to deliver the first dose of revelation. Best not to hide the unnatural stillness of the Fae. I am the other to her. A being whose kind she has only heard of in tales.

The volume of her cries makes my ears throb. "Help me. Help me. Fire. Murder. I'm being kidnapped."

Perhaps Artos's suggestion to end her life may have been the more prudent path.

She continues her ranting at full volume. "Did you drug me? Is this a perverted sex den?"

I nearly inform her no one can hear her then bite my lip, realizing such an admission might escalate her unease.

Taking a deep breath to stave off the rising discomfort in my breast, I force a tone of calm I do not feel and begin.

"I understand I have caused you distress, and for that I am not proud. You are neither drugged nor in a place where the desires of another will be visited upon you forcefully."

The level of Colleen's pleas for help intensifies, the timbre of her voice gouged with panic. Her movements become so violent that I fear she will do herself harm. Plain words of comfort are useless. Words of truth are my way forward. I will repeat them until she is capable of understanding what I tell her.

"I am Fae. You are, in a sense, my captive. I wish you no harm; however, I have placed your life in a position of some danger."

Her wailing does not abate. Sobs and tears punctuate her symphony of terror. I repeat the words a second and third time. As her skin deepens from a dark rose to purplish hues, alarm grows within my breast that this fervor will steal her coherency. Leaning my hands on the bed next to her, I draw closer to utter words I pray will revive her clarity of thought. "Will you hear me for Eala Duir's sake?"

At the mention of Eala's name, Colleen gulps in a breath nearly as loud as her cries. Her voice shakes with her next words. "Is Eala here? Did you kidnap her, too?"

I drop my head, letting my hair fall in a curtain around my face. "She is not here."

There is a moment of precious silence for me to gather my thoughts.

Instead of hysterics, anger colors her tone. "You're actually a Fae?"

"Not a Fae, I am Fae."

"You're busting me on semantics?" The woman roils with indignation but has somehow quelled her frenzy enough to scold me.

"You do not question my true nature?"

To my utter disbelief, she snorts. "Now you're accusing me of not believing in Fae? Frankly, asshole, it's a preferable explanation to you being a serial killer, or perverted sex dungeon kidnapper."

I am somewhat dumbfounded at this civil turn in her discourse. "While my intentions may not wear the light of honor, they are not dipped in the depravities of which you speak."

She gives a renewed lurch, testing her bonds. The latest failure seems to rob her of the last dregs of fight. "Then what the hell are they dipped in, and what does this have to do with Eala, Faerie man?"

I cock my head to the side, still not grasping her lack of incredulity that I am Fae, but forge on. "I have much to reveal to you of Eala Duir, Sionnach Loho, the fox, and their ties to my Folk."

Colleen closes her eyes for a prolonged blink. "Why am I not surprised goddamned Sion is part of this freaking nightmare?" She turns her head to me, and with a scoff retorts, "Spill it all, Faerie man."

I straighten up, still staring down at her. "And you will accept my confession of the fantastic?"

She gives a loud snuffle, clearing the evidence of her weeping. "Listen, dude, I'm Irish, like really Irish. Both parents were born in Wexford. My grandmother in Enniscorthy leaves milk, butter, and other offerings on her porch every night for your Folk. Our family honors feast day rituals. Hell, my aunt is sworn to the goddess Morrigan."

Colleen takes a stuttering breath before continuing. "I grew up hearing Eala's grandmother's folktales that were far from the simplistic versions in books, as if she had bizarre insight. Then there's Eala herself and her weird daydream vision things she called dream flashes. I can handle bizarre." Her voice hitches. "Eala's okay, right?"

I stare at Colleen for a moment before answering. This human may not be the simple canvas I believed her to be. "When last I saw Eala Duir, she was in good health."

Relief relaxes the tension in Colleen's face, but she does not speak. I seize the opportunity of her silence to begin my campaign. Hands clasped behind my back, I pace the room and unravel the tale of Eala being a gift to Finnbheara's human lover, Martha, to assist Sionnach in freeing the soulfall. I follow up quickly with Eala's bargain with the king to allow her and the fox to dwell in Tír na nÓg. Concluding, I share what I have gleaned from flashes in the connection I share with the white swan's essence. The mingling of our spirits enraged the king. Eala Duir has been separated from her fox, and although I do not know the true whereabouts of either, she lingers no longer in the Fae kingdom."

Colleen's silence stretches. I suppose such truths do challenge the limits of a human mind.

"Now, I shall—"

She interrupts. "None of this is about me or why I'm Faerie-spelled to your bed. Where in the hell are we, anyway?"

I stifle a grunt at her mention of hell. If only she grasped that in ironic terms, she has answered her own query. I lean against the door, sensing distance between us is prudent for the next chapter I will impart to her. "'Twas but to provide foundation for the current story in which we are both players."

Telling Colleen of my interference with her reality and the tricks I played on her mind, her life, and her emotions should not raise any sensation of note in me. She is a human, a lesser being. Yet...guilt, a state I have not felt often in my long life but seems to be a constant visitor since I entered the Cave of Cats, claws at me like a great beast. I falter when I illuminate the falsehood of our association when I acted as Robin Bright and used our seeming alliance as a weapon against Eala. After I finish the chapter where I supplied Eala with the vision of bringing Colleen through the mouth of hell, I pause, for it is not yet the most difficult admission I must make.

"You're a very twisted soul," Colleen whispers.

The insult lands harder than it should. I tell myself it is because of the precarious position I have put my Host in with Aodh, and nothing to do with this mortal's opinion of me. I pretend to ignore her bitter words.

Colleen's anger reverberates through the chamber in a writhing heat. "What is it you want from me, Faerie man?"

Now we are to it, the crux of the purpose I must wring out of her. "For the safety of my Host and the two of us, Aodh must believe you are bond-promised to me."

"Bond-promised?"

I suppress a growl of frustration. "Two beings committing to one another, a vow, an oath."

She hums as she weighs my scant explanation. The sound is fair music, sending pleasant vibrations through my body like an enraptured bee facing a garden of vibrant blooms.

"Like an old-fashioned betrothal?"

My focus snaps back to my captive. "Beyond that. You mortals would term it a marriage."

"Whoa there, this Aodh person—"

I interrupt. "Do not discount him as a mere person. He is a mighty God of the Underworld, King of Bráchthine, a Dark Prince of the *Daoine Sidhe*."

She squints through the dimness that is broken up only by flickering flames from wall sconces and the chandelier. "You're afraid of him."

I let out a dignified snort. "As any sane being should be. As you should be." Tension pecks at the control I strive to maintain. "Let us finish this." Standing at the foot of the bed, I cross my arms over my chest and glare at her. "Aodh covets you. I promise if I give you over to his keeping, you will not survive his brutal attentions. To protect you, it is imperative he believes we are bonded."

She grumbles, once again disrupting the flow of explanation. "Why do I find it hard to believe you're only asking me to go along with this to be gallant?"

"I did not claim such." I clutch the carved black footboard of the bed tightly enough to cease the blood flowing to my fingers. "Aodh desires Eala Duir to unravel the mystery of her making through the *beads of being*. He is certain that knowledge and possession of such ability will give him the power of creation equal to what Finnbheara holds. The kingdoms of Tír na nÓg and Bráchthine stand on the verge of war. Aodh only hesitates because he believes Finnbheara's use of the *beads of being* to create Fae gives the king of Tír na nÓg an insurmountable advantage."

I shake my hands to rid them of numbness. "Our future and that of my kin depend on Aodh's trust that I am unequivocally devoted to his cause. Proving a bond-promise between us is essential to that end."

Even though she is weary from struggling, Colleen attacks her bonds with renewed force. "You're an insane bastard to think I'd Faerie marry you to suck my best friend, my sister, into a trap for a horrible hell god to rip her apart and steal these *beads of being* swirling around inside her."

One flick of my finger would change this hellion into the docile, adoring woman I have cultivated over the last moon cycle. It is tempting, but I gain nothing but a borrowed reprieve.

Despite her previous abuse of her vocal cords, Colleen musters a new onslaught of shrieking. "The bad shit I've heard of your kind is true. You are self-serving, soulless fuckers who don't give a rat's ass about humans." A sob cuts through her rant. "I don't want to die, and I don't want Eala to die."

It is her words that die as she withers into a baleful bundle of sorrow. Colleen's bravado lulled me into a false sense of her strength. I broke this mortal with the truths I thrust upon her.

Her despair should be nothing to me. I turn my back to rid myself of her pathetic display, but this woman's anguish ripples through the air until it works its way through my skin to fasten around my heart. With no forethought, I whip around to face her. My voice is as raw and ravaged as hers. "I swear I will never allow Aodh's filth to touch Eala Duir."

Oh, gods and nature, what have I done? I spoke the deep secret no one can know, not my high command, not the Host, not Colleen. Yet her pain drove me to reveal the forbidden. This, above all else, may doom my purpose. I spring onto the bed and wrap a hand around her throat.

"You must never, never tell another soul what vow I have just given you. It will be the ruination of all." I clasp her shoulder and shake it. "Swear to me. Swear it. Aodh must not doubt my intention to bring Eala Duir before his throne."

Colleen swallows against my palm, and I ease my hold, cupping her throat as gently as a lover. Her eyes are wide and unblinking as she stares at my face. Slowly, she lifts her hand beneath her enchanted casing and wraps gentle fingers around my wrist.

Her touch sends golden warmth through my body. She does not weep or cry out as her gaze lingers on my eyes, my mouth, then my hair.

"I do know you," she whispers.

Impossible. I erased my enchantments from her essence.

I release her, sloughing off her hold on my wrist. "I assure you, you do not."

Colleen's hands press over her heart. Her breathing becomes rapid, and thin mist slides from her lips. "Come closer."

"Unnecessary," I say, but I cannot rip my gaze from hers. The delicate mist she creates from life's breath curls as it cuts a path through the air to my lips. I open and allow the sweetness of her to slide across my tongue. It is as lovely and innocent as a first kiss. I swallow the unexpected goodness.

"Please," she begs.

I find myself unable to refuse and sit beside her on the bed.

"Your hair has the colors of honey, sunflower, and burnt butter." She tries to touch the strands nearest my face, but my enchantments limit her reach. "It's weirdly perfect." Colleen gives her head a quick shake as if attempting to come out of a trance. "I know you," she repeats then whispers, "A deep knowing."

Her words resonate through my chest, my head, my very bones. I ache to dismiss this as the fantasy of a human enmeshed in the impossibility of stories, but I cannot, for I feel it too.

I feel.

I feel.

There is the tiniest bead of cold stone in my heart that is no longer made of ice.

I feel for this human.

"A deep knowing?" I ask, somewhat fearful her explanation will sour the revelatory moment.

She shrugs. "It's something Eala's grandmother would call an unexpected connection to someone you thought you didn't know."

I nearly protest that it is merely her essence sensing mine, but sudden doubt seizes me. I am uncertain how a human spirit tampered with as I have done to her's retains such knowledge. She is released from my influence. This should be the first meeting of our true selves.

Colleen's voice is calm. "What's your name?"

She does not call me Robin Bright. My essence opens to her and flares around me as if it is being called.

"Robálaí Geal."

This woman smiles warmly at me then repeats, "Robálaí Geal." My core grows hungrier with my name upon her lips. The night wanes, and I have yet to accomplish what I must.

"We must continue our negotiation."

She narrows her eyes, the dreamy quality of the last moments fading away. "Okay, we do the Faerie marriage thing, and then everyone is safe from the big bad god?"

"Bond-promise."

Colleen huffs. "Fine. Call it whatever. When this is finished and I go home, it's null and void. Right?"

Whether fatigue or fear weathers away my indifference, I cannot say, but a shudder of discontent seizes me at the thought of this human returning to her world. An honorable sort would tell her a bond-promise is as eternal as my Fae existence, but my honor can be fleeting. Additionally, such a revelation is not a wise move in our interchange. Let her believe she possesses a way out.

"I assure you, your heart will not be compromised in our arrangement. There is a geas upon me that forbids my heart from accepting the devotion of another." I tilt my head. "A geas being a—"

She flashes me a haughty look. "I know what a geas is, Faerie man."

My obfuscation works. To my relief, Colleen appears to accept the geas as an obstacle to the permanence of a bond-promise. I dare not reveal hers is a false perception.

"Next steps." She glances around the room, and her milky skin fades to an even paler shade. "Oh god, please tell me this bond-promise business is not a *slice your lifeline* thing. I can't handle bloody."

I slide a key into the locked door my hope is trapped behind. "A single drop of blood from the location of your choosing will suffice."

I watch her lovely throat bob as she swallows. "That, I can manage."

Still, I do not turn the key to free my hope since I have not told her all. "You agree then to enter a bond-promise with me?"

She wiggles and attempts to raise her knees. "Do you agree to let me out of this sparkly sack?" Her sigh is overly dramatic as she lies back. "I've dived into insta-relationships for less reason than protecting my best friend. So sure, I agree…for now."

Her callousness causes me surprising offense. I despair at my inability to enter a true bond-promise, and she treats its sanctity with no more respect than brushing a fly off one's shoulder. I enjoy a morsel of satisfaction in delivering the offensive final caveat to our bargain. "There is one additional requirement Aodh demands."

Colleen releases an exasperated breath. "Obviously, the stories of Faeries skating around the truth are no myth. What else does this hell-god clown want?"

There is no subtle way to elucidate this. I rescue the black box from the carpet where it had flown when I knelt before Colleen's prone form. A different wave washes over me, remembering my relief that the brutal act of heaving her into the bedchamber did not cause the mortal harm.

I detest the anxious fluttering of my heart as I show her the small container. "I must capture my bond-promised's sated cry of completion in this vessel."

Her brow furrows, then understanding dawns, reddening her cheeks. As she sputters, I remain unmoved. "Aodh expects you to fuck me until I come and stuff my scream in his box?"

"Crass but correct."

Beneath her charmed sheath, she extends a single finger in my direction. "You're not touching me. I can deal with the sham marriage thing for Eala's sake, but not that." She nods at the box and shudders. "It's sick."

Her agitation is baffling. "Never before has a human rejected an opportunity to receive my pleasures."

"I met you a hot minute ago. You dish out end-of-the-world-level shit, then want to jump me and make me scream for this Aodh's jollies. Real flattering, you ass."

We glare at one another. I break first and rage at her. "You will not protect Eala Duir." Rushing to the wall, I drive a fist into my enchantment. It sends a painful sting through me. "You agree, then reject. You are too complicated for a human. You—"

"Shut up, Faerie man."

"My name is Robálaí Geal," I roar and throw my body atop hers. "I could force my lust upon you, surpassing the filthiest of your mortal fantasies until you understand what you deny yourself." My lips graze her ear before my teeth rake over the same path. Colleen shivers beneath me. I brush my mouth along the length of her neck. The urge to throw her into an enchantment and play with her mind and body burns through my core.

I send hot breath across her collarbone, then along the exposed skin above her ruby-encrusted neckline. My nose skates lower, teasing the tip of one breast then the other until I feel her nipples plump with want. I dip my knee between her thighs and begin to slide her dress to her hips. The contrast of her satiny red underthings and black fabric of the skirt against ivory skin shoots delight straight to my cock. If this is the eve of our destruction, it is madness to avoid a tempting feast. I move my lips against the skin of her inner thigh, the tingle of the enchanted sheen around her heightening my desire. "You will beg for my attention." I slide back up her body to present my challenge eye to eye.

She half turns and manages to catch my chin with her elbow. "I said, shut up, you arrogant son of a bitch. If you dare try anything else, I'll snap your Faerie dick in half." Both our chests heave with heavy breaths. "Get off me so I can think."

I quickly comply, especially since the Faerie dick she just threatened seems overly eager to test her mettle. Stalking to a chair in the corner that matches the design of the great bed, I drop into it. Crossing one leg over the other, I fix my gaze on Colleen. "Do not linger on your conclusion. If we do not placate the Dark Prince by dawn, all will be lost." I bury every thought of the brief tenderness between us into a dark crevice of my mind. Ridiculous humans and their romantic proclivities. Curse my weakness of longing for something Finnbheara's geas ensures I will never know.

"Faerie man..."

I am stripped of too large a portion of my waning energy to counter her demeaning title.

She breathes loudly enough to irritate. "I have a workaround."

CHAPTER 13
THE FLIGHT

EALA

I sit facing the fire in Biddy's hearth while she changes out of her wet clothing. Robber Bright always hinted my Fae powers were beyond what my narrow mind imagined. I was so busy being pissed at his cryptic warnings, arrogance, and outright attempt at seducing me, I never took the time to let that information sink in. The magical communion I shared with Biddy and Alfie at the *lough* cracked open my curiosity about the possibilities of what I may be capable of.

I wish I could take a moment to sit here, let the fire warm me, and reflect on what an incredible experience my blossoming power provided, but I'm afraid to linger. When Sion and I dared to steal a few hours to pause and enjoy one another, it cost us precious time. My shoulders crack as I attempt to roll some of the tension from them.

Biddy calls to me from the far corner of the cottage. "I see your weariness from here, Eala. Eat a bit of stew."

"Thank you." I lift a wooden bowl from a shelf near the hearth. I ladle thick, savory stew, grab what looks like a horn spoon, and bring my humble meal to the table. A medley of herbs weaves through the steam, and my stomach growls loudly enough to raise a chuckle from Biddy.

As eager as I am to rush my new witchy friend to Loho cottage and get down to serious problem solving, I do have to eat.

"Should I fill a bowl for you too?" I ask Biddy.

"I'll fetch my own."

I'm torn in half, facing the crossroad of who to place at the top of my rescue list. Dread winding through my spirit like a poisonous vine warns me Colleen may be in greater peril, but what I've seen of Finnbheara's heartlessness contradicts that.

Sionnach must come first.

As much as I love Colleen, I don't want to continue down this screwed up path without the man who's given me more love, courage, and magic than my heart ever dreamt of. He's seen what the Fae are capable of longer than I have. With Sion by my side, we'll have a better chance of going after Colleen.

And what about Máthair? Is she back in the Glade of Chimes? Does she want to leave Finnbheara? There's something between those two. It might be nothing more than history, but I felt it in those final moments. I swear there were cracks in Finnbheara's marble shell when he looked at Máthair.

While lost in thought, I've gobbled my entire bowl of stew. Filling my belly gives me a nice burst of energy.

Low cooing rises behind me. The sound is so intimate, I feel as if I'm intruding. In an attempt at subtlety, I turn to see Biddy stroking the bottle like a lover, her lips inches from the glass as she whispers to it. The liquid inside roils and bubbles.

"This bottle holds part of my spirit," says Biddy, noticing my failed nonchalance. "I didn't know how much of me it's claimed until we were parted."

Her confession brings a fresh wave of sorrow to my spirit at the gravity of dragging another soul into my nightmare, especially when I've tricked Biddy into joining me. I push the thought away. I can't get to Sion alone. I'll do whatever I have to do.

"Biddy, it's time to go."

"There's a thing I'd ask of you, Eala of the Fae."

I've shaken the wise woman's reality to its core. I suppose she's entitled to just about any request she can dream up.

"Might your Veil carry me back to those I've loved and lost?"

The look of longing in her eyes breaks my heart. "Yes, Biddy, I believe it can."

"When this business of yours is finished, will you do such a kindness for me?"

I think of the moment I walked into the Loho cottage in the early 1800s and saw my grandmother for the first time since her alleged death in New York. Despite the dire circumstances we faced on that awful night with Olk, and even though she didn't know me yet, seeing Máthair again was truly a gift. If it's within my power to give someone else such joy, I won't deny Biddy.

"I promise I'll try."

"I thank you."

I pose the same question to Biddy that Sion asked me every time we were on the threshold of an impossible challenge. "Are you ready?"

The fire in her eyes is all the answer I need. This woman, this amazing witch, has more courage than I've ever possessed.

"Great. Let me explain the sorcery of a car."

I swear if Biddy turns the television on and off one more time, I'm going to smash it with Sion's fattest book, *Truths in Irish Folktales*. I thought her barrage of questions about the little she could make out in the dark on the drive from Feakle was challenging. Here, she's touched everything in the Loho cottage at least twice, making irritating noises with an endless chain of comments and inquiries. Wherever Sion and I traveled, I was nervous and squeamish about the unknown. Not Biddy.

In the moments back in Feakle, right before I willed the Veil to bring us to my time, my heart nearly stopped, terrified that transporting Biddy to a year beyond the end of her life could end badly, as in having to deal with a dead witch. Thankfully, my choice to give the Veil my blind trust paid off.

"How is it you're not more affected or nervous when these things must be incredibly strange to you?"

Biddy chuckles. "The first time a person sees something outside the natural boundaries, it brings fear and a need to shoo it off." She shakes her head. "Until you learn denial is a fool's errand." Biddy jabs her finger twice into the palm of her hand. "The second time, disbelief takes the lead, which does a person no good either." She treats me to a broad, knowing smile. "After the third time, you let in a bit of wonder and learn to take things as they come."

I appreciate her matter-of-fact approach to oddities that sent me into a tailspin when Sion first introduced me to the concept of the Veil and time traveling. I suppose when you live a life of magic, you're resilient when it comes to weird.

Biddy resumes her tinkering. Given her open-minded philosophy on the extraordinary, I share the time-bending encounters Sion and I weathered. I wait for each new otherworldly detail to surpass Biddy's wonder threshold and send her running off, but the witch is not fazed.

"I've been accused of consorting with druid spirits to bring about ill wishes, but never met one," says Biddy. "You've had the fortune to cross paths with four."

I wasn't counting, but she's right. "Pwyll, Cathbad, and his druidess wife were interesting to be sure, but I recommend avoiding any druid guardians in passage tombs."

The witch laughs. "Fine advice."

Recounting my travels with Sion makes my heart ache, fearing memories may be all I'm left with if we can't reach him.

"Have you ever had a vision or heard stories from Fae visitors about specific pathways into Tír na nÓg? You knew there was a Faerie door in the *lough*. Do you know of others?"

"I'm sure many hide in certain waters, but none save that one have shown themselves to me. Did your wanderer's tree show you a way in when we fetched my wee bottle?"

Shit. I was fixated on getting Biddy's prize back. I should have probed deeper for any opening into Finnbheara's kingdom, maybe a forgotten gate. "I blew it and didn't look for one. Let's put it on the list as a possibility."

I scribble *Biddy's Lough* on the pad of paper I set on the kitchen table.

"I've heard tell of caves leading to Himself's feast table."

"I'd rather leave caves as a last resort." I avoided the topic of Robber Bright and Colleen's abduction into Oweynagat. That particular cave leads to the feast table of a certain Himself I'm not eager to meet. The time doesn't feel right to bring up the vision Robber Bright sent of the hellmouth. Once we've tackled Finnbheara, I'll broach the subject of Aodh and the underworld with Biddy.

"Sionnach told me he was able to use the Veil to sneak into the Glade of Chimes to visit Máthair on feast days when Finnbheara was preoccupied." Most likely with revelry and debauchery. "Have you heard of any unique Faerie feast days? Maybe Finnbheara's birthday?"

I'd already poured through the Internet and Sion's books to try and uncover any Faerie-specific holidays apart from common Celtic celebrations like Beltane or Samhain. The closest sacred day is the summer solstice, and that's a month away. Too many awful things could happen to Sionnach by then if Finnbheara decides to punish my *anamchara* for my swift exit.

"No to that notion as well," Biddy says as she shoots down my latest suggestion and pokes at the coffee maker. "If the king means to keep you out, why would he leave any door open?"

I sink onto the couch with a growl and drop my head back on the cushions. Even they smell like Sion, which doesn't help the emotional soup sloshing around in my brain.

Biddy moves next to the hearth and studies me. "There's the possibility your man won't want to leave Tír na nÓg. It's said the weak human heart is fast won over by the place."

I gape at her then snap my mouth shut. God, maybe she's not off base. So many folktales share the theme of mortals not falling for Fae lovers alone but the land as well. What's not to love about eons of non-judgmental sex and never aging?

No, I won't accept that. "All the more reason for us to hurry." She tosses me a look as if I'm a deluded idiot. I jump to my feet, ready for a fight. "You don't know Sion and what we have. Our spirits, our hearts, our souls are tied together for all time. By choice. By love. He'd never trade the chance to come back to me for anything the Fae offered him."

I hate the pity on her face. "Girl, haste is the enemy of success."

"And hesitation could be the death of it. We've got to try something, Biddy. Maybe one of your spells can charm us past Finnbheara's barrier. If we have faith, it could work." The familiar scratch of yew branches against the back of the cottage makes me think of Máthair, the happy times she lived through right where I'm standing, and the faith she had in me, in her son, in the belief things do turn out for the best. I whisper her mantra of hope. "Faith is to believe what we do not see, and the reward of this faith is to see what we believe."

"Och," says Biddy, stamping her foot. "Don't be throwing that fool St. Augustine's words my way." She shakes a finger. "The stupid man also said witches don't have supernatural powers to call upon magic of any sort." She grumbles. "Your saint don't know true magic from a rotten egg."

The frustration I've been holding in explodes. "Then you suggest something, anything." I move to grab the blue bottle sitting on the kitchen table, but she sweeps it into her arms. "Have you even tried to use the blue bottle's magic to look for a gate, or is entertaining yourself with everything in my house more important?"

Biddy's hair falls free across her shoulders and begins to curl at the ends. A static crackle bites the air. I've done it now, pissed off a witch holding a bottle of Faerie juju.

Damage control. "I'm sorry, Biddy. Really. I'm going crazy not being able to decide what the next step should be. I know hundreds of stories of the Fae, but none of them feel specific enough to act on." I poke fingers into my temples. "Tracking down the right Faerie mound or path, mushroom circle, or standing stones to find a way in could take years."

The air calms. "Girl, do you think your woes left my reckoning? They have not. I do my best thinking when I'm moving about, letting thoughts stew in my mind."

"I'm desperate."

"That's plain to see. Your pain covers this place like creeping moss. I'm trying to break through the feel of it and be of use to you." She shakes her head. "I'd best be saying what's sticking with me even though it may be a blow to your aching heart."

"Please."

Biddy studies me, deciding if I can handle what she's about to say. "I've held the bottle to my breast and asked its help, but no answers come. I fear a plain and clear way has not shown itself because I don't believe it's just your king we'll be facing. If you challenge the gates of Tír na nÓg, I'm afeared Finnbheara's army'll be waiting for you by his side."

Oh, holy hell. Images of the line of Fae warriors I've seen every time I step foot in Finnbheara's kingdom flash through my mind, followed swiftly with memories of Robber Bright's Host of a Thousand Wings. They've defected, but the king surely commands countless others.

"Sorry to say, it takes an army to defeat an army, and we're only a Faerie, a witch, and a loyal *fánaí* tree, with nothing but noble intentions and a wee bit of power." She eyes me in her *I see right through you* way.

The cry bursting from my throat burns. I sense the truth of her words down to my fraying nerves. I can't give up, but she's right. Even if we find a way into Tír na nÓg, the battle is already lost. The weight of impossibility suffocates me. I stagger to the red wooden door of the cottage and lean a hand against it. "I, I have to get some air."

Without waiting for Biddy's answer, I leave the cottage and stumble over hardy wildflowers on my way to the fields. I thought partnering with someone who's dealt with the Fae and has her own magic would lead me to answers. Instead, I feel like I'm slipping farther away from my *anamchara*.

My sense of defeat leaches color from the land and the sweet smell of clean air from the sky. The helplessness I felt when I followed Sion out the window of the soulfall tower and he turned to sparkling light in my arms consumes me the way it did on the dawn of that fateful Beltane morning.

I'm falling again.

Warm wind spirals around me. My arms stretch wide to become white wings with the sprinkling of light gold freckles that cover my skin. The weight of grief is replaced by the lightness of parting from the earth as my swan takes over.

I fly.

Wings stronger than my withering heart beat in a steady rhythm as I rise toward the clouds. There is freedom in the sky. Burdens are shed as air strokes my white feathers. The swan does not doubt the sky. I do not doubt the swan. She is the magic and strength within me. We belong to one another.

I'm holding too tightly to the Eala I was, a safe, small, self-protected college professor who let my dreams only come alive in the folktales I cherish. Now, I'm the tale, and my sole limits are the echoes of an old life I must stop clinging to. It's time to let them go, and live fully in my own story.

As I soar above cliff, hill, and the land, hope travels beside me. Fear is a prison. Desperation is a shackle. The swan reminds me that hope is always there for the taking. So, I take it.

I welcome the wind's caress and revel in the contrast of cerulean sky and powder white clouds. My mind dismisses doubt and welcomes possibility. As Eala below, I could not stop the light of my spirit from fading. Eala, the swan, shines like the crystal sun in the Glade of Chimes.

I am renewed.

I won't let Finnbheara defeat love. I won't let Robber Bright steal what doesn't belong to him.

I am Fae.

I am swan.

I am power.

Below me, grasses sway where the wind leads them. Oh, to see my fox running across the land beneath.

The shimmer of a familiar crystal blue *lough* catches my eye, and I fly toward it. On its shores, I began to understand who I am. Even though Robber Bright was the wrong person to lead me into my new reality, he did open the door and show me what wonders lay beyond. He brought my *péist síoda*, my silk dragon, Cara, to me. We wandered through the Gem Kissed Forest until his true intention to possess me showed itself.

Drops of sunlight ride gentle currents across the lake. It doesn't wear a diamond coating, but it is pure beauty, nonetheless. I circle above the mystical waters of this Faerie door.

"Sionnach Loho." My voice rings out as the cry of a swan, a wordless song to anyone but me. "Don't lose hope. There's only water between us. I will find a way through."

The surface of the *lough* stills. A shadow moves over the water at a steady pace from one shore to the other and then back again. With each repetition across the *lough*, the shadow's edges become more defined until its outline is set. It's a man. He doesn't move with the fluid grace of a lithe Fae, but rather the solid step of one who works the land. I know this form as well as the wings that suspend me in the air.

Sionnach.

I stare longingly at the shadow arms that lift and carry. Arms that held me close and made me believe love is our greatest strength of all.

Beyond this *lough* is the Gem Kissed Forest. Is Sion truly there? Can I pass through the Crystal Gate within these waters to find him?

"Sionnach Loho," my swan cries again, but he doesn't look up.

I soar down to the *lough* and break through the surface. Diving deeper and deeper, I search for the Crystal Gate that leads to the Gem Kissed Forest. When I came through with Robber, I was so frightened, I closed my eyes. All I remember is Cara plunging into the water then Robber supporting me through the daze of crossing through the giant crystal chamber.

Is this gate barred to me as well?

All too soon, I lose breath and push to the surface. Shaking water from my feathers, I glide back and forth across the *lough*. Do I stay here and keep searching for an entrance to Finnbheara's kingdom that may be as impassable as the rest?

I clack my beak in annoyance. Here I am acting alone again when I'm not. Biddy is with me. Alfie is with me.

And who better to stand up to a Fae than another Fae? The clock has run out on my reluctance. It's time to delve deep into my Faerie spirit and discover just how much power Finnbheara and his *beads of being* have given me.

I fly to the cottage, invigorated by my swan's confidence and the unexpected hint of where my dearest love may be waiting for me. It's a place to target our efforts. When my feet touch the path near the front door, I transform into a woman and rush inside.

"Biddy, I think I saw Sion—"

The cottage is awash in a sapphire sheen. At first, I don't see Biddy until I follow a low hum and find the source of the light. On the bed, the witch lies as still as death. She's on her side, curled around the blue bottle, a mother cat protecting her kitten. The glass in her hands throbs like a captured sun, shooting vivid bright blue streaks in every direction.

I surge to her side and grasp her shoulder. "Biddy, oh my god. Are you hurt?"

Thankfully, this close, I see the rapid rise and fall of her chest. Slowly, a blue-tinted gaze lifts to mine. "Faerie girl, I may have found you an army."

CHAPTER 14
THE BINDING

ROBBER BRIGHT

I knead knuckles against my skull and vow to stock my chambers with elixir to quell the pounding in my head I suspect will be constant when dealing with this human. After brief moments of bidding my tumultuous thoughts to quiet, I lock my gaze on Colleen. "I do not understand your mortal term *workaround*. Have we not been working toward a resolution?"

Colleen strains to sit so she can see me across the bedchamber. "Ugh, take your magic trash bag off me, and I'll explain."

She can neither escape nor overpower me if I free her. It would take but the space of a finger snap to truss her anew if she proves violent. I flick my wrist, and her shroud bursts, sending gold flecks fleeing to the red glass leaf chandelier like moths to the moon.

Colleen propels herself off the bed in an instant. She smooths her dress then stares at it for a moment, absorbing her attire for the first time. "Huh," she remarks. "Nice. At least you have decent taste." Then she proceeds to shake out her limbs, head, and torso as if shedding water from a bath.

"Are you quite finished with this coltish dance?"

She sets her hands to her hips and tosses her hair over her shoulder. "Are you quite finished being an ass?"

The ache in my head extends to the tendons of my neck. I lift both hands to signal compliance.

"First, swear to me on whatever divine power Faeries worship you won't rape me."

I wince at the brutal term, taking offense. Forcing myself on anyone has never been necessary, but given I held her captive on a bed in a place unknown to her, delivering intimate touches, I understand her concern. "That was never and will never be my intention."

She does not look convinced, but proceeds. "What if…" Her skin blooms the color of the flames inside the sconces. "…Let me back up."

Colleen paces in a stunted circle on the other side of the room, keeping the bed between us. I recline then steeple my fingers on my knee in an attempt to put her at ease and reassure her I am not poised to leap up and ravish her. Although the thought is not altogether unpleasant.

She plaits her hair then shakes it to fall free before directing her attention to me once again. "Okay, here it is. The bond-promise thing is not an issue."

I nod. Relief softens the knots along my spine. "Noted."

"It's…it's the screaming orgasm in a box that's flipping me out."

I lean forward, bracing forearms on my thighs. "I promise to pleasure you tenderly if it will put you at ease."

Colleen wipes her hands through the air. "No, that's not…"

I grind my teeth at her inability to voice her discomfort in a straightforward manner.

"I haven't decided if I want you to touch me at all." The brightness in her eyes appears to contradict her words.

My frustration wars with a rising desire for this feisty woman. My jaw clenches painfully. She will turn me into a collection of aches from the crown of my head to my boots. I curse the flush of my skin and tangle of my tongue, preventing coherent words. Discomfiture on my part threatens to further stall resolution to our dire matter. I attempt to speak, but she cuts off my efforts.

"What if I touch…myself?"

She startles at my sudden growl. In truth, it is in equal part from her needless solution and my rush of lust at the enticing image of this woman naked on the bed before me, with legs spread, stroking slender fingers over ripe flesh to call her pleasure. I remain perplexed at her ongoing refusal of my attentions to bring forth a convincing cry of climax.

She shakes her head at my unease. "Will that work…if we do the bonding thing and then I give myself an orgasm for you to catch in your little cum box?"

I lean back in the chair and study the slate black ceiling with its veins of red lightning. Aodh demands the proof of ultimate pleasure from the one bond-promised to me. With the protection I sealed around us, he should have no way to detect what brought forth her cry. Still, it is a gamble.

"I am not sure. Is there no account in which you will allow me to summon your scream of ecstasy?"

Lust blossoms in her eyes, and I wonder what imaginings she harbors of me. If Aodh's deadline was not imposed upon us, I am confident my talents of persuasion would crush the walls of her fortress. Colleen is no maid. She has sampled human delights of the body. No doubt, the exquisite sexual experiences we Fae have to offer exists in tales known to her. Bold curiosity would surely overcome her resistance.

"I have another proposition." I do not temper the countenance of my lust. These hooded eyes and wry lips have earned me countless conquests of both Fae and mortal alike. It is gratifying to see her grasp the bed to remain standing. "If it eases your discontent, after we bond- promise, I shall wash the same brand of enchantment over you that encouraged your essence to welcome the affection of Robin Bright. You will know no fear. Everything that comes to pass promises to wear the guise of all good things. Your desire for me will flourish and be welcomed."

Her anger is immediate and vitriolic. "And be a damn lie. Mind controlling me to sleep with you doesn't constitute permission."

Apprehension pulses in my chest that my rebuffed offer may have damaged everything I hoped for with this woman. It is cruel that my fate and those I hold dear hang on the whims of a flighty mortal. As hard as I try, the stress and strain of our encounter colors my tone. "You misunderstand me. It was meant as a gesture to shelter you from discomfort after you agree to accept my pleasures."

"Yeah, I'll bet."

Faerie moon and stars, this creature plagues me.

"Tell me the truth, Faerie man. How much advantage did you take of my body while I was your compliant little puppet?"

A feeling far too close to regret sends painful pricks through my blood. Colleen has so little regard for me, she thinks me a true villain. It causes me unexpected displeasure that I am eager to allay.

Surprising us both, I cross the room and kneel before her. She does not resist when I take her hand and press it to the flame emblem on my chest, laying my hand over hers. "I swear by the Fae heart within my breast, nothing more than kisses have I stolen from you, and only in the presence of those I wished to bend to my purpose." I bow my head.

Her robust exhale tickles my scalp.

"I'm relieved. Still disgusted you used me to get to my friend, but relieved that's as far as you went." We stay in unmoving silence while precious minutes pass us by. When she speaks, Colleen's voice is gentle. "My gut tells me I didn't mind those kisses. I can't explain why I believe you or why I feel a bizarre connection to you when you swear you've erased whatever Faerie woo woo you used on me." She releases an irritatingly loud snort. "But I do."

The woman is reaching for purpose or reason in her extraordinary circumstance. I fear if I attempt to assist her, I will derail her erratic human thoughts, so I remain prone at her feet.

Finally, she raises my chin with her free hand. "It's insane to trust you at all, but since you gave me your oath you won't hurt Eala, I choose to believe you. For now."

Colleen scrutinizes me as if I am a riddle whose solution evades her. Our gazes meet with a silent agreement to go forward. Even though her faith is born of calculated logic and compassion for her friend, not me, I am moved by her loyalty. Is this *deep knowing* she claims to possess for me a catalyst for her leap of faith? It is not a human trait I comprehend, but something deep within me finds it alluring.

"Robálaí, I'm probably out of my mind, but as long as you agree to do the scream my way, then we're a go."

Her voice wears an authoritative tone that sends a rush of heat up my chest. Even in a circumstance foreign and reeking of danger, she is no demure, passive human. I smile at her use of my true name and the fine way it sounds rolling out of her pursed, blushberry wine-colored lips.

She looks around the room. "Walk me through your bonding. Are there required vows? Do we say them here, or is there a stone circle or Faerie ring we have to stand in?"

I chuckle at her human viewpoint of the workings of my world. "Perhaps a place with a pleasant view." I stand and take her hand, leading her back into the grand room of my suite. Her gaze darts around as quickly as a hummingbird taking flight.

"Wow, this is. Um, surprisingly elegant. The color scheme is too red and black for my taste, but the décor is definitely way out of my budget."

When we stop in front of the window, her movements freeze as if she has been encased in ice. I dart a glance at her chest to assure myself she still draws breath. My angle gives me a delightful view of the top swell of her generous breasts. I am flung back to the memory of my nose brushing their pert toppings tucked beneath her bodice. My half-hard cock is an inconvenience, given the solemnity of the ritual we are about to embark upon.

Her voice is breathy, which does not help my sensual agitation. "Are those mountains red? And made of glass?"

"I believe the glass for many of the adornments in this chamber and throughout the castle is hewn from those very peaks. Perhaps someday we will have the opportunity to venture forth and confirm such." The thought of Aillil ferrying Colleen and me on a sightseeing journey around Bráchthine is not altogether unpleasant.

She points into the gradient sky. "Is the orangey circle up there a sun?"

"You could term it thus. It is the light that constantly governs this realm."

Colleen switches her gaze to me. "Constantly? You mean there's no difference between day and night here?"

"Not by light or dark, but rather by hours and the sun's journey around the red glass mountains."

Her eyes take on a mischievous brightness. "Does the sun have a name like Hell's Beacon or the Great Scorch?"

The corner of my lip twitches. There is a wit about her I quite enjoy. "I will inquire."

She turns back to the scenery and strokes a finger down the glass. "Whatever it's called, the light it shines on the mountains sends rivers of gold from the top to the bottom." Colleen gazes at me, wonder not fear sparkling in her eyes. "Hell is not supposed to be so beautiful."

I nearly confess that the way she looks at me with such gentleness and awe may be the greatest beauty in all of Bráchthine. Instead, I give my head a hard shake. Her willingness to allow the bond-promise that will save my cherished Host may have melted some of my steel, but I must regain its full fortitude to survive in Aodh's realm.

This agreement between us is a contract. My geas-manacled heart may be hardened to love, but not loyalty. Despite the *deep knowing* conundrum she professes, I do not believe there is danger her human heart beats in my direction. Colleen is not doing this for the Host or for me. It is for Eala Duir alone that she proceeds.

"Humans created the hell you speak of to terrify your kind into obedience. It will serve you best to reframe your perception. Think of this not as your hell of torment and ugliness but another Fae realm beneath the others my Folk inhabit. Term it underworld, not hell."

She frowns. "Ruled by someone who sounds suspiciously like the devils and demons I've been warned about my whole life." Colleen grips my arm. "Do I ever have to meet Aodh?"

I pat her hand. "You have already done so."

It takes her a moment to absorb an encounter that has been extracted from her memories. "Was he beastly?"

I cluck my tongue. "It depends on your perception of beasts."

The woman huffs at me. "Does he look like you? Is he a pretty Fae with good hair and…these?" She reaches to brush aside strands to expose the sharp tip of my ear.

Again, the woman raises a smile to my lips. "I have never heard him described as pretty. No, the Dark Prince does not present as do my Folk. Once perhaps, but no longer." Describing Aodh's appearance might send her into a panic, but Colleen's healthy fear only benefits my control of her obedience. "He possesses a similar likeness of frame to other Fae and humans but wears skin of ash and eyes that shift between shadow and flame."

Colleen waves a hand to stop me and shudders. "So, not pretty." She lays fingers across her lips and flushes nearly as red as the chamber's décor. "Did I freak out when I saw him?"

I shake my head. "You were ensconced within my charm, thus shielded from fear."

She chews her lip, contemplating my admission. "Huh. Score a point for mind-control."

"It has its advantages."

For both of us.

The woman pulls from my grasp and fusses with her hair. "I always pictured wearing white to my wedding, a ceremony overlooking the ocean or in a room dripping with daisies." She humphs. "Guess a black dress and red glass mountains will have to do."

I bite my tongue to keep from substituting the term bond-promise for wedding. If framing what we are about to do in mortal terms moves her forward, so be it. Colleen is nervous and uncertain but gives no indication she will retreat.

"Shall we begin?"

In a breathy voice and with a hint of fear in her eyes, she says, "Okay."

I guide her shoulders to face me then ease us to kneel on the black rug covered in a pattern of red and gold leaves. She gasps when I pull a knife from a pocket and hold the blade point up. "Let us both prick a forefinger upon this Faerie steel so to offer our precious life blood to one another. I shall perform the ritual first so that you may hear the words and utter them in turn."

She rubs her lips together. "We don't need witnesses or an underworld priest to make it legal?"

It is apt she chooses this moment to swap her moniker of hell for underworld. I grasp her hand and twine my fingers through hers. "Blood speaks truth enough."

Colleen clucks her tongue. "My truth never included a Faerie husband." Her bosom heaves with a deep breath. "Okay, marry me, Robálaí."

I do not tame my words fast enough. "Bond-promise."

When she flashes me a look of unfettered exasperation, I smile. "If it is any consolation, my vision of destiny never included a bond-promise to anyone." Certainly not the mind-shredding fact that person would be human.

Her fingers tighten around mine. "A day of surprises for both of us."

My smile grows, and she answers with one of her own that supplants a modicum of my disquiet in what we are about to partake in. At least for the moment, Colleen seems to have discarded any resistance. I summon the peace of *Crann na Beatha*, the Tree of Life, to flow through my spirit then push my fingertip onto the knifepoint. When a bead of blood gathers on my skin, I speak words I thought forever banned from my lips.

"Soul that calls to mine. I offer you the essence of my life. Take this gift through body into spirit as my vow of bond-promise." I raise the glistening red drop to Colleen's mouth. Before I explain her part, her lips close around my finger. The soft sweep of her tongue to accept my blood sends strange currents of mingled fear and want through my body. As her gaze sears into mine, an ethereal cord unspools from where her lips touch my flesh, running up my arm until it pierces my chest and twines around my heart.

How can this be?

She is human. I am Fae. Even through blood and vow, I did not foresee this bond would bear the depth and trappings of destiny surging through my essence. Does she see this tether or is it for my knowing alone?

Colleen reverently slides her lips off my finger and stares at me with eyes as lush as the twinkling silver-gray moss that blankets rowan and elm in the Gem Kissed forest. Her pale skin wears the blush of joy, gracious acceptance, and a deeper intention that terrifies me. It is an effort to draw breath. This is the cruelty of Finnbheara's geas. The ritual conjures feelings in this woman for me. The geas murders any possibility my soul can return that affection.

I will resent her.

I will revile her for my inadequacy.

I am a robber indeed. A thief of emotion and trust.

She is but a human, Robálaí Geal. It does not matter.

My wandering thoughts miss the moment Colleen draws her blood with my blade. Her fingertip is poised before my lips as she says in a clear voice, "Soul that calls to mine. I offer you the essence of my life. Take this gift through body into spirit as my vow of bond-promise."

Without any guise of delicacy, I close my mouth around her outstretched finger, give a single hard suck, and release her.

I see how my perfunctory acceptance of her gift crushes her. She presented me with kindness, and I countered with disdain.

Her dove gray eyes glisten with tears. "Am I that disgusting to you?"

How do I confess it is not disgust but weakness she has roused in me? I thrust us onto the precipice of failure. My spitefulness may ruin her willingness to perform the very act that will deliver us from Aodh's wrath.

I capture both her hands in mine and stare into her eyes, willing the bond to reawaken that began to flourish between us as she so graciously accepted my blood. Her posture is rigid, and anger surrounds her in a simmering mist. She tries to pull away, until I implore her. "Do not think such, darling one.

You momentarily stole my reason. Forgive me. I lost myself in the enormity of our task." I am surprised at the quaver in my voice from the truth of my words. I mean them when I should not. "Even though we are forced into this union, its markings of grace overwhelm me."

Fighting the temptation to exert my influence over her to erase my thoughtlessness from her mind, I summon an expression of absolute honesty. Her shoulders relax. The shine in her eyes is not one of unshed tears, but rather undeserved understanding and forgiveness. It rankles me that she believes I am capable of weakness even as I play it out for the benefit of all. Thank nature, humans are far more malleable than Folk. If I had acted thusly with another Fae, I would find a dagger between my ribs.

Summoning a reverent tone, I repeat my vow. "Soul that calls to mine. I offer you the essence of my life. Take this gift through body into spirit as my vow of bond- promise."

With a wash of her blood still lingering on my tongue, I lean in and gently press my lips to hers in a mockery of what humans do at their bonding ceremonies. I mean my actions to be no more than a gesture to put her at ease.

Colleen has a different intention.

Whether it is the power of the bond we sealed, or a wish to convince ourselves what we have done is valid, there is nothing swift or ceremonial about our kiss. She opens to the pressure of our mouths upon one another as she presses her body into mine. I have no reason to deny her if she is willing. Perhaps there will be delights between us to capture Aodh's prize after all.

My arms cross behind her back. She is small of frame and easy to catch in my embrace. My lips slide over hers, appreciating the eagerness she offers. I allow her tongue to be first to foray into my mouth then meet it with a caress of my own, painting her with a dab of her blood. She tastes of spice and wicked intention. I lick her lips to give back a taste of the treat she favors me with as I relish the roll of her breasts against my chest.

Her mouth pulls away from mine to skate across my jaw and then down my neck as she settles onto the carpet, drawing me to lie upon her. I delve into my essence to assure myself that, in my passion, I did not inadvertently cast influence over her. I find no trace of enchantment that would compromise the scant trust I have built between us.

Hands thread through my hair as Colleen guides my lips to hers for fervent kisses. She laps at my tongue as if it is coated with sugar. My cock is pleased with this turn of events and flurries with sensation each time the tip of her tongue tastes mine.

I will leave the pace to my newly bond-promised as long as sensual explorations do not prevent us from meeting Aodh's deadline.

Without warning, she arches up against me with surprising force, and I yelp into her mouth. She giggles and rakes her fingernails over my ass before pushing me off her.

Sitting up, she wiggles away. "Okay, hubby, thanks for the jump start. Oooo, you got me going." Colleen gently smacks the palm of her hand against my cheek, pushes to her feet, and sashays into the bedroom.

My eyes are riveted on her swaying ass as my enlivened cock betrays any pretense of restraint. She looks over her shoulder. "Grab your nasty little cum box, and let's finish this."

No doubt this is some brand of retribution for my interference in Colleen's life. Call it revenge or restitution, whichever she intends, sets me aflame. Her brazen sexuality is worthy of a Fae. Has our bond given her this talent, or is it one she previously possessed? From her self-assurance, I guess it is the latter.

I find my way to my feet, daring to entertain the hope she changed her mind, and I will be invited to summon her scream. In my experience, once a human enjoys a sexual encounter with a Fae, they are ravenous to repeat the experience. Perhaps my time with Colleen here in Bráchthine will be more diverting than I predict.

I follow her into the bed chamber and shut the door behind us. I lay fresh fortifying charms upon the existing enchantment as an extra precaution to ensure our privacy. My senses tingle with the rising scent of female wanting.

Colleen glances around the room, first at the bed and then at an extravagant armchair, which is plenty large to accommodate coupling. She decides on the bed. I am left to imagine the satisfaction of bending her over the wide arm of the velvet-covered chair and forcing enticing sounds out of that sensuous mouth of hers. Given her saucy flirtations, I surmise this woman may enjoy the rough attentions I am willing to offer.

When she kicks off her shoes and crawls onto the bed, the skirt of her gown rucks up to show the back of shapely thighs. She is no waif. I grin. All the better. Her fair body will have no difficulty weathering the kaleidoscope of aggressive pleasure I prepare to deliver. My cock thickens in concert with my imagination.

Colleen moves to the array of pillows arranged at the headboard, stoking the lustful wildfire in my chest. Clutching Aodh's box, I move until my thighs rest against the side of the mattress and watch her. Anticipating the ways I plan to wring cries of pleasure from her sets my heart rampaging. I attempt to wait for her to crook one of her slender fingers to summon me closer, but my state of arousal challenges the patience I intended to maintain. Setting the box atop the duvet, I lean in to raise myself onto the bed.

Her voice carries a sharp warning. "What are you doing?"

I stop mid-motion, inadvertently rubbing my cock against the side of the bed, which only serves to dismantle my few remaining shreds of control. "Joining you, my darling."

For a moment, she seems to consider the offer, but then retreats farther into the nest of pillows. "That's not the deal." The finger she stabs in my direction mimics the warning of a blade. "For now, you stay there."

For now?

My face heats, its color likely surpassing every crimson splash in the chamber. Does this damnable woman taunt me purposefully? Power can be a wily beast, hidden inside the most fragile-looking vessel.

"When I'm close, I'll let you know and you can…" She twirls a hand at the box. Her skin blazes as dark as mine, and I suspect brazenness covers her discomfort. "…take whatever satisfies your buddy, Aodh." Anger rages across her face. "And nothing more tonight, Faerie man."

Tonight?

Colleen's qualifiers confuse me. She does not allow me near, yet her implications suggest…no, it is madness to ascribe any meaning to her careless words. The woman is out of her depth and flustered.

"Not Faerie man—bond-promised," I say.

"For fuck's sake. I get it, okay." She brushes a strand of hair from her eyes. "Now shut up before you destroy the mood."

Colleen lies back, closes her eyes, then raises and parts her knees. The black damask material of her gown bunches at her waist, revealing the inside of vanilla buttercream thighs. I run my tongue over my lips, wishing it were tasting her skin instead.

Slowly, she pinches one of her nipples through fabric then moves to attend the other. I take note that attention to those presently hidden delicacies is a desired step in her dance of arousal. My tongue and cock throb in unison, absorbing this knowledge through an ever-rising desire. As soon as I collect her cry of completion for Aodh, I will require my own solitary fulfillment… unless my bond-promised's resistance to my participation in her act of pleasure diminishes in the wake of her arousal. I release a silent sigh. Colleen made her stance on that particular point abundantly clear. My desire is of no concern to her.

I nearly choke on my next breath. While lost in my musings, Colleen's hand has ventured to the front of red satin. She strokes herself at varying speeds, first swiftly then with tortuous slowness. I see darkness spread beneath her fingers as the fabric saturates with her lovely juices. My mouth fills with saliva at the urge to savor their taste.

Colleen groans and sits up, removing her hand. "Shit, this isn't working."

I nearly contradict her based on the evidence before me, but the frustration pinching her lovely face keeps me silent.

"It's too weird." She flops back on the pillows then sits up, glaring at me. "Don't you dare say you can hop up here with me and make it happen." Her hand slaps the bed. "Or guarantee an orgasm by foisting enchantment on me." Balling her hands into fists, she punches the pillow. "I can do this."

This human has no idea of the assistance I can offer while still acquiescing to her edicts. I raise my hands as if revealing they are devoid of trickery. "Allow me to guide your pleasures by different means."

She assesses me with suspicion but does not object.

I restrain my smirk. "The voice can be as sensuous as touch. First, remove your underthings so you can experience the true response of your body as you proceed. In the game of arousal, skin craves skin above all."

Colleen eyes me warily but then reaches to shed herself of the red satin. A clench deep in my belly nearly cuts off my next words. Her sex glistens with hints of her lust. The temptation set between her thighs wears a similar blushberry hue to the one that adorns her lips, but in a deeper, more luscious shade. Dark curls shot through with streaks of the same auburn as her hair run wild over her mound. The Fae men and women I have shared pleasures with do not possess such an untamed landscape. The urge to twirl a finger through Colleen's delightful forest adds grit to my next words.

"You are lovely, my darling one. The sight of your ripening body is a wonder. Slide but one finger ever so slowly down your enticing valley to encourage the moisture already answering your touch."

She follows my direction.

"Again. Tease the rising tide of your desire."

This time her body squirms the slightest bit as she passes over the places I would prefer to be stroking.

"Does the awakening of your want intoxicate you? Bring it forth. Do you understand no one, man or woman, Fae or human could resist the beauty of your wanting?"

The movement of her fingers over her swelling sex increases in speed.

"Imagine another's hand sharing the journey with yours as you find that place where the hard knot of your pleasure cries to be fulfilled."

Colleen groans as her inhibitions begin to peel away.

"Dip into your deepest places and steal the liquid pearl of your pleasure."

Her body leans forward as she thrusts two fingers inside her blossoming entrance. Passions of nature, I wish to wrench both those dainty fingers free and replace them with my cock.

"Now paint yourself with your nectar. Draw circles to draw out your deepest need."

Colleen has opened herself wider as she twirls dripping fingers through her curls reaching for the jewel to unleash her ecstasy. Moans provide the music for her delicious readiness. Her hips push forward to increase the pressure. It should not be long now…for either of us. I pray my overwhelming lust will not cause me to fumble my task.

Before I can suppress it, my groan of anticipation joins with hers. Colleen's eyes snap open, and her gaze locks onto my arousal, quite apparent as it surges forward, testing the boundaries of my clothing.

"You want me," she rasps out. Her gaze hungry with the realization.

"Of course I do," I answer in an equally ragged tone.

"Show me."

I start to object, but she does not allow it.

"If I'm doing this in front of you, you're going to do the same. Dick out."

Every Faerie curse I know threatens to escape my lips. What is she doing to me? I begin to bristle at the inelegant request, but desire negates objection. I rid myself of my britches then my tunic. The black undertunic is short and does not prevent my cock from presenting itself fully for Colleen's scrutiny.

"Come closer," she says.

I move so I am as near to her as possible without climbing next to her. She swallows a gasp as she takes in my endowment. I watch her hand fall into a phantom grip as if testing her ability to wrap around my girth. She mimics stroking me, the flush of her skin deepening. My bond-promised's tone is more command than caress. Her next words threaten to finish me. "Pump yourself."

I run a hand over my cock. It shudders and pulses, pleading for more robust attention. Colleen's eyes are captivated by my length as my tip begins to shine with drops of my enthusiasm.

"Faster, Robálaí."

With my last measure of competence, I nudge Aodh's box next to her thigh as I follow her instruction. "This is what our bond-promise can offer you," I groan as my lower belly tightens. It taxes all my control not to drench the bed with my seed. "Show me what yours may promise me."

Colleen fixes her gaze on my strokes as she shifts her body to direct her plumped and sodden pussy at me. Primal urges surge within me. I long to grab her thighs and pull her to the edge of the bed to better destroy her need with my cock.

This infuriating human copies the pace of my frantic movements with greedy fingers against her own glorious sex. Our breathing and exclamations of impending release escalate in harmony. I must not lose self-control until I capture her ecstasy. I am stronger than this human. But seasons and snowfalls, I do not recall when pleasure has threatened my sanity as it does now.

Colleen sobs. "Robálaí, fuck, Robálaí. It's too much. I'm going to die."

The onslaught of her release is upon us. I manage to grab the box and thumb the lid open. Throwing myself on the bed next to Colleen, I lean over her. She grips my forearm as if I am her sole anchor to sanity. I ferry the cube to her lips, and she pours her scream into it. As soon as the sustained song of her ecstasy begins to wane, I trap it inside Aodh's vessel and with fumbling fingers, turn the handle to lock it. I flip onto my side, facing away from Colleen and set the black cube on the table next to the bed. With my own cry, I unleash, and my seed pours down the side of the blood red coverlet. The stream of satiny liquid catches the light of the flickering sconces.

My lungs pound with the effort of reclaiming my breath as I dwell in the aftermath of release. As my mind clears, the triumph of an accomplished task and the reprieve from Aodh's wrath it promises begins to lower my stress until I become aware my bare ass is pressed against the warmth of Colleen's thigh. I do not wish to incite her ire with this affront to her rejection of my touch. Before I am able to ease away, she rolls toward me. Gusts of her rapid breath heat my skin as the woman nestles against my back. I expected revulsion or anger from her at the conclusion of our task. It is this afterglow of quiet comfort that confounds my heart.

CHAPTER 15
THE HOWL

SIONNACH

"Ma, oh Ma." I'm weeping like a wee lad raising hell over a knee bump. I've battled medieval soldiers, fled demons, and faced the wailing death cries of the soulfall for two hundred years with a stiff jaw, but the sight of my mother reduces me to the last scrap of jam in the jar.

She strokes my hair, fingers snagging on the tangled mess of my curls. "Whist, *Mac*." Ma holds me at arm's length and checks me head to toe for blood or broken bones. "You look to be faring fine. What's brought on this grand flood?"

Embarrassed heat runs up my chest to my cheeks. "I thought you were a massive wolf come to wrap your teeth around my neck."

My mother eyes me as if I've gone round the bend. "Wolves knocking on the door to make stew of you, is it?" She swats the side of my head. "Sionnach Lóho, you've gone daft."

Her smile is warm as she teases, but I have no heart to match it. "Don't say such, Ma. Call me coward, but don't label me mad when Finnbheara's all but promised my mind's set to desert me in Tír na nÓg."

Her brows lower into the look of concern I've caused far too many times.

She studies me with a steady gaze then lays a hand to my cheek. "Aye, 'tis not a time for joking."

A chilling thought claims my bones. "Ma, are your wits in such danger as well?"

"No, *a stor.*"

"So, you and Finn—"

"Don't ask a thing about Finnbheara and myself. The time is coming soon when we open that door, but this isn't it."

I bristle at Ma's words but press my lips together and bob my chin in answer. The fact she's avoiding the topic means there's much I don't want to hear.

I grip Ma's shoulders. "Eala—has Finnbheara spoken of her to you?"

She smacks my hand. "Don't be bruising me to get answers, *Mac.*"

I lightly rub where I pinched. "Sorry, Ma."

She glances warily around the wood. "My time here is borrowed. Sit." Ma points to a log wearing a beard of glowing green and orange moss near the corner of the cottage.

I appreciate a moment to be a dutiful son rather than a frantic fool ranting about wolves and madness.

She blows a breath, and the loose tendrils of her chestnut hair dance around her face. "Listen well, *Mac.* Eala's return is all-important to the king, and he's not blind to the role you play. Use it to your advantage."

I scoff. "And how do you suggest I do that locked up with howling terrors and no company until the madness of Tír na nÓg claims me?"

The gold ring around her green glass irises flares. Her eyes are a perfect match to mine and Eala's, the mark of a *fánaí*, a Veil traveler. Is Eala traveling now, searching for a way back to me as I stand here in the Faerie realm?

Somewhere beyond the nearest copse of trees, a low rumble begins to sound. Ma's head whips toward it, and fear pinches the corners of her eyes.

"Och, I'm already discovered." She grabs my shirt and pulls me to my feet. "You must treat this land as a home, *Mac.* If you serve it well, it will sustain you. Find ways to keep your head clear and feed your belly." The pace of her words quickens. "Be alert for marks or signs of Fae deceit in all you see or touch." My mother presses a palm over my heart. "Keep this strong, fight any madness that comes for you, and trust in Eala. Trust your *anamchara.*"

Before Ma is lost to me, I blurt out, "Will I ever see you again, like this, as you were before the Glade of Chimes?"

Her eyes grow wild as the ground begins to tremble. "*Faix*, Sionnach, faith. Years of trial failed to ruin the way our Loho blood clings to hope. Let nothing do so now."

I pull her close. "I love you always, Ma."

As she presses a lingering kiss to my forehead, sections of the path in front of the cottage buckle, cracks running through their peaks. My mother and I have endured many partings in our long Fae-tainted lives. But more than any that came before, this moment bears the heavy sorrow of a last farewell.

"Goodbye, my dear Irish boy."

I reach for her, but my fingers slide through the mist she becomes in the Glade of Chimes. Ma's bitty haze flows between the collection of floating glass bubbles that range in size from a grape to a grapefruit, all shining with over-bright versions of colors. She bobs once over the moss and then disappears into a crevice on the closest pearly trunk.

I run to the tree and press my palms against it. "Ma," I wail as if my despair could call her back. Energy surges into my palms from the smooth bark, holding them fast to the surface. I can't move or draw my hands away. It's as if they've fused to the tree. My head swims and the forest blurs around me. I swear my spirit is drawn into the heart of the trunk then down, down, down toward a light far beneath its glittering roots.

There's no heaviness to my body. Deep within me, heat sparkles like a bucketful of shooting stars being poured over a night sky. I've tasted this magic before when my *anamchara* restored my Faerie gifts of becoming a fox and traveling through the Veil. Once again, I'm the essence Eala awakened in me.

Images of Alfie, the *fánaí* tree Eala and I share, waver through my mind like a shaft of light through water. Dancing through her slender trunks are the same tiny sparks that dwell among the boughs of Veil forests—Veil sprites. They flow in a golden river around a shadow until its shape becomes clear.

Eala.

I try to call out to her, but silence is all the enchantment allows. Does she see me as I do her? Is this truth or the wish of a broken heart?

The moment a drop of doubt poisons my thoughts, the tree releases me and I fall on my arse. Scrambling back to the trunk, I clutch its shiny bark, but there's no answer.

Ma told stories of *Crann na Beatha*, the Tree of Life, spreading its tendrils of hope, faith, life, and love through the earth. Its messages soothe those in despair, bring lovers together, and inspire belief in miracles. She swore the Tree of Life wasn't one tree, but many, whose roots became a single river across miles, time, and even realms. I stare at the tree that, apart from its strange pearly trunk, gives off no hint of being anything more.

I drive the heels of my hands against the sides of my head. My skull creaks as if it's been clouted with the business end of a peat cutter. "Och." Was my vision of Eala the very Fae trickery Ma warned of?

Stumbling to plant my arse on a log, I brace a weary head on open palms. My stomach knots. Was that truly Ma come to warn me, or Fae deceit? I dismiss the thought. She was no decoy. The worry in my mother's eyes was real.

I leap to my feet and pace. Entertaining doubt and fear will propel me faster into madness. I must let shadows pass through me but not linger. Closing my eyes, I picture the way Eala presses herself against my back in sleep with her pointy chin digging into where my shoulder meets my neck. That is no trickery, only peace. The glorious music of her voice plays in my ear.

We will best him, anamchara.

I hold to the memory of my swan until a loud groan from my belly ruins the sanctity of the moment. I'm knackered. With weary bones comes overwhelming thirst.

Water, I need water, and soon after, I'll need to find something to fill my grumbling gut. To stay strong. To stay sane. For Eala. Everything for Eala.

I study the forest with a different purpose. As if reaching out a hand to me, as Ma said this land would if I let it, a line of bushes bursting with blackberries, or fruit the spitting image of blackberries, forms a neat row alongside the cottage. I pick one, giving it a good sniff and lick. Not detecting the tingle or buzz of enchantment, I brave a taste. Sweetness pops in my mouth and trickles down my throat. After eating the one, I wait to see if I sprout wings or my ears pinch into points. Nothing so dramatic, just the growl in my stomach, nagging me to quit being a gobshite and get on with sending more berries into my gullet.

I search the yard for other food possibilities. There's a pile of broken branches behind the berries with bright sprigs of green crushed beneath. Nearby are several neat rows that could be vegetables I'm acquainted with or at least their close cousins.

"A gardener, are you?" I say to the absent proprietor of the cottage. There may not be a nice rasher of bacon in my future, but at least I won't be reduced to the likes of a sheep grazing on grass to survive.

Da taught me to clear a field of stones and build a wall with them, but it's my mother who showed me how to coax living things from the land. She saved me once from damnation by bargaining with Finnbheara for a chance to restore virtue to my soul, and now her lessons may save me again.

How long must I partner with this land? Days, weeks, years, goddamned centuries?

Without warning, a merciless gut twist sends me to my knees. White foam, like a stream breaking around rocks, fills my mind. With it comes a barrage of hopelessness. I collapse onto my side and start babbling. "I haven't lasted a single day without you, Eala *bán*." My tears flow into the soil beneath my cheek. The reality of enduring the cruel passage of time without my soulmate seeps like filthy sludge through the center of my bones.

I can't tell if it's night that's fallen over the forest or a blackness of the mind. Instead of a white highway of stars overhead, a splash of brilliant lavender brightens my darkness.

The will to carry on leaves me with the loss of light. I'm water disappearing into parched earth. Fate's been licking its lips for a taste of me since I dared to love Finnbheara's Treasure.

For a breath of time, that treasure was mine.

"Forgive me, Swan." My face rests against the dirt dampened with my tears. My eyes drift closed. I pray for this final sleep to take me swiftly.

A familiar howl creeps through the forest. I've not the strength to scurry into the cottage like a mouse to its hole. It's somehow fitting that, here in a Faerie forest, the mournful cry of an unseen creature should be the thing to sing me into oblivion.

A breeze blows leaves across my face as the beast lets loose a fucking banshee wail. I bolt up, smoldering with frustration and to my surprise find a daylight bright forest.

I shake a fist in the direction of the sound. "A man's trying to pass on here. Take your racket somewhere else."

When my unwanted guest doesn't give up, I push to my feet. "Feck off, you—"

Before I finish the insult, nasty shivers overtake my body. Following right behind is a belly heave that sends the bits of blackberry I swallowed flying out of my mouth.

"What in the bloody hell?" I run hands through my hair, feeling crumbles of soil fall from my curls, then brush more dirt off the front of my Faerie tunic. A minute ago, I was on the brink of giving up and giving in, inviting madness to take a chunk from my hide instead of fighting it off.

Who was the sniveling ass in the dirt? He was no more Sionnach Loho than I'm a flying cow.

My anger sizzles as a faint twinkle catches my eye. Damn, there's the slightest distortion in the air around the blackberry bushes. The cursed things were enchanted. Even with Ma's warning of Fae deceit still hanging in the air, I dove straight into it.

I shake a fist at the berries. "Oh, no, you don't, Finn." As soon as I speak the words, there's a pop, and the sheen around the bush dulls then disappears. I know as sure as my heart's still beating that Fae bastard tried to force feed me the first serving of madness with his devil fruit.

After spending a pair of centuries in Veil forests and the Glade of Chimes, I'm well equipped to spot a mark of the Fae if I take the time to look for it. I'm tempted to bang my fool head against a tree for being careless enough to stumble into the first trap Finnbheara laid at my feet.

The bastard won't find me so easily bewildered again. And for the love of every saint on a Sunday, I will fight the madness Tír na nÓg hurls my way.

"Forgive me again, Swan, for being a mallet-headed eejit." I lay both hands over my heart.

A new disturbing thought adds to the heap piled high in my mind. Since Robber Bright has turned against his king, I wonder how much danger Eala's in outside the gates of Tír na nÓg. I shake my head. Worry courts weakness that I can't afford. There's not a damn thing I can do except survive for Eala— for us.

Speaking of which, I painstakingly study the closest clump of blackberries for the sheen of Fae interference. I find no tell of Faerie fingers in the pie now.

I brave another berry. Sure enough, the intensity of sweetness I tasted on the first one is tamed. I make a mental note, *too sweet is sure to be sour in the end*. After stuffing more in the pockets of my britches, I set my sights on the abandoned bread on the table inside for my supper. If it was Faerie food before they left this place, odds are it isn't enchanted.

The still of the forest is broken again by a familiar howl. Hearing its lonely timbre without the terror of slavering wolves clogging my ears, it doesn't sound as much like a hunter's cry. Instead of cursing the beastie, I risk calling out to it with a note or two of my own.

It answers me straight away with more brightness and no shading of threat in its tone.

"Well, are you just another lonely bugger trapped in Finn's fancy fishbowl?" I continue to return its call. Aren't we a pair of forlorn fools singing a duet?

When the howl kicks up right quick with a more enthusiastic tempo, worry starts dancing in my belly. Assuming this tuneful conversation to be of the friendly sort would not be a wise man's first thought.

"Think, Sionny, think."

This is still a Fae forest full of tricks, waiting to have a go at me so I stop singing back.

The same chipper howl comes again, rising at the end like it's asking if I'm still in the game.

I'll not be fooled twice. That's a sure path to becoming someone's supper.

A rustling in the treetops starts as a distant scratching, but all too soon, there's no mistaking the branch rattling is coming this way.

I run hell for leather to the cottage.

CHAPTER 16

THE GIANT'S LAIR

EALA

Electric blue streaks meander back toward Biddy's bottle and then, with a loud *pop*, retreat to their cozy pool inside the glass. Only the mellow glow of late morning sun lights the cottage.

"How, who, where...what army?" I sputter as Biddy pushes herself up in the bed. "Did the blue bottle show you? Is it another Fae king or queen with a grudge against Finnbheara?"

Folklore speaks of distinct Faerie sovereigns for each of the Irish provinces. Other kings mean other armies. Ice chips trickle through my blood, remembering the day Robber Bright warned me that leaving Tír na nÓg always exposed his Host to dangers. Did he allude to potential attacks from other Fae monarchs? For the love of Sion's beautiful mop of curls, Faerie land grabs sound like bloody business.

Biddy stands, straightening her gray-blue dress, and makes her way to the warmth of the fireplace. "'Tis not of a Fae army I speak."

That's welcome news. I detest the idea of courting another duplicitous Fae royal with a bargain. But maybe...battle stories between mythological Irish kings and queens flash through my mind. Did I aim too low enlisting the aid of a human witch? Should I have Veil traveled to seek out a partnership with mighty Queen Medb or the great warrior, Cu Chulainn? Why stop there? The giant Fionn Mac Cumhaill may be able to snap the gates of Tír na nÓg in half and lift Finnbheara up by the scruff of his neck. That's an image I very much enjoy.

Sion and I have come face to face with real history and myth both. It's dicey but doable. Hell, I brought a long dead witch into this time through Veil magic. Who's to say I can't do the same with more formidable allies?

"Are you with me, girl, or is your head flitting among the clouds?"

The way Biddy keeps calling me "girl" with the faintest hint of mistrust rubs me the wrong way. I stare her down. "How old are you?"

"I've thirty years."

"It's not too long until I'm right there with you, so you don't need to call me "girl" anymore. Eala is fine."

Biddy smirks at me. Not the reaction I expected. "Looks like you put a bit of iron in your backbone out on your wee stroll, Eala of the Fae."

"Maybe I did." I drag teeth over my bottom lip. "And let's drop *of the Fae*. That designation may not be well-received by everyone we meet."

"Fair enough."

I twirl my wrists. "Back to the army. Details please? Where are they? Who are they? I need to prepare the best strategy to approach them."

She pets the bottle. "We two shared a look around. It's not a band of warriors we saw, but rather the way to find them."

Do all witches speak in roundabout riddles, or is it a Biddy-specific trait? "Go on."

The witch's eyes take on a gauzy trancelike look as she stares at nothing in particular. A strange hum winds through her voice as she speaks. "Seek the Giant's Lair within a glen of sacred oaks where some of these great trees bear acorns and others do not. It rests on the slope of Slieve Gullion, where both giant and goddess tested their fates."

Biddy sways a little as tiny sparks shoot through the bottle's blue liquid.

"Hewn into the trunks of these oaks are doors that reveal themselves once the shadows of the trees blend to create a carpet of black velvet at day's end. Before the last rays of sunlight disappear into the sea, each door in the lair claims a portion of the dying light. With this blessed adornment upon them, some reveal designs of gold or silver while others glow the copper of a blood moon."

I bite my tongue to stall the billion questions itching to come out.

"Behind these many doors lay countless wisdom, guidance, and strength of the ages. It's where the secrets of time and trial dwell. A soul may only open a single door. If their intention is true, the path they seek will shine before them with the collective clarity of all those who no longer walk this earth."

I speak quietly, testing if she's come back from whatever magic speak she'd drifted into. "Are gods and goddesses those who no longer walk the earth?"

"Gods, goddesses, druids, guardians, sages, kings, queens, warriors, holy men and women, mystics, and heroes have all come before us."

The intensity of her gaze makes me tentative to ask what she or the blue bottle, whichever is communicating with me, might perceive as a superfluous or obvious question. "And we can tap into their knowledge by opening magic doors?"

Biddy's amber eyes widen and smolder with an internal light. "One door and one alone."

"How many doors did you see in the lair?"

Biddy gives a shake of her head. Her tone shifts from supernatural messenger to a flesh-and-blood person. "Not many, but we must go to the glen and seek them. I believe, Eala, it's behind a sacred door we'll find your army."

"Slieve Gullion it is." I nod and quickly search the place on my phone. The timing here may be tricky since our target is practically all the way across the country to the Irish Sea and we're perched on cliffs above the Atlantic Ocean.

Shadows of the trees blending to create a carpet of black velvet at day's end makes it clear we need to hit the Giant's Lair at sunset. That's cutting it close to the start of the Celtic Day when the Veil allows me to travel. Luckily, this time of year, the length of twilight stretches a bit longer. If I call the Veil as soon as I feel the first prickles of its awakening, we should be able to make it from one side of Ireland to the other in time.

Better yet, I'll treat Biddy to the four-hour cross-country drive. We'll find the Giant's Lair, get our bearings, and wait for the day to end. I'll really blow her mind and take her to a chipper for lunch and introduce her to diet soda.

"Biddy, are you ready to see a bit more of my Ireland?"

"Oh, aye, Eala of the F—Eala."

I take in her tragically out-of-place clothing. She's a little taller and quite a bit stouter than me. One of my bulky knit sweaters should fit her, but I don't know if she's ready for my jeans. Sion's admired my ample ass on multiple occasions, but it doesn't hold a candle to Biddy's. With a belt, Sion's jeans might do for the witch.

A whiff of vanilla scent from our mattress's lady's bedstraw greets me as I head into the bedroom nook to grab clothing for Biddy's makeover. The memories it stirs are both lovely and punishing.

Sitting on the edge of the bed, I drift into the memories of Sion's loving touches I've savored here. How I long for those moments when our naked bodies, still warm from showering together, slip under the covers to preserve the heat in a carnal cocoon. His patch of foxy red chest hair would tickle the soft skin of my breasts. We'd growl and groan with wild kisses and tongues that tested and teased. Oh, the exquisite agony of anticipation as he slowly slid in and out of me until he could go no deeper, inciting our spirits to shatter in unison.

If I open my eyes, he will be here. We'll never have parted. Our souls will wrap around one another. I'll cry his name, and he mine. We will share promises and dreams.

"Eala? Is all well?" Biddy calls from the couch where she's turned on the television yet again.

I open my eyes, not realizing I'd shut them, eased onto my back, and slipped a hand between my thighs. Embarrassment flushes hotter, realizing how thoroughly I'd indulged in thoughts of making love with my husband while there was an audience in the next room. Shit, I'm still aroused, and more than a little wet, evidence that proves how potent sweet memories can be.

"Yes, just strained my back a little." I groan and stretch to cover up my indiscretion. Getting hot for Sion is a welcome improvement over messy sobbing. I take this as an encouraging sign that my body is catching up with the hope growing stronger in my heart after my vision of Sion's shadow on the *lough* and the insight from Biddy's blue bottle.

When I rummage through my drawer for clothing, the glint of metal catches my eye. Smooshed into the corner is my silver necklace. I lift the quarter-sized disk with the Celtic symbol for strength etched into its surface I found in Máthair's greenhouse in Manhattan. I'd taken it off after it snagged in Sion's curls during our lovely sex-a-thon when we returned home after striking our doomed bargain with Finnbheara.

I put the necklace on. The skeptic in me used to dismiss talismans and charms, but that was before my grandmother's ring sent me to Ireland, the Fae, and my soulmate. With the race to get Sion out of Tír na nÓg and Colleen away from Robber Bright, I'll welcome strength from anywhere I can get it.

We pull into a car park near the Slieve Gullion mountain on a road marked: *The Ring of Gullion, Area of Outstanding Natural Beauty.* The drive through the lush landscape to get here was transformative. It's impossible not to sink into a state of awe at the sweeping views as gently muted as chalk pictures of verdant hills and a sky crowded with clouds that continually shift across a cerulean canvas to offer endless celestial panoramas. The palette of cool colors is punctuated by breathtaking yellow blossoms of primroses and vermilion clusters of lords and ladies flowers. I'm adding this to my list of places to spend carefree hours with Sionnach once we're on the other side of this shitstorm.

Because I'm determined that time will come.

I sweep my gaze across the kiddie adventure play park in front of us and grumble. "This can't be right." I check the nav again, but this is the place.

Biddy stares wide-eyed as a kid skims down a zip line while others climb over gaily painted structures. There's a well-worn sign reading "Giants Lair" with an arrow pointing to a path.

I lean on the steering wheel. "Not the remote forest lair I expected."

Biddy peeks into my backpack, resting against her chest, which carries the blue bottle. "The potion is stirring up quite a whirlpool. We're where we ought to be."

The afternoon light wanes as day crawls toward evening. The park closes soon, and I already checked to discover there's no overnight parking. "Okay then. I need to find a place to leave the car. We'll Veil travel back here as soon as the Celtic Day arrives."

There's a loud commotion on the trail beside the playground. Someone dressed in a long hooded black robe, wearing an unflattering rubber witch's mask, emerges from the lengthening shadows. The mask sports a massive bulbous nose sprinkled with a plethora of warts. The mockery of Biddy's kind leads a band of kids and parents off the Giant's Lair path by pounding a gnarled wooden staff as tall as she is against the ground in a steady rhythm. With each thud of the staff, the crowd chants, "*Cailleach Bhéara, Cailleach Bhéara.*"

I glance at the authentic witch next to me and suppress a laugh at the disgusted look on her face. Biddy is as far from this "Hag of Beara" witchy impersonator as a bee from a buffalo. My *bean feasa* friend is quite striking, beautiful really, with her peachy hair, freckles, and strong-boned features. Not your typical apple-slinging storybook witch at all.

I nudge Biddy. "In the folktales I'm used to, the witch is usually leading the children into the woods instead of out of them."

My stab at humor is unappreciated.

Biddy grunts. "It's such thinking that's made my life a misery."

I feel horrible about my insensitivity. Even though I'm getting more comfortable around Biddy and continue to be impressed by her resilience, I need to remember she hasn't lived an easy life.

I bob my chin at the witchy parody. She's brandishing her staff at the kids who stick out their tongues in response before families head off toward the car park.

"They missed the mark there," I tell Biddy as I wiggle my cell phone. "My magic screen here tells me Cailleach Bhéara was said to be a goddess, not a witch. She's credited with enticing the giant Fionn Mac Cumhaill into a lake before turning the brawny fellow into a withered old man."

I point at the mountain. "There are stories that claim Slieve Gullion itself isn't a dormant…ah, sleeping volcano, but in truth a slumbering giant."

Biddy tilts her head to look at me. "So, it seems you are the learned woman you claim to be, Eala. I've heard such stories. It does my heart well to know they've lasted into your time."

Within the hour, we've left the car settled on the roadside not far from the park. I yanked us into the Veil the moment I felt the familiar prickles of the Veil sprites inside me as they awakened with the Celtic day. My internal companions weave trails of delicate heat from my neck to ankles. They've been especially peppy since my flight as the swan flipped a switch in my emotions, transforming crushing sorrow into a more adrenaline-fueled intention to get on with the business of saving Sionnach.

The sun is sinking fast as we hunker down behind a cluster of trees. We linger a few more minutes after the last visitor leaves the car park. The ranger locked the gates of the kiddie playground after finishing a final sweep of the Giant's Lair trail. Once her truck disappears down the road, I motion Biddy to follow me out of our hiding place.

We head into the Giant's Lair, which has been renamed *Fionn's Giant Adventure.* This tidy little wood is filled with whimsy. There are interpretations of Faerie doors carved into the base of trees, a smattering of Faerie houses rest among branches, woven straw figures that could be dancing elves or Faeries fill a little clearing, and small-scale rope suspension bridges connect adorably painted playhouses. It's a place to spark a child's imagination, but it looks nothing like the conclave of oaks Biddy described from her vision.

I pause near a huge stone sculpture intended to depict the creepy version of Cailleach Bhéara and shake my head. "We're off somehow."

When Biddy doesn't answer, I check behind me to make sure I haven't lost her on the trail. What I see nearly stops my heart.

Her peachy hair swirls around her head in a Medusa-like frenzy. Biddy's skin is as blue as the roiling liquid inside the bottle she holds in her hands. A ray of light from the setting sun stabs straight through her body and the bottle to light a path to the right of the trail.

I swallow hard. The witch is not entirely here. Do I touch her? Speak to her? Her chats with the magic in the bottle are getting more intense, and more frightening.

I startle when she screeches, "Go."

For less than a second, I debate whether she means go as in *get the hell out of here,* but opt for the other choice—to go down the path of sunlight piercing both witch and bottle.

Giving Biddy a wide berth, I follow the light. It stretches between the closely packed trunks of a row of birch trees. I carefully ease them apart to fit my body through. They acted like a curtain, hiding what lies just beyond—a gathering of great oaks.

The quintet of giants before me forms a circle, daring the last gasp of the sun to try and pass through the interlaced tapestry of their branches. Looking into the canopy overhead, I can't tell which limbs belong to which tree. The smell of both rot and life wafts from the sodden earth below, perpetually damp from spring rains. Overpowering both is the bittersweet, mossy aroma of the oaks themselves. True to Biddy's description, I spy catkin tassels that will soon contribute to the birth of new acorns dangling from three of the oaks, but not the other two.

I've entered the echoes of the forest primaeval where the air is thick with unmistakable magic. The Veil sprites dip and spin within me, delighted I've stepped away from the mundane into the enchanted, where they believe I belong.

This is the place from the witch's vision.

"Eala?"

I'm silent, refusing to disturb the energy coursing between my flesh and these elders of the earth.

Biddy joins me in the woody cathedral. "Look," she whispers and sweeps a hand across the forest floor. Sure enough, a black velvet carpet of shadow unfurls beneath our feet. Like frost across a jeweler's cloth, a layer of white sparkles, tinted azure from the bottle in the witch's outstretched hand, gleam on the dark ground.

The air in the glen expands as if great lungs are being filled, then a slow trickle of breeze twists around us, expelling the day and welcoming the night. At that very moment, rays of the sun breach any obstacle in their way and burst into the shadowy glade to bid a final farewell to the earth for the night.

We stand frozen in heady fascination as bright white-gold sizzling ovals appear and burn onto each of the oaken trunks. I hold my breath as the spots begin to shiver then dissolve into rectangular doors the size of a king's portrait. Each is made of elaborate metalwork with its own pattern of ornate abstract curlicues, designs of vines, flowers, leaves, or more angular geometrics. Below the center of each door, looping script drawn by an unseen hand appears. One door, one word.

Mind

Might

Mystery

Mettle

Motive

There are no knobs, knockers, or keyholes to be seen. No easy way to open these portals and reveal the answers within.

I approach each door, one at a time, careful not to touch. Before every possibility, I study the patterns and designs, hoping for some clue as to which of these not-so-helpful titles points to an army capable of standing up to Finnbheara.

"Take heed, Eala, before you choose, and remember magic is seldom straightforward." Biddy moves beside me and lays a hand on my arm. "What are you thinking?"

I point to the door of burnished bronze and its pattern of spirals that reads *mystery*. "This is the vaguest of them all. I'd never choose it." Moving on to the polished silver door with the serpentine botanical design, I shake my head. "*Motive* would be best for a person not sure of why they're trying to do something. Not the case here."

Biddy waggles a finger at the *mettle* door covered in shapes with harsh angles and corners. "From all you've told me of yourself, this is not what you'll be needing. I know your heart is near to breaking, but a weakling wouldn't seek the company of a witch."

I cross my arms. "That leaves *mind* and *might*. My first instinct says to jump on *might* since we need an army, but is that too obvious?" I look to Biddy for an opinion.

Her gaze keeps switching between the doors. "Aye, but oft times simple can be best."

I frown. "Says the witch who just warned me about magic not being straightforward."

"If we're speaking plainly, then *mind* points to wisdom, and wisdom is a powerful thing."

I stare at the gleaming gold door. The word *might* is surrounded by stars. "Power of the heavens," I whisper. Is that what I need? Celestial intervention to defeat my Faerie adversary. I certainly wouldn't turn it away. Of course, I need to choose might. I'm here to hire a damn army.

A flicker of blue from Biddy's bottle shines against the highly polished door of blackened steel promising *mind*. The movement of the light gives the curlicue pattern the appearance of rolling waves instead of an airy Rococo abstract. The barest tang of salty sea air prickles my nostrils.

"Wait," I say, holding up a hand.

My analytical brain goes into overdrive. *Might* without wisdom could be dangerous. It could mean aggression in a bad way, not just power. What if I open that door and unleash something uncontrollable without conscience?

An image of the awful scar Finnbheara gave Robber Bright rushes into my thoughts. There's a pair of Fae without any conscience. Finnbheara is the essence of might, and he's a morally gray, deceitful ass. Robber Bright has plenty of might with his Host of A Thousand Wings, and he used it to align himself with a terrible enemy of his Folk.

My stomach cramps with dreaded memories of that terrible picture from my childhood book with stories of Aodh, the terrifying underworld god who commands the might of fire and vengeance.

I pull my hands against my chest and back away from the *might* door as if it's going to reach out and yank me in.

"Biddy, bring your light closer to the black door."

She does, and the movement of the waves grows more distinct. What if it's not an army we need?

"Will you ask the blue bottle to show me Tír na nÓg?"

The witch holds the glass close to her lips and whispers the name of Finnbheara's kingdom over and over. I free my Faerie essence to wrap around the bottle. Magic recognizes friendly magic, and they willingly flow together. I send the name Tír na nÓg, through the connection. The image of crashing waves, the color of Robber Bright's strange aquamarine eyes, floods my thoughts. I experience the sensation of rising as the picture expands below me. The land that holds my *anamchara* and my grandmother begins to take shape.

As distance grows, so does my clarity of vision. Finely hewn headlands and cliffs do not herald the beginning of a vast continent I imagined Tír na nÓg to be. A rippling surf curls around the graceful arc and sway of a mass forged from purest white crystal.

Finnbheara's kingdom is an island, surrounded by a dazzling sea. Magnificent prismatic beams that could be borrowed from the walls of the Veil itself radiate skyward from thousands of points around the edges of Tír na nÓg. I defy anyone witnessing its glory not to choose this land for their eternity.

Of course, it's an island. The *Tuatha Dé Danann* left the island of Ireland to dwell beneath the earth. What form would their new home take other than the one they unwillingly left behind?

Ripples flow through the mystical illustration as my magic separates from Biddy's like oil and water. The witch takes long, slow breaths as she leaves the influence of our mingled powers.

I'm filled with a blast of energy and surety of what I'm meant to do. It's the wisdom and expertise I don't possess that I need most. The *mind* of an ally who not only knows the strategies of conflict, but who can command forces. A powerhouse to stand fast at the shores of Tír na nÓg and join with me as we blaze a path through the Faerie realm to my husband.

One by one, my Veil sprites burst into tiny flares as if crying *yes, yes, yes*. Whoever is on the other side of the *mind* door possesses what I need to show Finnbheara the price of disregarding the determination of a woman driven by love.

With new confidence in my step, I position myself in front of the black steel door. After laying both palms against its cool, patterned surface, I jerk my chin for Biddy to join me.

"It's not an army we need, Biddy. It's a navy."

With a witch at my right and the Veil sprites waltzing through my spirit, I shove the *mind* door.

It doesn't swing open. Instead, it spirals in on itself until it's no more than a pinprick of black against a deep groove of the oak's grain.

Biddy and I whip our gazes to one another. This can't be what's supposed to happen. Did I pick the wrong door? *Is* there a wrong door? In those final moments at his gates, Finnbheara said the merciless void of consequence waited for Máthair on the other side. Is this what I'm facing now—the true penalty of defying the Fae king?

Well, fuck him.

I pull from both my Faerie essence and the intensity of the Veil sprites popping inside me like firecrackers to ignite a surge of magic in my body. With a cry of blind rage, I jam my index finger against the black metal dot in the tree that was a door moments ago.

As the oak gives a wicked shudder followed by violent shakes, Biddy wraps both arms around my body. A huge gash opens in the trunk. There's a ripping sound as the tree splits and then a circle of its bark closes around us, smashing our bodies together. Our tiny cavity gets smaller and smaller. We're being swallowed into the heart of the mighty giant. A blue glaze from Biddy's bottle is our only light.

My words are lost to the deafening rumble around us. "I'm sorry, Biddy. I'm sorry."

I've barely rasped my last word when the sacred oak explodes in a blast of blinding white. If I'm being blown apart, it's surprisingly painless. The flash fades, and my body drops through a slate blue sky choked with billowy charcoal-tinged storm clouds. In less than the length of a heartbeat, I plop onto a clifftop into the middle of a water-logged patch of sea thrift flowers. The stalks of pinkish pom poms close around my body as if they were waiting to catch me. I welcome their cushion since an unforgiving hunk of rock taller than the cottage is less than a foot from my head.

The wind is brutal, preventing me from getting my bearings. Sea spray thick enough to blind pummels me. I scramble to my feet, shielding my face as best I can, and search for Biddy. Thank heavens she's only yards away, wiping a layer of drizzle off her face. My backpack no longer clings to her chest, but there's a huge lump under the sweater of Sion's I lent her. I'm relieved when she extracts an intact blue bottle from beneath drenched fabric.

We pick our way to one another and fall into an embrace. A strong gust of wind nearly topples us. Luckily, it whisks away the worst of the lashing mist. It takes us both a few minutes to catch our breath from whatever the hell just happened. When I brush a strand of soggy hair out of my eyes, Biddy's jaw drops and she grabs my index finger.

"What's this then?"

I pull out of her grip to wipe the newly-acquired sap dribble on my fingertip against my jeans.

Biddy snatches my hand again and holds my finger in front of my eyes. "Didn't see this mark on you until now."

"See wha—" It takes me a second to focus on the tiny inky black design there. It looks to be an old-fashioned skeleton key with a distinct Celtic knot as the bow. I rub my thumb against it, but it doesn't smear. I scratch at it with a fingernail and get the same result.

"You've been marked, Eala."

I stare at what's as permanent as a tattoo. It doesn't hurt. In fact, I can't feel it at all.

"Seems, your touch opened the door in the Giant's Lair."

I examine both hands to see if there's any more surprise body art, but there's only the key.

"I think I may have marked myself." I take a fortifying breath. "I pushed my magic into the tree when the door started to disappear, hoping I could bring it back or at least get us through."

Biddy tuts and nods to my finger. "Made yourself the key then, did you? Well done."

There's a loud *boom*—the familiar sound of sea colliding with the cliffs near the Loho cottage. I quickly scan the area. I'll be pissed if the *mind* tree carted us off home instead of helping.

There's no cottage or lighthouse. I don't recognize any landmarks. Craggy cliffs and jolly clumps of sea thrift flowers make up the landscape.

"Let's start walking and try to figure out where we are," I grunt. "And what *mind* we're supposed to meet up with."

"I hope it's got hot broth and a nice loaf of bread for us." Biddy shivers. "My bones are chilled clean though."

There's another *boom* followed by a low *hiss* as the sea below refuses to be ignored.

Biddy takes my hand, and we walk together, keeping well clear of the edge. Not far from where we were dumped, there's a massive granite formation blocking our view. We skirt around it and stop short, nearly toppling over a sudden drop-off.

Biddy and I exchange a look when an unexpected sound reaches our ears from below.

Singing.

It isn't loud or raucous, but rather warm and companionable. There's a convenient rock near the edge to hide us as we sneak a peek down to the seaside chorus.

This bend in the cliffs overlooks a snug cove. There, hidden away from the bay beyond, is a wooden-hulled ship, sails bound up nice and tidy. I take in the design. It's not a great tall ship but smallish, only two masts, with a silhouette paying homage to a Viking longship.

Standing at the bow with one booted foot on a crate, loose hair blowing in the wind, and a spyglass trained on the narrow opening of the cove is a woman whose build wouldn't be out of place on a rugby team. She's wearing a bright yellow *leine* under a forest green dress with a tight-fitting bodice and an extra-wide brown leather belt. The skirt flapping around her is full but not cumbersome. A thick plaid green shawl, so dark it almost looks black, is flung around her shoulders. The breeze off the water flicks the ends of the cloth. I notice small accents of orange, blue, and yellow thread weaving through the pattern.

Bits of a song Máthair used to sing to me come rushing back.

Up and down the waves she'd roam,
Mistress of both swell and foam.
For sailor, clan, and kin alike,
Her heart was true in love and fight.
See her coming through the mist,
With fiery hair that flame has kissed.
To queen afar she bent no knee,
Our Granuaile ruled brave the sea.

The ship, her masterful stance, and those amazing flame-kissed locks add up to one person—the legendary female sea captain, Grace O'Malley.

Biddy grins wide enough to show remarkably well-kept teeth for her time. "Well, Eala, seems you've found yourself a pirate queen."

CHAPTER 17
THE BROKEN

ROBBER BRIGHT

Any appreciation of my recent pleasure or relief in accomplishing Aodh's request is chased into memory by Colleen's intimacy. It should neither interest nor move me, yet I feel cuffed at her side.

Since the state of being bond-promised is foreign to me, so are the repercussions of entering into such a transaction. I am not blind nor ignorant as to the happiness a bond-promise grants pairs willing to partake of such an oath. Neither Colleen nor I chose this path for any reason other than to protect those we hold dear. She has contributed to Eala Duir's wellbeing as I have done for my Host.

Our agreement should hold no more emotion or investment than an assignment to bring apple-glazed pork to a Mabon feast. Yet, I am confounded that the sweet fragrance of her breath I smell even more strongly than the musk of our recent mutual release, burns the back of my throat. The sensation is as unwelcome as it is baffling.

I am all but finished with this human's contribution to my purpose here in Bráchthine, yet find myself mired in debate whether to leave her to puzzle out our transformed status alone or share my own conflicted feelings. Deciding my presence is more hindrance than comfort, I move to rise and provide her with privacy in which to expel her unruly emotions.

A hand upon my bare hip stops me. "Wait."

Withstanding another diatribe of her abhorrence of me is more than my weary soul can manage. There are scant hours before I must appear before Aodh with the insurance in the black box, so I will be seen as an ally and assume the place he has promised me. I crave rest and restoration of my wits.

"Don't go yet, Robálaí."

When I relax into my previous position against her, restoring skin-to skin-contact, I am reminded anew of our current exposure to one another. While my lust is sated at present, the nearness of her partial nakedness and memories of her enticing flesh might serve to spur fresh interest. Reaching behind, I find the hem of her dress and pull it down to cover her. I dare not turn and brush my cock against any portion of her skin.

Her voice is thin with exhaustion. "Did you get what you needed?" She inhales a stuttering breath and presses closer. "To protect Eala."

"I did."

"Good." I feel her turn away from me.

"May I leave you now, Colleen?"

We are still close enough that I feel the movement of her head as she nods. I swing my legs over the side of the bed and scan the carpet for my britches. They lay in a heap with my outer tunic. I redress before turning to Colleen.

I wish indifference partnered with me instead of concern as I take in the trembling she tries to hide. Curse this heart of mine that has grown unpleasantly softer since we crossed into Aodh's realm. I sit on the bed and place a hand on her back. "Allay your distress, my darling one. The service you have rendered will be of value to many."

She rolls back to me, and I expect her to insist I remove my touch. To my shock, Colleen presses her head to my hip as if seeking more contact. Surely, she reviles me after what I have demanded of her this night, a bond-promise and thievery of her ecstasy.

"Please don't ever make me do that again. It was demoralizing and embarrassing."

Out of generosity, I stroke her hair. "No, it was beguiling. You bore witness to the pleasure you roused in me." I rest fingers beneath her chin. "We are bond-promised, Colleen. Anything between us is acceptable. Do not think more on it." She is vulnerable, and I take advantage by pressing a kiss to her forehead. "I thank you for my pleasure."

"I can't do this, Robálaí."

I cock my head to the side. "Do what, my bond-promised?" I use the title as a reminder she is indeed tied to me and that we are beholden to one another now.

Colleen harrumphs. "Just use my name. No more 'darling one' or' bond-promised.' Let's be real. I'm a prisoner in hell, and you're going to do whatever you want to me."

I press a hand to my chest to quell the sudden leap of my heart. I am used to being called villainous, heartless, callous, but her resignation that I intend to do nothing but cause harm strikes a cruel blow. "You misread me." My words slip free without forethought, yet they are true and unexpectedly painful. "Your safety is as important to me as that of my Host." I stand, running a hand through my hair. "You are my bond-promised," I say as if the term explains all.

She sits up, staring at the rumpled bedding where I lay beside her then surveys the room. Falling back onto the pillows, Colleen crosses her arms over her face. "I can't handle this. I just can't."

Anger seethes in my core. Anger at this woman, at myself, at Aodh, at Finnbheara. This is an unconscionable predicament caused by calculations and manipulations that cannot be undone.

I grasp the box from the table next to the bed and stride to the door. Solitude is what I need to gather my thoughts and attempt to outrun the despicable guilt I am unable to rid myself of.

To my surprise, Colleen is off the bed, inserting herself between my body and the door before I escape. She grabs a handful of my tunic.

"Enchant me. Influence me. Charm me like you did before. I don't want to drown in fear or be aware of anything besides you in this place." She grimaces. "Especially that shitbag, Aodh."

I jolt in surprise.

Colleen digs her fingernails into my forearms. "When this is all over, I trust you to take me home and wake me up. Until then, slap your Faerie man magic on me and make me numb."

My reluctance shocks me. Her request is logical, even sensible. A shiver of unease passes through me. This woman with whom I am bond-promised, asks for the destruction of any memory of what we now share. It should be a welcome remedy, but it births sharp anxiety low in my stomach. Her actions pose a threat to our bond that I feel on a level deeper than rational thought.

Conflict rages in my breast. The safety of my Host is on stronger ground if this mortal is kept at bay in the seclusion she requests. Why does my essence prickle at the wrongness of locking her once again in a mental cage?

A smack to my chest pulls me out of introspection. "You manipulated me easily enough when it benefited you. Now it benefits me, so do it again." Colleen slams her eyes shut and juts her chin at me.

"I will do it for a kiss."

My bond-promised sputters as her eyes snap open. She gawks at me. I return the stare with equal surprise at my request. Deep in my soul, I need this from her as if the bond between us demands validation.

I do not give her the chance to answer. Caging her body, I press her back against the closed door and cover her mouth with mine. The meeting of our lips ignites a thrilling combination of resistance mingled with desire. We slide flesh against flesh, combat shifting to hunger. I thrust my tongue past her lips, and she grates her teeth over it with a moan of wanting before suckling on it as if starving for the very taste of me. My hand clamps on her nape to hold her in place as I draw her tongue into my mouth so I might savor and worship her in kind.

We break at the same moment, pulling apart. I have no doubt the fear in her eyes is reflected in mine. Our passion is unlooked-for and unsettling to us both.

Colleen covers her mouth with her hand and looks to the floor. "Do it now, Robálaí."

"Will you not accept my solemn vow of protection instead of a charm?" I cannot bear my bond-promised seeing me yet not seeing me through the glazed stare of one under a Faerie spell.

When she looks up, her gaze is more trusting than I deserve. After a contemplative pause, she nods. "Yes."

Starfall and moonshine, I want to kiss her again.

My bond-promised takes a shuddering breath. "Let's compromise. What if you enchant me just enough to sleep without nightmares about being stuck in the underworld?" Colleen lays a hand on my arm. "Until you come back to me?"

Come back to me.

Her words should not affect me so, yet they do. "Very well."

I pat her hand then stagger away, overcome by Colleen's presence alone and what passed between us this night. Waving a hand in her direction, I wrap her in the requested charm. "May dream and sleep upon your spirit flow. Heart and mind be free from fear of all that has transpired here."

As effective as a soothing caress, my words of influence erase the worry lines in Colleen's forehead. Her lashes flutter, and the fire in her eyes dims. A drowsy smile captures lips plumped from our kiss. "I'm so tired, Robin."

I catch her as her legs give out and she collapses into exhausted sleep.

Robin.

She called me Robin, not Robálaí. A loss I should not be capable of feeling clutches at my heart. This woman is not Fae and of no consequence. When the day comes and she is well rid of me, our bond will be nothing more than a memory she will not recall. Her heart will heal. I am the one cursed to forever carry the weight of our bond. One Finnbheara's geas bans me from ever embracing as anything more than an empty and meaningless inconvenience.

I glare at the woman in my arms whose alluring taste still lingers on my lips. It is the strain of Aodh and my purpose here that riles my mind into mistaking her as anything but a means to my success. I must hold fast to the truth that she is destiny's tool and nothing more.

I settle her into the armchair to sleep with no dreams of bond-promises, Aodh, or Bráchthine. I will instruct Aodh's servants to replace the bedclothes I soiled with my release. Their tongue-wagging alone will supply further proof as to our intimacy and the validity of Colleen as mine.

The thought of anyone in Aodh's household interacting with Colleen sends a hot plume of abhorrence through my blood. Certainty to keep my bond-promised away from any resident of Bráchthine unless I am present wars with the inkling in my head to hand the nuisance of her care over to Aodh's staff. The urge to restrict her exposure to those unknown overthrows convenience. Grinding my teeth, I demean my station by performing a menial cleansing spell on the bedclothes instead of necessitating an unwanted visitor to assume the task.

Not for the first time and surely not for the last, I regret bringing this human into Aodh's realm.

Leaving the bedchamber, I release the enchantments on my new quarters and open the door to the hallway. Satchels filled with my belongings and necessities for Colleen from Aillil's saddlebags are piled against the wall. I breathe deeply with relief. My trespass charms are effective here in the underworld. After hauling the leather packs into the bedchamber, I retrieve fresh garments. Before retreating to bathe and make myself presentable for the dawn audience with Aodh, I am drawn once again to Colleen. I brush my lips against her ear to whisper, "Within these walls dwell taciturn, until the moment I return."

I move to leave when she hums in her slumber. The sight of her body in carefree repose and the smile tugging at her lips fills me with the bloodlust of a worthy battle. I must not act on temptation nor ascribe it anything beyond carnal desire. I cannot care for another. It is decreed by Finnbheara's geas— the all too familiar cruel taunt that I may lust but not love.

A pair of underworld escorts waits for me at the bend in the corridor, not twenty paces from the door of my new chambers. Ah, guarded then, another sign of the mistrust I must erase from Aodh's assessment of me. The box with my bond-promised's cry of fulfillment sits in the pocket of my britches like a stone. I turned the crank until it could move no more to ensure the prize does not spill anywhere but in the presence of the contemptuous Dark Prince.

I suffer an uncomfortable pinch in my chest born of resentment that Aodh disallows me to traverse the halls of his fortress without being flanked by his soldiers. These men will soon learn the Host of a Thousand Wings is a force to be respected. Breathing long and deep, I assure myself that once Aodh's insidious request is granted, my access in Bráchthine will become unlimited.

Wearing a mask of pure viciousness, I sneer at the unwelcome guards. "Your king expects me."

Once again, I approach Aodh in his chamber of twisted branches. The Dark Prince languishes on his swan throne. There is no fire in his eyes this morning. Instead, deep within the shadows, I see two points of light that mimic the strange never-setting sun of his realm. Tucking this visage of a king at ease into the catalog of Aodh stored in my mind, I approach. My escorts remain at their stations inside the door.

It sickens me to be required to share what I hold in the small black box with Aodh. The thought of these two inconsequential idiots being privy to my bond-promised's ecstasy raises a murderous streak I usually reserve for times of battle.

I bow before my new monarch.

Aodh's voice is grit and ash. The mere sound of it causes my throat to dry and thirst to gather.

"As the time of dawn breaks, Robálaí Geal enters my presence. Your punctuality pleases me." He leans a menacing forearm on his knee that could be hewn from the smoldering stones of his castle walls. Unlike Finnbheara, who shifts his form between immense god and king as his mood dictates, Aodh maintains a constant bulk akin to my legendary Fae forebearers, images I recall from the gilded pages of tomes in the great library of Tír na nÓg.

Once again, I incline my head in deference to my new commander. "It is my honor to serve and obey you, Dark Prince."

"Do you bring your king proof of this obedience?" The menace in his tone is clear. The success of our fledgling arrangement and the future of my Host in his service hang on my answer. Inciting Aodh's displeasure could portend an end to my purposes, both overt and covert, that I have brought to Bráchthine. I will not allow that to pass. I am determined that, here in the underworld, my worth will be rewarded by Aodh. I will be elevated to a rank befitting my talents as a warrior and prowess as a commander of Fae.

I would have achieved the first seeds of trust from the Dark Prince upon our arrival had Colleen's presence not muddled everything. The King of Bráchthine and I struck an agreement. I am the one who altered the parameters by bringing an unexpected human to Aodh's court after my cocksure pronouncements that Eala Duir would be an easy mark. He is right to test me. In his place, I would do the same.

"Yes, as you commanded." I reach into my pocket. The moment my fingers clamp around Aodh's infernal vessel, another searing flush of possessiveness clouds my vision. "I hold in my hand the cries of my bond-promised's ecstasy."

My heart pumps scalding blood through every artery. Colleen's expression of fulfillment belongs to me, not Aodh. It is my right alone to drink the ambrosia of her pleasure, not this king.

My hand becomes a stone claw, repulsed at the thought of sharing the box's contents with another soul.

Aodh releases a grunt of displeasure. "Your hesitation raises troubling questions."

I do not play my part well. To cover my momentary idiocy, I nod in the direction of the guards. "The prize I bring bears the mark of an intimacy I shall not share with anyone but you, my king." I add yet another bow of subservience to sweeten my request. "May we not conclude our business without witnesses?"

The Underworld God eyes me with the very suspicion I fight to divest him of. "You protect the privacy of a human? Do I find the Fae blade I bartered for in our alliance wears a dull edge?"

I assume my haughtiest expression. "I assure you the sting and shine of my steel continues to blind those who look upon it." Thrusting my chin out, I continue. "The human is my bond-promised, my possession, the receiver of my sacred Fae oath. As is the custom of our Folk, no part of her is to be shared with any but those with whom I choose to do so. It is a dishonor to me for this subservient chattel to receive such a boon."

Aodh chuckles. "Your ire is up. Good. I require hearts of flame and thunder to lead my corps." With nothing more than a piercing stare from the king in their direction, the guards leave, closing the great chamber doors behind them.

As soon as we are alone, the twin suns embedded in Aodh's long, gaunt face switch their focus to me.

It is my move. Time to turn the tide of Aodh's questioning of my loyalty into surety that I am indeed pledged wholeheartedly to my new monarch. Flaying of my flesh would be less agonizing than the pain of turning the vessel with its precious contents over to Aodh, but I do it. I carry the weight of all who depend on me on these shoulders. Dealing with Aodh is dealing with the darkness of his demands.

Greed stokes the fire beneath the ash of Aodh's skin. The god glows a bloody red as he holds out a charred paw for the box. Every inch I extend my hand to deliver this precious token to my king threatens to crack my bones. It is torment to submit a treasure that rightfully belongs to me alone. Sweat pools along my forehead, rogue drops escaping to meander down the sides of my face. I neither comprehend nor accept this reaction. The bond-promise I entered into should mean nothing to me aside from the preservation of my Host's safety. What is this pain and fury writhing deep in the core of my essence? Does the bond-promise I swore to Colleen battle the geas that consumes my ability to feel?

Aodh's hell pales in comparison with the conflict in my soul.

My attention is drawn back to the Dark Prince on his black diamond throne as he turns the crank on his demanded tribute. His leer grows wider with each twist that brings him closer to the stolen prize. My fingers flex with the urge to brandish my blade and drive it through his blackened heart.

I hold my breath as the crank stills and the top of the box rises. Aodh opens his overlarge flaccid lips and seals them around the open top of the box. With a disgusting slurp, he swallows Colleen's scream of fulfillment. The Underworld God grunts as his eyes smolder in their sockets. A low hum rises from his chest as he savors the climactic cry of my bond-promised. I hold my breath to keep from vomiting on his black metal boots.

When the sound is spent, Aodh flings his head back and emits a lustful growl. After indulging in a long moment of satisfaction, he cracks his neck, levels his gaze at me, and licks his lips with a tongue as black as his tunic. "Delectable."

The King of Bráchthine is a swine. There are countless reasons my heart is hardened against Finnbheara, but never would the King of Tír na nÓg revel in the beastliness and base shamelessness of this Dark Prince.

Aodh stands proudly, palming his arousal. "You have inspired me, Robálaí Geal, to seek sport once again with humans. It seems boldness in their pleasures has escalated since last I stole a lover from the world above." He swipes a line of spittle from the side of his lips. "I am not one to withhold appreciation. Your bond-promised gives me a gift, so I shall bestow one upon her."

The lout acts as if Colleen's gift was freely given. His lustful brutishness raises my caution. "There is no need, my Dark Prince."

"Nonsense. You have your suite befitting your station. Thus, the mate of my general shall enjoy private rooms as opulent as that of a queen." Aodh dips his hatchet of a nose into the box and sniffs as if to drain any remaining echo of Colleen's pleasure.

In that instant, I vow never to allow Colleen to venture into Aodh's promised suite unless I am by her side. Curse the mystery between stars. This woman continues to distract me from my purpose. The mention of a queen draws the line of my interest straight to Queen Nuala.

"Will not your gracious queen disapprove of royal endowments bestowed upon a mere human?"

The Underworld God strides down the steps of his dais and drops his mutton roast of an arm across my shoulders. "Now, let us sow the final seeds of Finnbheara's demise." Without warning, he drives a fist into the center of the scar where the King of the Connacht Fae blighted the skin of my chest. "The ambrosia of revenge sweetens with time, eh, General?"

I nod. "Aye, it promises honey not bitterness."

He runs a hand through his ashy gray and charcoal mane. "Curses take many forms. Mine of transformation and yours of disregard."

I compare Aodh's plight to what I have endured at Finnbheara's hand, both to my flesh with the stroke of his blade and to my spirit with the geas condemning me to a life devoid of love. Aodh, his sister, and their twin brothers, the Children of Lir, shared their misery while they bided the years of their undeserved sentence. I bear my shame alone and act the lapdog to try and earn back Finnbheara's favor.

"We were both meant to be broken, Robálaí, but here we stand united to be the breakers of those who sought to break us." He pounds fists into the muscles of my upper arms and then strolls contemplatively around the chamber.

"I am certain our victory lies in acquiring the *beads of being*." He licks his scaly lips. "How Finnbheara will suffer as I disavow the King's Treasure of his great secret she bears. Once in my possession, I will combine that elusive power of creation with my magisterial essence to forge an army tenfold the number of Tír na nÓg. His legion of meager thousands will crumple beneath my ten-thousands. It is of tantamount importance you bring me Eala Duir without fail. Finnbheara's white swan will magnify the power of my black swan."

The prospect of Aodh gaining such power is daunting. A pit opens in my stomach, imagining the means this dark god will use to discover and extract the *beads of being* from Eala's Fae essence.

I have passed Aodh's first test, but it does not lessen the danger surrounding my Host like poisoned wind. Aodh cannot know I must wait until Eala summons me with the gold ring I placed in her possession. If I venture into either the human or Fae realms above to seek her, the wrath of Finnbheara will find me.

The Dark Prince's eyes lose the glow of his red-orange sun and ignite with virulent hellfire. "Until Eala Duir is mine, your Host shall be under my command."

I bow once again to hide my dismay at his implication. "We are already pledged to your service, my king."

The Underworld God flashes black, veined teeth. "You mistake my meaning, General. Until my faith in you is complete with the delivery of Finnbheara's Treasure as promised, your Host is under my control and mine alone. You shall no longer dictate their actions without my direct approval."

"You mean to treat them as hostages?"

Aodh sneers. "As incentive."

"What of our agreement that I command my Folk as an elite unit? They are not to be dissolved into the pool of Bráchthine's forces."

He glowers at my insubordination. "An agreement is only binding when both parties fulfill what they pledged. I have already afforded you leniencies with your human. There will be no more." Aodh turns and marches to his black swan throne.

I drop to one knee, so when he turns, he sees subservience. My time in Bráchthine already plagues me with increasing worry, unease, and worse— insecurity—but raw, unfettered fear now boils in my gut. Aodh has all but stripped my Host from me, the very Folk I have given my oath to protect. What of my bond-promised? Is she in any less peril?

Aodh is Fae. He dare not tread on such a sacred bond. Or do I dwell in the ignorance of hope?

Aodh is a Dark Prince.

Aodh is the god of a realm of sorrows and the death of hope.

I have no compass to aid me in my navigation of this land of red glass mountains and a mock sun that never sets nor rises. As quickening despair vanquishes the last of my hubris, a light no more substantial than the last gasp of a spent candleflame flickers in my breast.

Nuala.

Once queen of the lands above, and now queen of these lands beneath worm trail and badger den is the beacon cutting through the fog to guide me past this blackened rocky shore. It was always my shadow purpose, unknown even to Acacia and my high command, to seek Queen Nuala. I pray she who was stolen from golden sun-blessed glade and bower thrives.

I must find her and seek her counsel before I sink deeper into Aodh's mire.

"Leave me and go fulfill that which you have sworn to accomplish," says the Underworld God, clearly bored with our audience.

I rise, pound a fist over the sigil of Aodh's triple flame upon my breast, and turn to quit the throne room.

"And General…" says the king with sarcasm lacing every syllable of my rank.

In the smoky trunks of glass trees ringing his throne room, distorted reflections of Aodh's hungry glare surround me.

"…for each of Bráchthine's days that Eala Duir does not appear before your king, a pair of your precious *péist síoda* will I claim as the price for your failure." The beastly prince chuckles. "Or more precisely…*claimed*. For your penalty has already begun."

CHAPTER 18
THE NOTABLE TRAITRESS

EALA

I don't get three steps toward the winding path that leads from the cliff down to the cove where Grace O'Malley's ship bobs on the tide before Biddy grabs the back of my soggy sweater.

"And where do you think you're off to?"

"To get a closer look. Some hint as to where…" I chew my bottom lip. "Or when I should approach her."

She drags me behind the rock. "If anyone on that ship catches sight of these strange britches." Biddy pinches the pocket of Sion's jeans. "Or you with your odd talking, we'll be strapped to that mast faster than a falcon claims a wee mousie."

I point at the ship. "You do know who she is?"

I earn narrowed eyes and a crinkled lip from her for my question.

"Aye, Eala. I've said as much."

I glance across the cliff tops, hoping to see Alfie. There's plenty of generic peasant clothing we could slip into between her gorgeous white trunks. "There's our navy. The woman commands a fleet. In addition, she's famous for carting gallowglass mercenaries over from Scotland. Those guys are notorious for being bad ass."

I bark a laugh at Biddy's priceless expression of bewilderment as she mouths *bad ass*.

"Bad ass is a term from my time that means…" I search for the clearest explanation I can drum up. "A practically unbeatable fighter."

She nods. "A navy filled with bad ass it is." Biddy clamps her hands on my upper arms. "There's a fire in your eyes that spells trouble." She softens her stern tone. "I know you're hurting to get your man back, but a brazen lass like Grace O'Malley isn't going to be as hospitable to understanding your far-fetched dilemma as I."

Biddy's right. Her lifetime relationship with magic makes her open-minded. A practical pirate—not so much.

I gaze in the direction of the ship, disappointed. "Now that I know she's the one meant to help us, I've got work to do. I need to figure out the right point in time to approach her." My shoulders slump. "And what incentive can I possibly offer a pirate queen that's important enough for her to believe my story and want to join the team?" I wiggle my finger with the new key tattoo. "Hey, Grace, have I got a Faerie tale for you."

I spare a parting glance around the rocks at the Pirate Queen, who's now leaning against the side of the ship, stomping her boot in time with her crew's song. The Veil answers my call to take us back to Slieve Gullion.

The drive to County Clare is torturous. I feel as if I've been driving for days instead of hours. All I want to do is bury myself in Grace O'Malley research. Biddy proves to be a surprisingly good resource. She knows quite a few stories about the Pirate Queen. My favorite is the one where Grace's father refused to let her go to sea because she was a girl. Papa O'Malley claimed his daughter's long locks would get tangled up in the rigging, so Grace, the young spitfire she was, cut off her hair. Very ballsy move for the time.

Biddy swears the woman even gave birth to one of her sons at sea when she was captaining a ship in the thick of battle with Turkish pirates. Who's the bad ass now? She's definitely our gal. Grace is the *mind* filled with battle strategies to challenge Finnbheara on the sea.

Queasiness rolls through my stomach as I fixate on yet another complication. How large can the king's army or navy be? I picture Fae forces as antiquated and historic, balanced in numbers to what Grace can bring to the table. What if I'm wrong?

Dammit. More research to suck up precious time. Where do I even start looking for an estimate of the size of a Faerie army or navy? The only possibility that may hint at the size of Finnbheara's forces might be the *Leabhar Gabhála*, the Book of Invasions, but it's a mythical, fictional treatise.

I snort. Isn't Finnbheara himself supposed to be nothing more than a story?

Unfortunately, none of Biddy's yarns point to any vulnerabilities of Grace's I can exploit, since now I'm in the unscrupulous business of hoodwinking powerful women to join Team Eala.

For Sionnach, I'll be as down and dirty as I must. In the star-spattered sky, a waxing moon is just beginning to stretch its legs. How many days has it been since I abandoned my dearest love? Four? Five? My knotted stomach doesn't let up as I stress over the unpredictable passage of time in Tír na nÓg compared to mine. How is Finnbheara treating Sion and Máthair? Squeezing the steering wheel, I force my guilt not to run wild. I can't afford to backslide.

Nervous energy keeps me buzzing, but the day takes its toll on Biddy. She bunches up against the side of the car and starts snoozing like a champ. There's almost no one on the highway, so I spare half a glance to swipe my phone screen, searching for podcasts on the subject of Grace O'Malley to distract me on the long drive home.

I hit gold. Thank you, obsessive Pirate Queen fans. I knew Grace met with Queen Elizabeth, but there aren't many details of the historic moment, except that the Pirate Queen walked away with what she wanted. The podcast shares the arduous process it took for Grace to score the meeting with QE1. For a long time, there was little hope the girl chat would ever take place. The Brits hated the she-pirate, calling her "the most notorious woman on the western shores," "a notable traitress," and "the nurse of all rebellions." Not the person they wanted hanging out with their queen.

It's in Grace's specific goals for the royal meet-and-greet where I stumble across the nugget that'll get her attention. She was hellbent on pleading for the release of her son, Tibbott-ne-Long, from his imprisonment at the hands of the English. There's our common ground. Two women going head-to-head with a tyrant to free someone vital to their hearts. For Grace, a son, for me— the sun itself, the one who shines brightest in my soul.

Just as I used the truth of history to pretend it was in my power to guarantee Biddy an innocent verdict in her witch trial, I'll bamboozle Grace O'Malley into believing I'm her only hope to score an audience with Queen Elizabeth.

I used to be a decent person. Maybe someday, I will be again. The passion to do anything for the one you love rages in my blood. I'll lie for Sion. I'll cheat, steal, risk everything I have, and even who am I for my *anamchara*. My heart thunders with certainty. If it comes to it, I will even kill for him.

As Biddy and I tiptoe our way up the stairs of the tower house that is Granuaile, aka Grace O'Malley's castle, I steal a look out one of the few windows. A lovely shawl of mist clings to the hills of Clare Island. This particular stronghold of Grace's overlooks Clew Bay in County Mayo. Moonlight reveals the green-apple color of the island's peaks and slopes. It's quiet enough to hear the beat of a gull's wings. The only sounds are water whispering against the sand and the creaking of wood as Grace's galley ship leans to and fro in the tide.

"Grr –ahhn–u–whale," I whisper, practicing the correct pronunciation of the Pirate Queen's name one last time before we snatch her from sleep, and I propose my offer.

We slip into Grace's bedchamber. This woman is basically Irish royalty due to her high clan ranking and the impressive number of people loyal to her, but the room is not frilly. There's a large Elizabethan era bed with a huge carved post at each corner. We pass a shoulder-high chest of drawers inside the door. At the foot of the bed sits a dark wooden trunk covered in designs I can't make out. I'd love a closer look at it.

A single small tapestry stands out against the whitewashed stone wall where it hangs. It appears to bear a crest. My scholarly self wants to study and touch. What a joy it would be for our trials to be finished so Sion and I could use Veil wandering to do nothing more than visit and savor the richness of history.

Luckily, a nearly room-sized rug covers the floor and cushions our steps. As we carefully make our way to the side of the bed, Biddy thrusts an arm to stop me. She points at the strangest sight. A stout rope stretches from the bed

and across the snug room until it spills out the window. I examine the path of
the rope as it descends along the outside of the castle wall, then continues
down the slope of the small hill on which the tower house is perched and
stretches toward the bay. The tide is low, so it's not hard to find the rope's
destination—the wooden galley ship in the shallow sea.

I backtrack the rope's trail to the bed and nearly laugh when I discover it's
not tied to the bedpost, but to the stockinged ankle sticking out of the
bedding. We've discovered Grace O'Malley's trip wire. If anyone tries to mess
with her ship, she'll be the first to know when the rope yanks on her leg.

Biddy gestures to the opposite side of the bed from Grace's burglar alarm.
Once we're as close as we dare, I nod to the witch. She moves her mouth
against the blue bottle. When a gemstone haze surrounds the glass, Biddy
swipes her magic vessel toward the woman sleeping in the bed. A thin stream
of silvery blue serpentines away from the bottle then pushes its way between
Grace's lips. Her steady breathing shifts into a wheeze.

Again, Biddy whispers to her bottle then sets its base near the edge of the
bed on top of the thick quilt covering Grace. Nothing happens at first, and
panic begins to stir in my gut. The witch bends to place a kiss on the neck of
the bottle and wiggles its stopper free. When she blows against the rim,
threads the color of starshine spill out the top. As Biddy silently casts her
spell, the thin strands cross one another, weaving a fine, shimmery coverlet
over Grace's body. The filaments sink into the Pirate Queen until everything
but her head is encased in diamond-like armor. I marvel at the beauty and
intricacy of Biddy's work. The people who feared her power were on to
something.

Biddy caps the bottle and juts her chin in my direction.

My turn.

There's a glint of metal from under a squashed corner of Grace's pillow.
It's no surprise she keeps a weapon near at hand. From what I can see, it's a
scian, the Irish dirk, an incredibly effective dagger of her time. I've come
across plenty in my research and in museums. Even though I need to trust
that Biddy's magic diamond suit will immobilize the Pirate Queen, I still
choose to slip the stabby fellow free from its hiding place and out of Ms.
O'Malley's reach.

I should have figured anyone with a rope tied from her ankle to her ship
would be a light sleeper. It's a small miracle Biddy and I didn't wake Grace

before the spell was in place, but removing her weapon is a definite wake-up call.

Grace's eyes pop open. Their deep brown color, like the rich broth in Máthair's Guinness stew, flashes a murderous expression.

"Granuaile O'Malley, my name is Eala Duir Loho, and I have no intention to cause you harm. I'm here to ask for your help and give you mine in return."

To Biddy's credit, the diamond casing doesn't budge even though a wild-eyed Grace makes a noble attempt at busting through it.

I try to keep my voice from shaking, but even magically bound, this formidable woman's power scares the shit out of me. "I've a strange tale to tell, one that may sound like the rantings of a madwoman, but I promise you it's the truth."

Grace snarls at us, but thanks to the first of Biddy's spells, the pirate's sounds are muted so only we can hear her. This shocks Grace. She attempts to scream, but it degrades into nothing more than a gentle sigh.

I grit my teeth then continue. "My companion is the witch, Biddy Early."

At the word *witch* Grace stills.

"Her magic is of fair intent, benevolent and all kindness."

"Devils," hisses Grace. The sound of her muffled voice dies the moment it reaches us. She's pissed. Her gaze darts to her diamond shroud then back to me with pure hatred. Biddy was right. My bargain isn't going to be an easy sell to a leader of warriors and most likely the sea itself.

Time to rip off the bandage. "I am also known as Eala of the Fae."

For the first time, a crack opens in Grace's battle-ready vibe. I've delivered a shock.

"Rest assured, I am neither a deceiver nor maker of malevolent mischief as are many of my kind. I come to you with a bargain that will soothe the burdened hearts of us both." Sion is always so good at adjusting his speech for different time periods. I think I'm doing a pretty damn good job of sounding old school and Faerieish.

"Finnbheara, the King of the Connacht Fae, entrapped my husband in the kingdom of Tír na nÓg."

I have her active interest now. The poor woman probably decided she's having one hell of a dream. If I were in her position, believing my sleeping imagination had run amuck would be a thousand times more preferable than wearing a suit of binding magic and being gagged in my bed.

"Once I was welcome in the king's lands, but an understanding between us has soured. He locked his gates to me, his own kin, and keeps my husband hostage." Not technically the full truth, but enough for the sake of my goal to recruit Grace. We've traveled to a time of Irish clan conflict both within a single clan and against other clans. The concept of hostage taking and deal-making for their return is part of life. This woman, considered a clan chieftain herself, will speak that language.

"You also face the unjust circumstance of one you love held captive by others."

I see skepticism return to Grace's expression, but I ignore it. "I'm aware you strive for an audience with Queen Elizabeth, a nigh impossible feat, and are indeed being thwarted at every turn."

Grace narrows her eyes. Of course, these info bits are no secret. I'm sure she's been very vocal in her maneuverings to meet with the Queen of England. I go with that assumption as I continue. "The English hold your son Tibbott-ne-Long in their prison, just as the tyrant Finnbheara shackles my beloved. You desire to treat with her majesty for his release."

"This is known," Grace answers in her witch-controlled whisper.

I bust out an expression of sorrow which isn't much of a challenge considering I'm constantly pulled under by the weight of my own sadness. "Yes. The path you wish to take is known, but not its conclusion." That was nice and ominous. I pause for dramatic effect. Even in the scant light, it's clear Grace's sun-worn face pales.

"The witch and I have foreseen the outcome of your efforts. You will never meet the English queen, and never see your son again."

The finality of my statement hits Grace hard. The smallest hint of a tear begins to glisten in the corner of one eye but never falls. I'm guessing she's not much of a weeper. I've spent my life doing my damnedest not to cause other people pain. There's no satisfaction in doing it now. If there's such a thing as a Faerie hell, I've probably earned an express ticket with my stab-to-the-heart lies to Biddy and now Grace. My consolation lies in the knowledge Sionnach would do no less for me.

"'Tis doom you speak of in this my dark dream," murmurs Grace through the haze of Biddy's spell.

Yep, my dream theory is dead on. I'll keep that in mind. It could work to my advantage at some point.

"Nay, Granuaile O'Malley," I say in an almost reverent tone. "We have not come to be the harbingers of despair, but rather the light bringers of hope."

Biddy chooses this moment to use her blue bottle to enhance my words. It shines brighter and brighter until it appears as a ball of white fire, a literal light bringer to the dark room. Witchy perfection.

Even though I'm tempted, it would be egregiously over the top to raise my arms to the light, imitating the illustrations of those channeling the gods. I've got to avoid Grace calling bullshit on any part of my messenger of gloom and doom performance. "With the combined powers of Fae and witch magic, we will bring about the audience you yearn for. Beyond such, we shall redirect fate so your son will once again walk through this world a free man and back into his mother's loving arms."

As soon as I say it, I question whether or not Grace is a lovey, huggy kind of mom. She seems more the curt nod of approval type.

Just as I dare to be encouraged by the awe dawning across Grace's face at our grandiose offer, her expression dims into a scowl. The Pirate Queen's spelled voice is hot with accusation. "The price of such a gift is always dear. What do you and your witch demand of me, Fae, a blood price, land, or my soul itself?"

Biddy speaks up for the first time in our confab. "Only the devil himself is a soul-taker. We are none such villains."

I can't tell if relief or a fresh challenge flashing in Grace's dark sepia eyes. She's definitely a no-nonsense gal. Jumping in on the heels of Biddy's clarification, I add, "It's your battle savvy along with the fleet of ships and those you command, as well as the company of the gallowglasses you transport that we request. All so named will serve as a fair exchange to gain your admittance to the royal presence and freedom for your third son, Tibbott-ne-Long."

Grace huffs. "A dear price indeed. You've named barter goods but not their purpose."

My heartbeat skitters like a manic squirrel. Here comes the kicker. "We wish you to lead these forces across the Faerie sea and into the land of Tír na nÓg to confront Finnbheara and free my husband." The words tumble quickly out of my mouth as if the faster she hears them the better the odds she'll agree. I'm not sure my verbal barrage is even comprehensible.

I expect shock or a new flurry of questions. Instead, I'm met with Grace's hearty yet spell-stifled laugh.

"Och, this is a fine dream." She continues to chortle. "Faerie seas? Why not ask me to grow fins and challenge the mighty Kraken himself?"

Biddy leans to whisper conspiratorially in Grace's ear. "If calling us a dream soothes your spirit then name it such."

My witchy partner and I are on the same wavelength. Allowing Grace to buy into a dream theory may keep her from freaking the fuck out.

Grace tries to pull away from Biddy's closeness, but the witch continues. "You have our word that once all is set to rights, you shall awake to find our promise fulfilled."

There's a major flaw in Biddy's theory. Will Grace believe she's dreaming of things she has zero knowledge of? How do I explain the Veil, time travel, or the microwave in Loho cottage?

I pipe up with proactive damage control. "You'll see sights from a time yet to be. I speak of a future beyond your years."

Grace narrows her eyes. "Your persuasions are wrought from brittle leaves. Easily crumbled with a single closed fist."

Damn she's a tough one. "Believe what you must, Granuaile O'Malley, but we will have your answer now. Are a queen and a son a fair price for your savvy and might?"

Grace cocks her head to the side. "I've faced the foes of treachery and greed, false promises, and betrayal. Dark dealings all. This challenge is but the next of many my fate delivers. What is life if not a bend in the road or the far side of a monstrous wave beyond which you cannot see?" Her gaze bores into mine. "I do not cower in the face of possibility. Dream or waking, I shall partake of your bargain."

"You will?" My voice squeaks, wrecking my flimsy façade of a revenge-seeking Fae. Biddy grunts beside me at the misstep. I cover as quickly as I can. "What I mean to say, madame, is that I thank you. Our common purpose of freeing those we love shall be our North Star."

Here comes the make-or-break moment. I nod to Biddy, and she releases the spells holding Grace. A puff of sapphire mist pops from O'Malley lips. The diamond armor fades away. If the Pirate Queen grabs for a weapon or shouts for help, we'll slip into the Veil. She does neither, raising her hands to inspect them then sits up in her bed with nothing more than a hum of interest.

I feel the presence of the Veil a breath away, ready to yank Biddy and I out of trouble as I return Grace's *scian* to its owner.

The gesture pleases her. Without any fuss, she slips the rope from her ankle and slides out of bed on the opposite side from where I stand with Biddy. She doesn't shout or try to flee but lights a candle then goes about the business of dressing herself.

My apprehension doesn't magically disappear with a *poof*, but it eases ever so slightly.

"You speak of going beyond my time. By what means?"

I swallow to clear my throat of its stress clench. "I'm in possession of a Fae wonder. You've heard tell of the Veil between worlds?"

"Aye," she says, pulling on her boots.

"It goes beyond what the stories describe. It is a pathway through both time and place. The Veil brought us to you, and now you are very welcome to join us as we step back into its mystery."

"And what of my folk? Will I be lost to them?"

It's a fair question, but I don't want to waste time explaining the mechanics of the Veil to her. I can share details while we travel or once we get to Loho cottage and start to make our plan.

It's Biddy who steps in. "Eala of the Fae came to me from her time into mine. 'Tis a strange road leaving what you know behind for that which you don't. I took it on faith she was a person to follow."

Grace clucks her tongue. "And what did the Faerie promise you, witch?"

Damn, of course she'd guess Biddy was here as a result of a deal. This woman is not one to underestimate.

Biddy chuckles. "'Tis true I've struck my own bargain with her. I'll decide when we are better acquainted if I choose to share its character with you." Her demeanor becomes more serious. "I've many dealings with the Fae. Often, I've brokered a thing or two betwixt the Folk and my people. 'Tis true one must be on their guard with their kind, but I've never known a forthcoming Faerie to go back on a solemn promise. From what my eyes can see and my heart tells, Eala is of that ilk."

Grace listens intently to Biddy's affirmation of my character.

The bottle cradled in the witch's palms takes on a deep blue shade nearly as dark as midnight. "Know this. I believe her words and promises. Love fires her purpose. She will do what she must to honor it. Are not quests of the heart those which give purpose to us all?"

Grace wraps a plaid shawl around her shoulders that could be the very one we saw her wear as she stood on the bow of her galley. She moves decisively toward where I stand with Biddy near the door as if to leave by it.

I start to explain we'll leave via Veil, when in one swift lunge, Grace pulls my back flush against her chest and presses a dagger to my throat.

CHAPTER 19
THE GLASS BEAUTY

SIONNACH

When I sleep, I'm with Eala. I dream of stroking her feather-soft skin dusted with those strange gold freckles as we make love.

"My fox," she whispers.

"My swan," I answer.

This is what life—eternity—should be. Bodies pieced together like the perfect design of overlapping petals in a single rose, embracing the moment when eyes no longer see and the only sounds are sweet cries of complete surrender. We're as meant to be as tides or the wind.

"Fuck," I wheeze as I do every time the dream ends. I wake with a groan and a cock as hard as the stone pillar on the Hill of Tara. Tiny stars ignite behind my eyelids, shoving me none too nicely out of the threshold of bliss and into reality.

As I come fully awake and unsated, I listen for any difference in the forest's song. No concerning notes join the shush of leaves whispering their secrets to one another. After peering through the front windows to confirm the status quo of the woods, I drag my disappointed cock, still stiff from the pleasant images in my sleeping mind, down a wee slope behind the cottage. We both settle into the cool stream for a wash.

"There's a good lad," I say aloud to my now subdued shaft just to hear anything but the monotonous stirring of the forest.

It seems my howling partner has given up on me. Never thought I'd miss a beastie most likely musing whether my hide would go better with roasted potatoes or mash.

Solitude is my only companion. The great wind Finnbheara sends to devil the forest before his arrival to taunt me does not come.

My mother does not come.

Eala does not come.

Her absence unravels my soul.

If I were a patient sort instead of a runaway train, maybe I could stroll aimlessly through this undeniable paradise of color and feast on gorgeous fragrances. Instead, I drive myself to exhaustion, praying the work I do will keep my body strong—a key to preserving my sanity.

Today, I explore farther down the meandering forest path than before. It's a blessing the limp that's plagued me for more years than I care to count vanished when Eala healed me after that bastard Robber Bright tormented me by ruthlessly switching my body between man and fox back at Loho cottage.

I round the swooping bend beyond the tidy little row of abandoned cottages where I've gathered food and fresh clothing from what's been left behind. I'm determined Eala won't find a filthy ruffian when she comes for me.

I stroll alongside a circular clearing ringed with Faerie bottles like the ones near the cottage. In many tales, a captive or a prisoner marks the passage of time by notching the wall of their cell, knotting a rope, or stacking stones that will inevitably become their cairn. With constant sunlight here, except for the sudden darkness that came on when Finn and his cursed berry attempted to have a go at my mind, I decided to come up with my own way of counting. Collecting one of these pretty Fae bottles begins each of my so-called days. There are dozens or possibly hundreds of the glass beauties scattered about for me to choose from.

My bones are bitching especially loud from the long trek, even though I feel a pull to keep moving on. When I lift my shirttail to wipe sweat from my brow, it strikes me that these clothes droop off my body worse than before.

Despite my self-appointed physical tasks every day, I'm losing muscle. The thought of a nice lamb stew or beefsteak sets my mouth watering. Since I've not seen any sign of Faeries hell bent on fox hunting, maybe I'll give my red-furred beastie self a go and see what he can find in the way of meat.

At the far edge of the clearing, I come to a place where the trees are thicker, giving shadows more places to play, allowing the Faerie bottles to show off a bit more of their luminous shine. One of the buggers is more boastful than the rest. I stray off the path to pick it up.

This bright bauble escaped Finn's storm. No cracks run through its tapered sides, and the glass mushroom-shaped cap is firmly in place. Boredom drives me to pop the top and give it a sniff. I'm not eejit enough to taste the dark amber liquid inside straight away. Not since the Fae-tainted blackberries have I eaten anything until I've prodded and examined it for enchantments.

I've learned which particular rocks or hollows in certain trees wear the iridescent sheen of the Veil, a sure sign of mischief. At first, I was tempted to see if they were a doorway into the Veil that might snatch me away from here, but I felt no kinship toward the glimmer the way I did while tucked inside my magic pathway. I choose to steer clear of all rainbow shine from here on out.

When Eala spoke to the well sprite in Mick Ryan's village when we were chasing answers to Finn's riddle, the cursed Fae told her he was certain the king had wiped the creature's banishment from arrogant royal memory. I wouldn't put it past Finnbheara to do the same to me until he needs me in his scheming to claim Eala.

Eala won't forget me.

She'll come.

I hold my latest trinket up to the little sunlight that manages to poke through the boughs. Within the dark amber liquid, thin ribbons of something thicker wave through it. So quickly, I might have imagined it, tiny pinpricks of golden light flare and then die along the surface of the wee floating strands.

I admonish the bottle and set it on the ground then pace around it, squinting for any sign of Fae magic. "Tempt me with your pretty little sparkles, will you?"

High above me in an ancient oak with not-quite-right golden-brown bark and twinkly ivy climbing its trunk, there's a snap like a bitty twig caught under a boot. The itch of eyes on me prickles the back of my neck. I stare, but no other sounds follow. Maybe it's my howler watching me and deciding if it's time to crunch my bones before there's not enough meat left on them to matter. Best be turning back. I'm not keen on the feel of this part of the forest.

Switching my gaze to the bottle, I catch twin streaks of light piercing through its liquid and glass to cast a swirling pattern onto the matted moss.

I should leave the pretty piece be and grab a different bottle to add to the collection I keep on the shelves under the front windows in the cottage. I've fastened the shutters open to let sunlight brighten the spirited liquid inside the Faerie bottles. The lot of them add color and cheer to the empty place. They're restrained magic I can control by keeping their stoppers unbothered.

This bottle with its lively contents warns me to be wary and leave it behind.

Showing the wee glass temptress my back, I fully intend to return to the cottage. One step on, and I turn to it again, oddly reticent to walk away.

There's no subtle push of a Fae charm inching me toward today's bit of pretty glass, but my attention won't break from the thing. I cock my head to the side then search the ever-bright sky beyond the shadows. "Are you playing with me, Finnbheara?"

Is proper suspicion digging at me, or madness prowling to find a weak spot?

Even though this tiny urn may be the most unique I've found yet, many of the bottles I've gathered also catch the light in strange and beautiful ways. No two have yet to share an exact shape, color, or size. Finding new beauties gives me a small reason to venture out.

"Och, you're nothing but a fancy jelly jar." I reach for the bottle that's as round as a shiny Christmas ornament. It'll make a fine addition to my shelf.

Before I can grab it, the bloody thing rolls away from me into a patch of velvety moss colored parakeet green and apricot with dibs and dabs of bright purple. I stare at the boots I nicked from one of the other abandoned cottages. Did I kick the bottle when I moved off?

When I stoop to pick it up, my head reels. Dizziness sets the forest spinning. My hands heat from touching warm glass, but they don't burn. It's quite pleasing. My legs quiver, and I decide to take a bit of a rest here in the soft, spongy moss before going on my way.

"Aye, it's meat that'll do right by you, Sionnach, and chase off these episodes," I tell myself, chalking up the bout of weakness to my diet of pilfered stale bread, berries, and a veg or two. Maybe I've overlooked a smokehouse behind one of the cottages with a nice beefy haunch for the taking.

I relax onto my back. For once, the sky decides to treat me to the deep indigo of night. As before, there are no stars, only a streak of spilled lavender milk across the darkness.

I rest the bottle of amber liquid over my heart. The relaxation of sinking into a hot bath washes over me. I stretch my arms and legs like a star lily fallen onto the grass and hum, enjoying lazy indulgence.

Soft laughter trickles through the wood to jolt me out of my lagging about. I rise on an elbow to look around. "Who's there?"

No one calls out. Wee sparks burst around me, dropping painless kisses of fire across my skin. It's wonderful. Is this a hidden pleasure of resting under a Faerie night sky?

Fragrances of butterscotch and whiskey settle over me like warm mist, and I inhale greedily. There's nothing in the world more alluring than this mixture. Except for Eala's natural scent of growing things mixed with the sweet taste of her tears.

"Hello, Fox."

I twist my head to one side and find a slender woman in a gauzy gown surrounded by a golden haze hovering in the air between the trees.

Warning flares in my mind, and I shake off sluggishness to stand. "Who are you?"

The words are no sooner out of my mouth before she vanishes.

"What gorgeous russet locks you bear." I whip my head up to find a man much brawnier than myself in a calf-length tunic perched on a branch far above me. He's as shiny as the woman.

Every instinct tells me to get the hell away from the pair. Did they bring the darkness? When I turn to go, my feet refuse to move.

I raise my hands and chuckle as if enjoying the prank when I'm closer to nerves tying my tongue as tight as a bundle of hay. "Okay, you've had your go at me. I'll be on my way."

As soon as I speak, daylight returns.

Mother of the angels, did it ever truly leave? Am I seeing Faeries in the trees that aren't there? I take a tentative step, but my knees buckle and I sprawl back onto the moss.

The high-pitched laughter I heard moments ago is joined by chortles in a deeper, masculine tone before the duo starts chanting. "Russet, melon, fire honey…such bright strands fetch sacks of money."

The Faerie woman peeks from behind one side of a massive rock, and the man from the other. "See how his locks shine under the crystal sun," the woman chirps.

"Will you give us some of your fine curls, Fox?" asks her companion.

When I lay protective hands over my mop of hair, the two vanish again. Are my wits shivering, or are these Fae truly flitting about?

I push against the moss to stand and knock into an unseen barrier. I'm as helpless as a featherless bird.

The two Faeries fade into being in front of me. Their pronounced cheekbones and cutting angles of their features hold no beauty. I stiffen seeing the glint of a knife in the man's grasp. The both of 'em shimmer like jars of fecking fireflies.

"Human hair of such color and curl will fetch a healthy price," says the man.

In my Veil travels, I've outwitted or fought my way through enough situations to know my odds are shit.

"It's only fair to tell you, I'm here as a guest of Finnbheara. You might want to give a think to this bubble you've thrown around me and your intentions with that fine blade of yours."

For once, I'm glad Finn is such an ass when my words give the Faeries pause. The air around me gently thrums, and I risk a go at standing. Thank the last crusts of bread on my plate, I'm able to find my feet. I'm not thick enough to believe they wouldn't cage me again in the swish of a donkey's tail if need be. Running is a fool's errand.

"Och, 'tis true you'd be doing me a favor, helping me shed a bit of this." I run a hand through my hair. "I'm hoping my price isn't too dear for you."

Both Fae narrow their eyes and tilt their heads. Bargaining is catnip to these fuckers.

I fist a stingy handful of my curls. "I'm happy to part with this much. Anymore and my Fae wife, who's known hereabouts as Finnbheara's Treasure, will take it as an insult. She's fond of my ragged mop."

I've no notion of how far and wide news of Eala has spread in Tír na nÓg, but I pray delivering a double dose of ole Finn's potential displeasure will prevent my head from being shaved bald or worse, a slice to my throat and a grave in the Gem Kissed Forest.

The man tosses his knife from hand to hand. Let the fool posture. I kept my head around Finn. I can withstand these two wandering thieves.

The Faerie fellow's eyes gleam with trouble. "What price do you ask for your claret rubies, Finnbheara's guest?"

Think, Sionnach. What can these Faeries do for you that you can't do for yourself?

I could ask for food or better weapons. No, both reveal my weakness. If they think me vulnerable, what's to keep them from coming back for more?

What I need is knowledge.

"Nothing much. I'll ask a question of each of you. If your answers ring free of trickery, that will buy you the prize."

Their lips curl. "Agreed," they say in unison, sharing a pleased look that suggests I'm giving away too much for too little. Being rid of the two will be enough.

"How do I leave Tír na nÓg to return to the mortal world?"

The damn Faeries break out in guffaws, high-pitched enough to make my ears ring.

"Such a simple question for so fine a reward," says the man, swiping his blade against his metallic belt as if sharpening the edge. "You may only return to your realm with King Finnbheara's leave."

The woman continues to titter. "Humans truly are dimwitted."

I shrug as if their reaction is of no consequence, hoping my seething anger doesn't darken my skin. "I figured as much."

One question burned. Do I ask if they brought the false night or if that was my mind playing tricks? Do I ask about dangers here in the forest? Do I ask—

"How long before the madness of Tír na nÓg overcomes a human's mind?" I blurt.

The she-Fae giggles and bobs a few feet above the ground. "Time takes wing to swiftly maim as mortal minds does madness claim."

I smack my lips. "I'm gonna need a clearer answer to satisfy the bargain."

Instead of the pair giving up more detail, I'm shoved face-first into the moss with the man riding my back. His weight pins me to the ground. The Fae was so fast, I never saw the bastard coming.

"Your price has been paid," he growls, giving my hair a brutal tug. For a heart-clenching moment, I'm afraid he's going to tear it clean from my scalp. The whoosh of his slice screams in my ear as he shears off a hunk of my mop.

As soon as he's off me, I roll over, fists raised. The she-Fae has the bloody audacity to blow me a kiss before they fly off between the trees.

I scramble to my feet, jarred by the truth of how vulnerable I am. Searching around me, I see no sign of the godforsaken bottle that lured me to become a victim. I run fingers along the back of my head. Curse my tangle of curls. They prevent me from finding the extent of the cut.

Whirling thoughts send me stumbling for the support of the closest tree. There's no shimmering bottle, and I can't feel a clear sign of my stolen locks. Were those Faeries real? Is madness mucking about with my sanity? I didn't learn anything from those Fae that didn't already live in my head. I inhale the cinnamon scent of the bark, letting it quell my rising worries.

Rattled, I shuffle to the cottage like a man too deep in drink.

Time takes wing to swiftly maim as mortal minds does madness claim.

Heaven knows I'm determined to fight off the madness of Tír na nÓg, but what if I can't see it coming in time to know where to swing my blade?

CHAPTER 20
THE HIGH COMMAND

ROBBER BRIGHT

My audience with Aodh leaves me unsettled in mind and body. Muscles tick and quiver with rage as thoughts race with visions of *péist síoda* stripped from their riders. To undo any such affront, I must gather my high command and find my way to the dragon hold without delay.

If the Dark Prince seized my Aillil and Acacia's Eachna as his first penalty, I will storm into his presence and demand—

My roar reverberates throughout the corridor. I have no clout to demand anything of the Dark Prince. Aodh has not received the due I promised. By sacred rite of bargain, he is entitled to exact compensation from me until I fulfill that which I swore an oath to deliver.

I fooled myself into believing the arrival of the Host of a Thousand Wings would please him enough to grant me more time to bring Eala Duir to Bráchthine. I twist an invisible band on the ring finger of my left hand. How long must I wait for her summons?

I take several wrong turns through *Caisleán Bron's* corridors of blood red marble with jagged black veins. The iron sconces with serpent tongue-like flickering flames along the walls offer no aid in judging my whereabouts.

Aodh's castle is a disorienting maze. I slap my palm against the smooth wall. "Even your fortress, my Dark Prince, strives to torment."

When a corner bearing a familiar pilaster of burnished bronze with the likeness of four swans comes into view, I take a moment to calm the blood pounding in my ears before rounding the corner to my quarters.

A flurry of agitated voices greets me. My high command waits before the door, showing the respect of not barging into my rooms.

Artos's bellow reverberates in the hallway as I come into view. "Robálaí."

Nettle bounces nervously from one foot to the other as he flips his blade, deftly catching the handle with each revolution. "Impatience forbade us from tarrying in our chambers to learn of the outcome of your meeting with Aodh."

As I reach my Folk, Ciallmhar lays a hand on my shoulder. "It is done then?"

Acacia stands in stoic anticipation behind the Fae witch. When I give a curt bob of my chin, her amber eyes gleam with a warrior's readiness.

"Let us convene within," I say, pulling the door open then standing aside to let them pass. The three men enter my chamber, but when Acacia reaches the door, she shoves it closed.

The ferocity of her glare could force the mightiest foe to drop their sword at her feet. "I want to hear you utter the words, Robálaí Geal."

I doubt simplicity is what she seeks, but I try. "It is done."

She fists the neck of my tunic, drawing my face to hers. Her lips twist into a snarl. "Coward."

If she were any other of my Host, I would punish her for insubordination, but Acacia has a right to her anger. I have betrayed her heart again. She yearned for my bond-promise, knowing the acceptance of such an oath from my geas-blighted spirit would always be tattered and incomplete. I refused her. As if that were not damning enough, now I give her deepest desire to a creature she will forever deem unworthy of the gift.

Her fingers scratch up the back of my neck into my hair. She grabs hold and pulls my face so our mouths nearly touch. "Make me believe you."

Acacia's breath is hot and wanting. It slides over my parted lips and across my tongue. There was a time the taste of her breath would blind me with lust. There was a time I would sink my teeth into her bottom lip and growl her name. There was a time I would be inside her before another word was spoken.

That time is lost. Never to be found again.

My lips move against hers, not with a kiss, but a cruel blow. "I am bond-promised to the human, Colleen."

Her knuckles press harder against my windpipe as if poised to inflict physical pain as payment for the emotional pain I dealt her. Instead of harming me, Acacia drops her hands and retreats a step. I have never seen such an expression of defeat on this magnificent warrior's face. It steals a piece of my soul. "And you willingly wrung Aodh's price from her with your faithless cock."

That is what must be believed by all in Bráchthine. The Underworld God must never discover the deceit Colleen and I performed to obtain what was demanded of us. Not only is it dangerous to admit the truth to Acacia, but I harbor a new feral need to prevent anyone, even this most trusted soul before me, from intruding on the intimacy I've shared with my bond-promised.

"I did not wish to hurt you, Acacia."

She is upon me with the speed of a tempest. Her knee drives into my thigh, a finger width from reducing me to a gasping heap. "I wish to hurt you."

My cock jolts as if aware of the damage it barely escaped.

Acacia is well aware her attack purposefully falls just short of unforgivable. I grab my second's wrists to prevent her from committing further actions I must punish her for. I will not deny her the wrath of an abandoned lover, but an assault against a commander is unspeakable. "I have done what I have done for the good of all those I value above my own life. You must either accept that, Acacia, or resign your rank as my second."

Fight drains from her eyes. She crumples against my chest, and I wrap my arms around her. Only once in all our years as sworn comrades have I witnessed Acacia's tears. It was at the gates of this very kingdom when our queen, Nuala, was lost to us to spare the lives of her people. To be the cause of sorrow poignant enough to reduce this warrior to such a rare state darkens my soul.

I ache to comfort and lift her spirits to what they were a day ago, but I cannot. If only I could promise Acacia that Colleen will one day be gone from my life, and my former ties to my second will be as they once were. That is to give false hope. I am doubly fate-bound by geas and oath. Even if the mortal returns to her world, a bond-promise is severed only by death.

I stroke her hair that bears every color of the sacred soil of Tír na nÓg. "I do not ask your forgiveness, honored Acacia. Nor do I require your acceptance because, whether you believe me or not, I, too have not found the courage to fully accept the bond."

She sniffs once and pulls back, searching my face for falsehood.

"But I am now bound by the oath I gave to the human. I must honor it or spit on the tradition of our Folk."

Acacia swipes the moisture from her face and assumes the stance of one not to be trifled with. "You spit in the face of honor. Think on that every time you fuck your human trophy."

I back against the door.

Acacia bows, wearing neither the guise of a friend nor a former lover. Only a second to her commander stands before me. Indifference settles across her strikingly beautiful face. "Is my presence required with the rest of your high command, or do I already possess the information you plan to impart?"

Treasured affection that once warmed both my bed and my spirit leaks away like raindrops dripping off an acorn shell.

It would be heartless to force her to endure a second telling of what she now knows. Solitude is something I can give her in the hope she will find the will to remain at my side.

"There is troubling news."

Acacia snorts, as if what she just learned is not troubling enough.

I continue. "Aodh has pledged to take possession of our *péist síoda*, for each day I do not deliver Finnbheara's Treasure. I need you to investigate his actions. If possible, stall his claiming of any of our dragons." I share the distress evident in Acacia's expression. "If you discover either my Aillil or your Eachna has been touched, return to me immediately."

There is a fresh sting in my chest as I speak the names of our mated dragons.

She draws her brows together. "Why does the Dark Prince do this?"

There is no point in lying to her. "It is the penalty of my failure to bring Eala Duir to Bráchthine. Every day that relentless sun circles the red glass mountains, he will steal a pair of our beloved creatures. I say 'steal' because you must believe I would never give them willingly."

"Will they be returned to us once you deliver Finnbheara's Treasure to Aodh?"

"I will insist on it." A bold statement considering the abysmal lack of clout I have at present in the underworld.

Her countenance turns as icy as the glacial peaks of the Tearfall Mountains in the northerlands of Tír na nÓg. "Commander," she bites out with another bow then turns on her heel to stride down the hall.

I watch her go. The consequence of my decisions drove Acacia to sail from the harbor of our trust to a faraway port from which she will never return. Laying a hand to my chest, I anticipate the flood of pain I deserve for devastating the woman who came closest to reaching my hollow heart.

There is none.

Finnbheara's geas sees to it that my heart will never belong to anyone who truly desires it. Acacia yearned for what I am forbidden to give. I feel nothing more than a kinship devoid of passion for this noble lady.

Duty gnaws at me to go to see to our dragons myself, but I have entrusted Acacia with the task. Following her would only signal my lack of trust in her ability. I cannot add more damage to the now fragile cord stretched thin between us. With yet another burden on my spirit, I join the rest of my fellows in my chamber.

As the day wanes after too many bottles of wine and too little food in our bellies, Artos, Nettle, and Ciallmhar bid me boisterous farewells and depart for their own quarters. Despite Aodh's threatened control of the Host, per our ever-altering agreement, I continue to act as though I command their duties. A fragile state at present. Despite drink-laden minds, we outlined an ongoing training routine for the Host. It is essential to keep both Fae and dragons fit and battle-ready. Employing Ciallmhar's precious cache of druid stones, we have also devised surreptitious communication lines to run throughout my unit. The ways of Aodh and his Folk are far too great an unknown. We must stay alert as we assimilate in Bráchthine.

"Take your leave now, my fine fellows. After a respite, I will venture to the north tower and inspect the manner in which Aodh has chosen to house my high command. It is my responsibility to guarantee you are treated according to your stations."

Nettle grins. "And to commit to memory the quickest route to rouse us at any sign of concern."

Artos nods to the bedchamber door. "Or to drown in drink away from the scrutiny of your unintended tether."

I shut the door behind my lieutenants, cutting off Artos's thundering belch. The corners of my lips drift downward as the room falls silent. I feel Acacia's absence more acutely without the distraction of my fellows. The three promised to relay all we have spoken of so she knows our intentions and cautions. There is some solace she has not returned with concerning news of our *péist síoda*.

My gaze travels to the closed door of the bedchamber as it has done in constant intervals throughout the day. I prayed to the forces of luck Colleen would not wake and show herself. I am spent to the marrow of my bones from Aodh's demands and threats as well as Acacia's disillusionment. Thankfully, the mortal remained behind the door, and Bráchthine's wine proves bold and blessedly numbing.

Ciallmhar was the only one to inquire of Colleen. I explained that after all she has endured since leaving her world, she needs rest and rejuvenation. Respectful of the unfortunate circumstances surrounding our bond-promise, my fellows refrained from the usual ribald barbs one would expect from friends after a supposed night of consummation.

I fill a plate with meats, cheese, bread, and the strange black citrus fruit that grows from the smoky glass trees here in Bráchthine. Colleen must eat. I cannot add my bond-promised's fatigue or possible illness to the ever-growing mountain of concerns causing my back to bow.

Sudden dread fills me. Was my sleep charm too potent? Once her essence feels my protection near, she should have no difficulty waking. Is there a more troublesome reason she has not shown herself? Colleen is a human thrust into a dark Fae realm. The consequences of this change in her reality are not known to me. Humans unbound to Fae in Tír na nÓg are prone to deterioration of the mind. Do Aodh's lands escalate potential ills for Colleen despite our bond-promise?

"Robálaí, you fool." It is a fool's folly to have ignored her for nearly the span of an entire Bráchthine day. The memory of finding her in a motionless heap on the carpet after my brutish treatment of her last night surges like a plume of acid in my chest.

Abandoning the food, I charge through the inner chamber door. My gaze whips to the chair where I left Colleen. It is empty.

"Coll—" I bite off my cry when I catch the small figure in the center of the bed.

Slumping against the door frame, I catch my runaway breath. Colleen lies peacefully in the center of the mattress, her moonlight-fair complexion flushed rosy with sleep. Strands of hair shine the color of a red squirrel's coat in the gentle glow from the glass leaves of the crimson chandelier. Those long locks spread around her head like a silk fan. That same light stains her fine, plump lips a deep ruby. Dark bronze lashes kiss the tops of apple cheeks.

I always found her pleasant to look upon, but it strikes me in this moment how truly lovely she is. An opposite to Fae beauties with her face of soft curves instead of sharp angles. Colleen's cutting edges lay in the tang of her sharp-tongued words with their constant challenges and directness.

I murmur the title I gave her during our first encounter. "My peppered apple."

The apple is mine now. My cock rouses with the appeal of taking that thought to its conclusion. It seeks the satisfaction my debatable conscience still refuses to steal. I have stolen enough from this human. Consent may be all that is left to her.

The heavy black skirt twists around her legs. Her chest rises and falls, straining against the restriction of the gown's tight bodice. I am a thoughtless bastard not to have offered her one of the silk nightdresses in our trunks before delivering my hasty dreamless slumber charm.

I climb onto the mattress, careful not to create a dip that will disturb, and with painstaking slowness, unwind the fabric binding her legs. She sighs in her sleep as if grateful for the freedom and turns onto her side away from me. In this position, I am able to undo her lacings and spread the back of the gown wide to give her comfort. My gaze traces the graceful slope of her bare skin as it disappears beneath the skirt. With the lightest of touches, my fingertip follows the same path my eyes enjoyed.

Colleen's skin is as smooth and unblemished as the velvet of a newly blossomed petal. She radiates an intoxicating warmth I long to feel against my cool skin.

Restless in that space between sleep and waking, she shrugs out of the gown.

The heat she radiates in oblivious slumber wraps around me like a rope, drawing me to her. The beauty of a woman's form is far from a mystery to me. How is it my bond-promised's body speaks to mine even without words?

She is— My mind strains to find the word.

She is— I cannot yet define this indefinable sensation.

She is—My mouth fills with saliva, craving the feast laid before me.

She is—An invitation for insanity.

Breasts as round as a full moon rest upon her chest with peaks as lush as the ruby of her lips. My breath catches as my gaze travels to the curve and swell of her belly and hips. She has rid herself of the red satin sullied by our activities last night to bring forth Aodh's prize. The tuft between her thighs flutters like butterfly wings in the faint currents of air circling the room. I drop my head back, remembering the way her sex glistened with arousal and her unique scent of passion that could drive a man to madness.

My salacious need grows more insistent with each new luxurious discovery. I am ravenous to dig fingers into those fleshy thighs and open a path to drive my cock between them. I ache to fill my bond-promised with my pulsing length and drown her in my seed.

A moan escapes my lips, imagining too clearly how it would feel to slide in and out of her delectable slickness. The very sight of this inconsequential mortal consumes me.

"Robin?" she murmurs.

I slap a hand over my mouth to block the thunder in my chest from escaping at the sound of that insipid mortal name I wore. It rings as a vile curse in my ear.

How shall I prevent my obsession with this woman that threatens to take root? I am powerless to quiet its call.

Our bond belongs to Robálaí Geal. Robin Bright is who must die for all time.

Beg Robálaí Geal, to fuck you, Colleen, not Robin Bright.

"No," I cry then sink my teeth into the fleshy mound at the base of my thumb to bite off further outbursts.

If Robin Bright were truly a man other than a false skin I once wore, my sword would skewer his heart, and I would dance in the blood brought forth from the stroke. Then my bond-promised would no longer speak his name.

Colleen groans. "I'm tired, Robin. Stop fussing and come to bed."

My teeth ache to rip that bedeviled name from her tongue. Fuck my enchantment for allowing the return of a false Robálaí to her mind. She has yet to open her eyes and sense the predator at her side, slavering to consume her.

The hated name enflames my lust-fueled furor. To her, I must be Robálaí Geal, her bond-promised, not the mask I forced upon us both in my attempt to coerce Eala with my scheming.

Anger rages alongside my lust, both demanding total acknowledgement of our bond. How dare Colleen's human mind rob me of what rightfully belongs to me? I will not bear it. She must know me as the Fae she is bound to.

With savage ruthlessness, I rip my enchantment from her.

Her weak mortal body arches, lurching upward from the shock of the brutal shift into stark reality.

Nature curse me, I have done the unspeakable and harmed my bond-promised.

Awareness washes over her as she wakes. Colleen glares at her state of undress then at me, sliding backward to the black oak headboard. She reaches for the bedding and raises her brows. "You could have at least thrown a cover over me."

Her ire proves she is unharmed and not distressed to be laid bare in my presence. The beast within me resumes its hunt, dismissing my single moment of unnecessary concern. The urgency for her to say my name, to acknowledge who and what I am, crashes over me. I climb onto the bed, rising on all fours like the animal I have become, and crawl toward her before she is able to disappear beneath the sheet.

"Who am I?" I growl, teetering on insanity to hear her speak my name, my true name.

"Out of your fucking mind is who you are." She kicks at me. "What kind of a question is that?"

Her resistance is intoxicating. I take her tiny foot in my mouth, lick the scent from her skin then bite.

She thrashes to break free, and I pause to savor the way her breasts sway from side to side. Ever-increasing heat rises from her skin and through my clothing.

Fury crosses her face. "You were only supposed to charm me to sleep, not —" One hand darts to her sex, checking for signs of my intrusion into her flesh. Her shoulders relax slightly, satisfied she is untouched. "You're damn lucky, Faerie man, you didn't take advantage."

The sight of her probing fingers undoes me even more. The impulse to run my tongue over her skin and close my teeth around her stiff, inviting nipples drives me closer to her body, even as I detest myself for the urge.

I cannot want this human.

She is a distraction, a danger to my sanity. Whether it is the strength of Bráchthine wine or my unapologetic cock scrambling my wits—I do not care. Reason fails to find purchase through my overwhelming need. I continue to stalk my prey.

"Who am I?" I hiss through gritted teeth.

Colleen's glare might deter a lesser being, but I do not fear her wrath.

Her pupils grow larger. The raw tone of her voice bears a mark of the same hunger roiling within me. "My personal arrogant, aggressive kidnapper."

For the love of all the gods and goddesses who bless my Folk, this woman consumes me. She shows no fear. My bond-promised is built from might and grit to rival a warrior queen. The color on her face is as lush as a freshly split pomegranate. The sheen of sweat covering her body reflects flame from sconce and chandelier as if my bond-promised has been set alight for me.

I clamp fingers around her thighs and yank her beneath me. I am a cage and she, my captive.

With monumental restraint, I do not lower my body to hers, letting the wall of heat between us rage as wildly as our moods. Dipping my mouth to her ear, I clamp her lobe between my teeth. Words escape in a desperate rasp. "Who am I?"

I will not supply her with the answer that will calm the tempest in my blood. My bond-promised must name me, know me from the depths of her being. Until my true name comes from her spirit unprompted, my beast shall not be sated.

Double fists slam into my chest, catching me unawares and sending me onto my ass. She rises to her knees and cocks an arm back. Nature's bane, the woman aims to drive her fist between my eyes. Instead, she lunges at me to dig fingers into my thighs. Our furious glares lock. This is not resistance. It is a seductive battle.

I lift my chin in challenge. I have hungered for carnal pleasures but never been reduced to the starving fiend I become now.

I cannot quell this monstrous yearning to possess her completely. My true name upon her lips must prove to my raging soul we lay claim to one another.

To kill the madness that consumes me, Colleen must acknowledge and then reject Robálaí Geal to prevent the geas from taking hold and decimating us both. Forcing my body upon hers, the very thing she forbade me to do, will secure her hatred and protect her heart.

Lunging forward, trapping her once again between my arms until our faces are inches apart, I lock my unholy glare on her furious eyes. "Who... am...I?" I rave loud enough to rattle the polished granite walls of the bedchamber.

With the courage of a she-dragon, Colleen shows her teeth as she bellows. "You are Robálaí Geal, my fucking bond-promised."

She stretches the sound of my name like a curse, then gasps. I too lose the air in my lungs. The white surrounding Colleen's dove gray irises begins to swirl until light to rival the elegance of the Veil streams from her orbits straight into mine. There is a highway of brilliance fusing my astounded stare to hers.

"Robálaí Geal," she cries over and over.

My name upon her lips is the first sweet wine of early spring, the light of a full Veil moon upon a star-painted meadow, the sparkling sands welcoming the dawn tide of a Faerie sea. Within her voice lives my beating heart.

Tears burst from my eyes in a relentless torrent.

She is my life.

She promises to be the greatest pain I will ever know.

I must destroy her first to spare her the devastation of losing the love of the one she believes to be her soul's partner.

Colleen sinks her fingernails into my shoulders. Her breath is a desert wind on my face. "Robálaí," she calls out, this time to wake me from my trance.

My eyes focus to find hers aflame.

She stammers, clutching her heart. "What's happening?"

Confusion's blade sinks deep within my breast. Once the cut is made, clarity weeps from the wound.

The bond-promise speaks.

It is not merely a label, a title, or an agreement. It is awake and perceptive. Its binding is not a state to be set aside or dishonored. The bond-promise gives no heed to whether Colleen is human or I am Fae. It is the fusion of souls. The oath we swore out of necessity now demands to be embraced and acted upon, not in violence, but with reverence. It seizes our spirits with its blessed cataclysm.

The answer stalls in my throat. I must not explain but rather war against what has befallen us.

My wits tell me this is the single chance to overturn the destiny pulling us together in freefall. I cannot be soft. Colleen's consent that only moments ago I promised myself not to take from her, must be taken. There is no place for her tender feelings for me that our bond craves. If Colleen develops anything but hatred for me, that conclusion will be our ruin. Finnbheara and his geas have seen to it.

Her hands thread through my hair as if holding me in place will give her the answer she seeks to explain the gale building inside her…for me. I pray the storm has not yet broken, and there is still hope to send it off.

I embody the undesirable fiend she longed to detest before our oath and thrust her arms aside to loosen her grasp on me. Everything I do must disgust and spurn any drop of desire for me that my bond-promise struggles to rouse. I rip the tunic over my head, exposing my bare chest and the hideous scar blighting its flesh.

Colleen gasps at the mark of Finnbheara's displeasure. "My god. What happened to you?" She runs her fingers along the length of my scar before I snatch her hand away.

No. Her sympathy, her compassion, is the opposite of what I am trying to wring from her. I must be quick and merciless to milk hatred for me from her marrow.

I rise to my knees and grab Colleen's ass, forcing her naked body against me. Hot skin sizzles against hot skin.

"Robálaí, what are you doing?"

I thrust my hips to emphasize my words. "Fucking you."

I drop onto my ass and give her luscious cheeks a few squeezes before sliding my hands to her knees and forcing her to straddle me. Even through my britches, the length of my hot pulsing cock splits her folds.

She squeaks in surprise.

"Did you fool yourself that I had brought you here for any other reason than to use you, human?" I quickly raise and lower my hips in a barbarous stroke.

"You bastard." She slaps my shoulders.

I capture both her hands in one of mine. The rage in her eyes is exactly what I hoped for. "I will fuck you until you come and scream into my mouth instead of Aodh's filthy box and then leave you in this bed until I return to fuck you a hundred times. That is your only worth to me."

With her locked beneath one arm, I fumble with the ties on my britches with the other, hating every step closer to taking her against her will. It must be done. Her hatred born of my pitiless assault is all-important.

"You're a liar."

Her words halt my attempt to divest myself of clothing.

"A fucking Faerie liar."

My mouth hangs open in shock, allowing Colleen to crush her lips to mine and force her tongue into my mouth.

She groans through the kiss she initiated. "Why do you really need to fuck me, you Faerie liar?"

I try to push her off, but she clings to me, riding my still-clothed shaft. As much as I plead with my body not to make it so, her ardor fuels mine, and I dig my fingers into the flesh of her back. "I do not *need* to fuck you, human. My cock has earned the treat."

"Liar," she roars into my mouth.

Nature spare me, the savagery in her challenge drives my arousal close to ripping through the fabric of my britches to sink between her thighs. Colleen shifts to tug violently at my pants. The front seam splits, freeing my pulsing flesh.

"Why do you need to fuck me, Robálaí?" She forces my hand against her dripping cunt. "Tell me the truth." Colleen steals my finger and alongside one of hers guides both inside her.

"The need…is…not…mine," I groan as she slides our paired fingers in and out of her greedy opening. "It is the bond-promise. I cannot need you. I cannot want you."

Her teeth clamp onto my bottom lip. "Why do *you* need me, Robálaí?"

I force words through the taste of blood in my mouth. "I—DO—NOT."

Anguished tears come unbidden as I fight the tender words blooming in my soul. I will not scatter their blossoms over my bond-promised. The moment they meet the air, she will answer, and I shall be finished. Colleen will suffer from the decimation of my ardor. This desire that now consumes us will destroy her. She will never have me, but will yearn for my love until she takes her last breath. I am not the sole victim of Finnbheara's geas. It savages everyone who dares to seek my dead heart.

"Then why are you crying?" She opens her mouth, releasing her hold on me to run the tip of her nose through the tears drenching my cheeks.

"I am not."

She gives my hair a painful tug with her free hand. "Why do you need to fuck me?"

I growl through gritted teeth. "So, you will hate me."

This stills her, and she slides free of everywhere our bodies touch. "What?"

Her vulnerability renews my purpose, and I push her onto her back, separating her legs. "I will wrench hatred from you, body and soul," I bellow, taking my raging cock in hand, preparing to plunge inside her. There will be no tenderness. Only brutality.

I prepare to receive the brunt of her knee attempting to stop me, but instead she lays a gentle hand to the center of my scar. "Why do I have to hate you?"

The sight of my tears falling upon her breast and the delicate sound of her voice laced with so much gentleness and decency undoes me. I fall upon her, burying my face into her neck. "Because…damn my soul to the depths of Aodh's kingdom, I love you."

Love.

I love this woman.

Thoughts burn in my beleaguered mind. The first time I encountered Colleen, she was captivating in a way I had never encountered. Instead of possessing her for sport, I was drawn to explore the enticement. It was not only for the manipulation of Eala Duir that I continued to visit the peppered apple. I stole time to spend with Colleen alone, telling myself it was to strengthen the believability of our ploy. It was a lie. My bond-promised's presence held the foreign combination of curiosity and contentment for me that I found troublesome to resist. The pull toward her was inexplicably relentless.

Was my path to love this woman a cruel temptation from Finnbheara all along or something wholly unpredictable in the scheme of fate's amusement?

Colleen folds me in her arms, refusing to relinquish our contact. I still, focusing my entire spirit on this fleeting second of selflessly loving another before Finnbheara's geas murders our precious gift. That dreaded moment when every drop of true passion I feel for my bond-promised will be leached from my soul. A breath from now, because I dare to love, Colleen will pay the unrelenting price of a heartless mate.

"Robálaí, I lo—"

I lay my fingers across her lips and shake my head. She will hate herself for repeating the words I have spoken to her that will end us. "You must not speak the words."

She pulls my hand away. "If you won't let me say it, then let me show you what's in my heart. I give you my body willingly, Robálaí. There's no need to steal it."

Is it possible to share our bodies lovingly and be granted a few cherished moments before the geas finds me? A longing to worship and seal myself to my Colleen before my heart grows cold to her, chases the despair from my chest.

I roll onto my side, drawing her close, and slide a leg over her hip. I surrender in this battle between us and bow to the will of our bond-promise. Brushing a soft kiss against her lips, I welcome, however brief it may be, this beginning between us.

I ignore my fear of the oncoming emptiness the geas will visit upon me and give myself to my bond-promised. Not with the goal of cold satisfaction, but in celebration. A blessing of love for Colleen melts through my body. The sensation is foreign to me, yet every bit as welcome as a peaceful dawn after a perilous night of battle. I have never experienced such intensity of feeling or clarity of purpose in all the days of my long life. My affection for Acacia was a thin replica of this demand to be yoked to Colleen.

The bond-promise has birthed a new Robálaí Geal, and I do not yet know him. Yet, deep in my spirit, I believe Colleen knows him well.

"You are right, my love. There is no need for words," I say to Colleen, committing the sweetness of the word *love* lingering on my lips to a memory that in time the geas will transform into bitterness.

I caress her lips with my own. My savage lust is reborn as passion and longing. Just as the tip of her silky tongue meets mine, a violent pounding sounds on the door to the outer chamber. My inclination to ignore it is quickly extinguished when I recognize Acacia's desperate cry.

"Robálaí, come quickly. Our *péist síoda* are dying."

CHAPTER 21
THE FAERIE KING'S DAUGHTER

EALA

Of all the imagined dangers I conjured in my head during my travels with Sion, the reality of Grace's dagger against my throat tops them all. Now that I'm smack dab in the situation myself, every movie where the captive pulls off some fancy reversal move seems ludicrous. There's not a damn thing I can do but freeze and pray my blood isn't about to gush down the front of my dress.

Biddy's weight shifts as she starts to make a move. I stretch my eyes wide to hold her in place. Every sense tells me to let the Pirate Queen call the shots here. If she intended to kill us, she'd have signaled to her crew by now.

I hope.

I've never had to second-guess a bloodthirsty pirate before.

Grace O'Malley hisses in my ear. "I've oft wondered if the Fae bleed red."

A wide-eyed Biddy raises the blue bottle to her lips.

"Silence, witch. You'll find my blade is swifter than any spell."

"Please," I choke. "Decline our bargain if you must, but do not make a widower of my beloved husband." I feel cold metal against my skin. At the moment, it's the flat of her blade, not a lethal edge or point. I debate if the Veil can save me faster than the slice of the pirate's dagger. How did Sion survive two hundred years of his life being in constant danger?

Grace's stale breath slithers across my ear and cheek. "Listen well, I know the odor of treachery and betrayal. If such stench rises from you, Faerie, I'll have my answer as to the color of your blood."

"Understood," I manage to croak.

Grace's rough voice continues to spill into my ear. "For the sake of my son, I'll go with you, Faerie, but hear me well. At the first sign of mischief to myself from you or the witch, my blade will find its way back to this very spot." She jerks the arm beneath my breasts, caging me even tighter. "No tricks. Have I your word?"

It doesn't seem as if my word holds much worth, but if giving her what she asks calms her the hell down, she'll get it. "You have my promise. I won't keep secrets or intentions from you, and you'll retain free will to continue in our company or return home." The way the skin of my neck bumps the knife as I speak is incredibly disconcerting.

Grace grunts in response and, to my great relief, stabs the knife in Biddy's direction while keeping an iron-clad hold on me. "What of your word, witch?"

Biddy cackles. It's the witchiest sound I've heard her make. I feel a shiver run through Grace.

"Oh, you've my word to be sure," says Biddy with the nonchalance of enjoying a joke at a tea party. "But I might ask you, Mistress O'Malley, have you ever heard the tale of the pirate and the Faerie king's daughter?"

I flash *what the hell are you doing* eyes at Biddy, who remains unbothered.

"I have not," says Grace, bringing the knife back to my throat.

Biddy turns the blue bottle over in her hands. "As a show of good faith, I'll tell it now, to save you from the mistake you're making as we stand here. Does that suit you?"

"Speak, witch."

"First, you should consider removing your blade from the throat of this particular Faerie king's daughter." Biddy gestures to me.

When Grace's knife hand trembles, I see the tiniest flashes in my vision as I hit my limit of being brave. A momentary reprieve comes when the Pirate Queen lowers the blade and shoves me toward the bed. She blocks the door, now brandishing a sword. I grab the bedpost to steady myself, preparing to call the Veil if our visit goes any further downhill.

Biddy presses a reassuring hand between my shoulder blades as she speaks in a steady voice. "Surely you've heard of *Tuatha Dé Danann*?"

Grace narrows her eyes. "As have we all. Folk of the mounds, the Fae."

"Well," Biddy swipes her hand through the air in a careless gesture. "Royal Fae bloodlines exist within each of their separate kingdoms. The difference from monarchs in our world is that both sons and daughters are equally revered by the Folk. Some of the fiercest warriors of the ages are Faerie queens."

Grace nods. "Aye, Queen Mebh is known to me."

"So it goes, King Finnbheara of the Connacht Fae and his Queen, Nuala, were blessed with seventeen sons but no daughters. That might have been the way of it, but crafty ole Finnbheara possessed a magic known as the *beads of being*. One day, a former lover came to the king and pleaded with him to use his magic of creation to bring forth a child who would answer to both the Fae and human worlds."

I gape at Biddy. Why is she telling my story as a cautionary tale to Grace? I'm no threat.

"The king agreed and melded his essence with the *beads of being*. To his delight, this magic brought forth a daughter, the first princess of Tír na nÓg, who bore the grace of a swan and the stout heart of the mighty oak. To protect his cherished child, he placed upon her a powerful charm. Any who tried to harm the girl would find their body withering like the bark of the old tree. They'd soon become forever cursed as trunk and bough turned to stone where they stood."

With this last tidbit, Grace checks her hands then lifts a worried gaze to the storyteller.

"The girl was given to Finnbheara's former lover with the promise that the Faerie daughter would return to his kingdom once her purpose in the land of mortals was fulfilled. She grew into a woman of great beauty and courage. All who met her loved her as she brought light into the lives of those she touched."

Grace eyes me, clearly questioning her initial fear that I'm said Faerie king's daughter since her hands aren't withering or turning to stone.

"When the time came for the princess to return to her father's house, there was a rift between the regal pair, and she was shunned from the land of her making. The royal miss sought the aid of many with both natural and unnatural gifts to help her return home. Those who stood by her side were rewarded greatly, but there were two, a fallen priest and a pirate who wished her ill."

Grace touches the tip of her sword to the floor. "If the princess…parted ways with the Faerie king, surely his charm over her would no longer claim potency." She tosses me a glance dripping with sarcasm.

Biddy clucks. "So might one believe but ask the stone tree called *Priest's Trial* that rises on the road to Kilkee in County Clare if this is so."

The corrupted priest Jeremy Olk should be so lucky to have ended up as a stone tree instead of sludge dripping through Finnbheara's fisted fingers.

Grace frowns at Biddy. "And what becomes of the pirate and the Faerie king's daughter as your tale is so named?"

My witchy friend raises the blue bottle beneath her chin, casting a creepy glow across her face. "Ah, the ending of that tale is now left in your hands, Granuaile O'Malley."

For dramatic effect, I stare at Grace and rub the spot on my throat where her knife touched my skin.

Grace's gaze flicks between Biddy and me, her skepticism shifting into what I hope is a healthy dose of fear. She catches me completely off guard when the Pirate Queen drops into a deep curtsy, gaze locked to the carpet. "I beg your pardon, Eala of the Fae, for the false threat to your person. I swear there was no dastardly intent in the doing."

Biddy whispers in my ear, "Lucky for us, those who sail upon the sea are a superstitious lot."

Grace's voice is strained. "'Twas but to gain assurance of my own well-being."

I swallow to relieve the clench in my throat. "I respect that and choose in this instance to believe no true harm was intended." When Grace raises her head to meet my gaze, I bust out my stoniest expression. "I will not assume the same a second time."

The Pirate Queen's shoulders twitch. I silently applaud Biddy's brilliance. Even though I admitted to being Fae and Biddy demonstrated the strength of her spells, Grace still chose to hold a knife to my throat. The wise witch knew how to get right to the heart of our target's fear by sharing an impromptu tale that foretold unpleasant magical consequences.

It's something Sion would do.

Will I ever be able to read people as expertly as he and Biddy?

It's a strange feeling being the subject of a tale, even one made up on the spot. I'd prefer my story to feature a run of the mill human college folklore professor and the chronicle of her life with an equally normal curly-headed Irish farmer husband. Neither travel through time or become a fox or a swan when need arises. Fae, druids, underworld gods, and all manner of terrifying weaponry would remain confined to the pages of books.

I stare at the piece of living history bowing before me. Who am I kidding? I've faced paralyzing fear, possible death, losing my soulmate, and dickering dangerously with time, but the beauty, wonder, and magic in this journey go beyond the fantastic. I've seen things and met people that shouldn't be real, yet they are. Each encounter has made my life richer and changed me from a mouse into…maybe not a lion, but at least a much braver soul.

At the core of everything I've experienced, is the man who inspires me to embrace this bigger life I've fallen into.

Sion once asked me to take a single step with him and left it to me to take another.

I will take every step for you—with you, my dearest anamchara.

"Put your weapons away, Granuaile O'Malley," I say with authority. "And shore yourself up to journey through time."

Grace won't budge from the trunk of the yew tree behind the cottage. She let a few moments of amazement slip through her tough gal shell while we were inside the Veil. As soon as we arrived here and the first car drove by, she fell apart. The pirate keeps to the shadows, her posture tense and alert. I suspect she's considering where to bolt as if there were any place the privateer could escape to.

My patience is running thin. We should be inside with Biddy brainstorming a strategy to use Grace's navy to free Sion from Tír na nÓg.

I'm woefully unprepared for the fresh spike of fear brought about by the combination of frustration and gloomy visions of Sion's fate. I nearly double over and am forced to lean on the whitewashed wall for support.

I plan to get Sionnach out, but I have no idea how coming home will affect him. He's lived in the human world for two hundred years, but his time was controlled by Finnbheara. What if the king decides not to give Sion any more years outside of Tír na nÓg? I've got to factor that variable and Finnbheara's ego into our plan. What price will the king demand to leave us in peace?

From her post at the yew's trunk, Grace grumbles yet another curse about the evil of this place. That, coupled with my own worries, sets me off. "Oh, for heaven's sake, there's nothing evil waiting to sink its teeth in you. You're supposed to be the pinnacle of bravery."

Biddy was so easy, I deluded myself into believing Grace's adjustment would be just as successful. Of course, a witch would be quicker to accept the trappings of magic than a boots-on-the-ground pirate. Before Grace answers, I stalk to the tree, sword be damned, and jab a finger toward the road. "As I said before, they're called cars or trucks or who the hell cares." I shove aside the strand of hair sticking to my forehead. "They are not alive. The sound you hear is a motor, a device that allows them to move."

When I'm met with nothing but an unreadable stare from my guest, I pace in front of her, twirling my hands as I seek an explanation to drag her from behind the tree. "You use plenty of mechanics to hoist your sails or lift heavy cargo. Motors are just improvements on what you already know." I gesture at the road again. "These vehicles, ah…vessels are metal ships that don't need sails, nothing sinister."

Damn, I hope I can coax her into the cottage before a plane flies overhead.

She looks weary but maintains her tight-lipped demeanor and a firm hand on her *scian*.

What can I say or do short of shaking the pirate to knock her belligerent peg out of its snug hole? I want to slap my forehead when the answer comes to me. Where has my kindness gone? I think back on how terrified I was the first time Sion ripped me from my time into another. I barely functioned. My only strength was him at my side.

Who does Grace have? A near-frantic Faerie woman whom she has absolutely no reason to trust. Yes, I've promised her something dear, but as I learned in my travels, the concept of leaving your time and the reality of doing it are two entirely different things.

I reach a hand to Mistress O'Malley. Instead of chiding her like a freshman, angling for a grade they haven't earned, I owe her respect. This is a person used to being in charge, not relying on complete unknowns to rule her destiny.

As the Pirate Queen did before me in her castle, I drop into a curtsy.

"Granuaile O'Malley, I traveled through the ages to seek you above all others. Your deeds shine not with the greed often associated with pirates, but with loyalty to your kinsman." I pin my stare on hers. "You've walked dangerous paths, fought many a foe, and sailed vast oceans no woman before you dared. I am in awe of your intelligence, your courage, and the unshakeable honor you hold for those you love." I smile up at her. "If I haven't stated so before, these are the reasons I've taken you from your home, your time, your people. You bring with you the hope I fear is slipping away from me. With you by my side, that hope may be reclaimed."

I pray my speech is period adjacent enough to her timeline to make sense.

She studies me then gives a curt nod. "Pretty words are oft meant to distract, but I hear truth in yours."

I rise to face her. "I vowed not to lie to you, and will explain as clearly as I can the strange circumstances you find yourself in. You have my solemn promise I shall make all haste to return you to your home."

Again, I speak Sion's words that gave me the courage to overcome my fear.

"I'm asking you to take a single step with me. If you can bear that one, then take another."

She sizes up this latest request. Her sword sings as Grace returns it to her scabbard.

"Aye, I suppose I can do such." I expect relief but earn a scowl instead. I'm beginning to wonder if she ever smiles. "Here's a bit of advice. Do not name my hesitation as cowardice again. I've not collected victories from leaping headfirst into danger without first understanding the peril." She waves a hand over the fields. "You might have stolen me into Fae territory or other places I cannot guess," she scoffs. "I listened to the earth, the wind, and the sea just there." Grace gestures toward the cliffs. "I waited for their call, and once it came, 'twas in a language I know, saying all is well."

And idiot me thought she was hiding from a car. I won't underestimate the depths of this woman again. What she says is true. Grace O'Malley wouldn't be a legend if she'd led a careless, impulsive life. Talk about a sixth sense. The Pirate Queen probably has a seventh, eighth, and ninth sense as well.

"I apologize." I almost tell her that I should take a page from her book, but reframe the idiom. "I should follow your example instead of giving in to my lack of patience."

When I start around the side of the cottage to the front door, Grace follows.

"Granuaile, as you said back on Clare Island, maybe our situation would be more palatable if you believe it to be a strange dream. You'll be assured the time will come when you wake to the world as it should be. One where you are preparing to meet Queen Elizabeth and successfully free your son."

The dawn breeze dances through her hair. Thick strands shine crimson from the first hint of the rising sun. It gives Grace a carefree and less hardened appearance.

"Oft times…" I start my sentence with 'oft times' because when am I going to be able to use it again without sounding pretentious? "…I wish to believe all that's happening to me is a dream."

She scuffs her boots in the dirt. "I suppose I never imagined Faeries would seek the help of humans. In tales, they fancy themselves a superior lot."

A chuckle breaks through my pout. "That's the truth. They don't run short on arrogance." I step aside as we approach the red door of the cottage. "Granuaile O'Malley, you are very welcome to my home."

Grace sighs as she glares at the door. "And what new strangeness will I find inside your home?"

What won't be strange to her? The stone hearth? The natural plant-filled mattress? The list pretty much ends there.

I plunge into a recitation that begins with indoor plumbing and the refrigerator and ends with a description of my computer and cell phone, insisting they're not witchcraft. After constant interruptions from multiple piratical grunts, disbelieving comments, and a bounty of questions, Grace agrees to come inside.

"'Tis a dream, if need be," she repeats over and over as we enter the cottage.

Biddy, bless her, has a savory soup simmering on the hearth which still maintains the trappings of its original cooking capabilities from Máthair's time, such as metal arms and an iron pot. Grace prowls the cottage, squinting longer at some things, like the electric can opener and television, than others. There's a lot of head shaking and muttering.

Biddy takes particular delight in demonstrating the toilet. Done with her assessment of the place, Grace drags one of the two kitchen chairs over to the hearth to eat her meal, keeping weapons close at hand.

After dinner and a somewhat stilted conversation, the two women sleep, exhausted from what I've put them through. Biddy claims the bed, and Grace the couch. I stay awake at the kitchen table, pounding the keys of my computer. I've reached the state beyond exhaustion where sleep is as unwelcome as staying awake.

Given the days Sion and I lost when we slept while trying to solve Finnbheara's riddle, I'm terrified to drift off. What if I wake in a week or a month, or heaven help me, years from now in Faerie time? I tremble at dark thoughts of everything awful that could happen to Sion. Will Finnbheara beat him? Imprison him? Send him to wander alone in whatever wilds exist in Tír na nÓg? Would Faerie beasts decide Sionnach was food? Dwelling on these what-ifs is a recipe for a meltdown.

What about Colleen? Is time as unrelatable in the underworld as it is in other Fae realms?

I eye the stack of books with the sticky notes I've slapped on any page mentioning Tír na nÓg or Finnbheara's army or navy. I only found references to famous fictional battles in Irish mythological cycles. Specific numbers are never mentioned, just broad terms like *scores*, *legions*, or *multitudes*. Every map is a place in Ireland where these wars are said to have taken place. Once the *Tuatha De Danann* disappeared into the mounds, any new information pretty much dried up except in penned mortal fictions.

At dawn, Biddy lays a hand on my shoulder. "Have you found much?"

I snap at her. "Nothing of any use."

The toilet flushes, and Grace exits the bathroom, looking very pleased. I'm quite the short-tempered shrew as I bark at her. "How many people and ships will you command when we sail to Tír na nÓg?"

Her glare at my clear disrespect shifts toward anger, but then she zeroes in on the dark circles under my eyes and the sloppy braid I've twisted into my hair. Grace purses her lips. "Twenty or thereabouts vessels." She chews her bottom lip as she calculates. "Five or six thousand hands at best."

Six thousand. Where does that number fall in *legions*, *scores*, or *multitudes*?

I drop my head to the table. "I have no clue how many Folk Finnbheara has at his disposal. It could be six or sixty thousand."

Biddy steps in. "I heard wee chickens out the back window this morning." She looks at Grace. "Care to help me gather eggs for a fry?"

I fling a hand toward the rear of the cottage. "There's a coop down the path."

The two women practically fly out the door. Grace mutters something about surly Faeries.

I'm a shitty leader.

Why did I drag Biddy and Grace into this before I had any semblance of a real strategy? Biddy's magic and Grace's savvy are definite assets, but to what? I imagined once I'd gathered allies, their insights would lead me to formulate a plan. This challenge is a thousand times more enigmatic than Finnbheara's damned riddle. My need to find Sion is clear. Biddy and Grace's gifts are evident. It's my inability to put everything together that's failing.

I physically ache for any connection to Sion. When I open the door, Alfie's shivering leaves greet me. Percussive rhythms of waves splitting over massive offshore rocks and the sugary fragrance of sweet pea climbing a trellis near the corner of the cottage calm me enough to concentrate. My need for even the slightest glimpse of Sion consumes me. Pressing my key tattoo against her closest trunk, I pray this *Crann na Beatha* will show me another vision of my love.

For a moment, the twisting ribbons of Sion's essence float within mine then Alfie begins to waver as if she's made of water from a gentle stream. Gold threads undulate through her trunks and roots down into the earth.

"*Teach orm.*" I whisper the words in Irish etched into my wedding ring that once belonged to my grandmother, then repeat them in English. "Find me, Sionnach."

No vision of my *anamchara* appears. Instead, a jolt of urgency stabs me in the ribs. My eyes snap open as I clutch my chest. The Tree of Life's message is clear. I'm running out of time.

As shadows deepen and the start of the Celtic day draws near, Grace shares stories with Biddy near the hearth about dodging the English ships by hiding in the many coves and nooks around Clew Bay. I'll bet that's what she was doing when we passed through the door in the Giant's Lair to find her. At least she's not grousing about a mad Faerie woman who captured her out of time to bore her to death. Grace's rough storytelling cadence and delightfully foul language distract me from my fruitless research.

The Pirate Queen's tale grows even bawdier as the subject shifts to husbands and other sexual conquests. "Men deem themselves lords of the land and sea." She gives a hearty chuckle. "But once you get 'em on their backs and climb on board, their sword is at your mercy." Grace grabs her crotch as lewdly as any man fondling his package. "Women must never be afraid to seize what's theirs by rights." She grins, a gleam shining in her eyes.

Ah, so she does smile, just not at me, the Fae who stole her from her bed into my lair of abject futility.

They notice me lurking. "Biddy, can we show Grace the magical map you conjured at the Giant's Lair? Maybe she'll pick up on something we missed."

"Magical map, is it?" asks Grace in a tone that doesn't hide her skepticism.

She eyes the blue bottle with concern as she fidgets in the chair she's kept near the hearth.

After my failure with Alfie, do I dare ask Biddy to search harder for the Gem Kissed forest to try and see Sion? I decide not to. It will kill me if she finds the place and he isn't there. What if the shadow of my *anamchara* on the surface of the *lough* was nothing more than my psyche placating a lonely heart?

I may be able to travel through time, combine essences, communicate with a *fánaí* tree, and set the occasional Viking axe on fire, but none of those abilities are proving to be of any use in saving my husband. I'm doing everything in *my* Fae power, but clearly, it's not enough.

There *is* a Faerie I may have access to who possesses powers I lack.

No, I won't go there. It's foolish and dangerous.

Witch magic saturates the cottage in sapphire. Biddy's eyes are unfocused as the same map she conjured before of Tír na nÓg shines in the air above the blue bottle. Grace clutches her chest but doesn't take her eyes off the image.

"Does anything strike a chord with you, Granuaile?" She doesn't answer.

I approach the map of the island and study it for new details. There are none.

Biddy begins to wobble from the strain of sustaining the map, and I thread my arm through hers, adding my magic to increase her wattage.

"Gem Kissed Forest. Sionnach Loho." I chant, hoping my words have some effect.

The map gives up no secrets.

Biddy feels even more unstable, so I slide my arm around her back. "It's okay, Biddy. Let it go."

With a shaky hand, the witch stoppers her blue bottle, and I settle her on the couch.

Grace points to where Biddy's map hung in the room. "I've seen beasts of the sea to make the heart skip a beat, but the likes of that could stop it altogether."

Biddy tugs at my sleeve. "A bit of water if you please, Eala."

Rushing into the kitchen, I skid to a stop in front of a certain drawer.

The map failed us. My research failed us. My magic failed us. Despite my reservations, the time has come to consider the unthinkable. I yank open the drawer where I stashed the gold ring that's covered with etchings of waves and flowers. When I raise the band to study it more closely, firelight sets the metal ablaze.

He may be the most untrustworthy being above or below the earth, but if anyone has a score as massive to settle against Finnbheara as I do…

When I close my fist around the ring, the Veil sprites within me spin into clusters of tiny spirals. This battle to save Sion is one I was never going to win, even with the resources of a willing witch and a pirate queen. As much as I loathe what I know I must do, there is no other choice.

I will call Robber Bright.

CHAPTER 22
THE ATROCITY

ROBBER BRIGHT

Our *péist síoda*…dying?

This cannot be.

Colleen shoves me away, her expression as haunted as my own, but her voice is all command. "Go open the damn door, Robálaí."

My gaze whips between my bond-promised and Acacia's terrified cries.

"It's okay," says Colleen, shoving my tunic against my chest.

I grab her chin to bring her face to mine. "Whatever I do and say from this moment forward, believe these words are my deepest truth. I do love you with the very essence of my being, my cherished bond-promised. Time, fate, and a vengeful king may attempt to tear it from my heart, but it will never truly be gone, only sleeping." I kiss her fiercely, leaving her confused and gasping for breath as I pull away, racing around the room for britches without a split crotch and my boots.

It destroys me to do so, but protecting her is all-important, even if, when I next look upon my love, this fire in my breast for her will burn no longer. Finnbheara's geas licks its greedy jaws, waiting to spring.

Even as I begin to speak the words of the charm to spare Colleen the fear of dwelling in Aodh's kingdom, she shakes her head, as unwilling to break from me as I am from her. "Are you not in need of a charm for your comfort?"

She holds up a hand. "No. I'll be fine. Come back as soon as you can, and we'll figure out what comes next."

"Do not leave these rooms," I warn and dash for the door, sparing a final glance at the woman who will ruin my heart for all time. "Goodbye, my love."

Every moment the geas fails to find me is an agony, knowing all too soon, it will murder the love that has awakened a heart I thought forever spoiled.

The bed chamber door slams behind me as I throw open the main door to my quarters. Acacia's lovely sun-darkened skin is as pale as a milk flower blossom above her crimson armor. She flies at me, clutching handfuls of my tunic as she pushes me back into the room.

"Armor yourself."

I do not question the advice of my second, but I must know the reason. "Why?"

"Our resolution may not come without crossed swords."

I heave the metal breastplate over my head, snatching the wide bands that cover my forearms from elbow to wrist, a gift from Aodh, and my sword before following her into the corridor.

She hastens before me. "This is the swiftest way to the dragons."

With a final backward glance at the chamber door separating me from the woman I will harbor no morsel of love for when next I see her, I hurry after Acacia. We race to a curved stone staircase of the same blood red marble as the walls. "Acacia, please detail your grave tidings."

She swallows great mouthfuls of air, attempting to speak as we run. My warriors always keep to the utmost standards of physical condition. Her shortness of breath proves she came with all speed to fetch me.

"I sent word for Artos to tactfully alert the Host to armor and meet us at the dragon pens without drawing Aodh's eye."

Notes of warning fill my mind. "Why the pens and not the dragon hold?"

We hit the bottom of the stairs and speed down a corridor toward great glass doors infused with chips of red. "It is the breeding site of Aodh's *péist lasrach*, his flame dragons."

"No," I hiss. My stomach feels as if it turns to brittle glass, dreading her next words.

"Aodh's dragon masters are forcing their beastly drakes to breed with our drakainas."

The glass in my gut shatters, and my spirit becomes a butchered mass of cuts and blood.

"It is a horror, Robálaí, an atrocity. The species are not meant to be compatible, no matter the darkest spells the king's dragon masters attempt."

I am all sickness, disgust, and unfettered rage. My step falters, but Acacia drags me forward. We pass the outbuildings of the castle. In the near distance, across a field of deep russet grass, I see an enormous enclosure of gleaming black stone.

"This unholy mating is killing every *péist síoda* forced to submit to this horror."

As she speaks, the high-pitched death wail of a dragon pierces the air. It is not brief or cut short. The agonized keen continues to rise and fall as we draw closer. "Gods of the ancient ones," I cry out. "Will no one spare the creature?"

Acacia's tone is the thrust of a blade. "You have brought the unthinkable upon us, allowing our blessed dragons to fall into Aodh's keeping."

I am fueled by the agony of the cry and increase my speed. Acacia stays at my flank as I shout. "I would forfeit my life before allowing such wickedness. Aodh presses his advantage in the worst of ways."

A fresh wave of trepidation seizes my body, threatening to break bones. "Eachna and Aillil?" If Aodh dared to lay his fetid, charred touch upon my dragon, he will be the one splitting the air with his death song.

"No, thank nature in her goodness," says Acacia, and breath returns to my body.

As we swing around the corner of the long wall of the enclosure, we reach my Host, bloodlust and mayhem burning in their eyes. They are massed at the gate, a unit of Aodh's brutish soldiers blocking the way. Step by step, my Host closes in on the Bráchthine monoliths. The Host of a Thousand Wings are fearsome warriors, but I have not yet taken the full measure of Aodh's fighters.

"Hold," I command.

The Host halts their forward motion but continues to rumble with agitation like water threatening to boil over the rim of a cookpot.

My high command falls in behind me, all fully armored and reeking of battle fever. I advance, fists raised to the sky. "I am Robálaí Geal, a general who serves your king. You will open this gate. My lieutenants and I insist on entering your killing ground."

The ashy, charred skin of the largest soldier bulges over the edges of his forearm bands that bear the same pattern of bars and slashes as do the ones I wear. Quickly scanning the rest of the Bráchthine unit, I note no others are so adorned. He is of my rank, thus rendering us on equal footing.

I forge ahead to vanquish his refusal with a bluff. "Aodh has given me leave to oversee the breeding of my *péist síoda* with his *péist lasrach*." The phrase alone causes bile to rise in my throat. "Do I send my swiftest messenger to inform the king you take it upon yourself to rescind his assignment?" I raise a hand and snap my fingers. Immediately, a courier appears at my side. The Bráchthine thugs may appear to be chunks of hewn rock, but we are cannier soldiers with our arsenal of subterfuge and illusion.

"Order your Host back to barracks first," says my nemesis.

"You," I sneer in his face. "Do not command me."

I raise my hand again, and my runner readies to spring on his way to carry my complaint to Aodh.

A trickle of ash slides down the face of Aodh's general as he begins to smolder with a shadowed orange glow beneath his cracked flesh. "Only you and your high command may enter." The fool is reckless enough to clamp his scalding hand on the shoulder plate of my armor. "I shall cut down your Host if they make a single move to follow."

I thrust my arm up against his with enough force to send him stumbling. His shining red eyes widen, surprised at my strength. "What you perceive as willowy does not equate to weakness, General," I snarl as my four most trusted and I pass through the gates into a nightmare.

We face a large central pen with smaller pens around its perimeter. In the corner closest to us, four of Aodh's soldiers drag vicious-looking rakes through a steaming puddle of once beautiful iridescent scales and the tattered remains of cerulean silk wings.

Nettle gags as Artos unleashes curses both common and ancient.

It takes much of my wherewithal to hold my shock over this desecration at bay.

Acacia's horrified gasp and grip on my wrist pull my attention away from the tragedy before us. "Robálaí, stop them."

I follow her line of sight to the action in the far corner. Two of Aodh's dragon masters, marked by their armor of black and red scales mimicking *péist lasrach* dragon hide, attempt to soothe one of our beloved silk dragon females as a male flame dragon approaches her. The *péist síoda's* cry of distress sets off every primal attack instinct in my body.

The ground beneath me blurs as I streak toward the dragons. The *péist lasrach* drake raises high on muscled legs. Within its distended cock, the color of ash and shadow, a line of flaming seed surges from its base to tip.

I hurl a burst of magic at the drake. It hits the mark, and Aodh's creature is flung backward. A river of its molten seed sprays, coating the bastard's cock. It thrashes, attempting to rid itself of the burn.

Turning to the two dragon masters, I raise my weapon. "Remove your vile hands from my *péist síoda,* or I will roast your fucking cocks."

The men drop their ropes and flee. I rush to the dragon's side and throw my arms around her neck. Rubbing my face against her snout, I croon words of comfort in dragon speak as I stroke her.

She begins to calm. Suddenly, the dragon seizes violently then collapses. Her triple-spaded tail hits the ground with a deafening *slap*. I am aware of feet running toward me as I dive beside the fallen dragon. There is a massive scarlet-orange flash from inside her great body. The drakaina's scales flare far too hot to touch without scorching my flesh.

I try to reach for the suffering creature anyway, but am restrained by Artos and Nettle.

"You cannot save her," says Ciallmhar in a voice laced with deep sorrow. In a smooth and graceful movement, he cleaves the neck of the she-dragon, ending her suffering.

My soul is blackened with the knowledge we were too late to prevent Aodh's foul drake from claiming her. My assault only prevented a second invasion of his murderous, flaming cock.

We stand together as one, watching helplessly as the body of our cherished silk dragon melts into a pool of gore.

From what they perceive as a safe distance behind us, I hear the tutting of the dragon masters. "That drakaina was the sturdiest stock of all their females. Thought she would withstand the seeding."

The second humphs. "I think next, a smaller male flame beast with less robust seed."

"I think not. We will test their silk drake with one of our females."

I spin with the speed of a hurricane and clamp a hand around each of their throats. "This is the last of the *péist síoda* you will ever lay your rotted touch upon, abominable butchers."

As I squeeze, their pupils turn a sickly gray and their red irises begin to drain of color. I'm aware of my high command shouting my name, but they might as well be on the far side of the red glass mountains. I will kill these fiends as brutally as they slayed my blessed dragons.

I rage at them. "If my blade held fire, I would drive it up your asses to melt every organ within your cursed bodies so that you may endure the same death you inflict."

Their hands claw at mine, but vengeance gives me the strength of a god until a merciless blow from behind sends me to my knees. The walls of the dragon pen whirl. Glare from the blood-orange underworld sun sends streaks through my wavering vision, then blackness overtakes me.

The red I see upon my waking is not Bráchthine's false sun. Blood taints my vision from the gash above my right eye. The wound, as well as a collection of others, is courtesy of Aodh's metal gauntlet. The red-flecked obsidian simmering beneath his throne room floor compounds every blight on my body with stinging heat.

"You render my mightiest drake unbreedable then seek to strangle my dragon masters."

My ribs are the next recipient of the Dark Prince's boot.

"Shall I deem you the mad general, or are you merely the stupidest Fae in all of Bráchthine?"

I wipe blood from the corner of my mouth with the back of my hand. "Neither my king," I rasp.

"Your king." Aodh spits on the floor next to me and stalks to his swan throne.

I clear my throat. "Is my thrashing complete then, majesty?"

He whips back around to face me before ascending the steps, metal boots screeching against the thick glass floor. I brace for an encore of his displeasure. I have been thrice verbally dressed down and beaten for my trio of offenses: insolence at deceiving his general at the dragon pens, inciting my Host to potential violence, and interfering with his ghastly breeding atrocity.

I rise to my feet as I have done between each of his onslaughts.

He wags a menacing finger at me. "There exists a fine line between boldness and idiocy, General Geal."

After bobbing my head in a shallow bow, I straighten my dented armor. I crave a soothing drink of cool, fresh water from the stream behind my cottage in the Gem Kissed Forest. "Is it your desire to employ a general who will not defend his Host and their dragons? If that is what you deem as idiocy, then name me an idiot."

As he returns to his royal seat, flames dance in his eye sockets. It is boldness the king expects of me, so boldness I shall give.

"It was not in our agreement that you destroy my *péist síoda*."

He waves a dismissive hand at me and lounges on his throne. "Your failure to supply Finnbheara's Treasure forfeited your dragons. There is neither contract nor agreement on the fate of those beasts. I use the creatures at my pleasure."

I stride to the foot of the stairs leading to his throne. "Then let us strike such an understanding now. You will guarantee that any of my dragons forced into your keeping will not be used as chattel for your *péist lasrach* to fuck and kill." I fix him with a violent glare, that of a warrior unafraid to slay an enemy.

"Have you no foresight, General? Imagine the spawn of a *péist síoda* and a *péist lasrach*." A glob of blackened drool trails from the corner of his cinder-coated lips. "Think of it. The speed and agility of your silk dragons combined with the incendiary fire of my flame dragons would create the destructive power of the mightiest lightning strike. Together, our beasts will create a cavalry as potent as a vengeful god."

"You delude yourself. This despicable experiment is naught but a death sentence to my dragons. Nothing more than your greed-blinded folly."

Aodh rises to his feet, hand on the hilt of his great black sword. "You forget yourself, Robálaí Geal." He examines his handiwork on my face then smirks, convinced of his superiority, and sits. Relaxing once again against the breast of the likeness of a carved black swan, he peers haughtily down at me. Aodh drones on in a voice full of mockery. "Was it not you who sought a place in my kingdom after inviting the ire of Finnbheara?" He drums thick fingers on the arm of the throne. "If our situation does not please you, who is next on your royal roster, sir? Will you seek acceptance from the monarchs of Munster or Leinster once you've been expelled from Bráchthine?"

It is ill-advised, but I laugh. "And you forget yourself, Dark Prince. Do you not need my counsel and knowledge to best Finnbheara, the adversary you wish to destroy? Since there is no other queen to steal, it is only with force you will vanquish him."

Aodh sputters, and I am relieved my brazenness has indeed brought this king in check on our gameboard.

He recovers all too easily. "Not a queen, but a white swan, and her *beads of being* are the prize you promised. Eala Duir is the answer for me to create an army in the image of Aodh. It is by my hand and my issue we will vanquish the tyrannical king of Tír na nÓg."

Aodh upends the gameboard, and I am once again stripped of my advantage.

"You try my goodwill, Robálaí Geal. Soon, the price of your dragons will be insufficient. Perhaps your lovely second, the warrior Acacia, or…" He licks his flabby, chapped lips. "…your bond-promised will stay my anger at your inability to bring me Finnbheara's Treasure."

Does Aodh know he exploits my greatest weakness? "Defiling a bond-promise will bring a curse upon you, King Aodh."

"Fidelity is not an absolute in a bond-promise if a player is willing." He chuckles. "You know this well, Robálaí."

The urge to maim raises corded muscles across my arms and shoulders. I must not let Aodh see the toll Colleen's safety takes on me. Revealing the true depth of my devotion to my bond-promised weakens my position.

I force my attention back to Aodh and his treachery, already despising myself for the bait I shall dangle. "Aye, perhaps the threat of sullying my bond-promised would increase Eala Duir's urgency to come treat for her friend's release."

Aodh startles at this. "You would trade your bond-promised to lure Finnbheara's swan?"

I bow to keep from looking at this devil. "Only as a final resort to fulfilling my oath to you, my king."

It is vile treachery for me to speak of using Colleen as barter. Fate's worse punishment is too good for me.

Nature, forgive me, but since Eala fails to summon me, my ability to stall

Aodh from acting forcefully against my Host is perilously weakened. I truly believed her need to rescue Colleen from me, the Fae she hates more than even Finnbheara, would have brought her begging at my door by now.

I swore to Colleen not to harm Eala, but that may be a vow I cannot keep. The pact to present Finnbheara's Treasure to Aodh was key to accomplishing my purpose here. With the threat and shadow of Bráchthine's king fouling the very air around me, there may be no alternative but to sacrifice the white swan. If it comes to a decision to preserve Eala Duir versus Colleen and the Host of a Thousand Wings, my choice is already made.

And that choice will lead me into ruin.

CHAPTER 23
THE DECAY

SIONNACH

I listen at the door for the length of a preacher's Sunday sermon. I've known fear in my time. And a fair number of other lifetimes as well, but I've never been the fearful soul who's taken up residence in my skin since the ambush in the clearing. I huff, sending a spiral of dust into the air.

Real or not, the encounter sent a clear message: I'm no match for magic. That bald truth reduced a massive chunk of my confidence to rubble. I hate myself for jumping at every creak of a board or scratch of a branch. I'm less than I was before.

With my ear pressed to the wooden door, I only hear the familiar scrabbling of wee beasties through the brush. I call these critters rabbits since they've mostly got the look of the hares I know, with flopping ears and jittery whiskered noses. The wee things poke their heads out of the greenery to watch the lonely mortal man tend the cottage garden. These Fae creatures are covered with silver fur that catches the light like newly fallen snow. Little jewels hopping about. If I could trust these animals weren't one of Finn's temptations like that first tainted berry, I'd roast them over a fire, but my trust in anything here is in short supply.

I finally step outside. It's always plenty warm here, and tending to my self-assigned duties raises enough sweat to soak a shirt, so I've taken to not wearing one. Without a rope belt, my damn britches would fall to my hips. After meeting the wandering Fae, whether in my mind or otherwise, I've not gone past the yard. Non-enchanted berries and the limited vegetables I've coaxed from the house garden don't fill a man out much.

I run a hand over my jaw. I've not found anything suitable for shaving that wouldn't take off as much skin as stubble. Not that there's a need. The faint suggestion of growth where a beard should be is as thin as the rest of me.

Since I quit collecting new bottles, I don't know if seven or twenty days have passed. I continue to watch the sky for my Eala *bán* with her wings of flecked gold to come soaring over those treetops.

Protecting myself against any more unwelcome Fae visitors tops my list. Besides my three Fae daggers, I've got an arsenal of rocks and stout branches tucked inside the door.

I glance across the road to the line of bottles I carried out of the cottage, becoming fearful one of 'em will grow legs and come for me after that pretty glass bastard lured me into the clearing. I've no trust for anything touched by a Fae, and don't want those deceptive pretties anywhere near me, especially when I'm lost to sleep.

A wee slithery Faerie lizard with the color and shine of sea glass, who's only made himself known for a few peeks now and again, perches on top of the tallest bottle. It whips what looks to be more than one tail through the air. The fellow is no bigger than my hand, but I've no desire to get better acquainted with it. I wave my arm and shout. "Off with you, lad." He scampers away right quick at the sight of me. The beastie better not devil my garden.

"It's soup today," I announce to the trees and rocks. Grabbing a bucket from the side of the house, I make my way toward the stream to fetch water. "Good morning to you," I say to the simple herb garden I discovered behind the house. Every day with great care, I weed and water the clumps of fragrant leaves. "You're very welcome to flavor my soup along with those fine…those fine…" I stare at a bunch of feathery green leaves, searching for the name of the veg at their root. This is a bothersome thing, the forgetting.

Thankfully, the word barrels through the fog in my head. "Carrots." I waggle a finger at the small garden. "Don't be thinking you can hide from me, you orange buggers."

It must be bad sleep filling my mind with haze. Conversing with things that don't answer isn't madness. Who does a feller have a chat with if there's no one else? I figure plants are growing, living things. Ma would sing to her vines and flowers every morning. She claims it makes them feel wanted. Her singing always did such for me.

Out of nowhere, a blast of wind lifts the soil, burying the herbs with its violence.

"Och, for the sake of Ma's fine brown soda bread, what new harassment is this?" I clutch the bucket close in case I need to swing it at a Faerie head.

The wind isn't done with us. It rises again, causing a spray to shoot from the stream, spitting fine mist all over me. This is no natural blow. Something's coming. Eala spoke of the *Sluagh Sidhe*, the Faerie wind that split the air when Robber Bright and his Host were on their way.

I rush toward the front door of the cottage to duck inside.

Too late.

Finnbheara, or rather a doubled-up version of himself as tall as the cottage, is planted at my doorstep. His eyes, also twice as big and twice as disturbing, pulse a deep rotten plum color, bleeding a bloody crimson circle around the irises.

"Claiming that any portion of your mortal hide could enhance a Fae charm is an outrageous indignity." His voice cracks the bark of the trees unfortunate enough to be close to the raging king. He waves a familiar fat gold glass bottle at me. It's the one that the Faeries used to lure me off the path into the moss.

Whether it's the force of his anger, his unnatural dimensions, or my diminished state that's to blame, but I'm arse-clenching terrified. I cower back, ready to jump into the stream and swim for my life.

Faster than my eyes can follow, he shifts into his standard-sized Faerie package. Finn's hand shoots forward to grab my upper arm, killing any possibility of giving him the slip. As if I could.

This close, I can see the bottle in his grip is stuffed to the brim with my stolen curls.

Relief is the last emotion I expected to feel in the wake of an enraged king, but his hand holds proof I didn't hallucinate the hair-filching Faeries.

With a beastly growl, he shoves the container in my face. "Your wretched human hair was confiscated in the marketplace." He heaves the bottle onto the wagon-sized deep-brown stone speckled with copper flecks jutting out of the ground next to me. Glass shatters, peppering me with stinging flakes as my stolen strands escape into the breeze.

I may be curling in like a dry leaf, but I will not let Finn slap blame on me for this.

Damn the consequences, I punch down hard on Finnbheara's wrist, breaking free of his hold. Shaking glass off me, I glare at him. "If you'd look past the end of your nose, you'd remember I'm the one trapped. Any of your Faerie fuckers can show up and force their magic to steal whatever bits of me they choose then sell 'em in your marketplace."

Finn bares his teeth at me. Here we go. I've finally done it. This is where he pounds me into the ground. He'll leave my head sticking up like a pumpkin so the crows or whatever howls in his wood can peck my eyes out.

My anger fuels my gall. "Fate will make sure Eala knows you made me fair game for Fae sport."

Finn closes his mouth, and his eyes fade back to silver, although his pupils still shift between the size of pinpoints and tiny raindrops. "You were set upon?" He's genuinely gobsmacked. His gaze rakes the forest. "It should not have been so."

"Too right."

"I will see you are not troubled again."

"By anyone but you," I mumble under my breath.

He narrows his eyes at me but lets the insult pass. I'm sure that's the only concession I'll get from him for his false accusation. After a sweep of his hand, I'm clear of the glass splinters still clinging to me. The damn Fae keeps staring at me. It's unnerving as hell.

"You are not well." His gaze is fixed on my ribs showing plainly through my diminished hide.

Could this fool make my blood boil any hotter? "That's what comes of you dumping me here with Fae thieves, howling beasts, and spelled berry bushes."

The words are clear as daybreak in my head, but only the last two pass my lips as anything more than garbled grunts. Och, is the ass suppressing whatever he does not wish to hear.

He tilts his head to one side. "You speak nonsense."

"Nonsense. Nonsense. Nonsense." My blabber echoes Finn's words without my intention. I press a fist to my lips. What the hell is he playing at?

"If you're finished taking me to task for what others have done, Your Majesty, I suggest you feck off."

My voice climbs up and down the scale as if I'm humming a wordless tune. I try to repeat what I've just meant to say, but again words flow like the ranting of a fool.

I pound my fists against my sternum as if the action'll throttle plain words from my mouth.

Finnbheara continues to stare at me as if I'm an oddity sealed in a jar. When I continue to beat my chest, he crooks a finger at the vine trailing near my foot. It springs from the earth and begins to wrap around my wrists to end my self-pummeling. As soon as the thumb-sized leaves touch my skin, they loosen their grip and the vines retreat back to the earth.

Finn's eyes become the same green as the vine as it quivers against the soil. He slowly swivels his head to face me. "You are a friend to the Gem Kissed Forest. It refuses to restrain you."

This time, my words spill clearly. "I've been tending to what's been left behind." I'm itching to add, unlike what you've done to me, you imperious bastard.

"Ah, you've come back to yourself, I see." The side of his lip quirks up. "However briefly."

Back to myself? The chill washing over me isn't because I'm without a shirt.

He looks thoughtfully at the garden. "You've your mother's gift with the land's bounty."

I'm not keen on the way his expression softens when he mentions Ma.

"You'd better not have stowed her away without a care as you've done with me."

The king's eyes pop back to silver. "She is well."

"Then let her come to me."

The damn Fae grins. "I think not. The markings of madness come fast upon you." In a mocking tone, he repeats the strange tune I hummed when words were my intention. "Your mother does not deserve the distress of watching your decline."

"Ish nawa you—" I bite my lip to keep any more nutter sounds from spilling out. Is it true? Is this curse on my words the bright bloom of madness?

Finn ignores me, turning toward the road and flipping his hands like he's paddling across a river. A wide, squat silver tree stump fades into view. It's covered with plates of cheese, meats, fresh-baked rolls that make me start salivating, a pile of roasted potatoes covered in a layer of toasted crumbs, and a bowl of steaming creamy soup.

"Eat. You are of no worth to me if the wasting of your flesh continues." He tilts his head when I don't approach the feast. "Nor are you of worth to Eala Duir in this diminished physical state. She will not find you desirable enough to keep."

I chuff then speak slowly, having no inkling of what'll make sense or not. "You still don't understand, do you, Finnbheara? I'll always be of worth to my wife. You can lock me away and banish her from your kingdom, but we will never abandon the love between us in this life and far beyond." I shake my head and treat him to my most pitying look, hurrying to speak while I still can. "I've no doubt you've lusted or even longed for another. Although you may call what you've felt love, it's not something your fickle soul is wired for." My gaze rises to the sky. "Love isn't a passing state. It doesn't end or weaken as the body does."

It's my turn to be slapped into silence by the look of utter desolation on his face.

"I do not discount your words, Sionnach Loho." With another wave of his hand, a simple silver stool appears next to the table. The king sits, staring, unblinking, down the road. "I have a wife. There is love between us."

There's no sense of joy in his cold statement. Is he saddled with the missus by some Fae code of honor? Lord knows he's never been short on lovers, Fae or human. Including my mother.

His inscrutable face turns to me. "Our circumstances are not so different."

Has the sky fallen? Is great King Finnbheara about to blather about his marital problems to a man he'd rather roast over a spit than tolerate? The fella's expression is pathetic enough that I might muster a stitch of empathy if he weren't such a soulless, tyrannical bastard biding his time until my mind is full of cracks. Ma claims his heart ails, but I see no sign of feelings, only empty words.

I swallow hard, praying speech hasn't failed me again. "If that were so, you wouldn't be keeping Eala and me apart just to appease your over-bloated Faerie ego."

Any sign of the king's introspection vanishes along with his momentary pause in tormenting me. He moves so quickly, I see nothing but a faint stir in the air as he stands. "Eat, or I'll send one of my kin to force sustenance down your throat, Fox."

A visit from any Faerie but my wife is a bollocks freezing prospect, so I grab a hunk of cheese and take a bite. It's like nothing I've ever tasted. Notes of fresh honey wind through the salty, creamy, and buttery goodness, blessing my mouth.

Finnbheara flashes a quick, self-satisfied smirk at the obvious pleasure I take in the snack before his mouth forms a tight line. The typical glare of total disgust he wears for me returns.

"Your time here is short. Tensions rise, and the hour grows near that we go to war with Aodh."

I swallow without chewing and nearly choke. The prospect of lining up against Aodh's demon army sends sparks flickering through my vision.

The king nods once. "I shall not call you to arms as such. As I've said, you are cannon fodder, Fox. Do not fear battle. By the time you hear the sound of those great guns, you'll be a drooling simpleton with a mind as pliable as that cheese."

I set the uneaten half of the pale-yellow hunk back on the plate.

"You are intended for a single purpose—bait at the head of my vanguard to draw out Eala Duir."

"Draw her out. You locked your bloody gates."

"Never to her essence, only to the plague of her devotion to you. Without your interference, my treasure will see reason and accept her destiny at my side."

I'm puffing like a bellows stoking a forge. "It's you, not me, losing his mind. You've heard nothing either Eala or I said of our bond."

"You are wrong. I've heard all. That is why you are the perfect lure."

"She'll never fall for your tricks, Finn."

He stares down his nose at me, wrinkling it as if I'm a stink he can't be rid of. "What would you have me do then, oh, sage fox? Journey to her realm and discuss allegiance?"

I bark a bitter laugh. "She'd not trust a thing you say after the way you deceived her."

Finnbheara assumes that infuriating stillness of the Fae as he assesses my statement.

Sharp pain jabs at my temples. My sight dims as the feeling of an intruder slithers through my head. I tap my fingertips all over my scalp the way Ma taught me to ward off a headache. Does oncoming madness bring on a wicked sting?

Finnbheara stirs, and the ache disappears along with his movement. Och, the fiend was trying to sink into my spirit the way I happily allowed Eala to do. Can he speed up the weathering away of my sanity if he catches me unawares and slips in?

The immediate danger before me snaps back into clear focus. I can't be the *bait* this villain uses to force Eala into Fae servitude. "My wife will never be yours, devil."

His lips barely move as his stare knifes through me. "Issue insults, proclaim your righteousness, or cry to the wind, Sionnach Loho. These outbursts provide evidence of your oncoming insanity."

He's a liar. I'm not succumbing to the madness of Tír na nÓg. Fear, hunger, and exhaustion are what's banked my fire. I'll find a way to get rid of all three and come back to myself. I will use every wit given to me by time, fate, and faith to keep Eala from Finnbheara's grasp. I grind the heels of my hands into my temples as if the action could restore my lost reason.

The Faerie ass has the guts to laugh at me. "Yes, use your energy to fight the inevitable. It will hasten your decay."

Curses spring to my lips, but my ridiculous babble returns. I can't let him keep believing he's already won. Seeding his arrogance with doubt is my only weapon. I suck in a deep breath. Maybe if I sing my intention to thwart his plans, the words will come out plain. "There once was a king who all Folk, including the man himself, believed invincible."

Finn raises an eyebrow.

"But there were those who knew it was not so. They armored themselves with truth and honor that the king could not touch." I take a trio of steady breaths then continue. "The day for battle came…" My throat begins to squeeze tight, but I choke the words. "The day for battle…" I grasp my throat and keep pushing air through it. "The day…"

Finnbheara leans his pointy face close to mine. "The definition of madness, mortal, is to believe you can affect that which you cannot." His eyes twinkle as he begins to fade into silver smoke. "Whatever tale you were trying to tell, know this—I am the end of your story."

CHAPTER 24

THE CAPTAIN'S RING

EALA

I slip Robber Bright's ring into my pocket before the witch or the pirate catches me. Filling a glass with ice water, I bring it to Biddy.

"Oooo," she says in surprise when the cold liquid touches her lips. Whoops, another historical misstep.

"I'm sorry." I reach for the glass. "Let me get you one without ice."

Biddy waves me off as she takes another sip then rubs her lips together. "No need. The cold burn revives me well."

"If you don't mind, I think I'll go for a walk to clear my head." I probably should have said *take some exercise* or another old-time phrase, but I'm antsy and more than a little flustered at the thought of seeing my former Fae tutor and all-around ass again.

Even before going outside, I smell drizzle in the air. I grab Sion's flannel-lined jacket he keeps on a peg by the door and throw it on. Grace calls across the room to me.

"Only fools traipse through the dark without a weapon."

I have no patience to remind her I do possess Faerie power, no matter how undeveloped, or to admit to the pirate that I'd have no clue how to handle a sword or a dagger. I almost tell her I'll be fine, when Sion's whacking stick, a club with nails pounded into its round end, catches my eye. Yanking it from the umbrella stand, I wave the homemade weapon in Grace's direction.

"This'll do," I say and step into the night.

I wish I could see the stars. They've always been a source of inspiration and encouragement to me. The perpetual layer of springtime fog rising over the sea cliffs stretches across Loho land and blocks them from view.

I head down the path toward the far-off hill with the crystal *lough* at its base. It's not that I intend to walk all the way there, but I need to figure out how I'm going to meet up with Robber.

There is always the golden ring I slipped upon your finger.

I retrieve the ring from my pocket. Can it be as simple as slipping the band of gold Sion first glimpsed in his disturbing dream of the silver ship and its Fae captain who apparently had sex with me in the forms of Aodh, Robber Bright, and Finnbheara onto my finger?

Holding the ring near my fingertip, I struggle with how I'm going to start our conversation. Finding a way to Sion is my priority, but I also ache with the need to know if Colleen is okay. Then there's the matter of intel I need from the Faerie on the geography of Tír na nÓg and Finnbheara's forces. Will the prick even answer a single one of my questions? I'm sure Robber Bright has his own agenda.

Kingdom's strong may fall to shade,
Purged from light with bow and blade.
Misalliance takes its measure,
When this Robber steals the treasure.

The last words he spoke to me on this very spot play through my mind.

Steals the treasure

Once, I was Finnbheara's Treasure. Am I still something Robber wants to steal from him? Will connecting with the Faerie be the death of my freedom? I hold the ring at arm's length. Will using this so-called gift from Robber Bright ruin any chance Sion and I have of finding our way back to one another?

Or is it the only chance we have?

I want my husband back. I want the home we've made through the simple act of loving each other. My home with Sionnach isn't a cottage or land. It's what I feel in his kiss, his touch, his arms holding me to his beating heart. Whether we're body, spirit, or soul, we are that home.

I slide the ring onto my finger next to my wedding ring.

Raising my face to where the stars should be, I wait for the clouds to part and Robber Bright to come riding in on his mighty *péist síoda*, Aillil. Instead, I get an eyeful of rain.

There's no Faerie warrior or his damned Host to fetch me. I wrench the ring from my finger and heave it onto the path. "Damn you."

Instead of disappearing back into the realm of dreams and threats, the ring sticks to the damp ground. I'm tempted to stomp it in deeper. With my version of Sion's derisive grunt, I retrieve the gold band and wipe it clean on the jacket's sleeve.

I glare at Robber's so-called "gift" through the wet hair plastered to my face and scream at the ring. "Now what, you son of a bitch?"

My impotence claws at me. Everything I try turns to shit. As if reflecting my fury, a faint red cast fades across the gold band.

More of Robber's words come back to me. He said this ring was the key to finding him. At Finnbheara's gates, when the turncoat Fae's essence split mine wide open to show me Colleen perched with him in Aillil's saddle, he told me exactly where to find him.

Oweynagat. The Cave of Cats.

The mouth to Aodh's underworld hell.

I look at Sion's cudgel that I dropped in the mud and snort. Yeah, like the whacking stick would do me a lick of good against the Dark Prince, Fae God of the Underworld.

As if anything could.

I call the Veil. It surrounds me with a thousand colors and thrums of power. Nearby, Alfie sways ever so slightly within the passage. I pat one of her trunks. Laying the ring on my palm, I show it to the Veil. "Oweynagat."

The bubble-thin walls of the Veil shudder, then the brilliance of myriad colors dulls. Damn, my mystical partner makes no secret that it doesn't want to take me to the hellmouth.

Before asking again, I slip Robber Bright's ring back onto my finger. Searching for calm, I will my Faerie essence to rise within me. When my Veil sprites begin to dance, I whisper, "Oweynagat."

There's a loud snap, and the Veil becomes a tight box made of thick sheets of glass with rainbow light streaming in a thousand tiny waterfalls inside the panes. This was Sion's Veil, rigid and strong, before I found him and taught him that life is better when you embrace flexibility.

I thrust my hand with the ring toward one of the walls. A ripple of my Fae energy flows from my shoulder, down my arm to my fingertips. "Take me to Oweynagat."

Still, the Veil refuses.

I search all around, addressing my words to no specific spot but the entirety of the Veil. "Please, do this for my *anamchara*. You know Sionnach. You've been his ally through his trials and years of fighting. Don't fail him. Don't fail us."

The immovable wall before me reflects a strange sight. Behind me, Alfie is glowing with a barely perceptible gilded tint. The key tattoo on my finger begins to flicker in concert with her light. The color of the mark changes from black to the same faint gold of the *fánaí* tree.

I switch the Fae ring to my index finger and watch the key brighten. Within Alfie's trunks, branches, and leaves, a thin molten rivulet moves up and then reverses direction. I'm drawn to the liquid magic flowing to and fro through the Tree of Life.

I'd lost faith that my key tattoo had any other purpose other than opening the door in the Giant's Glen when it later failed to connect me with Sion. Clearly, the mark I now wear has more to offer. Was it a loss of faith that kept Alfie from restoring the vision of Sion this morning? I believe more fervently now in the key on my flesh, the tree, and the magic we all share.

Lifting my hand with the tattoo and the Fae ring once again, I drift over to the Tree of Life and rest my fingertip against her bark. This time I don't demand or even request. I wish.

"Oweynagat."

The Veil telescopes down until it holds me like a marble in the palm of its hand. It slides over my body, painting me with its endless hues. When I try to move, invisible fingers tighten around me, as if I'm precious and the Veil will protect me from any who want to hurt me.

I am Finnbheara's Treasure. Aodh is his greatest enemy. Even in his anger, does the King of the Connacht Fae shield me from the gates of his Fae nemesis?

"Oweynagat," I repeat the word like a mantra from a place of human awareness and then from the depths of my Fae being.

Slowly, the Veil assumes its tunnel form with Alfie at her station next to the churning vortex I consider its picture window. I can't discern anything on the other side.

I frown at the ring. "If this is a dead end, you're getting melted down."

Pulling the jacket tightly around me, I step out of the Veil into a soggy field. I dig into a pocket for the flashlight Sion keeps handy, but it's not there. Thankfully, the growing slice of the moon and starlight allow me to see.

Two steps in and suction from the muck almost pulls the sneaker off my foot. I groan and yank it free.

The online pictures of the Cave of Cats glamorized this muddy ditch leading to the hellmouth. The mound ahead of me wears a bare, scraggly tree with branches reminiscent of outstretched claws. Under the tree is a hole. It's the size of our cottage door, but nothing more notable than a nondescript, unappealing hole.

Where is the gaping maw from the vision Robber Bright sent me? Where are the flames—the bloody glow and craggy rocks that could take a bite of me?

I squelch my way to the supposed entrance of Oweynagat and peer into it. It's as pitch black as Robber Bright's soul.

When I lift my finger to check the ring and key tattoo, their combined light brightens. Hmm, seems I brought a jerry-rigged Fae flashlight.

I bend in half to stick my head inside. Once I'm through the hole, I stretch my mini torch ahead of me, praying the cave opens up. The Faerie glow reaches less than a foot. I can't see a damn thing beyond.

Grabbing the rocky sides of the opening, I yell as loudly as I can. "Robber Bright." Nothing. What a shocker that I don't get a satisfying result from this talisman of an unreliable Fae scoundrel. Channeling Sion, I try again. "Robber Bright, get your ass out here."

I'm wearing the bastard's ring in front of the place whose name he ominously blurted when he kidnapped my best friend. So, where in the name of every fucking untrustworthy Fae is he?

I slap my palm against wet stone. If he's not coming to me, I'll have to go inside and try calling him again.

A wave of lightheadedness hits me as I absorb the fact that Eala Duir Loho is willingly entering a hellmouth.

I lower my head and sink into a crouch. The moment I'm through the hole, all I see is red. Not just red—fire. It stretches in a sizzling arch over my head. Stinging sweat pours into my eyes from the heat, making it nearly impossible to see. I step out from under the arch, and thick ashy air sets off a coughing fit that gives me an instant raw throat. It's every burnt smell I've ever experienced—wood in a fireplace, candle wax, campfires, and even the nasty reek of hair singed from a curling iron.

It's damn hard to breathe. Tiny particles block my airways, and I gasp for each breath. If I take another step, I'll suffocate.

I spin back to face the flaming archway at the cave mouth. The air within its frame wavers like heat off an asphalt playground, giving off the hideous smell of fresh tar. My options dwindle to either melting underneath the arch or choking to death inside the cave.

Robber Bright will get his wish to steal Finnbheara's Treasure by killing me.

A fresh wave of heat surges from the tunnel behind me. When I turn, I nearly retch from fear. A huge creature, the evil antithesis of a beautiful *péist síoda,* speeds toward me. Instead of the delicate satiny blue wings of the silk dragon, jets of fire shoot from this beast's metallic black scales, each defined by gleaming, blood red outlines.

There's not just one. As they get closer, I see another pair of these nightmares behind the one in the lead.

I hurl myself at the fiery archway, holding my breath as I punch through it and out of the hole. Landing in the mud, I sputter and scramble as fast as I can along the ditch.

When I steal a glance over my shoulder, any ridiculous hope of escape dies. The mound, the skeletal tree, and the boring hole have vanished. A massive maw with teeth of stone and fire blots out the sky. Surging through the opening are two gargantuan warriors in crimson armor with the sigil of Aodh's triple flame in the center of their chests.

CHAPTER 25
THE GENERAL

ROBBER BRIGHT

Filthy from the mauling of Aodh's guards and bloody from the blows of the Dark Prince himself, I drag my body to my quarters. Alarm seizes me when I find Acacia, Ciallmhar, Nettle, and Artos seated around the huge table before the window, their postures tense and rigid.

"How did you get in?" I bark, more from distress than opposition to their presence.

They mirror one another's look of confusion as they rise and surround me. Voices spill over one another.

"The door opened freely to us," says Nettle. "We assumed that was our sign of welcome."

Freely? I swear I laid charms upon my quarters.

Acacia digs fingers into my arms and shakes, heedless of my injuries. "What did Aodh say of his murder of our *péist síoda*?"

"The Host has been confined within their barracks," Artos booms.

"Friends," says Ciallmhar, his volume overriding the others. "Let the man speak." His gaze rakes over my bruised and disheveled form, eyes widening at my battered armor and face then adds his own question on the tail of the rest. "Do you bear the unforgiving ire of Aodh?"

My gaze flashes to the door of the bedchamber, which remains closed. My entire being screams to confirm that Colleen is unharmed, and Aodh has not struck at me further through her.

Nature's bane. She remains fully ingrained in my heart. The geas surely prowls but does not attack yet.

I raise a hand for silence, attempting to stagger toward the door as I strive to offer them solace after the catastrophic horror at the dragon pens. "I assure you, I did not leave the king's presence without securing a stay in his misuse of our blessed *péist síoda*. He will continue to peel dragons from their riders but will not use our cherished mounts in his insidious breeding experiments." I omit that the gain of a brief respite in Aodh's foul practices came at the cost of my Host being held as little more than prisoners until I fulfill my promises to the Dark Prince. If I did not truly believe my Folk were safer in their quarters than among the soldiers of Bráchthine after the near collision of our forces at the dragon pens, I would have struck a different bargain.

"Be grateful he has not demanded restriction of my freedom or yours." I turn to the coolest head of my high command. "Ciallmhar, keep flawless count of the dragons Aodh filched and the ones he…slaughtered." My rage rekindles. "We will demand recompense."

Again, I attempt to move to the bedchamber, but Artos lays fisted knuckles to Aodh's sigil on my breastplate. "Fuck recompense. It is vengeance we seek."

The crushing weight that tortures me for the decision to bring my Host to Bráchthine threatens to break my bones. I tragically underestimated the depths of Aodh's capacity for dark intentions.

I have much to alter. Plans that once were flawless have become shot through with deadly fissures. But before another breath is taken or word spoken, I will lose my reason if I cannot feel my bond-promised's heart beating.

Acacia's words are bitter as she exerts her warrior's strength to reclaim her hold on my forearm. "We knew he was a base devil, but you swore service to him would be no more trying than our days under Finnbheara's banner." My second increases her pressure on my arm. "We follow you, Commander, not the God of the Underworld. Where is the respect and recognition not given by the King of Tír na nÓg? Into what darkness have you truly led us?"

No quick answer will serve the gravity of her question, nor do I possess the will to attempt one in this moment. Tearing out of her hold, I hiss through a jaw of iron. "Leave me. Await my summons. See to our Folk and our dragons."

Storming across the room, I throw open the door to the bedchamber hard enough to wrench it off its hinges.

The room is empty.

The door to the bath is open, revealing an equally unoccupied space.

I burn, surging into the main room before my high command has a chance to follow my order. "Where is my bond-promised?" I roar.

My fury shakes the window glass. The faces of my friends show no sign other than apprehension at my outburst. I do not pause, but pound into the hallway, searching for one of Aodh's ever-present guards. I move with all speed until my hands are at the throat of the luckless fellow near the junction of two corridors.

"Where is my bond-promised?" The usual simmering hues beneath his cracked skin shift to purple, and I loosen my hold before I kill him without getting an answer. Colleen would not venture into these halls on her own. She has been taken from me.

Humans tell tales of Fae with the pointed teeth of beasts. Never have I wished such lies were truths. Sharp as knives or as blunt as spoons, my teeth will rip the throat from anyone in Bráchthine who lays their foul touch upon my bond-promised.

"Given your display at the dragon pens, I suggest you unhand my guard and demonstrate you are not as untamed as your animals, General Geal."

I recognize the voice of Aodh's general, Dóite. Releasing the palace guard, I spin toward my unsavory equal.

He is not the least bit cautious of my obvious violent intent. The hound flicks a fallen ash off his armored shoulder. "My king wishes to inform you that your human—"

"My bond-promised," I growl, making sure the bastard knows of Colleen's rank.

He acts as if I did not speak. "Has been escorted to the quarters generously gifted to her by his majesty."

"Take me there," I say with no pretense of anything but deadly purpose. I curse my carelessness in believing my enchantments alone were strong enough to repel Aodh's intentions. I should have enlisted Ciallmhar to combine his magic with mine in the hopes of keeping Colleen protected in my rooms.

"Exactly my purpose, General," he drawls in the gravely tone common to the Folk in this realm.

Seething, I fantasize all the ways I will make the Dark Prince scream as I follow the smug mouthpiece of Aodh down private steps behind a black steel door to the level of the palace below mine. As we pass from stair into corridor, the sight causes me to halt. There are no red marble walls nor grand halls. We are in a circular room no larger than my cottage in the Gem Kissed Forest with four opaque, thick glass doors. The walls here are of gleaming white silver bearing a pattern of leaf, vine, and bud. The preferred emblems of Finnbheara's court. Above each door is the black diamond sculpture of a swan. This chamber bears the hallmarks of both Tír na nÓg and Bráchthine.

My heart thunders in my chest. Is my queen, the revered Nuala, behind one of those doors? Did Aodh house Colleen near one who might provide a gentle hand in this bedeviled realm?

Finding my queen would be the greatest of blessings, especially now as Aodh's castle walls close in around me. Nuala will possess wisdom that I am in dire need of. She will give essential counsel to reverse my fortune. Apart from myself, the queen is whom I trust most dearly to keep my bond-promised from harm. Even after the geas returns my heart to stone, Nuala's compassionate nature will ensure Colleen a royal shroud of protection.

Queen Nuala is the power most equal to Aodh in his Castle of Sorrows.

The general raps once on the door to our right. I do not wait for Colleen's answer but force my way into the room. The sight before me chars my soul.

Aodh lounges on his side in the center of an enormous, canopied bed covered in sky blue coverlets and festooned with the spring blooms of Tír na nÓg. He's clad all in black silk, a long-sleeved shirt and equally flimsy trousers, form-fitted to his mass of muscle. Cinder-gray and black hair falls loose over his shoulders. The flaking ash of his skin shows through the neck of his shirt, hands, and bare feet. His long, gaunt face wears a predatory grin. Deep-set eyes flare with dancing crimson flames as he meets my gaze.

In the crook of his arm, Colleen lounges against him, wearing the black gown trimmed in rubies that I dressed her in for our journey to Bráchthine. She assumes the dazed look of the enchanted. My brilliant bond-promised pretends to remain under my charm, bravely enduring this obscenity.

The Dark Prince shifts. Through the insubstantial fabric of his pants, the press of his monstrous erection is visible as it perches atop Colleen's hip.

I hiss through my teeth. "To violate the bond-promised of another against their will grants me the right to do worse to you than what I did to your fucking flame dragon."

The Underworld God chortles and strokes Colleen's hair. "If my reckoning is correct, has not a single hour passed since you offered this sweet to me?"

A flicker in Colleen's eyes betrays horror at her proximity to Aodh and the cock using her as a shelf. I pray her trust in my protection gives her the strength to maintain the charade.

"You misheard my intention, sir."

Aodh feigns surprise. "Did I?"

It is only then, I notice the trembling of Colleen's hands and the fluttering of her bodice from a racing heart.

She is close to breaking.

"I will thank you to remove yourself from my bond-promised." I give a sharp bow. "My king." I school my anger so as not to give Aodh any reason to act against me or Colleen. There is no doubt in my mind that this is further retribution for my offenses at the dragon pens.

The Dark Prince waits for me to give him cause to continue my punishment. To bring me to heel, the vile god would not hesitate to force me to watch him batter my bond-promised with his ashen cock.

"And I shall accept our misunderstanding, sire, is due to my lack of clarity at our meeting."

Aodh gives a luxurious stretch that points his stiff cock straight at the flowery canopy. Before swinging his legs over the side of the bed, he drops a slovenly kiss on Colleen's temple. I catch sight of her fingernails digging into the meat of her palm.

"Farewell, Lady Colleen. May this be but the first of our tender sessions."

She remains silent.

"Ah, well," sighs Aodh, then pinches her cheek. "When next we meet, I will remove the restraints of vapidity my general has placed upon you, and we shall enjoy a more productive interchange."

I bow again, my gaze pinned to the swirls of green and lavender in the carpet to mask the intent to slay a god smoldering in my eyes.

As soon as he and his general leave, I heave the door closed and slam a barrier charm on the room.

Colleen lets out a soul-rending wail. I am the cause of her agony, leaving her vulnerable and unprotected instead of wreathed in a thousand enchantments of safety. What a fool to believe the Dark Prince would consider my quarters sacrosanct.

I leap onto the bed and raise her skirt, examining her thighs for blood or other signs Aodh defiled her all too assailable flesh. Thank the ancient gods and goddesses of the Folk, I find nothing.

Colleen flails like a wildcat. "Get me away from his disgusting smell." She sobs as she rages. "That fucker stinks like burnt popcorn in a microwave."

I do not understand her words, but their meaning is clear. She wipes at her nose over and over as she shoves her way off the bed to the door. My bond-promised is in hysterics.

I approach her as I would a skittish hatchling silk dragon, holding one hand in front of me to show I mean no harm. "Colleen, it is over. Aodh is gone."

When the door will not open, she claws at it, still screeching. "Take me to our room, Robálaí."

My essence explodes around me, its edges sparking as it reaches for her. I lower my hand and retreat to put distance between us. It takes incredible strength to stall my essence so its oncoming power does not add to her debilitating panic. It resists my efforts and continues to strain toward Colleen.

I speak with great urgency. "I need you to follow my instructions. By my oath and honor, what I do for you now will only serve to soothe your blighted spirit."

She whips around and presses her back to the door. Her face is blotched, tears shining atop its mottled color. "You promised to keep me safe, but it all went to shit." Her arms bend before her as if to ward off any advance as my Fae spirit inches closer. "How can I believe anything you say when it's clear you're not strong enough to keep that sickening creature away from me?"

There is no time to bandy words. My essence will not be kept from folding my bond-promised into its shell. "Stop speaking, Colleen." The harshness of my tone silences her. "Something beyond your current comprehension is about to transpire. Listen well. The spirits of those bond-promised know each other beyond the twining of words or flesh. Your spirit, your essence as the

Fae name it, is in turmoil, and mine as your bond mate refuses to be quelled until it guides yours to peace."

Her body jolts as the leading edge of my essence slides across her skin. "You may know it as love, but our bond takes the simple term and carries it to something deeper and richer. I beg you to close your eyes and let the world fade. Find the place that dwells inside you between waking and sleep. I wait for you there."

I can say no more before the radiance of my Fae core floods her consciousness, searching for its partner. Her legs refuse to hold her. I catch her in my arms and stumble backwards at the ferocity of our spirits bleeding into one another. I have never experienced this intensity of power, not in the bloodlust of battle or the exhilaration riding my *péist síoda* as we challenge the wind. My back crashes against the wall, and I slide to the floor, keeping hold of my beloved.

Only once before have I opened myself like this to another when I coaxed Eala Duir's strange essence to mingle with mine. My purpose then was less than honorable. To take advantage of her lack of Fae wiles, I shared but a minuscule token of what she desired, the ability to restore the Fae gifts to her lover. I had planned to strike at Finnbheara through his treasure, by luring her into a tryst. I knew full well the king would consider her sullied once she had partaken of pleasures with me.

I was the embodiment of delusion to attempt such a betrayal, and the blow fell upon my heart, not Eala Duir's. As our essences mingled, the purity of her love for her mate shone like the first winter snowfall on a mountain top, untouched and radiant. I was drawn to the scarlet ribbons flowing through her Fae spirit that were not of her creation, but rather enduring proof of the spirit cleaved to hers—the fox. The two, Fae woman and mortal man, were one, not in body, but in soul.

Witnessing such a union, the great love Finnbheara's geas would forever deny me, fractured my wits. In that moment, hatred for the king consumed me. Blind with greed, I sought to use my talents of illusion and deception to steal the passion woven through every wisp of Eala's essence for myself.

A power rose in her to demolish my ill intentions. It was then I knew Eala Duir was a Fae flame with the power to scorch and burn.

This woman in my arms, the human, my bond-promised, does not scorch or burn. She incinerates. Our essences are so completely melded, one is not discernable from the other. We are not bodies. Together we form a galaxy of tightly packed stars that glow with a single blinding light.

Colleen

My mind screams for her.

Robálaí

Her answering cry holds no fear but rather determination, possession, blessed surety I have only glimpsed once before between Eala Duir and her fox.

I must stop this. If our essences do not maintain their own separate fires, it will destroy both of us in the end.

Shards burst free from my heart, igniting new pulse points down my spine and through every drop of blood as our souls prepare to fuse for all time. I must plead with her not to allow this final act of joining that guarantees her eventual heartbreak.

I am helpless to resist, because I yearn to share my soul.

I cannot breathe without her.

I cannot love, Colleen. I am cursed. Your heart will know nothing but endless suffering in the face of my indifference.

You do love, Robálaí. You have loved. You will love.

You do not know me. I manipulated, influenced, and enchanted you until your mind became separated from the truth.

Colleen's essence shines as if the lovely dove gray color of her eyes was forged into precious silver. It gleams, racing in nimble revolutions until her spirit entraps mine in an inescapable web. I float in a womb filled with the aquamarine mist of my essence and her shimmering grace. She holds me in a rarefied embrace. It is bliss I do not deserve, but I lap it up like the dog I am.

Images shiver within the mist, faint at first, but then ribbons bearing both the colors of Colleen's eyes and mine twist and weave around me. Proof of essences forever joined. As Eala has gifted her fox, this woman, this incredible, unforeseen gift sears her human soul to my Faerie spirit.

Thoughts as sheer as the finest silk and just as delicate continue to caress my soul.

> *I do know you, Robálaí Geal, by any name. Knowing is not only in the mind. I*
> *have always known you're not like me. I felt your magic from the*
> *beginning. It sang to me and I listened. It reached for me, and I took its*

hand. You don't understand how a soul searches for its perfect echo because you're afraid. I'm not.

Our essences become smaller and smaller until they are no larger than the head of a pin, before they burst into millions of droplets of aquamarine and dove gray that coalesce into a curtain of gentle light. Instantly, images begin to play across its surface, and I see myself through Colleen's mortal eyes.

We stand in front of Eala Duir's cottage and I call Colleen my peppered apple. She stares at the pointed tips of my ears. Faerie – Faerie – Faerie drifts through her mind, then... I've found you, My Faerie – My Faerie – My Faerie. Eala tries to pull her from me, but Colleen's essence flares around her like an aurora, reaching for mine even at this first encounter.

We sit on the porch of the same cottage and share tales of the loneliness fate visits upon us both. It is not the mortal clothes upon my body she sees, but the bare skin of my chest and the scar cutting through my flesh. She shows no alarm. Colleen's essence accepts my imperfection and the burdens of my soul, smoothing every surface with a featherlight touch while the light of her spirit croons a lullaby to me. Her mortal mind pierces the curtain of enchantment to my truth. I hear her call to me. There you are, My Faerie – My Faerie – My Faerie.

We ride upon the back of my péist síoda, Aillil. Before us, the hellmouth covers us with its unholy breath. She sees a Fae warrior clad in Aodh's armor with a flame sigil upon his breast. Her mortal body trembles but her essence whispers to calm the anger, fear, and conflict in my spirit. I tighten my hold on her fragile human body. Her heart speaks—I know you will protect me, My Faerie – My Faerie – My Faerie.

We are on our knees before the great glass window in my chamber of Aodh's palace, swearing the bond-promise to one another. Her mind, her spirit, her soul is as clear as the first note of a songbird calling the dawn. You are home, My Faerie – My Faerie – My Faerie.

And then, like the last downpour from a rain cloud, our joined essences fall. They hit the ground in a splash of spectral brilliance then disappear. We are back in the Castle of Sorrows in each other's arms.

"How…" I gasp, feeding my lungs with air. "Did you know me? I never allowed you to see…to know I was Fae until the oath of bond-promise became a necessity. My magic and strong will both prevented it."

Colleen takes my face in her hands. The pad of her thumb carefully strokes my swollen cheek. "Sometimes love *is* the magic, you stupid Faerie man."

"But when I first woke you from the enchantment, you did not know or accept me."

This provokes a thoughtful shine in her eyes. I attempt to still my racing heart while she contemplates. A smile curls her lips as she lays a palm to my breastplate as if she can sense the rapid pace of my heartbeats. "Easy there, fellow."

I lay my hand over hers.

Her gaze drifts upwards as she formulates a response to my questions. "It's like…" she chews delicately on her lip. "…there were two parts of my mind, the one with both feet in the world I've lived in my whole life that insisted what was happening to me was bonkers, and the other half trying to slap sense into the first to tell it *this*…" She rubs her nose against mine. "…*you* were my true reality, and things are finally the way they're supposed to be."

"Not bonkers."

Colleen's explosive laugh is a burst of light through the shadows of this day. "I love hearing 'bonkers' come out of your fancy-talking Faerie mouth." Her mocking expression shifts into something much more tender. "My Faerie." She captures my still-astonished lips in the most loving kiss my multitude of years has ever known.

I break the kiss as gently as it was delivered then brush my mouth along the smooth shell of her ear and whisper, "I do not comprehend how fate allowed a union such as ours."

Colleen's fingers thread through my hair, pausing to pinch the sharp tips of my ears. "Guess fate isn't as almighty as it pretends to be."

The touch sends a jolt straight to my cock that is acutely aware of the ass nestled atop it.

Colleen gives a little squeak, feeling the none-too-subtle twitch between our bodies, and then my naughty vixen wiggles against me. Heat radiates off her skin, raising prickles along mine.

"Speaking of which…" Her heavy breaths push her chest against me as she draws my mouth close to hers. "Call yourself my bond-promised if Faerie language insists, but I'll call you my husband."

I move my lips against hers. "Call me your knave, brute, bond-promised, mate, husband, or devotee. All will serve." I push any thoughts of time beyond this from my mind. Now is all. No next moment, hour, or day exists. Now, we are together. Now, we claim each other's hearts. Now, my every imperfection belongs to this perfect woman.

Colleen is aggressive with her kiss, demanding my tongue to meet her challenge. When she breaks it off before a morsel of satisfaction from her welcome assault is allowed to take hold, I groan. She presses two fingers to my lips and grinds her sweet bottom even more deliberately against my rapidly hardening cock. "Hold that thought." Colleen tosses a look over her shoulder at the bed, her face tightening with disgust. "Not in here. Not on the bed where that shithead groped me."

She slides off my lap to stand and moves to the door of an adjoining room. "Your stinking charcoal briquette of a king said this room is mine as well."

I do not understand the title she gives Aodh, but I am certain it befits his villainy. Accepting her outstretched hand, I rise to my feet, but before she can open the door, I sweep her up into my arms and steal her mouth with a ravenous kiss until she pushes me away to draw breath. Only then do I throw open the door and carry her through.

Colleen kicks it shut and takes her turn at ravishing my mouth, her tongue sweeping round and round in a relentless rhythm that has me straining to keep pace with her. I entertain no doubt, she will prove a delightfully savage lover.

My feet sink deep into a carpet so plush and pliant it rivals the lush field of silvery green grass covering the meadows of Tír na nÓg. We enter a sitting room with white marble walls covered in feminine touches of flowers and delicate furniture I am in no state to thoroughly assess. I aim for a white velvet settee bathed in the rosy glow from Bráchthine's sun. Its blood-orange light streams in through a single wall of glass overlooking tawny plains beneath sculpted red mountains.

"Wait, Robálaí." She scrutinizes the evidence on my face from Aodh's beating, testing the damaged spots with careful touches. "You're hurt."

"Not enough to matter." I prove this to her with a kiss equal to her savagery, not sparing any portion of her mouth, teeth, tongue, lips…

She runs a fingertip along the corded muscle in my neck. "I'm convinced."

Setting my darling upon her feet, I strip the gown over her head and lick my lips at the slap of breasts against skin as the beauties are freed from their restraints. Her sole covering is a pair of provocative black lace underthings from our trunks. The thought of my bond-promised choosing to wear this enticement with me in mind stretches my cock to a greater length.

I graze a teasing touch from her navel down the front of the lace without exposing the prize beneath. Colleen grabs my finger, her gaze locked on the arched tongue hungrily stroking my bottom lip. "How long is your tongue?"

One of my hands flies to her ass, the tips of my fingers barely teasing the sweet valley in its center as I slam her body against mine. My free hand seizes the silky locks at her nape to tug until my lips hover above hers. I trill the mating call of a silk dragon, "Allow me to enlighten you." Smashing my mouth against hers, I drive my tongue past lips and teeth to lick her spicy tongue straight down its center. I do not stop there. Pressing deeper, I tease the back of her throat, forging a path my cock yearns to follow.

Colleen releases an indulgent moan that coats the inside of her mouth with the taste of her peppered apple goodness. The volume of her pleasure increases, sending ripples down the length of my tongue, inspiring me to roll it into a pulsing cylinder that traps hers with a squeeze before reluctantly sliding free.

She jumps into my arms, locking her legs around me, and drives her own sharp tongue into my ear.

My battered ribs ache with her attack, but I ignore their protests.

She growls between wicked swirls of her tongue. "I need more of your bare skin. Then you're going to show me what else that fucking incredible tongue can do." The woman slides her legs down mine, stroking my arousal with the front of her black lace and the soft mound within. She leans back, offering me her pair of plumped and eager nipples. Dessert before the meal.

Colleen may be the boldest lover I have ever taken to my bed. "Yes, General," I say, peeling her off my chest, before spreading my hand between her swaying breasts to press her onto the settee. I could bury my cock inside her and burst before she finished saying my name, but our first joining must be more. I have shared my lust and my body, but never my love. This shall be nothing less than my all. I will discover every way my bond-promised revels in pleasure before I sate myself.

I should not have expected my peppered apple to accept my guidance. Colleen does not remain on the settee but continues to the carpet, taking my britches along with her. Obediently, I step out of them. She twirls the discarded clothing thrice over her head then sends it flying against the glass wall. We laugh at the absurdity of her display. Her gaze falls to where my cock remains trapped beneath my armor. In a single burst of magic, I open the clasps and let the crimson plates fall to my feet so I am clad only in my black under tunic.

Colleen kicks the armor. "Ow ow ow." She grips my shoulder and hops on one foot, grabbing her unhappy toes with her other hand. "The metal looks light, but it's as hard as a rock." Her hip collides with the shaft pressing against my stomach that at present may also be mistaken for stone. I yelp, shielding my cock against further onslaught.

She stills. "Oh god, I'm so sorry." A mischievous smile claims her plump lips, and she pulls my hand away. Her fingers tickle my swollen tip trapped beneath the fabric. "Did I hurt you? Let me check." Crouching in front of me, she lifts my hem and replaces her fingertips with a kiss.

I think I go blind for a moment as she slowly licks the evidence of my enthusiasm. "Nature's bane, Colleen." It takes all my forbearance not to push my cock between the ripe fruit of her lips.

"Looks fine to me." Trailing a finger along the length of my thick, thrumming vein, she giggles. "Much nicer up close." The low feminine growl that follows sends another surge of blood to increase my girth. "And bigger. You'll do."

"You will be my undoing," I force through gritted teeth.

She sets both hands on my abdomen under my tunic. "I plan to be."

Her touch begins to slide up my chest. I know the moment she feels the difference between the warmth of my unblighted flesh and the frigid span of scar, spanning my torso. I have not lain with another since Finnbheara left the mark of his ire upon me. It is no badge of honor, but rather a testimony to my dishonor.

She flips the tunic up, forcing my arms to give way, and pulls the garment over my head. Without speech or meeting my gaze, my bond-promised presses her lips to the scar and kisses. She repeats the action until every piece of the ruined flesh has received her tender acceptance.

I scorned the concept of destined love as a youth. Once Finnbheara's geas was upon me, there was no point in changing course to accept its existence.

I believe it now with all that I am. My destiny slept until this woman ripped it from slumber.

"Now, husband, now," she whispers, stepping away from me to lie back on the settee.

Catching her ankles, I slide her until she's seated at the very end, facing me. I kneel between her legs and cradle her breasts in my hands. I suckle each in turn, curling my tongue to seize her nipple and pull until she groans with a combination of pain and delight.

"Harder, Robálaí, harder." I grin then dive back, adding teeth. She pulls my head closer to her chest. "Suck me until I scream."

I obey. When her cry is finished, she drops her head to my shoulder, panting. I release her breast from my mouth with a *pop*. Her skin glistens from my attention, nipples hard and plumped nearly to the size of my cock's crown.

"Holy mother of all orgasms," she pants into my ear. "I've never come so hard in my life."

"Oh, my darling, that was but a prelude." Bless the talent of females to welcome crests of pleasure as constant as waves to the shore. I grind my lips to hers, allowing her taste to flow down my throat. With enough speed to raise an alluring squeal from Colleen, I raise her knees to send her tumbling back onto the settee. Driving my face between her thighs, I press a lick up the lace covering her slit then continue to her navel. The way her skin pebbles from my long taste increases my hunger for my bond-promised.

"Off, off," she moans.

When I start to pull away, she slaps the side of my head. "Not you, damn it." She grapples for the lace, which I gladly tear off her body instead of waiting for her to remove it.

I chuckle against her quivering ripeness.

"I'm going to come again," she rasps.

Cupping her with my hand, I give a gentle squeeze. "Not until I allow it."

She bolts up to sitting, her slickness coating my palm. "I'll come as fast and as often as I want to."

I press her down and take her clit in my teeth as I answer, "Yes, General."

She shall command me for all time. As her body trembles with a combination of laughter and need, I flatten my tongue to its full width and length and bury it inside her.

The song my lovely bond-promised sings now has no words, only a tangle of breath and the notes of her rising ecstasy. I pump my tongue deep, curling and twisting as I drink her flowing juice. I seal my mouth to her sex and suck in time with my roving tongue.

"R-R-Robal-ahhhhhhh," she wails as I demand her release with my mouth.

My cock throbs against my stomach, already weeping with approval. I fear the exuberance of its arousal may prove too much for Colleen's petite dimensions. One arm is flung over her eyes as she works at recovering breath.

Apparently, I remain still too long, for her legs trap my body and she sits again. "If that's what your tongue is capable of…" The point of her petite tongue slides over her thickened bottom lip. "…show me what else you got, Faerie man."

The invitation and burning lust in her eyes do indeed undo me. I return her once again to her back and guide her body up the settee. The scent of her arousal unleashes more hunger to gorge myself on the feast between her thighs, but a primal need overpowers the craving.

I slip along her body through the sweet layer of sweat coating our skins. My voice is rough and untamed. "I do not wish to cause you pain only pleasure."

Her hand sneaks between us. Fingers strain to wrap around my shaft and Colleen giggles a triumphant breath when she achieves her goal. "You think very highly of yourself, husband." A surprised "Oh" escapes her lips when she explores me from root to tip. "Someone's gotten even more enthusiastic."

I take her earlobe in my teeth. "If it is too much, I will stop."

She rakes fingernails down my back. "You'll do nothing of the sort. I can take you, Faerie man. All of you." Her legs circle my hips, and she guides my cock between her folds, sliding her parted slit along my length. She gushes in a hot torrent around me. I may not last long enough for my size to deter either of us.

As one last measure to allay my concern, I sink one finger inside her, then two. When she opens to my touch, accepting a third, the last of my control is destroyed. I swap fingers for my tip and tease her entrance until she whimpers.

"If…you…aren't going to—"

I answer her threat with a roar as my length surges forward. Her slick walls tense around me for the briefest moment then bloom to accept my hammering cock. I push in until my base crushes against her hot flesh.

Colleen arches against me as if to beg for more. I pull back and deliver a second merciless thrust. She grabs my ass and pounds our bodies together, hissing in my ear. "I told you."

Damn this woman. She will best me in all things. I withdraw again and match her ferocity with my own. Her long, slow moans ride my movements as I quicken my pace, adjusting my angle so her hungry clit receives its share of the friction, climbing to explosive levels between us. My cock throbs with relentless pressure, thickening to painful dimensions as if daring Colleen to reveal her limits.

She grinds out her words. "I'm about to—"

Nature, bless me, I love the way she announces the onslaught of her climaxes. Any further thoughts fracture when she clenches around me with the force of a warrior goddess. When she lurches forward, I claim her mouth to consume the raw screech as she explodes with release.

Instead of melting into the aftermath of her pleasure, she bucks her hips to mine as her body squeezes my cock. "Come with me, you damn Faerie man."

Her command sends a monstrous pulse through my cock, and seed bursts from me with enough force that I arch my back, driving my hips forward to remain locked inside her. We howl in tandem, as tremors seize us both and cling to one another as if the next great wave of pleasure will tear us apart.

"Don't let me go. Don't let me go," Colleen sobs against the skin of my neck.

"Never, love. Never."

I will every realm above, within, and beneath the earth to cease the forward motion of time, so I may dwell forever in this moment.

CHAPTER 26
THE ELIXIR

SIONNACH

O nce the king leaves, every bit of good sense warns me to avoid Finnbheara's food. Whether it's a compulsion from that bastard of a Faerie king or the specter of starvation overpowering what's left of my good sense, I eat.

Initially, I blamed my agitated mind and twisting words on the Faerie cheese, but it's not muddling my thoughts now.

Or is it?

Was Finn having a go at me to make me believe the madness is taking hold? He seemed to catch my words clearly enough when he wanted to.

I carry a hunk of toasty brown bread to the side of the cottage. Is it newly baked from a Faerie oven or warmed by the perpetually shining sun?

Does it matter?

Knowing anything for certain matters.

Standing at the edge of the garden, I point my bread at the patch. "Carrots there. Carrots. Carrots." I'm taking the magic of three to the bank. "Potato at the end. Potato. Potato." I aim my bread pointer farther down the row. "Turnip. Turnip. Turnip." Wait. Is that so? I rush to the leaves and kneel in the dirt. Yanking the fat, round root from the ground, I stare at it. "White, are you? Yesterday you were purple."

Were they? Are turnips white or purple?

Damn it, if I hoped the garden would provide a measuring stick for the strength of my mind and body, it's failing me.

I search for the herb garden, but can't find it. "Where are you, wee buggers? You were here yesterday." I search the ground. "Or was it this morning I saw you?"

Taking a bite of bread, I chew with my eyes closed to paint pictures I know to be real. As sure as I am of anything, I swear I've visited the herb garden since awakening. A memory of blowing dirt, spraying water, and an unfriendly wind leaks into my mind. "Och." I shake a fist at nothing since the fool I'd like to hit isn't here then address the buried herbs. "Sorry Finnbheara's tempest of a calling card deviled you."

I toss the bread aside and frantically dig the lines and clusters of leaves free. "There ya are." Running a finger over a sprig of rosemary, I nod. "Soup, I was making soup before the bastard showed up."

Memory is a fine thing. I don't appreciate it enough.

Standing, I reach for the bucket I dropped when the king came to call. A sharp pain shoots through my back. As I rub the aching spots, I try to piece together what I've done to my body to cause such soreness. I've tended the garden, but that's not much.

I run my hand over my ribs. The meat on my bones has diminished. Did Finnbheara comment on my wasting frame? Try as I might, no clear memory of his words comes to me.

Fuck all. This is a puzzle with blank pieces.

Without fetching water, I stomp to the silver food stump. I grab the bowl of creamy soup and drain it dry. It's annoyingly delicious. I sneer at the cloudless sky and holler, addressing my unseen jailer. "I'll eat your food, Finn, and feed my mind as well as my body."

My voice comes out disturbingly loud. Am I raving?

I stare at the empty, baby blue stretch above me. My life in Ireland was filled with magnificent skyscapes of clouds. Layers heaped in great piles from creamy white to tabby cat gray that every so often let rays of sunlight, surely born of heaven itself, break through to bathe the land in their golden touch.

Were there ever such things here? The Veil forests are still. Breeze hardly disturbs the air unless Finn is making hisself known. Am I shut in a box of a never-changing sky?

I grab handfuls of hair. "Why are you tormenting yourself with such thoughts of beauteous yesterdays, Sionnach Loho?"

My fingers bump against my head as tremors overtake both hands. I hold them in front of me and stare. They shake of their own accord, not of cold or fright. Clenching the pair of 'em into fists doesn't stop the trembling. Am I losing control of my body as well as my mind?

A picture as vivid as if the scene was playing out in front of me locks my feet to the ground.

I was a lad young enough to cling to Ma's skirts. We were inside a dim cottage much smaller than ours, and she held a cup of healing tea to an old man's lips. His hands shook as mine do now, so he couldn't hold the cup. He drank only a bit before throwing his head back to wail, *"They're laughing at me, all of them."* His eyes bobbled, showing mostly white, as his gaze tore around the room. *"See them there, striking my mind like a hurling ball with their Faerie sticks."*

"Mad Michael," I whisper. Yeah, that was what they called him. The man scared the stuffing out of me. My fingers doing a jig sets me to wondering if he was truly mad or if Michael got on the bad side of a Faerie same as me. Based on his rantings, I'm inclined to blame the Fae.

I clasp my hands together and send a prayer to anyone who'd be willing to take the time to listen. My knuckles crack from the bending, but as quickly as it came, the shaking stops.

I stretch my fingers. "Mad Sionny is what they'll call me if Eala doesn't find me soon."

Has it already been too long? Am I heading down a path that only leads in one direction?

"Don't think such nonsense, you fool." I shut up. Talking to plants is one thing, having a chat with myself is another.

If Faerie sport is watching mortals go mad, they're more heartless and heathenly than I believed them to be. With no Fae to punch, anger sends me running toward the line of Faerie bottles I've stowed in the grass on the other side of the path.

I stop dead in my tracks when a beautiful sight rises in a clear space between the trunks of two Faerie trees. Slender white, sloping trunks. A pattern of dark green triangles whose design spells out my name next to Eala's in the language of *fánaí* trees. Branches filled with graceful leaves shiver a greeting.

"Alfie," I murmur, approaching my *fánaí* tree with an outstretched hand.

Just as my loving fingertips promise to touch her sweet bark, the vision of my beloved friend fades away.

I gawk then call her name. Jogging this way and that, I search for Alfie among the trees and brambles of the forest, but she's gone.

I find myself before the row of Faerie decanters as if I never moved from the spot in the first place.

"To the devil with all your kind." I cry and kick the largest bottle that's filled halfway with pale mint liquid the color of gin with a squeeze of lime. Its glass mushroom stopper flies free, and the Fae potion glugs into the grass. I'm aiming for a taller thin one next in line, filled nearly to the top with pink liquid, when the blades surrounding the felled vessel shoot up as high as my waist.

"All Ma's saints help me," I say, covering my eyes. "Now, I'm truly seeing what can't be."

I've almost made it to the cottage door to hide from this Fae bedevilment when I stop myself, turning to examine the newly sprouted grass. "For the sake of your fox's furry arse, Sionnach Loho, you're in a Faerie forest. Who's to say what can and can't be?"

Retracing my steps to the line of bottles, I lift the one I kicked over. There's a tiny bit of Faerie elixir still pooling inside it. I take the glass to the herb garden. Holding it over the rosemary, I tip a few drops onto the plant. Sure as I'm my father's son, the rosemary doubles in size. I move along to an ailing fennel and dump more of the pale green stuff on it. Same as before, it plumps and preens, the picture of botanical health.

Running my finger along the inside of the spout, I collect the last little puddle of liquid. If it didn't kill the plants, it won't kill me. When I pop it in my mouth, there's not much taste to it. More than water, but not the nip of gin I hoped for. As soon as I swallow, there's a strange flutter along the skin of my upper arms that have turned flabby from fading muscle. The movement raises an itch. A moment later, my skin tightens not more than the width of a pinkie finger as my bicep underneath stretches like it's yawning awake.

"Ha. A plant am I then?" I stare at the empty bottle. "So, that's how you make yourselves hale and hardy, Faerie folk. No hard work for you, just a nice glass of this cheating muscle juice now and again." I mime a toast. "*Sláinte.*"

Once again, curiosity draws me to the line of bottles. Instead of kicking them over, I dribble a bit of their insides onto the grass to see what comes of it. The pink liquid from a tall skinny one only bubbles and smells of juniper berries. Don't need my guts fizzing. I kick it over.

A tamarind-colored potion, as I decide to call these magical drinks, doesn't bother the land when it releases a puff of air that sounds like a low wail. I'm leaving that one be. The next could pass for a well-aged whiskey, but it withers the grass.

"Steering clear of you as well, mate."

I come to a nice stout decanter filled with the minty fake gin similar to the first. I hold it up to the light, deciding if it's a match for the one that made the plants grow. Carrying the bottle to the stump of food, I set it next to the buttery honey cheese and plant my arse on the ground.

"What do you say, pal? Are you going to give me back what Finn's lack of hospitality took away?"

How many stories have I told in Corrigan pubs over the years about the dangers of indulging in food and drink from the table in a Faerie kingdom? I grunt. "Don't think the caution applies when you're stuck here for good instead of waltzing in and out for a single night's revelry."

A memory I wish would leave my mind of the hair-stealing Fae and the glass beauty they plunked onto the road to tempt me spikes my heartbeat. This bottle doesn't have the same pull. Before I booted the Faerie potions out of the cottage, this decanter kept company with me for days. Maybe weeks? And caused no harm. It's been biding its time at the edge of the forest, exactly where I took it, and hasn't moved since. None of these bottles let loose so much as a bubble until I bothered them.

I tear off a hunk of bread and top it with the cheese. While I munch, I'm smitten with the way the Faerie potion catches the light. I'll stick to a fingertip's worth at a time to test it. The first drops didn't hurt or give me the sicks. Taking the liquid a bit at a time will help me judge whether or not to keep going.

Gazing across the road at the rest of the bottles, I wish for one to restore more than my body. If only Faerie juice could return even a small portion of the courage and confidence those bastards who ambushed me took away.

To fuel my rising uncertainty, the distant howling creature who's been off and away for a bit chooses now to start up again. I strain to call a clear memory. Did Finn say he'd keep danger from visiting me? Och, even if his words rang between my ears clear as a bell, I'd give nothing that bastard said any worth.

I eye the bottle again. At least if I get some of my strength back, I may gain enough energy to run from trouble if need be.

Popping off the mushroom cap, I dip a finger in the spout and then suck down the potion, coating my skin. Shivering, quivering, and itching start before my upper arms stretch the tiniest bit. I keep at it, growing myself back to what I was. It's slow going. Sometimes, there's nothing more than a stitch to my skin with no notable result.

Whenever I tip the glass, the tiniest bubbles rise inside the bottle. Not a troubling fizz like the pink potion, but a wee dance.

The wail calls to me again. I sing to it, figuring there's no harm in reviving our conversation if the beastie stays put. Any sign of its approach and it's into the cottage with me.

As I prolong our duet, I risk a bigger taste of the flavorless gin. A greedy sip sets off a ruffling under my skin. It's not painful, just unsettling. The effect outlasts the rest to the point that I consider stopping. The flutters end abruptly. I pinch forearms that seem firmer.

Grabbing the mushroom cork in my hand, I stare at the bottle. "Should we take this up again tomorrow, lad, or press on?"

Frustration answers. How long will I have to go at sipping until I'm fully restored? This pace is slow enough to make a man beat his chest and call for a bigger pour. "What the hell?" The stuff isn't doing much to me. What's throwing back a hardier swig going to hurt? I've felt nothing ill so far.

I chuckle. I've never been a patient man. Maybe not wanting my recovery to plod along like an old plow horse is a sign I'm coming back to myself. Grabbing the bottle, I take a couple of generous swallows. The liquid slides down my throat quite fine.

I set the bottle aside so any rippling doesn't cause me to spill its restorative contents. I've barely let go when a ramrod hits my gut, and I double over. The side of my head hits the silver stump as I fall. A hot trickle of blood runs down my face.

I curl into myself, grabbing my stomach, waiting for the sick to come up my throat, but instead, the forest starts spinning. My skin feels as if it's splitting apart in a thousand places.

My folks did raise a fool. Eala will never forgive me for taking this eejit's path.

The critter wails its part, but I've got no answer for it as time, place, and Sionnach Loho are scraped away to nothing.

A mouthful of icy water wakes me. I spit and sputter to find myself neck deep in the stream. My teeth rattle so hard, I've surely cracked a few as I'm seized with violent shakes.

The noises coming out of me are nonsense, but they're not meant to be words. Curses are grunts and groans. I've got to get free of the water or I'm a drowned man. The bank isn't steep or wide, but when I try to reach for it to pull out of this hellish dunk, my arms flop like the ears of a hound. My vision melts into a slate gray blur.

Something plunges into the water near my arse. Drowning isn't to be my destiny. It's being swallowed by a Fae water beast.

There's a tug on the back of my britches, and I'm dragged up the bank onto a patch of grass near the water. I will my head to turn and see what's huffing and snorting behind me, but my body isn't answering my brain's request. There's nothing for it but to close my eyes and wait.

Something like the scratch of a dry twig slides along my cheek. It tangles in my hair and gives a rough yank. I moan at the pain, and whatever's preparing me for dinner stops its poking. I'm a shivering cat plucked from a lake. Warm mist covers me, and the air smells of Ma's cherry pie.

There's a nudge at my shoulder. Och, the beast prefers its food live and wiggling. Sorry, pal, can't oblige you.

With a thump, something big and blissfully warm drops onto the ground next to me, pressing against my side. If I could open my eyes, I'd do it, but I've not a lick of energy for anything but lying here like a discarded sack of rubbish. Staying blind allows me to believe I'm in my home place on my mattress of lady's bedstraw with my *anamchara* gathered in my arms.

Goodnight, Eala *bán*, beat your great white wings to fly me where stars are born from the fire of lovers' passions. With that lovely wish, shadows claim me.

CHAPTER 27
THE QUEEN'S ECHO

ROBBER BRIGHT

Colleen's slender fingers alternate between twirling through the hair on the unscarred portions of my chest and petting the length of the smooth, silvery damage I wear across my flesh. "Do you know your chest hair has as many colors as your lovely Faerie locks?" She reaches up to pinch a strand of hair near my shoulder. "You're a living paint chip of every blond shade with the teeniest bit of silver sneaking in."

I kiss her temple. "I do not know this paint chip."

"Do Faeries paint?"

I nip her finger. "Of course. We do not chip but rather crush fruits and the leaves of plants and trees to create pigments."

"Well," she raises onto one elbow. "Humans buy paint at big ass stores. There are cards with a bunch of different variations of a similar color on each called paint chips." She rubs her delightfully swollen lips together. "There's really nothing chippy about them."

I lie back on the settee and clasp my hands behind my head. "We have much to teach one another."

She slaps a hand to my chest. "That's for damn sure."

I remember the strange phrase she used for Aodh's stench. "What is the stink you named a burned microwave?"

Her head, hair still slightly sweat-dampened from our exertion, nestles against me. "Burned *popcorn* in the microwave. It's a super nasty smell you can't get rid of."

I grunt. "Fitting for Aodh."

Colleen grunts in return. "He also smells like a dog just pissed on a dying campfire."

I sit up, carrying her with me. "Insulting Aodh is a pastime I quite enjoy..." I leave a lingering kiss on her alluring lips. "...among others, but our interlude of stolen passion and mirth must end." I run a hand through my hair. "I have tarried too long. Dangers are brewing that I must attend to."

I detest the fear seeping into Colleen's expression. "Dangers to me?"

For an instant, I consider lying.

My hesitation supplies the answer.

She wrinkles her nose. "I figured we were in deep shit when cinder boy snatched me and brought me here."

I answer by tucking a strand of hair behind her ear, using comfort to confirm.

Colleen sighs.

I adore even the simplest of sounds from those lips, but her callousness is a concern. "I do enjoy your fire, love, but for your safety, you will need to mind your speech and continue playing the innocent doe."

She glares at me but then softens. "Yeah. I understand."

I sit straighter as the enormity of my troubles comes flooding back. "I do not trust Aodh's gift of these isolated quarters. It is best for you to remain in my chambers." Rising, I gather my sullied clothes and dented armor, a stark reminder of Aodh's cruelty. "The Dark Prince has proven he will not hesitate to strike at those I care for."

Colleen reaches for her dress on the carpet near the settee. She swings it at me, catching my back. "Those you *love*. It's a very nice word to use, especially when I know you love me." She moves to stand in front of me, resting her palms against my chest. "And you know I—"

My hand closes over her mouth more roughly than I intend. "Do not speak the word to me."

She bites my hand.

"Colleen, I am gravely serious." My tone is met with narrowed eyes. When she opens her mouth to protest, I cover it again, more gently this time.

"Please, my darling. I beg you not to say the word confirming your heart's truth. You know of Finnbheara's geas against me."

She does not sink her teeth into my flesh. Instead, my bond-promised closes her fingers around my wrist to lower my hand. Anger leaves her.

I bracket her face with a tender touch. "If you ever declare such feelings of your heart precisely and aloud…" My throat tightens, and I cannot finish.

She touches a fingertip to the corner of my eye, catching a tear before it can fall. "You think the geas will kick in?"

I nod.

"And you'll stop loving me."

Closing my eyes, I drop my chin to my chest. "I fear that will be the conclusion." Finding some modicum of courage, I meet her gaze. "I do not understand why I have been allowed these fleeting moments of joy with you." I take her hands. "You are my eternal beloved. My bond-promised."

She shakes our joined hands. "Maybe that's it. The bond-promise overrides the geas."

Nature's torment, I loathe my next words. "If it were so, dear one, I would have entered into a bond-promise for no other reason than to thwart Finnbheara's curse and spite the king."

She turns her back on me. "Go ahead and tell yourself that, Robálaí."

I nearly laugh. The great Fae warrior Robálaí Geal has no clout with his bond-promised mortal. My humor dies abruptly as I know what I must say next. "I do not wish to injure your heart, Colleen, but in truth, I believe the geas to be only delayed as it winds its way through the roots of the earth until it finds me here beneath the ground."

She shimmies into her gown then turns to me, arms crossed, hurt evident in her dewy eyes. "Well, pardon me if I think your theory is bullshit or dragon shit or whatever." Colleen flails her arms. "Would it kill you to get onboard?"

I wrap my arms around her to tighten the black ribbon lacings on the back of her gown. "I am sorry." Where is the harm in giving her hope, even if I have none myself? "I will not lose faith."

After a moment of hesitation, she slides her arms around me, lifting her chin to meet my gaze. "Agreed. I won't say the L word to you, and you don't give up on us."

I kiss the top of her head. "I accept your bargain."

She huffs. "It's not fair you're allowed to say what you feel, but I can't."

I pull her closer. "If it is of any solace, your essence never hesitated to express what your words dare not."

Colleen gazes up at me. Her expression is a breathtaking picture of devotion. "Good. Now, let's go home, Robálaí."

Home

How I ache to whisk Colleen to my cottage in the Gem Kissed Forest, where she will be forever safe and protected. Oh, to share the wonders of Tír na nÓg with my love.

Colleen stoops to retrieve the remnants of her lace underthings. "Probably not a great idea to leave these lying around for a hellhound to sniff." She frowns, inspecting the shredded fabric. "Or what's left of them." Catching sight of herself in the mirror atop an ornate dressing table, she groans and pulls fingers through her hair. "Serious rat's nest going on here." Colleen reaches for a brush on the table. When she brings it to her hair, my heart stops.

The handle is made of glass to look like the looping branches of a blushberry vine. I tear the brush from Colleen's hand and turn it over to check the emblem on its backing.

"Of all the ancient gods and goddesses," I breathe.

"Robálaí, what's wrong?"

I hold the design up for her to see. "This is the crest of the queen." I swallow the painful lump in my throat. "Queen Nuala of Tír na nÓg, beloved wife of Finnbheara, sacrificed herself to Bráchthine as the price to end a terrible war and broker peace between the realms."

Dragging Colleen by the hand, I burst through the door into the circular antechamber and rush to the first door next to the ones leading to the suite Aodh had designated for my bond-promised. Given the presence of the queen's belongings and the styles of these rooms, so different in design from the rest of Bráchthine's limited palette of red, black, and gold, I am hopeful this is Nuala's private corner of Aodh's kingdom.

Turning to my love, I smile. "Prepare to meet a most gracious and brave lady."

I give a polite knock. When no one answers, I repeat my action with more determination. There is nothing but the echo of my fist against the door.

"My lady, queen," I call in too loud a voice to claim subtlety. "Queen Nuala, are you within?"

Colleen fidgets next to me. I sense she is all nerves in anticipation of our audience with royalty, who, unlike Aodh, is deserving of our respect. "Maybe she's not in there," she whispers.

My bond-promised voices the fear rising at my center. "Perhaps she is just at rest." Or somewhere in Bráchthine, forced to remain on the arm of Aodh as he parades her around his kingdom as a perpetual spoil of war.

Colleen clasps the ornate gold handle and attempts to open the door. I pull her hand away. "It is not fitting to enter a royal chamber without permission."

She grumbles. "You don't know that's what this is." To my dismay, she lays her ear against its surface and pounds on the pristine door. "Hello." Looking at me, she shakes her head and shrugs. "Don't hear a thing."

I may be committing a punishable act of disrespect, but the sense that something vital is amiss drives me to land a brutal kick against the door. It flies open to reveal a sitting room much larger than the one in Colleen's suite, but this one is draped in shadow. A musty smell reveals air not disturbed for an age. Instead of the far wall being made of glass, curtains of silver watermarked silk are drawn over a pair of windows reaching to the ceiling.

Colleen sneezes from the thick dust in the air. There is a tall writing desk of white lacquered wood between the windows. Carvings of vines and leaves circle the legs and frame the entire piece of furniture. In the center of its topmost shelf sits the crest of Finnbheara's queen.

With a sweep of my hand, I brush the curtains aside to let in more light and rush to the desk. On it is a single sheet of paper with elegant writing.

A candle burns to wake the light,
One steadfast flame to challenge night.
If bright doth silver brilliance show,
The blood of blessed life will flow.
If wick be bare and cold at bay,
My spirit bright forever fades.

I trail my finger through the gray dust coating the crème-colored sheet. I know my queen's hand from scores of her missives. The message is a passage known to our Folk. Its meaning shakes me to the center of my soul.

If Nuala is here in Bráchthine, if she…if she…lives, the silver flame of a candle from Tír na nÓg will continue to burn in these rooms I believe she once occupied.

Colleen's voice calls from the adjoining room. "Robálaí, this is a bedroom with no windows, and it's super dark. I can only see from the light in your room. I found a fancy closet with a billion poufy dresses." She returns to the sitting room with an unlit candle in a gold filigreed stand bearing the queen's crest. "It doesn't look like anyone's been in there for a while. I don't suppose you have a match." Colleen chuckles. "Can you light the candle with your magic so we can poke around more?"

I stare at the blackened wick. This cold candle once bore a flame.

If wick be bare and cold at bay,
My spirit bright forever fades.

If the candle shows it once shone with the silver flame of Tír na nÓg, then it is the harbinger of my queen's demise. If the red flame of Bráchthine rises, there is still hope. I yearn to walk away and remain in ignorance, but it is not a choice I am bidden to make. Knowledge may be pain or confirmation of dread happenings, but it is necessary.

I take the candle from Colleen's hand and blow a gentle breath on the wick, willing with any good fortune that may yet linger in my breast for it to ignite with ruby fire.

It shines with a silver flame.

I fall to my knees, and the candle gutters out.

My queen is dead.

Colleen rushes to my side and grips my bent frame. "Robálaí, what's wrong?"

Sorrow steals my words. I point to the writing desk. Colleen leaves me. No time seems to pass before her sudden intake of breath breaks the silence. She brings the note to where I remain unmoving and picks up the fallen candle, switching her gaze between the two items. "But don't Faeries live forever, especially Faerie kings and queens?"

I swallow over and over until the way is clear for words. My voice is cracked and broken. "No. We Fae do not die as humans do, but our lives can be ended in other ways, such as war or by another's hand."

I rise to my feet and stare at the human who has become the silver flame of my life. She cannot stay in Bráchthine. Not Colleen, nor my Host, nor our *péist síoda*. My inadequacy did not perceive the breadth of decay in this realm and its deceptions. I took Aodh and Finnbheara as opposite sides of a coin, both Fae kings equal in deviousness, greed, and power mongering, but also dedication and devotion to the Folk under their rule.

It is a deadly misassumption.

A strain of unquenchable evil runs through Aodh. The Castle of Sorrows and indeed Bráchthine itself hold nothing but despicable calamity for all who pass through their gates.

My queen is dead.

Dragons have died.

The Host of a Thousand Wings are prisoners.

My gaze falls to Colleen, the embodiment of my helpless heart.

My true purpose in coming to this cursed realm dies with my queen. We all must flee the grave peril of this place. What can I bargain with Aodh for the lives of those dear to me? Colleen's words ring through my thoughts. Not dear to me...those I love. How the fates have shifted when Robálaí Geal is driven by love.

"Come, my darling one." I take Colleen's hand in mine, and with a final bow to my once grand and gracious queen, I close the door on the last echo of Queen Nuala.

Colleen is blessedly silent as we hasten toward my chambers. This has been a day of horrors for us both.

A brutal constriction of the chest stops me, and I let out a strangled cry.

"Robálaí?" Colleen runs her hands over my body as if searching for an undiscovered injury.

"Aaaach," I moan and grab my head as the unseen grip eases from my chest. Stumbling, I lay a hand against the wall as a scream blasts through my skull.

"Robálaí Geal."

The voice in my mind is not Colleen's, but I know it well.

Eala Duir calls me.

The threads of her essence dwelling in mine flair, and I see through her eyes.

Finnbheara's Treasure stands before Oweynagat.

Eala Duir has come.

Again, the game curves in on itself.

Shaking my head, I seize Colleen's hand once again. "Run."

As we arrive in the north tower at the rooms of my high command, I pound on each door. Ciallmhar finally answers his. His concerned gaze falls on Colleen.

"She is well," I answer curtly. "Call the others to my chambers and await my return. Time has become our enemy."

"Robálaí," whispers Colleen, unable to mask her fear.

Ciallmhar's head switches between my bond-promised and me.

"She knows all," I hiss then take Colleen's chin in my hand and stare into her eyes. Knowing we have precious seconds, I crash my mouth to hers for a brief burning kiss shot through with my complete and total reverence for what exists between us. "Goodbye, my love."

In parting, I grip Ciallmhar's shoulders. "Use your powers, dear witch, and protect her at all costs, especially from the Dark Prince." With those words, I take my leave.

Aillil senses my approach in the dragon hold and snuffles enough steam to drape his stall in a hazy canopy the color of ripe berries. There is no time for saddle or armaments. Slipping the bridle across his chest, I leap upon his back and we soar to the hellmouth.

It is both surprise and relief that Aodh does not stop me. Has he already discovered Eala's nearness? If she is his prisoner, I have lost the only leverage left to me.

But how shall I levy her if she is not taken? Reason tells me turning her over to Aodh will not expunge the danger of my Folk. I am not in the Underworld God's favor after thwarting his wishes both at the dragon pens and his attempt to seduce my bond-promised. I fear that beating me and limiting my Host to their barracks are but a preamble to further punishments for my disobedience.

Eala Duir must be used to my advantage. She is the winning hand I will not yet reveal.

Summoning me alone is evidence of her desperation. Despite my promise to Colleen, if I must barter Finnbheara's Treasure for the lives I bear responsibility for, I will not hesitate. The King of Tír na nÓg holds nothing but disdain for me. What will one more act against him matter? My heart strings play a melancholy note. Once love for my bond-promised is extinguished by the geas, it is better for us both if Colleen hates me for my oath-breaking.

The way ahead is shrouded in smoke. Its source is the belching breaths of a trio of flame dragons stopped just inside the fiery arch that marks the entrance to Oweynagat. One soldier holds the reins of the riderless pair of beasts. His comrades, with weapons raised, venture forward.

Without hesitation, Aillil and I barge past the flame dragons on a course to run down the foot soldiers. "Halt," I bellow. "I am General Robálaí Geal of King Aodh's high command, and I order you to return to your posts."

I may not hold any rank for long after my trespasses, but it suffices now. Spinning Aillil around, I face the soldiers. In my first turn of luck on this dark day, they bow to me.

"Do you not require us at your back, General?" The soldier's voice reminds me of a boar's grunt.

"I thank you for the offer, but my subtle dealing here is at the Dark Prince's bidding. You are dismissed."

They pound fists to their flame sigils and return to their dragons. I dare not pass into the human realm until I hear no further sign of their nearness or see the reflection of dragon flame upon the dark walls of the Cave of Cats.

I guide Aillil through the boundary between Bráchthine and the land that serves no king. Eala is close to Oweynagat's entrance and looks to be swimming backwards through the muddy sludge of a ditch. When she catches sight of Aillil, the fright in her eyes eases until her gaze finds me upon his back. Her expression hardens, and hatred ignites the gold ring around her green glass *fánaí* irises.

I assume the arrogance and nonchalance of the Robber Bright she expects. "Do you require me to fetch you unsoiled garments?"

Eala clumsily uses a rock embedded in the side of the ditch to prop herself up and manages to find her feet. She shakes mud from her hands and proceeds to rage at me.

"Where did you take Colleen, you bastard? What have you done to her?"

Given her my heart and soul.

I flash a lazy smile. "She is well and happy to be with me." Not a lie, but certainly not the full truth.

"Does she know who she is, or are you still brainwashing her?"

The insinuation rankles me, and my composure slips before I can temper my tone. "Your friend is in complete possession of her mind."

Eala strides toward me, brandishing her finger like a dagger. "Oh no, you don't get to be pissed."

Resuming my air of indifference before my tongue loosens to my detriment, I lean a forearm on Aillil's sturdy neck. "So, you summon me for a reprimand." I raise both hands. "I stand chastened. Farewell, Eala Duir." I begin to turn Aillil, but my erstwhile student lunges forward and tries to throw her arms around my dragon's thick neck.

For a panicked moment, I fear his jaws will snap her arm in two. Instead, he pushes his snout against her shoulder, snuffling a greeting. Of course, she is known to him as the *péist síoda*, Cara's rider and therefore friend to the Host. I feel a pang of regret from separating the young female dragon from her kin. Better to be a lone creature in a land that can sustain her rather than what might have befallen her at the hand of Aodh.

Eala strokes my dragon's neck, daring me with a glare not to move. *"Hello, Aillil. Please inform the ass on your back that he isn't going anywhere."*

I nearly fall off my mount hearing the dragon speak fall from her lips. She is the second woman to confound me in the space of a few hours.

"Ah, the language of the péist síoda rolls off your tongue. You no longer fight your Fae spirit?"

She releases Aillil and wipes a sleeve to chase a lock of her pale, mud-drenched hair off her face. "There's no point in denying it anymore." Eala eyes me suspiciously. "How did you know that? Still poking your nose into my essence where you don't belong?"

There is no time to banter. By now, news of my exit from Bráchthine will be chittering throughout Aodh's network. It will reach the king soon enough. We do not have the luxury of a tedious pace. I slide off Aillil's back.

"Why did you summon me, Eala Duir?"

"First, tell me why you gave me the key to summon you, Robálaí Geal?"

I must tread with caution. "I considered the occasion might arise when you, like myself and my Host of a Thousand Wings, may wish to embrace alternate options of allegiance."

Her shoulders rise as she calls breath to her lungs. "And reject Finnbheara's dictatorial rule as you've done?"

"Yes." I do not elaborate.

"Aodh is your new king."

I nod.

"And serving him is a better situation than serving Finnbheara?"

Her expression is hope itself. It is not in my interest to crush it. "We are adjusting."

"And you swear by...by..." Her gaze lingers on Aillil's ruby eyes. "...your dragon, that Colleen is with you willingly?"

"If you require proof, I will open my essence to you so the truth will be clear."

Eala backs away, waving her hands in front of her. "No, we're not doing that again. I thought Finnbheara was going to skin me when he..." She whirls her fingers on either side of her head. "...sensed your mindprints smeared all over me."

Ah, now we get to her purpose. "So, you come to ask for my aid to escape the King of Tír na nÓg?"

"No." She takes a step forward and sets her hands to her hips. "I've come for your aid to fight him."

I stare at this unexpected proclamation.

She grumbles. "Drop the Faerie statue impersonation so I know you're listening."

A single blink seems to satisfy her. "Finnbheara locked me out of Tír na nÓg and kept Sionnach. I have to get my husband away from there, and I need you to tell me how to do that."

Ah, the separation she reveals confirms the despair I felt from her essence when the Host first entered the Cave of Cats. Eala may not be trapped under Finnbheara's thumb, but her fox has not escaped the king's pinch.

"Is there a way to sneak in and rescue him? Or will I need to fight my way in?"

I cross my arms. "Those are two different circumstances. Equally fraught." I press my lips together. "If the king holds Sionnach Loho, you are correct, force is required to extract your fox." I tap a finger to the side of my nose. "Without knowledge of where Finnbheara keeps him, it is nigh impossible for you to *sneak* in and hunt undetected."

"I believe he's in the Gem Kissed Forest."

My brows shoot up. "Why?"

"I saw a shadow vision of him on the lake you took me through to get to the Crystal Gate and into your forest."

Scratching my chin, I turn to study the sky and think. This meeting with Eala continues to tilt in my direction. She names the single place in Tír na nÓg where I can grant her the power to enter. Finnbheara has no knowledge of the Crystal Gate. Once my rift with the king increased in its seriousness, I created the gate and kept it secret from all but my Host. We felt it prudent to retain the means to travel into or out of the kingdom without drawing the eye of our monarch. By the grace of the ancient gods and goddesses, I pray it still remains hidden from him.

"I do not guarantee your success or safety, but I agree to share the key to the Crystal Gate with you. Know this, you, Eala Duir, may pass freely between Finnbheara's realm and yours through this means, but it remains a Faerie gate and will sense the king's hold on the fox. Your mate will be barred from passing out of Tír na nÓg."

She is shaken but quickly composes herself.

"I am sorry, Eala."

Finnbheara's Treasure eyes me warily. "And what's your price for sharing the key?"

More evidence Eala Duir cants in the direction of the Folk. "Aodh desires an audience with you."

"Are you out of your mind?" She points to the Cave of Cats. "I'm not going back in there."

"It is the price to pass through the Crystal Gate."

Her breaths come in short, shallow puffs. It is easy to see the need to join her fox is all-consuming. "And what's the price for you to help me fight Finnbheara if that's what it takes to get Sion out?"

"You say fight, Eala Duir, but what forces do you bring against the Fae?"

Her mouth stretches into a sly smile. "A pirate navy of six thousand." She frowns. "But we don't know how to get to Tír na nÓg by sea or what numbers we'll face in the fight. You can tell me both."

"A human navy against a Fae navy." I shake my head. You speak of a guaranteed slaughter.

Her face falls, but then lights again. "If we have the Host of a Thousand Wings on our side—"

I raise a hand to stop her. "I can grant you passage to the Faerie seas and Finnbheara's shores, but it will not be enough for a victory."

As she looks to the sky, starlight reflects off the tears welling in her eyes. "Then where else am I supposed to find enough strength to stand against Finnbheara?"

I clear my throat to get her attention. When she drops her gaze to me, I bob my head toward Oweynagat. "Aodh commands such a force."

Eala shakes her head and backs away. "No. I don't want anything to do with your new boss." She throws her arms up. "I knew this was a waste of time, but I came to you anyway. Robber Bright wouldn't know the right thing to do if it bit him in the ass. You have no heart and don't care about anyone but yourself." Again, the *fánaí* ring blazes in her eyes. "You belong with Aodh."

If she only knew the cruel blow her words dealt. To be aligned with the creature of cinder and slaughter I now know Aodh to be is to cover my soul in eternal shadow.

Behind her, the Veil bursts into being, spreading its color and light across the field. There are mere seconds before I lose her.

"Wait, Eala. Allow me to propose a more agreeable parlay. Call it a show of good faith."

Her glare is nearly as potent as the Veil's brightness.

"I will give you the key to the Crystal Gate and swear an oath on Colleen's life that Aodh means you no harm. I also agree to stand by your side during your audience with the king until such time you pass out of the underworld and back to your realm." The lies scorch my tongue.

The Veil's luminescence reflects off the silver borders of Aillil's scales, setting him aglow. Eala stares at the dragon, refusing to meet my gaze, but I see she listens intently.

"I promise you these things, and all I ask in return on this night is for you to consider meeting with my king." I am as treacherous as the Underworld God himself, a fitting general for a Dark Prince.

The pooling of our essences grows weaker with passing time, but I can still sense conflict and agitation below her forced stoicism. She is tempted.

"Test me, Eala Duir, to see if, regardless of who I serve, my word is true."

Slowly, her attention shifts to me. "Fine. Give me the key to the gate, and I will consider—" Her gaze hardens into a keen stare. "Speaking with Aodh, on my terms, not his."

Oh, that this trickle of a Fae believes she can make demands of the God of the Underworld would almost be amusing if all our futures were not threatened. "I accept."

Eala holds her hand palm up as if I will produce a key from my pocket to fit into the lock of a Faerie door.

"As abhorrent as I am to you, it is necessary for you to come close to receive the key. It is made of words, not metal."

She steps to the very edge of the Veil, reaching inside to clutch the branch of a white poplar tree just inside the portal. "You come to me."

Eala Duir is no fool. The Veil will act as her armor against my mischief.

Masking my desperation, I approach her and lean my lips as close to her ear as I dare and whisper the words to open the Crystal Gate no one outside my Host has ever been privy to.

"I don't understand you."

The language of dragons may be hers, but not the ancient words of our Folk. "Memorize it as the notes to a song in a tongue not known to you. Do not try to make meaning of it."

She nods, and I repeat the phrase, singing it this time.

Again, she shakes her head. "Not yet."

The back and forth stretches between us until eventually she sings the complete key to me. Her version is not flawless, but I am confident the Crystal Gate will recognize its proximity to the unique progression of ancient words.

"Yes?" I ask.

"Yes," she answers then furrows her brow. "Robber, you need to promise me one more thing or this whole deal's off."

I scoff. "You give me nothing substantial thus far, yet you attempt to bargain for more?"

"Not attempting…demanding. You owe me. I'm separated from Sionnach because Finnbheara turned into a monster because of you. Your betrayal set him off, and when he sensed your essence hitchhiking in mine, he took his anger out on the people I love."

I slash a hand across my chest to remind Eala of the scar that lies beneath. "The king's vengeance is never fair to look upon."

"Is any king's?"

The truth of her words sinks deep into my soul, a warning that I must hasten the progress of this contract.

"What is your demand?"

She strives to convey strength by assuming an almost military posture, but it does not hide the toll of recent events on her spirit. "Robber, I assume Finnbheara's Veil is closed to you, but does Aodh have a portal you can use to travel through human history?"

"Yes."

She mutters something unintelligible then lifts her chin. "I stole two people from their natural time to help me. Swear an oath, if I don't meet you here tomorrow, you'll return both women to where they belong."

Eala does not yet grasp that she will never know if I kept this promise if she is indeed unable to fulfill it herself. Finnbheara's Treasure is willing to accept my word. It is a fair turn in our dealings. "It shall be done. May I know their names?"

"Biddy Early and Grace O'Malley. You'll find them at my cottage."

The witch's name surprises me. "Mistress Early is known to the Fae. She has oft served as a liaison between Folk and humans."

She nods. "Okay then. Meet me here tomorrow at the start of the Celtic day."

"Eala, when you return, do not attempt to enter Oweynagat. Hail me from this spot. I will hear you and come."

She moves to enter the Veil, but stalls. "Bring Colleen."

Her caveat catches me off guard. If I agree and do not deliver, I shall lose all I gained with my ploy. I don my mask of arrogance as if the request is nothing more than a nuisance, and cloak my answer in deceit. "If it is safe. I assume you care as much for your friend's well-being as I."

"You know I do." With that, she and the Veil are gone.

I drop my head against Aillil's neck. He trills and wraps his tongues around my wrist. I finally have progress to report to Aodh. Nature willing, it will confirm my ongoing value to the king. Although situations are no less dire, it is a small shift in my direction to buy precious time to plan how best to proceed for the salvation of all I endangered by bringing them into Bráchthine.

The Crystal Gate will open.

Eala Duir will return.

CHAPTER 28
THE CRYSTAL GATE

EALA

The moment I step out of the Veil, next to a blooming cluster of cerise-colored trumpet lilies near the cottage, the loud bickering of Biddy and Grace greets me. I need a minute to collect my thoughts before facing them. Adrenaline geysers through my chest from my meeting with Robber.

If my vision in the *lough* was real and the duplicitous Faerie isn't setting me up for a trap at the Crystal Gate, I'm going to find Sionnach. I may not be able to bring him home yet, but to see him, touch him, and know he's alive will boost my courage to keep moving forward. I rub my thumb across my necklace, hoping to absorb some of the Celtic symbol of strength's power. Courage and strength together make their own kind of magic.

Sion's knowledge of what happened after I left Tír na nÓg could be a vital piece in the decision whether or not to risk a meeting with Aodh.

Aodh.

Do I dare make a deal with the closest thing to the devil I'll ever know? Folktales of soul bargains too often have devastating ends naïve humans never saw coming.

There's the story of the barren wife who begged the devil for a baby and then bore a creature with horns and other horrors of its true nature she alone could see. The child killed everyone in the village who spoke a contrary word about the devil and forced his mother to boil them into a stew as food for her demonic spawn.

I recall the saga of the harp maker who bargained for enchanted strings to make his instruments the most sought-after in all the land. Once the devil granted his wish, the man could never rest from his work and died before his fame took hold. The story claims the craftsman vanished into hell and now builds harps that play magnificent melodies the devil uses to lure other desperate souls into his ignominious deals.

I play back my promises to Robber Bright and breathe a sigh of relief. I've only agreed to consider a meeting with Aodh, nothing more.

What about Colleen? How high will Robber and Aodh's demands be to free her from hell?

I can't begin to unravel Máthair's situation. Hopefully, Sion will be able to fill in some blanks.

As eager as I am for my swan to fly to the gate, I need to brief Biddy and Grace on what I did and what I plan to do. A chunk of dried mud on my collar tickles my neck, and I flick it off. Meeting Sion, looking like I've just lost a mud wrestling match, doesn't paint me as the picture of competence. I'll grab a quick shower, change, and be at the Crystal Gate before the moon has fully risen.

I stamp my muddy sneakers on the porch and decide to strip off every stitch of my fouled and grimy clothes. I'm about to push the latch and announce I'm home and naked by choice when the Pirate Queen rails even louder. "You mean to serve me flowers for my supper, witch, or is it a spell you're brewing?"

Biddy blasts right back at her. "Once these dahlia tubers are roasted and covered with sweet syrup from the petals, you'll stop looking for spells 'round every corner."

Grace grumbles. "What have you witches got against a nice roasted hare?"

Throwing the red door open, I yell, "I've got news," and streak to the bathroom. That stops the argument. I'd bet a handful of the money Sion hides under the floorboards that Grace is checking to see if I have Faerie wings.

On my mad dash, I catch a glimpse of the pirate lying on the couch with her dirty boots propped on its arm and Biddy hovering over the fire.

How would Sion react to a pirate's soiled boots on his sofa in the cottage he keeps so tidy? Will my husband and I ever have the chance to worry about something as mundane as mud on the furniture?

After the fastest shower on record, I open the door, releasing a cloud of steam into the bedroom. Pulling on fresh jeans, Sion's navy-blue thermal shirt, and a Kennard Park University hoodie as fast as I can, I dart into the main room of the cottage.

The two women stare at me with raised brows. Grace is on her feet while Biddy attends to her cooking.

"News, is it?" Grace prods with a scowl.

"Bottom line," I say, sitting on a kitchen chair to pull on the waterproof hiking boots I wish I'd worn to Oweynagat. "I've made a bargain with another Fae. He's given me the password to a secret gate to get into the forest in Tír na nÓg, where I believe Finnbheara is keeping Sionnach."

Biddy drops her spoon. "A bargain," she whispers. "Oh no, Eala."

I shake my head. "Don't worry, I didn't promise much."

The witch comes to stand in front of me, arms crossed and an extremely unhappy expression on her face. "Everything is much when you're dealing with the Fae."

Grace joins Biddy to double-team me. "I've no fondness for the sound of this."

"You forget," I say, double knotting my shoe. "I'm Fae."

"Och," Biddy waves a hand at me. "You're a Fae still in the nest who's not yet flown." She cocks her head. "And what other Fae have you bargained with?"

Damn it. All I want to do is get to Sionnach. I've tiptoed around the parts Aodh, Robber Bright, and the underworld play in this, but my gut tells me it's time to come clean. I slap my knees and stand. "You'd both better sit for this, there are things I haven't told you yet."

Grace blasts a string of curses so unique I wish I had time to write them down. "Fae are always hiding a trick or a lie. This one is no different." She slides the dagger from her belt, but after flashing a glance at Biddy, switches it to a less threatening position.

As soon as the blade catches the light, my Veil sprites dive into my bloodstream and begin to pulse. The result is instant and entirely new. Unmistakable threads of light flare from my body, brightening the room. Both witch and pirate take a step back.

A dab of fear and a dash of awe from the team can only help my case. "It's true that I'm newly acquainted with my Fae heritage, but underestimating any Faerie isn't in your best interest." I gesture to the couch. "Sit."

These two stalwart women don't choose to argue with a Faerie light bulb. Where do I start? Might as well begin with the Fae elephant in the room.

"The Faerie I hold an impending bargain with is Robálaí Geal, or Robber Bright, as I prefer to call him. Although I've seen no brightness in his soul. He is made of shadow and deception." I flick a wrist. "He was assigned by Finnbheara to show me the way to my Faerie gifts. In the end, he betrayed me and his king to align with…"

Do I blurt Aodh's name or use one of his titles? Which will they be more familiar with? Or…can I show them? I think of the stories Sionnach sent me in the flames of the hearth throughout my childhood. If I share Aodh's myth wrapped in a tale instead of labeling him *the* devil, will his involvement be easier to swallow?

I still and let my essence encompass the Veil sprites.

Will you paint my story with shadow and flame in the hearth?

Tiny wisps rise out of my body and bob over to the hearth. Okay, that's a yes.

I move next to the fireplace and gesture to the flames. "I'm a keeper of story, tale, and myth. Here is one you must know to understand the totality of mine." It's easy to fall into my professor lecture cadence. "Lir, god of the *Tuatha Dé Danann*, was blessed with a beloved wife and from their union, four children."

Biddy and Grace lean forward when six human figures appear in the flames. From their silhouettes of flowing robes and Lir's crown, I can tell the Veil sprites know this story. I brush aside the uneventful middle to get to the end faster. "After Lir's wife died, he claimed her sister's hand. The second wife was of a jealous sort and did not favor the offspring from her predecessor."

I don't go into the scholarly speculations that Aodh and his siblings weren't the angelic victims many versions of the myth make them out to be. In fact, a handful of pretty horrific actions are credited to the quartet.

"She plotted to kill the Children of Lir but the courage to murder failed the stepmother. Instead, she cursed the four to dwell within the bodies of white swans. Many tales claim the rage within these souls charred their feathers black."

The flames climb high as the shadow of a chariot charges forward bearing a woman with a raised sword. Smoke streams from the tip of her blade, transforming into four light gray swans. One by one, each darkens to the color of coal.

"For hundreds of years, the siblings haunted the *loughs* of Ireland, singing their laments with the voices of the children they once were. All who heard them carried a stone of sorrow within their hearts."

The shadow swans fly through the flames, the swells of a stormy lake dip and crash beneath them.

"One day, a man not of the *Tuatha Dé Danann* heard their strange song. He was pledged to a different god, a King of Heaven, not the gods and goddesses of the Folk. When this newly forged holy man begged his King to end the suffering of Lir's children, they shed feather and beak, becoming aged men and women."

Biddy and Grace listen, occasionally nodding their heads at this old chestnut of a myth.

The Veil sprites paint the transformation in smoky gray strokes.

"Curses may be broken, but are never forgotten. They shape the souls who bore them."

The flames flare and turn black. Biddy and Grace both gasp.

"While three of the siblings accepted peaceful ends, Aodh, eldest son of Lir, rejuvenated and seized the throne of the underworld to forever reign with a heart filled with hate, greed, and the vow of vengeance against all who challenge his power." In the middle of the black fire, the red-orange triple flame emblem of Aodh that I first saw on Robber Bright's underworld armor appears. As if marching through a mighty gate, the inky shadow of a warrior bursts through the center flame and thrusts his arms high to threaten the ancient gods themselves.

I change my tone to something more conversational, but every bit as serious. "Aodh is the sworn enemy of Finnbheara. The son of Lir is the king Robber Bright now serves in the underworld."

With a rush, the Veil sprites leave the fire and return to me, leaving familiar orange hearth flames in their wake.

Biddy's face is ashen. "You treat with the devil?"

"No, I've never spoken to Aodh...directly, just Robber Bright."

If Grace is shaken by my potential dealings with Aodh, she doesn't show fear. "Speak of your association with more clarity, Faerie. You've spoken to the devil *indirectly*."

If clarity is what she wants, I'll deliver. "Aodh is not the devil you know. He's a Fae king like Finnbheara with...a navy."

The Pirate Queen clacks her teeth. "You would ask us to fight on the side of hell?"

I'm done with this. I've got to get to Sion. "It's not the hell you think you know, damn it. Aodh was the son of a Fae king who now rules his own kingdom. I don't deny the Underworld God is dark and dangerous, but he's our only choice to gain a Faerie navy at our back. A navy that knows how to get to Tír na nÓg."

"For a soul price," hisses Biddy.

"No one's asked for anyone's soul." I brush a strand of hair behind my ear. "Let me worry about the price of any bargains I make with Robber Bright involving Aodh." I grab one of Biddy's hands and one of Grace's. "I swear on my soul, neither of yours is in jeopardy."

The pirate yanks her hand free. "You risk your eternal soul for a man."

I step away from Biddy to face down Grace. "My soul is already claimed. Sionnach is my *anamchara*. You may not believe souls are destined. I tell you now, we share a bond that most claim is legend or myth, but they're wrong. We aren't halves of a whole, but rather we form a unique light, a completely new entity. I call him husband, soulmate, but neither does justice to what we are. We are a single moonbeam, the dazzling light of spirits woven together."

Biddy's voice is quiet. "I have known love, but never that."

A crackle from the hearth is the only sound in the room. I break the silence. "Granuaile O'Malley, has there never been a man or woman you would fight and die for?"

"I take your meaning," she says with a clipped voice.

"I'm going to leave you both for a while to go to the *lough*. I'll try to get into Tír na nÓg and, fates willing, my *anamchara*. There's a chance I might not come back."

Grace's eyes flare with all the violence I believe she's capable of. "And what of us? Are we now cursed to be prisoners of your time? You've bargained with us, too, Faerie. Was your word nothing but mischief of the Folk?"

The woman is truly terrifying. I blow out a slow breath and breathe another in so I don't stammer when I deliver news I'm sure they won't like. "Everything I've promised you both will come to pass. Outcomes are set in motion. Believe me or not, but time will prove my vows were made with truth and honest intention."

I'd love to squeeze my eyes shut and not suffer their reaction to this second part, but I do my best to stare down the pessimism in the room. "If I don't return by tomorrow night, the Faerie Robber Bright will see to it you both are returned to your times without harm. He is bound to our oath."

They're both stunned, but at least Grace isn't pointing a weapon at me. That's progress.

"I have every intention of returning, but before I go, I want to say…" Whether from fatigue or the gratitude I feel for these two women, I can't tell, but it's rough to get out my next words. "Thank you." There's so much more they deserve, and hopefully, I'll be given the opportunity to properly express my gratitude. "Goodbye."

With a tight-lipped smile and an even tighter chest choked with emotion, I turn toward the door.

"Oh, no, Eala Duir. You'll not leave without me," says Biddy, springing to my side.

"Biddy, I'm not going to take you into Tír na nÓg. It's too dangerous."

To my surprise, she motions to Grace. "Aye, but there's no harm in seeing you safe to this Faerie door of yours. We fared well together at the last one, did we not?"

The Pirate Queen remains near the hearth and grunts. "I've nothing to offer a Faerie door. I'll keep the home fire burning."

Biddy frowns at her.

"Let her stay," I tell Biddy. "If all goes well, she'll get her moment to be by my side."

The witch nods, and together we leave Grace behind. I'd planned to fly as my swan, but with Biddy along, I call the Veil to take us to the shore of the *lough*. Its waters shimmer more brilliantly than the light of the waxing moon warrants. Flickers of silver light rise and hover just above the surface.

"Biddy, there's one more thing I need to prepare you for." I'm glad Grace decided not to join us. My transformation into a swan on top of everything else she'd learned tonight would be quite a shaker. "To get to the gate, I need to be in a different form."

"Oh?" She sounds more interested than worried.

I point to the path near the end of the lake that barely qualifies as a road. I've only traveled it on the back of a silk dragon or as my swan. "Follow this path to the cottage. I'm sorry, but it's a long walk. Once I've gone, don't linger here. If I don't return, you can't miss meeting up with Robber Bright."

"Fine." She takes a long, appraising look at me. "Good luck to you, Eala of the Fae."

"Thank you, my *bean feasa* friend." I pull her into a hug.

"I'll watch until you've gone."

When we pull apart, I crinkle my lip. "Aren't you curious about the form I'll take?"

Biddy smiles. "Eala, the meaning of your very name being swan, answers any wondering."

I smile back. "So, it does."

I walk to the shore and stare into the *lough*. If I speak the words Robber gave me, will I be able to see the gate through these enchanted waters? I'm not sure where to aim. It'll be helpful if the darn thing lights up like a beacon.

Tapping into my Fae essence, I begin the phrase. Halfway through, the faintest iridescent ripples begin to swirl on the surface near the opposite shore. I'm so excited by the sight, I bungle the rest of Robber's words. The glimpse of what I pray is the gate disappears.

"Shit."

Again, I concentrate on the gentle ebb and flow of the lake's surface. My essence mimics the movement of the water. I will the words of the key to flow through my mind as silver ink across a deep blue sheet of parchment, then read them in a low singsong.

The weak shine of the ripples returns, and this time I don't break my focus. As I come to the final pair of words, it fades again. Damn it. Did I mess up the order? I'm sure those were the words.

On my third attempt, I switch around the last two words but still fail. No, I'm sure I had it right before. Or am I? The words of the key jumble in my memory. I'm losing it. Did Robber Bright charm the phrase so it's impossible to use again once it's been spoken? No, that can't be it. He wants me to succeed so he will gain my trust.

"Eala?"

The note of concern in Biddy's voice doesn't help the knots in my stomach and throat. I need to walk off my nerves and try again. I rejoin Biddy. "I'm pretty sure I saw the gate, but I'm not correctly speaking the words to open it." I shake my head. "I thought I remembered the phrase, but I was wrong."

Biddy smooths a hand down my hair. "Whist, whist. You're working yourself into a fine fit."

Her touch is as calming as one of Colleen's hugs.

"Where's this gate you speak of?"

"Over—" I start to point, but without the telltale light, I have no idea where the gate is. The far shore and swaying water are one big blur. I slap my thigh so hard it burns. "I saw it. I just can't remember where. The damn Faerie gate is teasing me." I'm sure I sound as crazy as I feel.

"Will you let me lend a bit of help?"

My geyser of anger fizzles out, and I fight back a sob. "I don't know what you can do."

Biddy leaves me to flounder in my distress and walks to the edge of the water. She tips a single drop from her blue bottle into the *lough*. Like ink bleeding across paper, a neon blue gleam blossoms over the surface, making the water transparent. At the base of the hill on the opposite shore, the reflection of light hitting crystal rides the current.

"You found it."

"Magic found it. You forget, my blue bottle, like you, Eala, is also of the Fae." She pats my shoulder. "Now go back to the moment when you learned the words of the key and find what you're missing."

I summon the memory of Robber whispering the words of the key. That's when it hits me. I was grasping Alfie's trunk while I listened. The strength of the Veil flowed through my spirit and mixed with his voice.

Alfie.

Is it possible? Could my *fánaí* tree, this sacred chain in the great Tree of Life, hold memory?

I walk trancelike until the toes of my boots touch the lapping water and call the Veil. Without needing to look, I sense Alfie behind me and wrap a hand around her closest trunk. "Sing with me, friend."

I begin the song of the key to the Crystal Gate in a language just out of reach, but that I know without a doubt is embedded deep in my Faerie essence. This time, the words come to me as if Robber Bright still whispers in my ear. Just as I finish, there's a loud *whoosh* and a circle of water rises in a spinning spout from the *lough*.

I don't spare a single second before becoming my swan. With the beat of my wings, I rise in an arc beneath the stars then plunge down the center of the watery tunnel and into the Crystal Gate.

CHAPTER 29
THE NESTLING

SIONNACH

A smell like I've snuck my nose in a pile of burnt sugar rouses me. I've had an easier time opening my eyes after a night of too many whiskeys. It takes a good knuckle rub to wipe away the bit of crust gluing my lashes to my skin. I manage a squint. The light is the blessed dim of a gloaming before night takes hold.

My body aches as if I were on the losing end of more than a few fists. There's an unfriendly scratching at my back. When I brush off the poke, my hand closes around a long twig.

It's then that I prop myself on an elbow, stretching my eyes the rest of the way open.

"What in the name of Ma's shortbread biscuits?"

I rub my eyes again as if that's ever made a daft sight any clearer. I'm in the bedroom of the cottage, but not on the bed I have yet to sleep on, much preferring a place on the rug before the hearth. My sorry self is plunked in the middle of the nest wedged into the corner of the room. Trailing vines act as a curtain of sorts to block out the sunlight slicing in through any crack it can find in the main room. I'd locked the shutters back in place, creating as much of a fortress as possible after those Fae had at me.

I'm in nothing but britches with leaves and flowers piled over the rest of me.

Memories slam into me—talking to the garden, my shaking hands, mind spinning like a whirligig.

"Sionnach Loho, you fecking fool," I grumble as the recollections of drinking from a Faerie bottle and nearly drowning in the stream are next to visit me.

I pat my chest and britches. I'm as dry as a bone and warm to boot. Wait. Someone dragged me out of the water. I blink over and over as if that'll wake my mind. No such luck.

"Och." I grab my head. Trying to think is like being stabbed in the ear with a pick.

Through the pain, recollection flares. Finnbheara doesn't want me dead. Not yet, at least. He leaves food for me. Could it be it was his hand that hauled me from the stream and onto this nest that some massive bird built in the abandoned cottage?

I drop back down, not having the will to bring anything else to mind.

"Sion."

Ah, now there's music to mend a broken soul. The memory of Eala's voice calling me brings no pain. I close my eyes to allow the sound of my name upon my *anamchara's* lips return me to sleep.

"Sionnach Loho."

I spring to a sitting position. This can't be.

"Sion, are you here?"

Is her voice more torment from the Folk, or a cruel trick of my battered mind?

I crawl over the edge of the nest and hurry as best I can to my armory of sticks and stones. No fucking Fae will bother me again without tasting the whittled point of my homemade spear. Crouching beneath the shuttered window, I keep still.

"It's me, Eala. I'm here, *anamchara*. I'm here."

Maybe there's nothing out there. My mind has decided to start telling its own stories. Moving as slow as sap in winter, I ease up to peek through the first slat of the shutter.

Eala, my Eala *bán*, for none other could make my heart burst in my chest, stands across the road, inspecting one of the Faerie bottles I knocked over in the grass. The stick falls from my hand. The clatter brings Eala's head round to stare at the cottage.

"Sion," she breathes as quietly as ice melting.

I open the cottage door and step into the sunlight.

Eala cries, "*Anamchara*," and before the word is finished, leaps into my arms. Her limbs fasten around me like ivy twining up the trunk of an oak. She frantically kisses my brow, eyes, cheeks, and jaw, checking they're all there, murmuring perfect words of love. But I'm no oak. Even though I cling to her, I've not got the strength I once did. Stumbling backward, I bump against the cottage and lose my grip on her.

"Tell me it's you, my fox. Tell me you're real."

Eala's fallen from my arms but keeps hold of my shoulders. I bury my face in her perfect feathery locks until my lips graze her ear. "Aye, swan. What's left of me is real." I drop kisses from her temple to the corner of those pouty lips and linger there. "Are you truly my Eala *bán*?"

To the depth of my soul, I ache for this to be a truth before me and not another Fae cruelty. She feels like my love, the scent of my home fields and hearth lingers in her hair, and this voice never fades from my dreams, but the days of trusting my mind are sailing far away.

The woman holds my face in her hands with a loving touch as dear to me as my own breath. "Sionnach Loho, I am your Eala *bán*, your *anamchara*, your soulmate, your partner in every time and place, your heart, your wife."

"Wife," I repeat with the reverence due a saint. It's not a word any Fae would use in their trickery, as they do not honor our blessed vows. "Wife… wife…wife," I say over and over, pressing a kiss to her lips with every saying of it.

She answers in kind, "Husband…husband…husband," until we finally sink into a kiss neither Fae nor fate would dare deny us. I'll kiss my woman until time forgets itself and doesn't allow dawn to break or days to wane. Ours is an eternal kiss, a promise to the ages that one shall always know the other. This is the gift of *anamchara* that will live forever in our souls.

Eala's hands run down my chest as one kiss blends into the next. When her touch finds its way to my ribs, she steals her lips from me and stands back to take in my dwindled carcass. Seeing the shock in her eyes, I stare at my sorry state. Instead of adding meat to my bones, that cursed Faerie potion made a scarecrow of me.

Eala's voice is mostly breath. "Holy hell, Sion. What happened to you?"

I pull her to me. "Seems Tír na nÓg is not kind to humans, especially those Finnbheara considers a splinter in his thumb."

She pinches me all over, measuring the damage. "But it's only been days. How…?" Fingertips run through the light stubble on my face that's not grown a whit since we parted. Her brow wrinkles when she sees the silver stump still plenty crowded with food, ruling out starvation as the culprit.

"Days for you, love," I say. "I've no measure of time here without night." I jerk my chin to the sky.

Her brow furrows. "What do you mean?"

"There's never a moon here, only sunlight." I snort, remembering the odd darkness that fell once when I ate the berry and again before the Faeries cut my hair. "Except in my untrustworthy noggin.'"

Eala shakes her head. "That makes no sense. Robber Bright showed me a Faerie moon." She narrows her eyes. "Finnbheara," she growls. "He's keeping the lights on to screw with you."

I wobble a bit.

Eala catches me flagging. Her lovely face softens with concern. "Tell me what's wrong with you, Sion."

"I'll tell you all, love, but if you don't mind, I need to rest a bit." I take her hand. "Come inside."

She glances about the cottage as I lead her through the door. "This is where you've been staying. It's gloomy." Eala starts poking around with more interest than I ever showed the place.

I'm too weary to follow her, so I sink onto my familiar spot on the rug before the hearth. There's a great ache and crack in my bones when I lean back on my elbows. "Oof."

In a flash, Eala cuts off her snooping to drop down next to me. "That did not sound good."

I drop onto my back. "Truth be told, love, there may be beauty for the eye to see, but nothing's truly good in this cursed land."

She lies with me and pulls my head to her chest. The thumping of her heart is a wondrous thing.

"Oh my, love." Eala rests her cheek on my hair, and fingers slide softly through the matted mop. "Tell me everything?"

I rest a hand on her leg. "The short of it is, both my mind and body are falling apart. Finn's had a fine time telling me how Tír na nÓg robs a human fella like me of his senses."

"I don't understand."

The look of me and my words give her a fright. I hold up a trembling hand for her to see. "My mind and body are going the way of a river running dry. Finnbheara's keeping me at the edge of life so there's enough left of my bones and breath to draw you to me and, in turn, to him." I grip her thigh, trying to stop my shakes. "He's off to war with Aodh soon, and I'm to be the one bringing you into their Faerie knuckle supper." I hide my face against her breast. "I'm sorry, my darling, but after that, I fear I'm done for."

She grabs my chin, twisting me to look at her. "Don't you dare believe such nonsense, Sionnach Loho." Tears flow freely down her cheeks. She hugs me tighter. "I should have stayed and fought by your side, not run out of Finnbheara's cursed gates. This is my fault."

I rustle the strength to sit and snug her on my lap. "Don't you dare believe that nonsense, Eala Loho."

We're still as tears fall from us both. Hers from sorrow at what's become of me and mine because I've not the strength to hold them in. I rub her back. "You've come now, my lovely swan. If you'll have what's left of your husband, we'll go off home."

Her sudden wail pierces my heart.

"I can't take you home, Sion. I'm the only one who can leave." Her gaze skitters to the shuttered window. "I have to be careful. Finnbheara can't find me here. I'm sorry. I'm sorry. I've been trying so hard…"

She's wrecked. I won't let my devastation add to her misery. I stroke her hair. "I know, my brave *anamchara*. Don't fret over ole Finn. He's got no reason to come around until the war with Aodh catches fire." I grunt. "Whenever the bugger does lower himself to visit, the man makes a big show of it with thrashing winds and such. We'll hear him coming." I look into her eyes. "How fast can you be gone, love, if he does blow in?"

Eala shows me the black tattoo on her pointer finger. "Fast. This will take me straight to the gate." She taps a thumb to it. "When I made my way through the forest to you, I laid this finger over my heart for a hot second. The touch sent me right back to the spot where I entered Tír na nÓg from the *lough*."

"That's a useful bit of Faerie magic," I say, kissing her finger with the wee key. Before I can ask more about the new mark on her, she dissolves against me, curling in on herself, a right mess of weeping.

"Oh, my Sionnach, how can I leave you again?"

As if answering her keening, my beastie howls from the forest. Eala's sorrows cut off with a sharp gasp, and now she's the one shaking. Her gaze locks onto mine, "Cara?"

"No friend of mine, love. Just another lonely fool stuck in Finn's pretty cage."

She shakes her head. "I'm not saying friend in Irish. It's her name." Eala's off my lap and to the front door so fast, she nearly knocks me over. "Cara," she hollers to the forest, then utters a bunch of clicks, trills, and hisses.

A great whirring and buzzing fill the forest. Out the open door, clouds of dust roll by. Eala's back at my side, helping me up. "Come with me." She's glowing as bright as a Beltane bonfire as she drags me along with her. "Look," she says, pointing at the sky. "Cara's here. I thought Robber Bright had her."

Only one part of what she said makes any sense to me, *Cara*, the name of the silk dragon that Fae bastard brought to Eala as a gift from Finn.

My wife's got a death grip on my arm. "Wow. She's grown."

In the bleached sky above the treetops, a creature as grand as Pegasus is coming fast for us. There's a haze of blue about her. A wonderous hide that looks to be encrusted with jewel dust shows through the nimbus. The dragon releases a howling cry I know well.

Here in the middle of a Faerie forest with my *anamchara*, I sing my answering notes as Cara floats to the ground in front of us.

Eala throws her arms around the dragon's neck as its snout bats the top of her head and then the top of mine. The dragon's tongues are all over Eala before it treats me to the same with purrs and chitters.

Eala's off and weeping again. "Oh, you beautiful darling." She switches her gaze between the dragon and me, making those strange clickety noises.

Full of anguish, I rest my head in my hands. I'm losing Eala's words. They're turning to nothing but gibberish. Finn's stealing everything from me.

"Sion, Sionnach, what's wrong?"

My head snaps up. "I thought…I couldn't understand you."

"Oh god, I'm sorry." She drops kisses across my face. "When there's a dragon around, I think I'm speaking English, but it comes out in words that sound like a form of ancient Irish. It's a Fae language the *péist síoda* understand."

When Cara clicks and huffs, two tidy wee clouds of berry-colored steam billow from her snout. Eala looks at me, surprised. "You've been singing to her?"

"This one's been putting up quite a howl. I had no notion what was making the noise. I thought maybe singing back would keep me out of its belly."

Eala looks horrified. "A *péist síoda* would never eat you."

I shrug. "Everything else here has it in for me." My legs start to fail me again, and I slump against the dragon. The hide looks like armor of turquoise and purple scales, the colors of the Veil's carpet, each with a silver outline, but they're as soft as a knitted blanket.

Eala grabs for me, but it's her Cara who trills and grabs the back of my britches to hold me up, snorting wet mist all over my bare back.

"Sion, why is Cara calling you her nestling?"

"Bless this howler's hide." I rest my head against Eala's *péist síoda*. "I think your beastie here saved my damned skin."

Eala says the creature's name, which is the last word I make sense of before the two of them have a noisy chat.

Eala's eyes go wide. Her skin flushes. "You drank from a Faerie bottle, Sion? What the hell? Do you even listen to the stories you tell about the consequences of doing something so stupid?" She shakes her head. "Cara said she stuck you in a stream to wash it out of your system and then put you in Aillil's nest."

"Well, bugger me. I've been squatting in a beastie's cottage." My knees start to feel as if the bones in 'em have turned to jam. "Never thought I'd be grateful to have dragon teeth close to my arse."

Eala slings my arm around her shoulders and helps me to the cottage. "Uh, Sion. Aillil is Robber Bright's dragon. You've been squatting in Robber's cottage."

"Wouldn't the bastard love that?" I growl as I stumble alongside Eala with Cara close behind us.

My love helps me to the bed in the room with vines and what I know now to be a dragon's nest. I'm too knackered to protest.

"Sion, Robber Bright and his Host left Tír na nÓg to serve Aodh in the underworld."

"Yeah, Finn's piss and fire about being betrayed, coupled with the day we saw Robber Bright kitted out in Aodh's armor at Loho cottage, confirmed well enough the Fae bastard ended up in hell." I manage a snort. "Where he belongs."

All at once, as if saying the word brings on my own personal hell. The edges of my sight start to darken, a sound like a hornet trapped in my head sets off a wicked ache, and the damn shakes take over my body. Eala's asking me about gates and Robber Bright, but I can't make heads or tails of her words through my agony.

She stops talking. My dearest love curls her body around me. If I'm to go, at least the last thing I'll feel is the sainted warmth of my *anamchara* against my skin.

Her voice cuts through the buzzing. "Find me, Sionnach. Find me as you did before."

Dreams are wondrous things. There's no hurting, and impossible is not part of their language. I'm settled onto a bed of flower petals as soft as lamb's wool. Golden dust swirls around me. Or is it light? Has Heaven decided it's where my soul should finally rest?

It's not the pearly gates or Saint Peter that call to me. Something far more brilliant melts into my golden halo. It's frost and heat all at once. My heart is held gently in a loving touch. The colors of the Veil flicker beyond the gilded light and its strength pulses through me. It's a fitting goodbye for the years the magical path and I spent in each other's company.

Wings as white as an Easter lily brush over me, tending to every ailing bit. A whisper dances around me like the breath of a sleeping babe. It speaks not in words but caresses the blights in my mind until the ache fades away.

This is peace, the place a soul can rest.

"You're untouched by any Fae cruelty. You are whole."

A final blessing to end my endless days.

I am Sionnach Loho.

Beloved son.

Veil guide.

Wanderer through the paths of time.

Saver of soulfalls.

Husband to a Faerie woman who burns with the goodness of a bright soul.

A tickle in the center of my chest brings back the light. Eala's fingers trail through the patch of hair she loves to play with.

I grab her hand and press her palm flat against my chest. "Is it beating? My heart?"

Eala moves my hand to kiss the very place thumping like mad beneath my skin. "Strong as ever."

I sit up, carrying her along, and stare at my arms. They're not wasted thin. I press along my chest, abdomen, and ribs. Muscles, firm and fine, bunch back where they belong. My sight is clear. My mind doesn't hum with the threat of madness.

I stare at the room. I'm in Robber Bright's fecking bedroom in the Gem Kissed Forest. Finnbheara's only keeping me here to steal Eala back into his kingdom. There's a dragon outside the door who saved my life.

I clutch Eala to me. "Oh, my wondrous Faerie maid."

She ducks her face against my neck. "Oh, Sionnach. I didn't know if I could find you this time. I sent my essence to yours, but it was like flying into a churning storm cloud—the angriest gray I've ever seen and full of brutal lightning."

I let a fluff of her hair fall through my fingers. "But you kept at it."

"In the middle of everything, I saw a silver circle. It grew larger and larger until I knew what it was, a simple silver ring with the words *teacht orm* written on the band."

"*Teacht orm*…find me," I whisper.

"Find me," she answers back, and lifts her left hand for me to kiss the silver ring that brought us together.

Whatever god or goddess blesses this woman with the strength of her love, I bless those holy folks right back.

She runs her hands all over my chest then up the sides of my neck. Eala draws her lips to mine and dots them with a light kiss. "How do you feel?"

I press my hands into her back. "Like I was falling then caught by a cloud."

Eala laughs. "Seriously." She starts up her patting again, leaving none of my body unexamined.

I catch her hand. "I may not be a fan of the Folk, but this gift you have of setting me to rights is a miraculous thing."

"It is, isn't it?" She smiles, and I would be fine with the world ending right now.

"I love you, Sionnach Loho." It's no gentle kiss she steals from me then. Her velvet tongue sweeps through my mouth like she's painting memories no madness dare touch. One of her hands holds the back of my neck in place, daring me to pull away, while the other is pulling at her clothes.

I laugh into her hot mouth as she makes a tangle of getting naked. "I can help you with that, love."

She lets me free. While keeping my gaze locked to hers, I peel away her jacket then slide off my waffle weave shirt she's wearing. Her lovely buds already strain at her bra. She reaches behind to lose the lacy wrapper, and there she is, bare from waist to those beautiful green glass *fánaí*, Veil traveler's, eyes we share.

I ravish the perfect pout of her lips, giving her a hot thrashing with my tongue. She's every drop of honey I've ever tasted. Her hand threads through my hair, stroking and pulling like I'm the only thing keeping her from floating into the sky.

"I love you. I love you. I love you," she moans into my mouth, and I return the favor.

We sit on the bed, pressed together with no space between us. Eala tucks onto my lap, her legs squeezing around me without mercy. The pounding in her chest is as strong as the wings of her swan in flight. With every beat of hers, my heart answers with equal force. Our skin rages with the joyous fire of our reunion.

My tongue draws a path down the front of my swan's gorgeous neck. I rest an ear over that lovely place where her life's blood sings to me. With a slight turn of my head, her hard nipple slides over my tongue. I fill my palms with her heavy breasts and knead her hot, silky flesh until she groans my name and steals my mouth away again.

The sound of her rising need drives straight to my cock. Eala pushes her hips forward so the pressure of my length is right where it belongs. I let her rock against me, losing myself to the rhythm, and drop my head back. If there ever was a version of my life without this woman in it, I never want to imagine it.

I thread my fingers into her hair. Suddenly, I imagine losing her if Finnbheara drags her into his battle. My hands begin to tremble.

She pulls away. "What's wrong, my fox? Do you need more healing?"

I drop my head against her chest. "There are things your healing can't touch, like my uselessness against magic." I meet her gaze. "How can I protect my wife when I've got no control over any Fae that comes along to pin me to the ground with a flick of their finger? You're married to a weakling, Eala."

The soft pads of her thumbs caress my jaw. "I most certainly am not." Her eyes narrow. "Sion, did Finnbheara hurt you?"

"He's deviled me to be sure, but it was a different pair of Folk who waylaid me to steal a bit of my hair…" I draw in a long breath. "And a sight more courage and confidence I've yet to find again."

My swan's skin turns as red as a fire flower. The muscles in her neck become an iron rod. "I'll cut off Finnbheara's dick for putting you in danger."

The satisfying image of Eala slicing through the royal member with a sword brings a smile to my face and steadiness to my hands. "Seems you've enough courage for the both of us."

"Sionnach Loho, you are my courage, and I'm yours," she says, crushing her lips to mine. Eala restored my body and mind, now she gives me back my soul. When her lips part mine, there's bravery in every breath gliding over my tongue. I deepen the kiss, drinking in her strength. My battered confidence will find its way home for the sake of this woman.

Eala stands to shred her jeans. When I stare in renewed wonder at my wife's beautiful body, she guides my hands to her shoulders. "I need your touch, my darling fox."

I skate my fingers down her arms until they twine with my swan's. Our gazes meet, and she lifts our hands to her breasts. I let the warmth of her skin soak into my palms and slowly rub my thumbs over her lovely plum-colored peaks before slipping my fingertips along her sides to the dip in her waist then the curve of her hips.

Eala hums when I travel toward the silk of her inner thighs. My cock thickens as the heat from her core flows over my skin. I move higher until my fingertip sinks into the damp fabric of her panties. When she bends to slide them free, my desire drips like rain falling beneath my flesh.

I open my knees to pull her closer, keeping a slow pace as I slide my grip around to her ass. With Eala, I'm not a weakling. Palming her sex, I find her enticingly hot and wet, fluttering with desire for me.

All my dreams of loving her, only to wake without my swan in my bed, come crashing back. Finally, they become reality. One at a time, I allow each of my fingers to savor the slickness of her cleft, reveling in the fiery deluge her body gifts me with.

"Sion, damn that's brilliant."

My cock grows harder as I languish in the feel of Eala— her words, the desire flaring inside me when I reach the swell of her pulsing bud.

I show no mercy as I bite her lip and scrape my teeth over her tongue before nipping her ear then her shoulder. Using both hands to stroke her inside and out, I coax my swan into feverish need. The quiet little grumbles and moans she makes send another rush of want to my cock. I pause to drown in the notes of her pleasure. I'll give and give until lust destroys her.

She climbs back onto my lap to greedily capture every bit of what my touch offers. My mouth tastes its way to her heavy breasts. I grind teeth into her flesh as I bury my fingers inside her with one powerful push then another and another. She gasps through panting breaths until her climax clenches around me hard enough to snap bone.

"Yes, love, yes." I slide my fingers out of her and pull her flush against the cock that's beating a thunderous rhythm as it strains to find its way home.

Eala responds to the call, slicking the front of my britches with her pleasure as she grinds her still blooming petals against me.

Her voice pours into my ear. "More, *anamchara*, more."

I growl and flip her onto her back against the mattress, pleased I've the strength to do it.

Her eyes dart to the impatient bulge trapped inside my britches. I slip 'em off to give her an unobstructed view as I take myself in hand and stroke the fine fellow. He obliges me with a surge that brings a cry to my lips. I feel power rising in my spirit. No one's taking a thing from me now. I'm doing the giving and damn glad of it.

I kneel between Eala's legs and drive her wider with my knees. Sliding a hand under her lovely arse, I lift her blushing sex even higher and guide my leaking tip in circles around her opening. She shines as my beads cling to her. I drop lower to swipe my tongue across her flesh, taking in the taste of us both. The joining of our flavor is far more delicious than anything that's ever slipped across my tongue.

My balls pulse, warning me I'd better get on with things. With determination, I flip Eala face down. This wondrous swan knows what I need and lifts her hips high. I lovingly spread her as if I'm coaxing a flower bud to show me what it's to become.

With a blinding need to be inside the greatest joy the gods ever gifted a fool like me, my cock sinks deep into her body. I brace my hands on her shoulder and pull her to me. She reaches to wrap fingers around my wrists, with the promise never to let go. At each thrust, I cry out, "*Anamchara, anamchara,*" until I've no voice left. My cock gives a violent throb, and I drive deeper into Eala as seed surges from me into its sacred home.

I rock with gentle strokes until I've completely emptied myself then collapse onto my side, cradling Eala's body to mine.

She pets the side of my face. "Always yours, only yours," she whispers.

"Always yours, only yours," I answer, and press my lips to hers.

There's more kissing, lovely kissing, but all too soon, Eala tenses. Hollowness grows in my chest, knowing she can't stay. Despite her assurance she's able to escape Finnbheara in a blink, we've already taken too great a risk. The time may be growing short until the king's next appearance.

I ease her away from my body. "We've made a fine mess of Robber Bright's bed."

She snorts, "Good for us," then clasps my hand in hers. "I have to go, Sion. It kills me not to take you with me."

It's killing me, too, but I'm not going to add any more troubles to her mind than she's already suffered by coming here. "I know, Swan."

"I need you to listen now and not go mental on me."

I love the way she uses my words. I give her back some of her own. "Promise I won't freak out."

Eala laughs. I send up a wish to any power listening that this will not be the last time I hear the sound of it.

"Robber Bright is going to help me get you out of here."

I let go of her hand and swing my legs over the side of the bed. "And you don't want me to go fucking mental?" I shake my head and turn to her. "Eala, Finnbheara is on the brink of war with Aodh, and he's dragging me into it. Robber Bright is lying to you. He's Aodh's man. He won't do a damn thing to help anyone associated with Tír na nÓg."

"Robber Bright is the reason I'm here at all. He told me the way to get to you."

I slice my hands through my hair. "How is it you're even talking to that bad penny?"

She sits up, eyes blazing. "The details don't matter. Please trust me on this, Sion."

Oh, but there are loads my swan is keeping from me. As much as I want to wring it out, she's asking for trust. It's about all I have left to give her, no matter how it knots my guts not to know why she's dealing with Robber Bright. I kiss her temple. "I will, Swan."

"Did Finnbheara give you any idea how long it'll be until he goes after Aodh?" She chews her lip. "Or when he suspects Aodh will make a move?"

"Not long, I think."

Eala grunts. "I suppose that's as specific as any Faerie timeline." She slides off the bed and, to my great disappointment, reaches for her clothes.

I grab her hand to stop her, taking one more long look at her perfect body. "You're so beautiful, my Eala *bán*."

She leans in to kiss me. "So are you, my fox, body and soul."

I let her go and watch her dress, finally tugging on my britches. She grabs my hips and pulls me to her. "I'll come back soon. Really soon, I swear. I'm going to meet with Robber now. Then I'll be able to tell you how everything is going to work."

Robber.

I hate the way she says his name as if the bastard is anything but a bloody devil of a liar. Doesn't matter what I like or don't. Eala believes he may be our only shot at slipping through Finnbheara's trap.

She stares up at me with every hope in the world swimming in her eyes. "And it *is* going to work."

CHAPTER 30

THE LAST LESSON

ROBBER BRIGHT

The sight of my empty chambers sends the frigid wind of dread through my soul. Where is my high command? Where is my bond-promised? We were to meet here. Did I foolishly believe the quarters of a general in Aodh's high command would be the safest place for them? Nature, curse me. This might be the worst place for them to be if I have fallen completely from Aodh's favor.

"Unmask if you are in this room," I call to the empty suite. In the presence of danger, one of Ciallmhar's witch spells could cast a shielding. There is no distortion in the air or *crack* of a charm's end. If their absence signifies Aodh's anger at my breach of his hellmouth and harm has come to them, there will be no redemption for me.

Aillil and I flew as swiftly as the churning winds of a sea storm to return to *Caisleán Brón*. It was not fast enough.

Furtive knocking unlike the pounding of Aodh's lackeys, sounds against the chamber door. I throw it open to find Artos red-faced and breathless.

"Come," he says, dragging me by the arm. In a low, furtive hiss, he says, "We thought it more prudent not to linger in your rooms with the latest goings on." When I start to question him, he throws me a look that begs for silence. There are more guards than usual lining the hallways. Artos speaks for their benefit. "We need your approval, General, on our proposal for integrating the Host of a Thousand Wings into the Dark Prince's fighting forces. The high command waits with your strategist."

We stride with purpose down hallways. As we reach Ciallmhar's door, it swings open, our footsteps loud enough to announce our arrival. Artos's bulk is barely inside before Nettle throws a concealment charm over the room. Ciallmhar follows with a fortification spell.

Colleen flings herself into my arms. I wait for the rush of annoyance that heralds the onset of the geas, but still my heart soars at her touch.

The rest of my high command descends, and I motion for Colleen to sit.

"Is what the human says true?" asks Acacia, her voice infused with both venom and desperation. "Is Queen Nuala dead?"

I look at the stricken faces of my friends, regretting that in my haste to meet Eala Duir, this desolate tiding did not come from my lips. "Yes. There is sad proof in the queen's own words."

My second flicks a dismissive hand in my bond-promised's direction and then Acacia disregards her completely. "The sacred verse and the candle the mortal spoke of?"

A surge of protectiveness runs through my veins. "*Colleen* sits here in our company," I say. "Do not exclude her from our council."

"It's fine," says Colleen.

"It is not fine," I say.

Acacia forges on. "Did you truly try to escape Bráchthine?"

My mouth drops open in surprise. "What? It is ludicrous to imply I would abandon you, my most trusted, the Host, and…" My gaze locks with Colleen's. "My bond-promised."

"Speculation travels fast in the palace," says Nettle, leaning on the edge of the table.

Acacia drives a fist into her palm. "Your visit to Oweynagat was not well received."

"You should have informed us you were going to the hellmouth," says Ciallmhar quietly. "We were caught unaware when General Dóite questioned us."

I run my hands through my hair. "There was no time." I steal a glance at

Colleen. "Eala Duir summoned me. I did not dare hesitate and give Finnbheara's Treasure the impression I ignored her call."

My bond-promised rushes to my side. "Is she okay? Did you bring her here? Oh no, is Eala with Aodh?"

I wrap an arm around her. "She fares well." Addressing my most trusted, I continue. "Listen, friends. With the death of the queen, everything is altered. We will forfeit our purpose here in Bráchthine and flee."

Artos's gruff voice rumbles through the room. "Forfeit? For what? Finnbheara won't have us back in Tír na nÓg. We will be reduced to the existence of despised Fae wanderers without loyalty or kingdom." He punches his fists together.

"We forfeit to keep our lives," I say. "Aodh's treachery goes deeper than my worst premonitions. Those of us in this room, the rest of the Host, and our dragons are a meager breath from destruction." I pull Colleen more firmly to my side. "We are all leaving this realm. I go now to placate Aodh. Be ready to fly at a moment's notice and get word to the Host to do likewise." I turn to Artos. "Can you retrieve the dragons Aodh has stolen from us?"

Nettle is the one who answers. "If it can be done, I will see to it. I can become more insignificant to the eye than any of you."

I clap him on the shoulder. His trickery does surpass us all. "Thank you, Nettle."

Acacia's eyes seethe with rage. "We are under guard, General. Do you mean for us to fight our way free?"

I swallow hard, detesting myself. This fateful journey to Bráchthine is compromised because, in my arrogance, I both underestimated Aodh and, against all wisdom, fell in love. "I hope it does not come to that, but we will do what we must."

"What have you become, Robálaí Geal?" Acacia's question is filled with the bitterness of one betrayed.

Who have I not betrayed? I openly denounced Finnbheara. I led my Host into the underworld beneath a canopy of lies, promising a destiny preferable to the one they faced in the service of Tír na nÓg. I convinced Colleen that I am capable of protecting her. Eala Duir believes we are to ally and challenge the most powerful Fae king in any realm.

All for a deception I still must keep sealed within my breast.

If I thought them all better off without me, I would join Queen Nuala and fade from this existence, but I set the doom of too many souls in motion. I must be the one to set everything to rights.

"I have become nothing more or less than I have always been, Acacia. You swore oaths of obedience to me. I hold you to those now." I look at each of my high command in turn until every head bows. Anger roils in Acacia's gaze until she lowers her eyes, coldly accepting a loyalty she once celebrated.

Colleen clutches my arm as if she does not agree to follow my command and will not let me part from her. I sweep her into my embrace, consuming her mouth with the passion of the inferno blazing in my chest, then leave her with only that wordless farewell.

There are triple the guards at the doors of Aodh's throne room. I am now perceived as more wildcard than the sycophant he desires his newest general to be.

I must appear eager in reporting my progress to bring Eala Duir before the fiend. The Dark Prince must believe my loyalty to him grows.

I hoped to find Aodh draped across his swan throne, the picture of confidence in his superiority to all things under Bráchthine's sun. To my great consternation, his fire-blackened ass barely touches the royal seat as he sits statue-like and alert to match the swan behind him.

"If you come with more complaints or demands, I advise you to hold your tongue," Aodh barks as I approach the throne.

I drop to a knee at the base of the steps leading to his dais. "On the contrary, my king." The title tastes of acid in my mouth. This beast is not my king, nor will he ever be. "I have come to report excellent news."

Aodh blows a cloud of cinder that drifts to the floor in a pile. "It had better impress me, General, since news of your exit from Bráchthine does the opposite."

"Not an exit, a rendezvous. I crossed the threshold of Oweynagat to treat with Eala Duir."

The God of the Underworld leaps to his feet and roars. "And yet she is not here before me."

Keeping to my position of supplication, I raise a hand. "Fear not, Sire. The wheels spin faster, bringing her ever closer to your keeping through willingness instead of force."

He juts his chin forward. "It matters not how she arrives at my castle steps."

"Is it not true that if she is taken against her will, it may compromise your discovery of her origin and how the *beads of being* wrought her?"

"I possess the means of gleaning that which I need."

I suppress a shudder born of hatred for this queen killer, and apprehension of the horrors the monster plans for Eala Duir. Rising without waiting for leave from Aodh, I clasp hands behind my back to appear unconcerned. "I have experienced the character of Eala Duir's essence and beg you to accept my counsel that prolonging possible damage to Finnbheara's Treasure will only yield greater benefits to you, majesty."

Aodh's charred form drops onto his throne, never shifting his glare off me. I am well practiced at presenting an exterior in conflict with my interior thoughts and give him no outward cause to question my sincerity.

"Your majesty, I regret the disappointment I have caused thus far in your service."

Aodh grunts at my obvious understatement.

"I will make amends, delivering an Eala Duir willing to align with the foe of her greatest enemy, Finnbheara. Imagine the bounty in store for you from Finnbheara's Treasure. Through her, the *beads of being* will surely give you more than the means to create the greatest fighting force in any Fae realm. You shall gain knowledge of her maker's weaknesses. Also consider the eternal torment it will cause the King of Tír na nÓg as he endures the sight of Eala Duir by your side through the ages."

Aodh strokes his grossly long, pointed jaw. "If it is as you claim, I may better know my enemy by controlling his creation." He chuckles. "Puncturing but not shattering her Faerie core could prove enlightening."

I flinch at his brash debasement of forcing a connection with another Fae spirit without invitation. "Offer her the generosity Finnbheara withholds as you have done for me, and I do not doubt she will not simply allow but welcome your essence into hers. Within that joining, the *beads of being* that dwell within her spirit will reveal their mysteries to you."

If a lie could take a life, this one would surely claim mine.

Aodh uses his stare as a threat. "In what form do you suggest I offer my generosity?"

"By retrieving her human mate from Finnbheara's grasp."

The God of the Underworld narrows his gaze. "By what means?"

"Nothing taxing." I study my fingernails, feigning that the conversation has begun to bore to me. "Eala Duir has used the Veil to enlist a pirate navy from human history that she believes is mighty enough to challenge Finnbheara."

As I hoped, this amuses Aodh, and his swinish chortle rings throughout the throne room. "Pitiable ignorance."

I pretend to contemplate, then assume the tone of an advisor. "But being of Finnbheara, Eala Duir is a Fae possessing formidable power which she may attempt to lend to her piratical navy."

My statement gives Aodh the pause I hoped for.

I shrug. "Still, if she does not succeed in imbuing her human legion with that power, Finnbheara may reclaim his treasure as soon as she enters the Faerie seas." I click my tongue. "Eala Duir, along with the *beads of being*, will prove more challenging to obtain once she returns to Tír na nÓg."

Aodh fondles the handle of his sword. "Which bodes ill for you, General."

"Dark Prince, I am convinced this is the time to act. Lend your navy to stand with Eala Duir. Once her mate is retrieved, then she will be yours along with six thousand hearty humans you can press into the service of Bráchthine to do with as you will." I shrug. "You wish to use the *beads of being* to fortify your numbers. Convert these six thousand into shadow soldiers loyal to Bráchthine. A laudable and instant increase in force."

Aodh wags his thick, ashy finger at me. "You have intrigued me, Robálaí Geal. Perhaps your trespasses of late may be overlooked with this web you entice me to weave."

My hubris-ridden actions threaten to condemn not just Eala Duir, but scores of others to damnation under Aodh's merciless, murderous tyranny, but even the craftiest of spider can fail to weave an infallible web.

I long to return to my high command and Colleen to glean the progress of the Host's readiness to flee, but Aodh demands my presence in his war council. I suffer the boorish and vulgar demeanor of General Dóite and the Dark Prince's additional advisors as the tedious session purloins the entirety of Bráchthine's day.

The earthly sun is newly set when I arrive outside Oweynagat without being able to spare a moment to commune with my Folk. It is before the appointed meeting time with Eala Duir, but I appear early so she does not reach our meeting place and find me absent. Her mortal moon wears a broader smile than last night.

My long life has faced many trials and dangers, but my association with Eala Duir throws it into a maelstrom. I curse Finnbheara's Treasure, who escalated my rift with the king and drove me to Bráchthine.

I collapse onto the seat of the dragon-sized stone half-buried in the ground.

I cannot curse her.

Without Eala Duir, Colleen would not exist for me.

Without Eala Duir, love would not exist for me.

Without love, my life would continue as nothing more than a passionless plod through time.

Perhaps the white swan is more treasure than curse.

A blinding torrent of color crashes to the ground, a comet falling to earth. Surging from its center with her Fae power pulsing in a radiant blaze, Eala Duir charges me. Surprise and the force of our collision knock me backward off my seat.

She lands a respectable kick to the side of my knee before I regain my footing. I catch her fisted hands before they meet my armor.

"You bastard," she rails. "You didn't tell me Tír na nÓg drives a human crazy. You knew that was happening to Sion."

Her foot lands a blow against my shin. "Peace, Eala. Madness is only a danger if a human is not within the protection of a Fae."

She rips from my hold and stalks a short distance as she continues to rant. "And whose fucking protection did you think he'd be under? Finnbheara's?"

I tighten my grip. "Yours. Are you not bonded to the fox?"

"As *anamchara* and husband, but neither protected him."

I pop my lips. "Ah, yes. Those are mere human bonds, not Fae."

Eala speaks to the sky. "I didn't know if I could heal him. His essence…his mind…" She grabs handfuls of hair from the sides of her head. "…was crawling with a million burnt silver spots." Her voice falters. "I don't know if I got rid of them all."

Imagining the horror of discovering such a blight in Colleen's beautiful essence sends a painful shock up my spine.

"Please, Robber. I have to get him out. Finnbheara told Sion he's ready to go to war with the underworld. He plans to use Sion in the fighting to get his hooks back into me." She sets her jaw. "There's no time left, and I'm in over my head. I can't even get into the Fae realms without you, and we need more power. Take me to Aodh. I'm ready to bargain for his help."

"No—"

Eala halts my attempt at elaboration. "What do you mean no? Damn it. Isn't that what you asked me to do?"

I look at Oweynagat. Aodh's spies are surely just inside the flames. "Lower your voice and listen well. We both stand at the edge of a precipice."

"What—"

"Your Colleen is in unspeakable danger." There is fire in Eala's eyes. "Not from me. You do not want to hear it, but I love her. Not by enchantment or influence but with purity of heart. I beg you to allow me to show you the truth of this."

Forcing into another Fae's essence without their permission is a grave offense, but I will do it if Finnbheara's Treasure refuses to let me in. It is essential she see that where Colleen is concerned, I do not lie.

Eala's eyes widen. "You love her?" Her brows lift with swift suspicion. "I swear, Robber Bright, if you take advantage of me like the last time—"

"I vow on Colleen's life and the bond I now share with her that you need not fear my influence."

"Bond?" She scorches me with a look of utter hatred. "What bond?"

"Please, Eala. Extend me this modicum of trust." Turmoil pinches her features as her gaze dissects me. Finally, with a nod and a grimace, she closes her eyes.

I summon my essence and command it to join with its fading shards that remain in hers.

As our Fae spirits flow together, Eala grasps my arm.

"I feel her…Colleen…" She stammers the rest of her thoughts. "…her joy… her love for you." Eala's eyes pop open, and she stares in disbelief. "Colleen loves you."

She has barely spoken the words when a shower of ice falls upon my spirit. I hear Colleen's cry in my mind grow fainter and fainter until it is silent. My heart gives a single mighty beat, sending such agony through my body I fear I may not survive the onslaught.

Eala shakes me. "Robber. Robber, what's wrong with you?"

My heart calms, returning to the cold, empty organ that woke ever so briefly until Finnbheara's geas now finds me through the words of his treasure. The bond-promise Colleen and I swore did not prevent this inevitability. There is no sorrow. Only the hollowness I know well.

"Yes, she loves me." My tone lacks emotion. I no longer find any remnant of love for Colleen in my spirit, essence, or soul. My mind tells me I did once, but no longer. Our bond-promise is now the shackle I feared. The sooner I carry out the plan I must with Eala, the sooner I do not have to bear witness to the pain clouding Colleen's bright dove gray eyes that my indifference will bring.

"Colleen, along with my Host, must leave Aodh's kingdom. The home I promised here is a false one. Fate willing, my Folk will not be called into this first conflict of the war between Fae kings. Once you have prepared your folk to sail to the Faerie seas, bring the Veil here. I will send Colleen and my Host to you. Carry them to the Gem Kissed Forest before you take your place in the battle to save your fox."

"Them? Aren't you coming?"

I hesitate, but keeping my grim possibility from Eala serves no purpose. "That is my intention, but it may fall to me to create a diversion for the escape." For an instant, I detect a hint of something apart from loathing in her eyes.

"You make it sound like a done deal. Won't Aodh insist I show up on bended knee to beg for his navy?"

I shake my head. "I shall be your agent in the negotiation. Aodh heeds my counsel where Finnbheara is concerned and will send his navy." She need not know I have bartered her essence and her freedom as the price of this bargain.

"Tell me exactly what Aodh will ask of me after the battle. I'm not stupid enough to believe there isn't something serious he wants."

"The God of the Underworld wishes to enlist you into his service to taunt Finnbheara and to learn what he can from you about his enemy." There it is, a veiled half-truth, but not a complete lie.

"And Sion will be safe with me?"

"It does not concern Aodh who accompanies you into Bráchthine." I fail to elaborate that once Eala forfeits her freedom to Aodh, the fox's life will last no longer than the length of a single thought.

She chews on her bottom lip, considering. "I know you and Finnbheara had your issues, but Robber, when he called for you before I left Tír na nÓg, I swear it sounded like he was calling for his best friend. Well, until he learned you backstabbed him. He called you the king's man and kin."

I skirt the issue of being named *king's man*. "Finnbheara sees all Folk who dwell in his lands as kin. It does not define our value or lack of value to him." Only when she stares at my hand do I realize I am tracing the trail of the scar beneath my armor.

"You became a traitor because Aodh values you more than Finnbheara."

A corner of my mouth quirks up. "You found me out, Eala Duir."

"When I left Sion and Máthair, uh, Martha behind in Tír na nÓg, I thought I'd be able to go back when Finnbheara cooled off. Never imagined swords or ships with cannons would be involved when I met him again." Her mouth falls into a hard line. "The king is as heartless and cruel as every tale ever told of him."

"Do not take every story of Finnbheara at face value."

She eyes me with the suspicion I have come to expect and admire from her.

"I'm only agreeing to this for three reasons, Robber. First, you were honest in sending me to Sion, and second, because you didn't take Cara into hell."

"She is your *péist síoda*. I did not have the right."

Eala tuts at me. "As if personal rights matter to you."

"The third reason?"

Eala faces me with the boldness of the Folk. "I always planned to free Colleen from you once Sion was safe." She scoffs. "It's ironic you and Aodh of all people are the ones making that possible."

"As you wander through your long life, Eala Duir, you will discover the unexpected is a constant companion."

Eala taps her lips. "That may be the truest thing you've ever said to me." She sighs. "If I choose to accept Aodh's bargain and stay in his kingdom with Sion…is hell as bad as they say?" She tilts her head. "It may be the only place Sion and I can live together where Finnbheara can't reach us."

The ground beneath us gives the faintest shudder. I know it for what it is. Aodh's soldiers approach through the Cave of Cats.

"Call the Veil, Eala. You must go soon."

Instantly, the Faerie path appears, and I see resolve settle in her expression. "Tell Aodh I'll accept his invite for Sion and me to live in this realm if he sends his navy as backup to help us free Sion from Finnbheara." She blows a sharp breath. "Do I need the pirates if I have the hell ships?"

"The forces of Aodh and Finnbheara are well matched. The human navy will give you the advantage."

Eala begins to wilt, a flower under too bold a sun. "Can this truly work?" She turns her wild eyes on me. "Robber, how am I going to bring a human navy into a battle with the Fae without them dropping dead from the…" Eala flails her arms. "…weirdness of it all?"

"You must cast influence over them."

"Six thousand people?"

I urge my mind into swift contemplation.

Eala is faster to the mark. "Is there something Biddy Early, the witch, can do to help?"

Ah, therein lies the solution. The Fae witch, Ciallmhar, once influenced a human army in the final days before the *Tuatha Dé Danann* crossed beneath the mounds. "Ask your witch to call forth a mist. Imbue it with this instruction: All that comes to pass in your endeavor shall not strike the humans as strange but commonplace. Let the haze fall upon your forces. If you hold fast to this intention in your essence, the Fae influence will remain until you remove it." I step closer. "Keep its purpose in the forefront of your mind even as you face the challenges laid before you."

"Do I need a specific chant or rhyme to make my influence go live?"

Her phrase may be strange, but her meaning is clear enough. "Use clarity in your words to make the purpose clear, and all should be well."

Eala bumps the heels of her hands together as her eyes dart in rapid movements, evidence of her frantic thoughts. She grasps my arm. "Wait, how will I meet up with Aodh's ships, then what has to happen to draw out Finnbheara's navy, and how will I get to Sion?" Eala releases me. "This is impossibly complicated."

She knows not how close to the truth she speaks. Neither Eala's untried powers nor her witch's spells can protect her humans from enchantments that will surely hail from both Finnbheara and Aodh's Folk during the battle. There is but one remedy for this.

I must address each of her fears in turn. "All of Tír na nÓg will sense the approach of the Dark Prince's fleet. You say Finnbheara plans to thrust your fox into the battle. Find him there."

I dart a look behind me, but Aodh's shadows have not yet discovered us. "There are two more tasks before you. First, return to the Gem Kissed Forest and seek the bottles of dark coral-colored elixir that smell of juniper berries. You must cut bread into cubes enough for the humans who sail with you. Add a drop from the bottle onto each morsel and insist every mortal consumes a single portion. This will protect them from Fae enchantments striving to work against you on the Faerie seas."

"Won't that negate the influence of my protection?"

I shake my head. "No, the elixir acts as a shield against ill will alone, not fair intention."

"Sion has been collecting Faerie bottles. Hopefully, he's found the right one. How many do we need?"

"You need only find one." I put my hands on her shoulders. "When the liquid runs low. Ask it to replenish. You have such power. Let this be my last lesson to you, Eala Duir."

The trembling grows stronger, and Eala notices. Our time grows short. Fear shadows her bright eyes.

"Robber, is there time to accomplish everything you're telling me before Finnbheara decides to start the war—prepping the bread, mustering and protecting Grace's fleet, saving Colleen ..."

I nod to the Veil. "There sits time itself, Eala Duir. Use it well." I tap her temple. "Call upon your magic. I know you fear what is not easy or clear to you, but this is the time to cast doubt aside."

"I wasn't made for this."

I smile. "Were you not, Finnbheara's Treasure?"

Eala's essence hums with the weight of her emotions. The time for lessons has passed. The white swan must find her own strength.

And now, the salvation for those I have thrust into peril. "Here is the second of your tasks. When your forces stand at the ready, alert me with the Captain's ring by calling directly to the ribbons of my essence that dwell in yours. Bring the Veil to carry the Host and Colleen away from the underworld. I promise Aodh's ships will be awaiting your arrival at the edge of the Faerie Sea. Amass your fleet off the coast of the Aran Island, Inishmore, near the place called Poll na bPéist, the Serpents Lair, and speak these words..."

The approaching flame dragons of Bráchthine cause a thickening in the air. Eala frantically glances between the cave and the Veil. Her words tumble out. "I almost botched the words to the Crystal Gate. Can I speak the words in English so I won't forget them?"

I am frustrated she still resists her knowledge of our tongue. "Say these words: *I Eala of the Fae call to the Folk of Bráchthine. Receive us in our mother sea.* They will transport your people across the realms."

"Much easier," she mutters then repeats the opening charm with perfection. "Not like the gobbledygook I had to use on the Crystal Gate." Suddenly, Eala's gaze burns into mine with even greater urgency. "Can you make it any easier for me to get through the gate with this?" She raises a finger with the tattoo of a Fae key on her flesh. "I had to use my *fánaí* tree to remember the words to open the gate, and then this little beauty helped me get home."

I stare agape, grasping her finger. "You bear the mark of Queen Nuala's key."

The skin between her brows creases as she swivels her finger to look at the tattoo. "Queen Nuala?"

"The Queen of Tír na nÓg, now lost for all time." With the vicious heat of Bráchthine billowing into Eala's world, I cannot spare a single borrowed moment to share my beloved queen's tragedy or the significance and power of the mark. I squeeze the white swan's finger that bears Nuala's emblem. "Touch this key to your temple and the words to open the Crystal Gate will flow through your essence."

The rumble of voices pours from Oweynagat.

"Go now, Eala Duir." I shove her none too gently into the Veil.

CHAPTER 31
THE BEAST OF TIME

EALA

I Veil travel back to the banks of the *lough* in County Clare and lean against the trunk of an oak near the water's edge. My stomach seizes, absorbing the gravity of the battering Sion's been forced to endure in Tír na nÓg from Finnbheara and other Fae.

He'd never have faced those nightmares if I hadn't left him.

How much cruelty lurks beneath the surface of Faerie gifts?

My own misuse of magic sends a wave of chest-crushing anxiety through me. I didn't magically bind Grace, but I certainly encouraged Biddy to spell her.

I lay my palms against the oak's bark. "I don't know if you are part of *Crann na Beatha*," I call to the branches. "But as you're part of this earth, I trust you with my vow. I swear to never use my Faerie gifts to steal the freedom of another being or to cause them fear or harm."

My lifeline tingles. I remove my hands from the oak to find matching threadlike trails of whiskey gold flare then spill down my palms and the bark of the tree before the lines fade.

Crann na Beatha acknowledges my oath.

Shoring myself for another plunge through the Crystal Gate, I touch the tattoo to my temple. The words of the key come to me as easily as my name. I've never heard any folktales or histories about Queen Nuala's mark. Maybe Aodh has a big fancy archive I can poke around in. I wish there were any other way to save Sion besides having to join Team Aodh, especially since Robber seems hellbent on getting his Host and Colleen out of hell.

The timing of this latest act in Robber's traitorous habit of defection better not lose me Aodh's navy.

I should have asked more questions, as usual, when dealing with other Fae. With my focus on getting Grace's navy into the Faerie seas and Robber spouting off a list of must-dos to make that possible, I missed some huge red flags…every one of them marked with Aodh's triple flame sigil.

It's a chilling reality that the god of the underworld himself may provide answers to my questions sooner than Robber can.

What other choices do I have at this point? Absolutely none.

I pass through the Crystal Gate with ease and retrace my steps to Robber's cottage. When I don't see Sion or Cara anywhere, my stomach folds in panic.

"Sionnach," I scream and bang on the cottage door, trying to push it open. The damn thing doesn't budge. Is Sion inside, too hurt to come out? Did madness and the wasting of his body creep back in the moment I left? Has Finnbheara already come for him?

Robber accused me of being a coward with magic. I'm one hundred percent in favor of holding hands with my power now. The tiny iridescent glass bubbles, bobbing in the air between the trees and above the path, catch my eye. If the Faerie bottles hold magic, why shouldn't those?

I spy a tennis ball-sized sphere stuck beneath the branch of a tree next to the cottage. The glassy bauble's light reflects off a trunk that looks as if it's made of pearl. When I grab the ball, the damn thing is almost too hot to hold. I toss it from hand to hand and rush back to the cottage door. Bringing the orb close to my lips, I whisper to it the way Biddy does to her blue bottle.

"If you need something to burn—burn this." I heave the bubble at the door. It splatters into rainbow paint across the image of a *péist síoda*. The dragon carving begins to glow like the coals of a campfire. There's a sizzle and then the whole door turns to ash and collapses in a pile of iridescent dust.

"Sion." I tear through the opening. The bedroom door is closed. Thankfully, it opens without a fire bubble. I rush in to find a very distressed silk dragon and my husband clawing out of a huge silky cocoon the color of Cara's scales in the middle of the nest.

"Eala, I was so afraid you couldn't get back…I…fuck all," says Sion. Breaking free, he scrambles over the ring of woven leaves and branches to clutch me to his chest.

I run my hands through his hair and kiss him soundly, igniting a massive need in me that'll take longer than a single reunion to satisfy. I reluctantly break the kiss. His jaw is covered with a soft layer of fuzzy stubble the same color as his copper and garnet curls that wasn't there hours ago. I take it as an encouraging sign the toll this place was taking on his body has stalled if not stopped altogether. "Thank goodness Finnbheara hasn't come for you yet my dear dear Irish boy."

"Amen to that my dear dear Amerrrrican Faerie girl."

Cara bumps me with her snout, and I scratch her neck, frowning at the odd dragon pouch in the nest. "I'm glad to see you're taking care of each other."

"Cara's belly scales send out this wee beastie sleeping bag when it's time to close my eyes. It's brilliant. Inside it, I'm not plagued by dark dreams of going mad."

I lean into him. "Every night? How long since I left?"

Sion's gorgeously familiar derisive grunt is the sweetest sound in this forest. "Not night exactly. Two maybe three sleeps." He looks at Cara as if she has answers he doesn't.

My stomach adds another fold. "It's only been hours for me."

He can't hide his look of distress. "I'm beginning to think time is the cruelest beast under any sky."

I tuck my head beneath his chin to steal a moment of comfort. "It's certainly never been our friend."

Sion's voice thins, making me look up. "I don't think I'll be here for long, *anamchara*. Finnbheara's been loading his kitchen stump outside with extra food. It's my cue that swine of a king may be heading my way soon." He motions toward the front of the cottage. "He means to fatten me up so I'm an easier target when Fae arrows start flying."

I slap his chest, relieved to find tightly packed farmer muscles solidly in place beneath the shirt he's pulled on. "Don't talk like that, Sion." I both hate and love his sarcasm. It's a sign my husband is finding himself.

"Sorry, love. 'Tis truly a blessing to see you once more before the storm, Eala *bán*." He strokes the side of my face and rocks us gently. "So, love, did you speak with Robber Bright?"

I can tell he's struggling to temper the hatred in his voice. It's eating him up that Robber is the reason I was able to get to Sion at all. My husband's feelings for the Fae are as transparent as glass.

"Did the villain give you a way to pluck me out of this mousetrap before Finn springs it?"

"Not...exactly." My voice catches.

His body tenses. "That's a no, then." He eases my shoulders back. "Seems your husband is off to war then, Swan." He forces a smile. "At least thanks to you, I'm doing it with a clear head." His gaze turns wistful. "Do you think there'll ever be a time when fate's not trying to force us into a goodbye?"

I grab a handful of the Fae fabric of his shirt with sparkly silver thread running through it. "Yes. I do, and I believe that day is coming."

Sion perks up. "I've heard swans boast quite a temper. Sounds like yours is brewing."

I want to keep talking. I want to kiss him. I want to make love with him, but he's right. Time is a cruel beast.

"Sion, I need to find a Faerie bottle filled with pinkish elixir. Have you seen one?"

"Aye, just there across the path." His face flushes. "But I kicked the shit out of it."

"You broke it?" This can't be. I'm on the verge of calling up the navies of a long-dead pirate queen, not to mention the God of the Underworld, and might be fucked because the man I'm trying to save can't control his temper.

"Tipped it. The potion fizzed and stained the grass around it. Bad stuff."

"No, it's good stuff, and we need it. Show me." I grab his hand and drag him through the opening where the door used to be.

"Where's my door?"

I'm pissed and happier than I've been since the night before Finnbheara snatched us back into Tír na nÓg. Bickering with Sion is the most wonderful feeling in the world. Well, almost. I'd rather be lying skin to skin as he touches me in all the ways that make me forget time.

Cara wiggles out of the empty door frame, snorting her displeasure at being ignored.

"Go find your breakfast," I tell her and make a shooing motion. After a scratchy kiss to my cheek with her triple tongues, she shrinks into her snaky form and scampers up a tree trunk.

"Will you look at that?" Sion stares after her, astonished.

"You've never seen her do her thing?"

He snorts. "I've spotted a wee lizard the color of your dragon skittering about." He shakes his head. "Och, to think she's been looking after me all along, and I had no appreciation of it."

"Cara's a keeper."

Sion smiles. "She's dear to you, and you to her."

I tilt my head. "Given your cozy sleeping arrangement, I'd say you're dear to her as well, nestling."

He smacks my bottom then gives it a squeeze.

Curse, the beast of time.

"Now, dragon baby, show me the elixirs."

"Just there," he says, pointing to a tall unruly tangle of grass.

"Maybe the one you kicked wasn't it. Robber says it smells like juniper berries." The low rumble coming from Sion doesn't bode well. "Damn it, that was it, wasn't it?"

"How was I to know it wasn't more devil juice from these soulless Fae?"

Sion sounds strong and beautifully belligerent, far from the broken soul I found wasting away here in the forest. I just wish the content of his words were different.

I tug at his sleeve. "Help me find it."

We root around in grass much taller and wilder than any of the patches around it. I find a bottle with the tamarind-colored liquid that Robber told me allowed the Fae to speak to dragons. He'd said I wasn't ready to taste it then, and now I don't need it. I'll let that tidbit sink in after we find the elixir to prevent Grace's sailors from falling victim to the Fae.

Sion tears up handfuls of grass. "Why do you need the bewitched Faerie poison?"

"Robber says if I put a drop on a cube of bread and the humans eat it, they'll be free from Fae enchantments."

He huffs. "Seems I chose the wrong bottle." He heaves another chunk of grass onto the road. "And what humans are you set to protect, love?"

I straighten so I can look him eye to eye. "The six thousand men and women that will sail with Granuaile O'Malley into the Faerie seas to face Finnbheara and save your arse."

Sion goggles at me. "The Pirate Queen?"

"The very one."

He lunges for me, gripping my upper arms. "Eala, even with a drop of Faerie magic in their guts, you're leading humans to a slaughter against the Fae."

"Cannons kill Faeries, Sionnach."

He's enraged. "Not if they're dissolved into a mound of melted iron by magic first, Eala."

"I've got a witch on board, too. Biddy Early and her legendary blue bottle. She got it from the Fae. It's full of their magic. She can protect the cannons, I'm sure of it."

"Eala, listen to me." He gives me a little shake. "One famous witch casting spells, no matter how powerful, won't be a match for Finnbheara. Swear to me you're not foolish enough to do this. How will you even get to the Faerie seas?"

"Robber told me how to go to the Serpent's Lair on Inishmore and cross over from our seas into the Fae's."

Sion's curls bob furiously as he shakes his head. "I'll not have it, Eala. This is exactly what Finn wants—you to come after me. He'll not let you go free again."

What he doesn't say screams louder than what he's saying—that Finnbheara will make sure Sionnach Loho is out of the picture once and for all. The king won't let my *anamchara* survive.

"He won't be able to touch me. Grace's navy isn't the only one sailing with me."

Sion's arms drop to his sides, and he tries to back away from me. "No, Eala. Tell me you didn't—"

I grab the front of his shirt to stop him. "I made a bargain with Aodh. His ships will join forces with us. We'll have plenty of Fae magic on our side."

All the color drains from Sion's face. "What did you promise the devil bastard for his aid?"

"That I…we, would live in his kingdom and work as advisors to him against Finnbheara." I cradle his strong jaw in my hands. "We can make a home there, Sionnach. Mythology suggests it's just a different flavor of Fae realm, not the hell of lava pits and brimstone used to terrify us as kids." His skin chills beneath my touch. "I'm sure it's not anything we've ever imagined, but isn't staying together all that matters?"

He pulls away to plop down cross-legged in the middle of the path. The movement is so much like the first night he took me into the Veil forest, a lump rises in my throat. I squat in front of him. "Sion, I followed you when you tore me away from everything I knew into an entirely new life. Now, I'm asking you to do the same." I pull him to his feet and throw my arms around his neck. "Will you do whatever it takes to be with me?"

Sion presses his lips to my forehead. "Of course I will, Eala *bán*."

He rubs his long, straight nose against my little round nub of a nose Máthair always called a Faerie kiss. If I'd only known how true that was.

My fox growls. "I don't have to like it, though."

We hold one another while the breeze sends the leaves into their subtle dances and light reflects off the gemstone bubbles filling the space between the trees.

I scratch a finger through his sprouting beard. "Sionnach Loho, if this crazy plan doesn't succeed—"

"Don't you say goodbye to me, Eala Loho. It's a thing we will not do."

I lay my hand on his chest and feel his heart beat strong and steady against my palm. "If we'd only been given a hundred thousand heartbeats to love one another, Sionnach, that time would be as perfect as a long life together."

"Eala, I've always known there was a magic in you beyond Faerie kings or the glorious way the Veil wraps you in its arms. To think, I'm the fool you've chosen to share it with is almost more than a man can bear."

He drops to his knees and wraps his arms around me, pressing his cheek to my stomach. "I thank you...I worship you for blessing me with the gift of your glorious soul." He lifts his face to look at me with eyes filled with drops that shine like crystal. "You've always had mine and you always will."

I stroke his hair. My tears are the first to fall. "Your love, Sionnach, is every color, the first note of every song, and ..." I run a thumb over his cheek. "Every breath of my spirit." I drop to the ground with him and fold him into my arms. "I thank you for this life of extraordinary joy."

Sion braces his hands on either side of my head and brings my mouth to his. The kiss that's not a goodbye is possessive and relentless. I dig my fingers into his hips as the strokes of his tongue burn against mine. We demand the beast of time's submission. If it reaches for us, we will bloody its selfish hand.

Finally, we stand, hands clasped together. I shake my head. "It's probably ridiculous, but when I first saw the beauty of this place, I imagined we'd make two homes, one at Loho cottage and another in a Faerie forest."

He sighs. "Not ridiculous, love. I've often thought how grand it would be to share a home with you on the land living in my blood, where those who came before spent lives of both toil and great happiness."

"Ireland is more than a place, isn't it?"

Sion kisses my temple. "Aye. It's a power that knows your heart, and it'll give its own right back to you if you listen to its song."

"That must be why the Fae never truly left the island. They just continue to love the land where they began from a different vantage point." I sigh. "And speaking of the Folk you're so fond of…"

Sion mutters, "Fucking faeries."

I slap his arm. "Except for me."

He brings my hand to his lips. "Except for you, *anamchara.*"

When we face the Faerie bottles hand in hand to search for magic, Sion's curse is the opposite of what I want to hear. He holds out a tall, thin decanter. "God help me, this was the one with the juniper berry potion. I'm dreadful sorry, love."

I take the empty container from him and stare at it.

"There are more bottles down the road and scattered in the forest. We'll find another with the same pretty pink juice in it," he says.

Disappointment and hopelessness twine together to crawl up my insides like a thorny vine. If I can't protect Grace's people, how can I ask her to go through with this? Will Aodh's navy be enough without her twenty ships and six thousand fighters? I don't want to say anything that will make Sion feel any worse than he already does about dumping the elixir, so I just nod.

I'm about to toss the bottle into the grass when I notice a fat drop of bright coral pink liquid clinging to an inside corner.

You have such power. Let this be my last lesson to you, Eala Duir.

Robber's words linger in my mind, encouraging me. I press my lips to the glass the way Biddy does when she speaks to her blue bottle and whisper the word, *"Fill."*

The tiny bit of elixir begins to bubble. The scent of juniper berries fills the air as pinkish liquid slowly rises to the neck of the bottle.

Sion stares at me, then a wide smile breaks out across his face. "You're always a wonder to me, Eala *bán*."

I return his smile as liquid starts to dribble over the top of the glass onto my finger. "Get me a stopper."

Sion fumbles around in the grass and retrieves three mushroom-shaped crystal corks. The second one fits perfectly.

Holding the bottle in my hand, I meet his gaze. "I have to go, *anamchara*."

He wraps his fingers around mine, capturing my gaze with his green glass eyes. "I know, my love." Sion leans in until our foreheads touch. "Hold this kiss for me until I ask for it back." Our lips press together ever-so-lightly.

We've said all that needs to be said with our bodies, our tears, and our love. He turns and walks back to the cottage.

From somewhere deep in the Gem Kissed Forest, I hear Cara's melancholy howl.

CHAPTER 32
THE MUSTER

EALA

When I slip into the cottage along with the dawn light, Biddy snores from the bed while Grace curls up on the couch, sword on the floor nearby. Her hand dangles just above the weapon, a pirate queen always at the ready for action. Sure enough, a creaky board under my foot sends her to her feet, blade in hand.

"You're back well before the hour," she says through a yawn so loud and unrestrained, I'm surprised it doesn't wake Biddy.

"Go back to sleep, Granuaile. We've a busy time ahead of us." She gives me that unreadable stare of hers then drags the chair by the fire to the kitchen table. Grace sits and nods at me to take the other chair.

When I do, she leans a forearm on the tabletop. "Saw your man, did you?"

"I did."

"Is he well?"

Didn't expect much interest from her, seeing as when I shared my soul-deep love for Sion earlier, Grace was far from moved. No pirate buy-in for my *anamchara* confession.

I set the bottle of Faerie elixir on the table and pull my hair back, wishing I had a clip to keep the stray wispy nuisances off my face. "It's complicated. He wasn't when I first found him." There's no way I'm going to go into detail with Grace about my healing essence. "The Fae kingdom can be challenging for a human."

She studies the bottle then wrings her hands. With tight lips, she meets my gaze. "I ask your pardon for not accompanying you to the *lough*."

I start to brush her off, but she leans in. "Being useless does not settle well with me. I saw no purpose in being there when you've your magic and that of your witch."

"Don't trouble yourself. We managed fine."

She nods to the bed. "The witch's weary bones tell a different tale."

I glance at Biddy, feeling guilty for her long trip home on foot. "She had quite a walk back here."

"My heart is not made of stone." Her gaze drifts out the window. "I took in the words about the love you share with your husband." Piercing brown eyes as rich as dark roast coffee lock onto mine. "I loved my husbands in all ways of devotion and loyalty." She sighs. "I love my children. Would not be sitting here with a witch and a Faerie if I did not."

I want to reach across the table and take her hand, but she's far from the warm and fuzzy type. Instead, I sweep my arm across the cottage. "I'm sorry this is so hard for you, Granuaile."

She grunts in response, no admission forthcoming.

"Biddy took the strangeness in stride."

The Pirate Queen straightens her arms, leaning back in the chair. "Och, I suppose those with magic seem to ease into whichever place they please."

Her features tense when I laugh at her inadvertent rhyme. "Careful there. You sound as if you're casting a spell."

Oh boy, does that earn me a glare. Grace pounds a fist to her breast. "The only powers I possess are those granted me by the sea, my O'Malley blood, and the steadfastness of those who stand at my side."

"All enviable," I say, and go to the cupboard, grab the whiskey bottle, and pour amber spirits into two glasses. This seems more her speed. I raise my glass, and she taps it with hers before tossing back the whiskey as I always imagined a pirate would.

"Home. Love. Families. None of it's easy, is it, Granuaile?"

She pours herself more whiskey. "Aye to that, Eala of the Fae."

We clink again.

"I expect you would like to take a bit of sleep," says Grace.

I should be exhausted from emotion, traveling, terror, Robber Bright, and the awfulness Sion's endured, but oddly, I'm not. The more my essence and magic seem to come alive, the more energy I have.

"I've had enough of it to suit me." Grace jerks her head at the couch, and I realize she means sleep, not whiskey.

Biddy makes a strange gurgling sound and then sits up as if she's been pulled by a rope. "Eala? Back, are ya?" She joins us, eyeing the bottle of Faerie elixir. "Let's have it then. Tell your tale."

I slouch in the chair. "The first thing we need to do is get enough bread to make at least six thousand cubes for Granuaile and her sailors to eat."

Both women wear matching goggle-eyed looks that make me laugh. I tilt my head to Grace. "Are you ready to go sailing in my metal ship?"

Grace lasted about a block in the back seat of the car before she bellowed about being trapped in the belly of a growling beast and insisted on returning to the cottage. Time travel is not for everyone.

As Biddy and I set out on "take two" of our bread quest, my heart feels as if it's surrounded by a circle of hammers all pounding on it at the same time. How in the name of Máthair's herb garden am I going to find enough bread to cut into six thousand cubes? What kind of bread should I grab? Loaves? Baguettes? Then, cutting it into cubes, even with Grace and Biddy's help, will be a massive investment of time we don't have.

"Eala, you idiot."

Biddy swivels to stare at me, no doubt baffled by my outburst.

In a sudden smack-myself-in-the-head revelation, I realize the version of bread cubes in my world are croutons.

Biddy's eyes roll back in her head when we step into the first Tesco Superstore. I've never heard someone say, "Goddess save me," so many times as she gawks at packaged meats, produce bins, and the vast selection of Keogh's crisps. We buy a dozen flavors of the snack to try. Biddy's torn between the Cashel Blue Cheese and Barbeque Whiskey crisps as a favorite.

We drive for hours, hitting every Tesco from Limerick to Cork and a few further inland until we arrive back at the cottage in the late afternoon with roughly 400 bags of croutons.

Now, Grace stares at the lines of paper towels we've unrolled across the cottage floor. Every inch is covered in drying, dark pink cubes. "What happens if the portion of your Faeries drink in these is off?" she grumbles.

I finish asking the decanter to fill for hopefully the last time. We've dunked roughly six thousand croutons in a bucket filled with the elixir, soaked them for a few minutes, then poured the whole mess through the row of colanders lined up in front of the cottage before bringing the works inside to dry.

"Robber Bright said a drop, not exactly a precise measurement, so saturating the croutons will have to do."

I ignore Grace's huffing to turn to Biddy and point to a collection of croutons near the end of a row. "Okay, do these."

Thank fate, the witch knows a spell to dry the gooshy cubes without allowing the elixir to evaporate.

Grace rubs her sore back. She's been bending over to grab dry croutons and pour them into our twenty plastic buckets. We'll need to smuggle our elixir-doused bread into wooden barrels for distribution on the ships since plastic and the sixteenth century do not make good bedfellows.

I peer out at the sky. We've only got about an hour before I pull Grace and Biddy into the mother of all Veil-hopping Celtic days. "Granuaile, why don't you soak in the tub? Biddy and I can finish here."

A sneer almost makes its way to the Pirate Queen's face before she gives up and shrugs. "Will you show me again how to draw the bath?" She huffs. "Not keen on scalding my hide as before."

Once Grace is settled in the tub and all the croutons are in buckets, I collapse onto the couch. "Okay, Biddy. I'm ready."

She brings the blue bottle over and sits next to me, easing the stopper free. I grab my cell phone from the end table and unplug the charger. "How did mankind survive without the Internet?" I mumble as I pull up the website I found earlier with a list of Grace's numerous castles where we'll drop in on every ship in her unsuspecting fleet.

"Here goes, my friend. Let's make a pirate map."

Biddy waves a hand over the bottle, summoning a wisp of cerulean steam. Using her waltz with mist and magic, she whispers the name of every O'Malley castle I list into the haze. Grace adds several more secret docking inlets to the witchy map when she comes out rosy-cheeked from the bathroom.

When I repeat the name of our jumping off point to leave the human realm, The Serpent's Lair of Inishmore, Grace cringes.

I look at my two companions. "Promise me you won't try to make sense of what we're about to do." I almost say 'because it'll make your head explode' but catch myself. "It'll drive you mad." I lay a hand to my heart and speak words I hope will be reassuring. "I've traveled through time and learned to accept it as a gift, not something to fear." I latch onto Robber Bright's claim as he pointed to the Veil, *There is time itself, Eala Duir. Use it well.* I sure as hell intend to.

Okay, time, prepare to be slapped across the face. We're going to Veil travel back three days to muster Grace's fleet and instruct them to meet us at the Serpent's Lair today before dusk. Once everyone is accounted for, the Pirate Queen will give the order for her people to enjoy their crouton rations.

The sun blazes low in the sky behind the lighthouse on the cliff's edge. I set the last of twenty plastic buckets, one for each of Grace's ships, on a cart I found in the shed behind the cottage. My plan is to wheel the croutons into the Veil. I've never tried to bring anything but Alfie and small artifacts with me before. I hope the mystical transit has no objections.

Grace adjusts her thick shawl around her shoulders then tucks it into her belt. Her bright yellow *leine* will certainly make her easy to spot at the bow of *an Capall Mara Bán*, the White Seahorse, her flagship that will lead the O'Malley fleet into the Faerie fray.

I raided Alfie's huge canvas bags of period clothing to scare up facsimiles of Grace's outfit for Biddy and me. The witch kept digging around, claiming she wanted a proper pirate hat with a swooping feather. Grace scoffed at the notion. Given the reaction, I take it she's a more practical than flashy sea captain.

I swipe a sleeve across my forehead and inhale the mixture of wildflowers and herbs that flourish around the cottage, many of which are so familiar to me. When I lived in New York City in an apartment on top of a high-rise hotel, the fragrances mingling in Máthair's adjoining greenhouse always said home to me. They're here with me now, and I've added salty sea breeze, cozy drifting peat smoke, and Sionnach's deep, earthy scent to my definition.

Grace clears her throat, glaring at the buckets. "Before we step back into your Faerie world, give me one of those potion breads. I will not subject my people to Faerie deception without first partaking of it myself."

As if Faerie deceit would ever involve the manual labor of dousing thousands of croutons. She has a valid point. It's important to test the cubes on a human lacking Fae or witch magic before we feed them to six thousand sailors. After what happened to Sion when he drank elixir, I should have been more wary of Robber's instructions.

I gesture toward a bucket. "Help yourself."

Grace plucks a cube out of the closest batch and holds it between her thumb and forefinger, turning it to examine all six sides. She pops it in her mouth, chews, and swallows.

Biddy and I watch in silence. Tension twists through my chest like a corkscrew into a wine bottle, but the Pirate Queen shows no ill effects from the Faerie snack.

I test a little magic push of my essence to make her stumble just a smidge, but thankfully, it has no effect. Thank you, crouton.

Next, I practice exerting my influence and say, "Nothing you see in our travels will seem strange to you, Granuaile O'Malley. You will accept it as plain intention." This isn't magic to hurt but only to protect, so I'm not breaking my vow to the Tree of Life. As I finish, there's the slightest sideways twitch of her head. Pointing to Alfie, I say, "Watch the tree in front of my window." When she follows my instruction, I call the Veil and ask the *fánaí* tree to shift from her earthly position to a perch just inside the prismatic portal.

Grace gives no reaction other than pursing her lips when Alfie, my conduit to the mysterious *Crann na Beatha*, disappears then reappears inside the Veil. The Pirate Queen doesn't show a stitch of unease, surprise, or distress. She walks toward the Veil as if it's her standard mode of travel. Score bonus points for my Faerie influence. Here's hoping her six thousand sailors take to my charm as easily.

Once my two teammates, Alfie, and the croutons are safe inside the Veil's front door, I do my damnedest to swap doubt for determination. There's nothing left to do but forge ahead. Biddy opens the blue bottle and coaxes the shimmering map into being. I lay my fingertip with Queen Nuala's mark against the image of Grace's castle on Clare Island and allow my mind to drift into the magic of the Veil.

My hair hangs in limp, wet strands around my face as I grip the swaying rail of the latest wooden-hulled galley ship in our nautical odyssey. As with all our previous encounters, I hang back and watch Granuaile O'Malley, the great pirate queen, give instructions to her captains. No one openly argues with her, although to the man, they're a bit ruffled that she doesn't give a direct answer to the same question that arises every time.

What is the purpose of this venture, Granuaile?

Despite her avoidance of their curiosity, everyone she speaks with shows respect and near worship for Grace.

It's impressive.

It's intimidating.

I stretch the muscles of my influence over sailors to carry wooden barrels to where Biddy waits on docks or shores, so they don't react to the plastic buckets we've brought through the Veil to dump into the barrels.

The captains of the two ships we've gone farthest back in time to meet were the most skeptical. They've been tasked with retrieving gallowglasses, mercenary human fighting machines from Scotland, to round out our numbers in case ship-jumping hand-to-hand combat becomes a factor. If humans exist who are able to stand against Faerie warriors, I'd put my money on the gallowglasses.

Grace beckons to me, and we walk the gangway to where Biddy waits at a dock on Galway Bay.

"That's the last," says the commander of the pirate fleet, gazing thoughtfully at the White Seahorse. "Will you not leave me at her helm? I've done all you've asked, Eala of the Fae. Surely that earns enough trust that I'll not betray you. I, along with those loyal to me, shall arrive at the Serpent's Lair to fulfill my oath."

I feel awful not granting her request, but with all the Veil jumps, there are technically two days between now and then. I can't risk that a storm or encounters with enemies will prevent any of her ships from the rendezvous. If we arrive and there's been a problem, I'll use my *fánaí* advantages to fix it, but Grace's voice of authority by my side might also be needed.

"I trust you, Granuaile O'Malley, but I don't trust the forces, natural or otherwise, working against us."

Biddy lays a hand on Grace's shoulder. "It will only seem like moments before you're reunited with this ship that makes your eyes shine with pride."

Wind whips hair across my face, and for an instant, I'm alone behind the curtain. But I am not alone. These two brave women stand with me, both true to their word and the promises we've struck between us. I would have failed in my struggles to save Sionnach if they hadn't lent their magic and might to my crusade.

A Faerie, a witch, and a pirate go to war—the perfect beginning of an epic folktale. One I hope to write and add to the canon of myths, tales, and stories that shape my origins, my life, and my love.

Then there is Robber Bright. The being I trust least beneath the heavens is the final link in this impossible chain to save my *anamchara* and my best friend.

I won't abandon Máthair, but she's proved she can strike her own bargains with the Fae and continue to survive. When Sion and I are together and Colleen and the Host of a Thousand Wings are free, we'll find a way to save my grandmother from Finnbheara.

I bat my hair aside, but it flaps back in my face. I groan. "Biddy, as soon as we're in the Veil, will you please braid this mess?"

It's what Colleen would do for me.

We make our way behind a line of trees. I call the Veil, and we are on our way to war. Grace stands apart as Biddy deals with my hair.

After I fulfill my promise to Robber Bright and open the Veil for Colleen and the Host of a Thousand Wings to get the hell out of hell, I'll be on the deck of the White Seahorse, standing between the souls I ripped out of time in the name of love. Wrapping fingers around one of Alfie's strong, unfailing trunks, I send my gratitude into the heart of the Veil traveler's tree, the Tree of Life, who has been a faithful constant in my unexpected life of wandering and wonder.

Suddenly, it feels as if my entire being is drawn into the tree. All around me, the spectral light of the Veil flares in countless bursts. A flood of energy crackles up from roots and through bark to ignite my essence.

"Alfie," I scream.

I'm in the Veil, but its walls fly past in a blinding blur.

Flash.

In the streaks of light, I see Sion in front of Robber's cottage in the Gem

Kissed Forest, shielding his eyes from a viciously bright glow falling from the sky.

Flash.

Finnbheara appears in front of Sionnach, the king's white-gold armor blazing like the sun.

Flash.

A great fog boils through the forest, obscuring the two men.

Flash.

The forest is still. Nothing stirs. The silver stump covered with food has disappeared.

Sionnach is gone.

CHAPTER 33
THE DARK BLOW

ROBBER BRIGHT

Instead of meeting Aodh's furious stare as the God of the Underworld storms off his dais toward me, I fixate on the great black swan sculpture at his back. I crave the satisfaction snapping off the wingtips of the Dark Prince's throne would bring.

This king is eternally wretched by choice.

No wonder the god's skin continually flakes to ash as he allows pieces of his soul to fester from the ancient blow dealt to the Children of Lir.

He pauses on the last step, drawing his onyx sword as if to send it through my body. "Again, you pass through the gates of Bráchthine without the company of my guard," hisses Aodh. My latest breach of his arrogant control sends the crimson flames in the king's eyes into a tumultuous spin.

The guards who confronted me outside the mouth of Oweynagat have delivered me to a god filled with rage and fury. Hatred for this monster churns in my breast, challenging the necessity to keep a cool head.

"And as before, it was to earn the trust of Eala Duir so I may fulfill my promise to you."

He glowers, the smolder beneath his charred flesh emitting licks of flame. "You openly defy my orders and go without my trusted swords of Bráchthine.

And as before…" Aodh throws my words back at me. "…here you stand alone in your arrogance without Eala Duir."

Alone, he says. The God of the Underworld stands as one perpetually alone from all who might once have truly cared for him. Where are the siblings who suffered alongside Aodh? They did not allow the misery of fate to shape them into vessels of dark madness. This king could have crafted a kingdom honoring his torment. Instead, all in his realm are mired in the despair its sovereign uses as an excuse to justify atrocity and cruelty—the killing of a queen and his never-ending hunger to destroy, destroy, destroy. There will always be challenges between the Fae kings that may lead to wars, but those are struggles for power, for land, for wealth. Not thirst for the agony of others.

I need to throw water on Aodh's flames before they consume me. "The bargain is struck. Eala Duir willingly accepts Bráchthine as her dominion."

The Dark Prince pauses.

"The largess will be fourfold for you, sire, once the ships of Bráchthine sail at the back of Eala Duir and her earthly forces. You will overpower Finnbheara in this first strike of the new war. Afterward, she who was once the treasure of your rival will sail her ships to the shores of your kingdom. You seize victory, six thousand souls for Bráchthine, the white swam, and the *beads of being* dwelling in her essence."

And now to point Aodh's attention away from my transgressions.

"Ready your ships, my king. Eala Duir's fleet approaches the gateway to the Faerie seas. She will soon call for you to open the way."

Aodh grabs me by the throat. His fingers feel like smoldering coals against my skin. "This will be the end of your defiance, Robálaí Geal. Do you understand?" I fight to breathe the charred air spewing from Aodh's lips. "If Eala Duir does not follow through with what you claim, your life and your Host of a Thousand Wings will be the first casualties of war. Your bond-promised…" Words force their way through his clenched teeth. "…shall be my whore until I have ridden her to a slow and agonizing death."

The Underworld God is truly beyond any redemption of fate. His horrible words strike fear in my soul for Colleen. It is not passion-driven, only the will to spare anyone from such an unspeakable death. Instead of the promise of joy she once was, my bond-promised now resides as a cold pebble in my heart.

He shoves me and I fall, clutching my bruised throat.

Aodh's eyes are incendiary as he strides past me. "General Dóite," he booms to his man at the door of the throne room. "Call the fleet to arms. I shall command the Red Glass Hammer."

I do not speak, praying to any gods and goddesses of the ancient ones who have not forsaken me that Aodh does not send me to the dungeons of Caisleán Brón or bid me sail with him. I must retain enough freedom to send my Host and Colleen out of the gates of Bráchthine and through the Cave of Cats to Eala Duir while he and his legions are distracted.

Just as he is about to pass through the great black oak doors, he turns back to me. "There are eyes on you, Robálaí Geal, with spikes of burning iron behind them.

The woeful screech of a *péist síoda* I know as dearly as my own soul sounds outside the doors. Aodh's dragon masters force my beloved dragon into the room. Chains and ropes bind Aillil so his movements are dictated by the will of his captors. One of the brutes slices a blade across the creature's throat. The dragon bellows as loud as a breaking storm, sending clouds of steam into the faces of the men holding him. He tries to buck then kick his powerful legs at the bastards, but Aillil's restraints are too effective. Thankfully, the cut is only shallow enough to produce a weak stream of aquamarine blood, the same color as my eyes, to spill down the creature's neck.

One of the masters sneers at me. "We are Aodh's spikes of burning iron, but it is your dragon and not your worthless hide that will suffer our scorch."

When I make a move toward them, the other brandishes a metal rod with fire burning at its tip and tilts it near Aillil's eye.

"You ruthless bastards."

The other flashes a hideous grin. "For every act of yours that displeases our king, we will melt a pretty scale from this beast."

Aillil stands as proud as he is able within his bindings. In the tongue of the *péist síoda* that no one dwelling in Aodh's kingdom possesses the wisdom to speak, I say, *"For the actions I will commit sending you into darkness, I beg your forgiveness, blessed friend. I am sorry, my brother."* There is no doubt that my blatant defiance in orchestrating the Host's exodus will sentence this magnificent being to death.

He answers in a raw trill. *"Our path together ends, but you must go on."*

I bow to my dragon then leave him in the hands of devils.

Aodh knows the bonds we forge with our dragons. He believes holding Aillil hostage will cow me. The God of the Underworld does not understand true loyalty, the willingness to forfeit one precious life to spare another. Aillil gives me his blessing to do so.

I will not weep. I will honor my mighty *péist síoda* drake's sacrifice.

Now that my dragon is a hostage, I am not accosted by Aodh's soldiers as I return to Ciallmhar's rooms. The high command is armored, and Colleen is cloaked. Nettle is not with them. My bond-promised tries to run to me, but I raise a hand to stop her. Artos gently restrains her. My cold expression raises distress in her eyes, and she does not resist him.

My gaze lingers on her. Deep within, my soul is not at rest. It pushes against my essence as if trying to break through a barrier as unmovable as the steel doors of the Castle of Sorrows. Only when I look away, the pressure does not threaten to overtake me.

Acacia stares at me and then at Colleen. Pity is plain across her fair face. She knows the look of my hollow heart well.

I turn to my Fae witch. "Are the Host and the *péist síoda* ready?"

Ciallmhar answers. "I gave Nettle a druid's stone. It will heat in his palm when the Host is to mount and prepare to fly to the gates of Bráchthine."

I give a curt nod. "No one touch or speak to me."

Colleen's mournful whimper is a hot sting in my ear.

"I must have silence to listen for Eala Duir's call."

I will sense Eala's summons like lightning from an angry cloud. It is Colleen's voice and touch I can no longer bear.

I stand before the hearth fire with my back to my Folk, straining to ignore the cracks forming in a heart that should not be capable of breaking.

There is rustling behind me as they settle in to wait. Mere moments pass before I clutch my chest. Eala's call doubles my heartbeats. Had she hailed me any sooner, I might have been in Aodh's presence and risked him discovering the machinations of our escape.

"Heat your druid stone, Ciallmhar," I say, drawing my sword and facing my high command. "Kill anyone in our way."

Two guards at the end of the hall are the first to die. Heading away from the commotion of soldiers gathering around a corner to jitter about the launching of Aodh's fleet, we take the spiral stone stairs in the rear corner of the palace. It is not until we reach an iron door studded with circles of red glass leading out of the fortress that the next quartet of Bráchthine soldiers are cut down by the combined strikes of Artos and Acacia.

Colleen calls to me on the stairs. When I answer with an icy glare and the slash of my hand across lips that once claimed hers in passion, she does not try again. Ciallmhar keeps her close to his side as the rest of us stay alert for more guards.

We make it unmolested to the opposite side of the barracks from Bráchthine's blood-orange sun and its perpetual revolutions around the red glass mountains. The Host of a Thousand Wings blends with the shadows of the tall black stone structure.

My high command mounts their waiting dragons. There are already double riders on a dozen creatures due to those *péist síoda* destroyed in Aodh's wicked breeding experiments.

Acacia leads an agitated Eachna to my side, her face grave. "Robálaí, where is Aillil?"

I reveal nothing. "I will ride with you."

Turning to Colleen, I grasp her trembling shoulders. "I am sorry to have brought you to this place where joy is forbidden to exist." Before she speaks, I call to Ciallmhar. "Take my bond-promised to your saddle."

Soon, Colleen will be with Eala Duir, who I pray will lead her back to a human life where one day our bond-promise may fade enough to grant her happiness and love untainted by Finnbheara's geas.

I mount my second's dragon then extend a hand to hoist Acacia into the saddle before me. She points off to the left. "If we keep to the eastern shadows, there is a steeper path to the far side of Bráchthine's gates. It may buy us some measure of time before we are set upon."

I raise my fist and thrust it in the direction Acacia determined. The Host of a Thousand Wings takes flight, and we soar across burnished sands toward the gates. When we crest the path to the wall of blackened bones, a dirge plays through my mind for our fallen Folk.

"Robálaí, they come," hisses Acacia. Streaming up the main road, the dark blot of Aodh's approaching *péist lasrach* legion flies in our direction.

I call to the warrior at my flank. "Artos, lead the Host through the Cave of Cats. Leave our best fighters with me at the rear. Eala Duir and the Veil will be waiting for us." I spare a moment to judge the speed of our enemy.

The bulk of the Host streams past me. We do not contend with Aodh's showy red rain. That spectacle is only for those entering his kingdom for the first time. As soon as the last row of our fiercest has crossed beyond Bráchthine's gates, I spur Eachna to follow.

The whirr of *péist síoda* wings at their topmost speed is deafening within the cave walls. Still, Acacia twists to angle her mouth to my ear and shouts. "I am confounded. What are you about, Robálaí?"

I cup a hand around her ear and breathe my words into it. "I am still the king's man, Finnbheara of Tír na nÓg."

I feel her body go rigid before she shifts to face me. "You lie to those who have sworn their lives to you and nearly condemned us to a land of horrors? This cannot be. This cannot be."

"I will explain all when we return to our rightful kingdom."

My second slaps my face with a flesh-stinging blow. "This is my last hour in your service, traitor. I will never speak to you again as long as I draw breath."

I would welcome the slice of her blade across my throat. Blessed dragons died. I have betrayed those I value most because I refused to doubt the efficacy of my gifts of duplicity and how they would prevail against the Dark Prince. I was a fool indeed to believe Aodh's conceit a weakness easily exploited. I scoffed at risk, and others will pay with their lives, and…their hearts. Colleen's face bursts into my mind's eye.

All for what? To win back a place at the side of a king who denies me the esteem I crave like a begging dog?

I bartered with souls that did not belong to me. How is my spirit any less diabolic than Aodh's?

We flee through the curves of the Cave of Cats. Even with the superior speed and agility of the *péist síoda*, reflections of the pursuing *péist lasrach's* dragon fire begin to shine between the licks of flame in the walls of the cave. I urge Eachna on with greater speed. Acacia adds her pleas to Aillil's mate. If only I rode beside her with my cherished dragon, so Eachna was not burdened with two, outrunning our foe with would be a certainty not a deadly gamble.

We take a curve sharply enough to cause Eachna to cry out from what must be a strain on her muscles. Before us is the arch of fire. Beyond Aodh's hellish portal, the splendor of the flowering Veil lights the sky in a magnificent borealis.

Between the shining promise of our escape and the cave's opening, steel sings against steel. A cluster of my warriors cut at Aodh's guards from dragon-back, maintaining an opening for silk dragons and their riders to escape over the bodies of three fallen *péist lasrach* the enemy piled under the arch to hinder the Host's exit. A great curtain of steam rises from the carcasses.

"Robálaí, to your right," screams Acacia, as the gleam of flame off an onyx blade slices through the air.

I slide from the dragon, with my sword in the lead, knocking my opponent back and cry "All Host to the Veil. All Host to the Veil." I pierce the neck of Aodh's soldier with my blade. Blistering heat surges up my weapon all the way to my grip from where it contacts the warrior's smoldering Bráchthine hide. An unyielding flare scorches flesh like wildfire. The intensity causes me to drop my sword onto the rocky ground.

A wall of fiery wind slams into me from the flames engulfing the tunnel behind us as our pursuers close the final gap. Skin boils across my back. I fight the blinding pain. Screaming with murderous rage despite my agony, I grab an abandoned sword at my feet that lacks the red glow of hellfire, and force another Bráchthine soldier against the cave wall. My onslaught creates space for Acacia and Eachna to leap over the bodies of the fallen flame dragons and through the haze of the creatures' dying breaths.

"Go," I shout to the handful of my Host still standing as the last of Oweynagat's guards fall. The small cadre of underworld fighters I faced before at the entrance to the Cave of Cats has become an entire unit, no doubt ordered to guard the hellmouth after my last unsanctioned visit.

By my quick count, there are close to a dozen of my Host dead on the ground alongside Bráchthine foe. There is no time to collect their bodies. I commend their souls to the ancient ones then turn toward the blessed avenue of our delivery from Aodh's kingdom. Eala Duir stands at the edge of the frantic churning edges of the Veil portal's entrance, clutching Colleen to her breast. Artos, Ciallmhar, and Nettle are alongside them, waving the rest of our Host into the passage. Acacia is last to join the high command, wheeling Eachna around to face Oweynagat.

When I make to leap over the tangle of death to stand with Finnbheara's Treasure, my name flies from the lips of those who wait for me, looks of horror upon every face. Instantly, their terror is made real as a burning sword buries itself into the flesh of my already ruined back, its tip severing my spine. I crumble like dried clay.

Reaching an arm to Eala Duir, I send my dwindling essence to hers, crying through our connection, *"Close the Veil."* As the blessed path of light begins to fade, I search for the white swan's spirit with the last of my strength. *"Do not go to Aodh,"* I repeat the warning, praying she hears my call until the shadow of Aodh's soldiers hides the stars and the Veil disappears.

CHAPTER 34
THE VEIL AWAITS

EALA

The horrid image of Robber Bright replays in my head. His body glowed a deep, bloody orange like an ember of fire. The Faerie's brain-splintering cry to my essence forced me to close the Veil before Aodh's terrifying forces could follow us.

I swear I felt Robber try to say more. His message was lost when a shadow as black as unlit coal obliterated the entire hellmouth of the Cave of Cats until it was just a small opening in a Roscommon farmer's field.

It's amazing how long and wide the Veil passage lengthens behind me to accommodate the Host of a Thousand Wings. My body trembles as badly as the near-hysterical Colleen in my arms. The music of violins and bells plays triumphant music. I count Thirty-plus silk dragons and riders glide past then cluster in a wide space where the Veil expands for them. The pastiche of dragon scales is as stunningly beautiful and as varied as the colors of the Veil.

As we're cut off from danger, buzzing from *péist síoda* wings softens from a high-pitched screech into the contented hum of bees delighted by a field of blooms. I wish I could steal even a moment to absorb the gratitude that my best friend is free, but the shadow of Aodh, God of the Underworld, looms over any happiness. I've just witnessed the brutality of his warriors and

Robber's decimation. This is the realm and its king the Host has just escaped, and I'm about to pledge my loyalty to them.

Dread wraps iron collars around my Veil sprites. They struggle to move within my essence. Aodh must never learn I brought the Veil to rescue the Host. I can't risk beginning our relationship with a betrayal. Not that I hold much hope that the partnership will ever be anything but disturbing. I'll accept the cost of a bleak future if it reunites me with Sion.

Finnbheara has set this eventuality in motion. To save my soulmate, I must go forward.

"I thought the Veil was lost to us," says Artos, a near giant, who I've just learned is part of Robber Bright's elite.

"How is it we could enter?" asks Nettle, a skittish, skinny Fae who looks like he should be selling cheese rather than stabbing people with a sword.

"Tell us, Ciallmhar," says Acacia, the Fae woman with an attitude. I remember her from the Host's visit to the cottage. "Was not our affinity to Tír na nÓg severed, wise witch?"

Biddy takes Colleen from my arms so I can speak to the Faeries. My friend is so screwed up with grief, she's beyond speech. My witch friend raises her brows as if she's the *wise witch* expected to answer. This Ciallmhar, a very serious-looking Faerie, another one of Robber's closest soldiers, who's been stoically watching the Host pass into the Veil, lays his palm against the undulating wall. "Never severed, only hidden."

"You're a witch?" I ask him, surprised. I didn't know there was such a thing as a Fae witch. A rush of sadness runs through me at the realization I, too, will soon be severed from the Veil.

"I am, Eala Duir," says Ciallmhar. "We owe you our thanks. May I now overtake your burden of guiding the Host through the Veil?"

"If you can act quickly, please do." This detour must end so we can get back to Grace's fleet. Sion's probably strapped as a figurehead to the front of Finnbheara's ship.

Ciallmhar sings the word *home*, then pushes it into the Veil. In a gentle downward slope, a second Faerie path extends off the main passageway, answering to his wishes instead of mine. The way is open to carry the Host to the Gem Kissed Forest. Heaven knows what Finnbheara's going to do when they show up.

Without Robber Bright.

The four Fae in his leadership team stand shoulder to shoulder, staring into the space where my Veil window slammed shut. We all witnessed the horror Robber endured, but they don't say a word about it. I can't bear the wrongness of just letting the trauma pass. "Is there any possibility Robber Bright is still alive?"

"The commander pays a dire cost for his betrayal," says Acacia in a voice as frigid as winter snow.

Colleen comes to life with the vehemence of a cat avoiding water. "Robálaí is not dead." The cat looks poised to claw every hint of pity from the eyes of the Fae, but fight suddenly leaves her. "Not dead, but—" She clutches her temples. "He's fading. I sense his body blowing away like flakes of ash." Her eyes roll up, and Ciallmhar catches her before she falls, lifting Colleen into his arms.

Artos faces the others. "If he lives, we must return."

"It is sure death to step into Aodh's realm. In the absence of Robálaí, the command is mine. No one shall return," says Acacia.

It's pretty damn clear Robber Bright wanted to be free of Bráchthine. It wasn't only Colleen and the Host he was helping to escape. Robálaí Geal was fighting his way out of the cave.

Colleen's quiet weeping signals she didn't pass out. My dearest friend is the personification of a broken and bleeding heart.

I turn on Acacia. "Are you that hard-hearted? It's cruel to prevent others from going back who are willing to take the risk."

She glares at me, but I'm not under her command.

I answer her pissy attitude by ramping up my anger. "You're standing here free, Acacia, because Robber Bright saved you. Don't you dare leave him to possibly suffer a more ghastly fate than what we just witnessed." I wave a hand at the other Faerie warriors while maintaining a furious gaze on Acacia. "If you won't go after him, give them the chance to."

It's clear from their expressions that Artos, Ciallmhar, or Nettle would go back in a hot second.

I point a finger at her. "You may have written him off, but these companions and this woman he loves haven't."

Acacia stares at each of them. Unblinking eyes that shine with defiance and lips pressed into unyielding lines telegraph that one or all of Robber Bright's friends contemplate going against her heartless orders.

Artos grits his teeth. "A single rider may escape Aodh's notice as his attentions will be on war. Since the Host has fled Bráchthine, the Dark Prince will not think any of us foolish enough to return. I will go."

Ciallmhar carefully shifts Colleen into Nettle's arms. "The commander would never leave any in the Host to perish atop the unforgiving sands of Bráchthine. I will go."

Nettle rests his head against Colleen's. "Lend me a concealment spell, Ciallmhar, so I might travel as nothing more than a whisper in Aodh's lands. I will go."

For the first time, Grace pipes up from behind Alfie. I'm damn glad I already influenced her. Even the hardiest of souls would be done in by burning hellmouths and a parade of silk dragons.

"Loyalty will always find its due reward," says Grace.

Acacia, the lines of her face as unforgiving as stone, barks, "I shall not rescind my orders. As I commanded, the Host of a Thousand Wings and Robálaí's human bond-promised will return to the Gem Kissed Forest."

I'm stunned into silence by her complete lack of compassion. How can the Fae stand to live their long lives with hearts of ice? My gaze sweeps over the warriors, torn between obedience and the loyalty Grace speaks of. I amend my thoughts. There are some Fae not built of ice, granite, and malice.

With stone-faced acquiescence, Robber's soldiers mount their dragons. In a whoosh of wing-whipped air, the *péist síoda* take flight down the path created by Ciallmhar.

"Colleen," I cry and start after them.

Biddy grabs my arm. "Let her go, Eala of the Fae. You'll find your way back to her."

From Nettle's arms, Colleen just stares at me, then she too vanishes down the tunnel as Ciallmhar's branch of the Veil closes behind them.

Sion, Colleen, Máthair, Robber Bright, and all too soon Biddy and Grace... will there be anyone left in my life to give a damn about?

"Time to go, Faerie girl," says Biddy, clutching my shoulder. With my heart freezing over from the sorrow of Robber's end and watching Colleen ride away, I ask the Veil to carry us to the deck of the White Seahorse.

CHAPTER 35

THE SANDS OF BRÁCHTHINE

ROBBER BRIGHT

My mind switches from black to gray then black again. My body is numb, and I suspect that is a mercy. One not granted me for long as a burning drop falls upon my cheek and eats through flesh and bone. My brain screams to my hand to paw at the pain, but my limbs do not respond.

Above me are the interlocking smoked glass tree branches that trail across the ceiling of the throne room in Caisleán Brón. Red glass leaves drip black fire that sizzles when it hits the floor…or my skin. Brutal fingers grabs me by the hair, lifting and twisting until my body spins and the hideous face of Aodh comes into view inches from mine. He spits a simmering glob into my eye, robbing me of half my sight. "You canker of festering pus."

I force words from my battered mouth. "Queen killer."

"Your bitch queen provoked me as have you, Robálaí Geal. Like Nuala of Tír na nÓg, a traitor of your same ilk, your body will rot on the sands of Bráchthine. May your soul be banished from every realm of our forebearers as you are cast into the merciless void of consequence. I will feast and glory at this triumph of reaching into Finnbheara's heart and stripping from it two vital pieces, both queen and kin. Let your essence wail for all time as you endure the true potential of fate's cruelty."

Aodh licks his lips. "Know this, king's fool. You are the instrument of your beloved Finnbheara's ruin. The silver king will soon fall when Eala Duir and the *beads of being* are mine."

His despicable threat chases me into utter darkness.

The stench of roasting flesh wakes me. It is my skin that cooks under the blood-orange sun of Bráchthine. The scrape of drifting crimson grit across my face is the only proof I have not yet passed beyond this life. Aodh has dumped me here, as promised, to smolder until I am nothing but ash.

My decrepit body does not move. I am limited to the view straight above me. The warm hues of the underworld sky are stunning. Aodh's ruined soul does not deserve such beauty. Dying as I gaze up at this gradient of deep amber and ruby-tinted light is a better end than I deserve.

The scratch of boots against the earth disturbs my journey into death. "Grant me the mercy of the gods and goddesses," a voice whispers near my head. I know it. Queen Nuala calls to my soul from the void of consequence where Aodh's brutality has banished her.

A face of glorious bronze skin drops close to mine.

It is not the queen.

It is my cherished second.

"Can you move at all, Robálaí?" Acacia whispers.

I move parched lips, forcing what few words I can through them. "I am dead. You must leave."

"You live, Commander. I have come to take you to her...to your bond-promised. If you must die, you will do so in her arms."

Bond-promised.

I mouth the name still alive in my heart as the rest of me fades.

Colleen.

Battle-strong arms lift me, and my head falls back like a child's sugarvine doll. The position brings the sight of a great nearby mound into clear view.

Acacia follows my gaze as the weak drone of despair spills from my slack lips. She immediately whispers words of a charm to stir the dusts of

Bráchthine and cover what lies next to me. She is too late. I see every burnt and tattered blue silk wing that will never again lift the body of my beloved dead dragon into the sky.

Acacia carries me toward Eachna. Aillil's mate releases a long, low, keen so quiet it barely disturbs the air.

Despite the unspeakable and unforgivable circumstances I forced upon her and the Host of a Thousand Wings, my ever-loyal second croons just as softly as her dragon to me. She gifts me a single tear.

"Sleep now, Robálaí Geal."

CHAPTER 36
THE DEATH OF DECEIT

SIONNACH

I've not been given a speck of the fine Faerie armor that covers Finnbheara from above his pointy ears to his toes. The silver-white metal is stamped with vines, leaves, and flowers that I now recognize as the ones growing wild in the Gem Kissed Forest. There could have been a reality where I'd spend my days learning the names of every plant and how to care for them if this crooked villain of a king had kept his word to Eala and granted us a home here.

My arse is charmed to a silver stool in the corner of the same war room I saw before Ma dragged me away after Eala disappeared through Finn's gates. If I can call it a corner or this a room. With the mist, it's like being in the middle of a cloud with no walls and a floor you may as soon fall through than walk on.

Ole Finn stamps around his massive magical map table, barking orders and huffing as loudly as Eala's dragon. I squint at the flickering seas, straining to see if Eala and her pirates have joined the party.

Soldiers stream in and out of the mist that drifts through the room, collecting orders and grousing about odds and such. At a lull in the hive, Finn leans on the edge of the table and hangs his head.

I gain satisfaction from interrupting his moment of pause. The fool doesn't deserve a single drop of peace. "A decent man would at least let a fella say goodbye to his mother." The request isn't just to rattle Finn, I've a need to know if he's made Ma's life a misery because of the blind hate he has for me. Can she return to the little bit of calm she'd grown to accept in the Glade of Chimes, or did Eala and I rob her of that solitude by riling the king? He's claimed she's well, but I believe him as much as I believe a crow would pass up a shining coin to feather its nest.

Finnbheara never opens his gob. The king fades into the fog. Did he even hear me? I'd wonder if he left me behind to join the upcoming battle, except, he needs me front and center to trap Eala.

In a flash, Finn returns to his table with Ma by his side. After setting a hand on his arm, she leaves the king to come to me. Her long gown of silk is stamped with the same pattern as Finn's armor as if the bastard's marked her as his. Waves of dark hair fall freely across her shoulders. My mother opens her arms. "Sionnach."

I struggle to meet her, forgetting I'm plastered to the stool.

Ma whips around to the king. "For decency's sake, Finnbheara, let him go."

The bastard doesn't even look up, but a push from behind sends me to the ground. The mist was hiding the white stamped metal floor of the war room. It's not as forgiving as the silver green grass near the gates.

My mother holds out her hands to help me to my feet. She holds me close, laying a hand to the back of my head. "These curls are the dearest thing in all the world," she says, letting them fall through her fingers.

Lucky those wandering Fae didn't snatch every hair from my head. "Not my faithful heart or fine singing voice?"

She pulls back. "Certainly not your runaway mouth or stubbornness." We share a smile and the twinkle of our green glass *fánaí* eyes. Our happy moment doesn't last.

"At least the bastard is letting me say my goodbyes to you."

Ma hisses to quiet me and glances at the king. "His mood is foul and full of worry. I'm begging you not to provoke him, *Mac*."

I lower my voice. "Do you know he means to use me to draw Eala back here?" She nods. "Ma, he doesn't intend for me to be with her. He's all but said the battle will take me."

The gold ring around her irises flares wide until I can't see anything but gilded shine with single black dots in each center. "No."

"Don't raise a fuss, Ma. We know Finnbheara'll do what he'll do. I need a promise from you that if the bastard allows it, you'll care for Eala once I'm gone. She loves you as I do, and you'll need each other."

"Sionnach, nothing is certain until it is."

I try to give her a smile that says I believe her words, but I've not got it in me. "If a fox had the nine lives of a cat, I'd be glad of it." I lean in to kiss her cheek. "I don't know how to share the bounty of gratitude in my heart for all you've done for me and for my Eala. If not for you, I'd have passed from this world without knowing the love of an *anamchara* and never had a woman to call wife. It doesn't matter how short a time Eala and me were given, it carries the fullness of ages. Thank you, Ma. I love you so."

We clutch one another as her body trembles. She doesn't try again to convince me that there may be any other end than the grim one that's finally come for me.

A massive pressure fills the air, enough to set ears to bleeding. Rainbow light spills through the mist, sending the thin fog clean away. I see now we're in a bit of a glade, not a room. Its border of clear glass trees defines the space.

A woman mighty enough to kick my sorry arse stands at the edge of the trees with a bundle in her arms and the shine of the Veil at her back. As she steps toward the king, he releases a sound I've never heard from those royal lips and strips the helm from his head. Finn's cry is filled with enough anguish to split his Faerie moon.

"Brave Acacia, this tragic sorrow you bear cannot be." Great King Finnbheara rushes forward, taking the body of a man from the she-warrior. He drops to the ground and clasps the Fae to his breast, weeping and rocking like a man who's had his soul cleaved in two.

Next to me, Ma lets out a shocked gasp.

"Robálaí. Robálaí." The king wails to the rhythm of the name, gently guiding strands of hair from the man's face.

Of things both holy and cursed. It's Robber Bright in the arms of the king. His clothes are in shreds, and what I see of the body beneath is a horror. Skin blistered and burned, oozing the black ichor of the damned.

With words strangled by grief, the king speaks to the Acacia woman.

She answers in equally low tones, but she's easier to understand than the sobbing mess of a king I never thought to witness. "The Host of a Thousand Wings fled Bráchthine at our commander's bidding when Eala Duir opened the Veil to us."

Eala.

The look of torment on Acacia's face sets my gut to churning. "My king, we believed he perished at Oweynagat." Her voice starts to fail her. "Robalaí's bond-promised swore he lived still but that his life would soon scatter across the plains of Bráchthine."

Finn rests his cheek against Robber Bright's blood-matted hair.

The warrior clears her throat and pushes on. "Finnbheara's Treasure bade me to return to Aodh's kingdom to retrieve the commander for the sake of his bond-promised."

She inhales a stuttering breath. "I cannot forgive Robálaí's betrayal. I do not owe the woman he joined with in bond-promise or Eala Duir any debt, but nor could I leave the rider of my dragon's mate to rot in Bráchthine. It is a gift from the ancient ones that even waning essence still dwells within this man."

Bond-promised? I can't make sense of these Faeries. A page has been ripped out of the book I'm trying to read here.

Finnbheara dismissed my *anamchara* bond with Eala, but is the bond-promise the soldier speaks of a Fae version of something equally sacred to what I have with my wife? If so, another heart is set to break in this cursed kingdom.

Finn's head snaps up, fury raging in his eyes, spilling silver tears. "There is no betrayal here, Acacia. Robálaí did not lead the Host into Bráchthine for any other purpose than to bring my queen home."

The Fae woman gasps and clutches her middle as if she's trying to keep her guts from leaking out.

Finn's broken voice is replaced with a regal roar. "Robalaí's pledges to Aodh were false. They were but a ploy to open the way barred for centuries against Nuala of Tír na nÓg that prevented my queen's return to her rightful place by my side."

Stories and tales blast Finn's infidelities across time. For a king who doesn't keep his cock in his pants, a mission to save his wife must be about his pride, not love.

The soldier, Acacia, rasps her next words. "The Host was ignorant that our true purpose was to rescue your beloved queen."

Beloved?

"Robálaí and I were the sole bearers of such knowledge. The extent of Aodh's powers to glean that which others do not wish him to know is a mystery. The risk was too great. Through the strength of his pure *Tuatha Dé Danann* bloodline, Robálaí Geal alone held the might to keep the quest secret. Weakness from but one of the Host would spell the doom of all."

I'm still chewing on *beloved*. I'd think they'd call the queen esteemed, revered, or some other fancy Fae phrasing. Finn claims to have loved, but his claims are as reliable as sandals in a snowstorm.

The king's eyes shift from silver into slate gray, ringed in black splotches that look like storm clouds, as he glares at Acacia. "Has your anger killed all compassion in your spirit? You say Robálaí lives, yet I detect no attempt at healing." His gaze sweeps the glade. "Where is this bond-promised?"

I would've been glad to kill Robber Bright with my own hands more than once, but no man deserves the horrors the Faerie suffers.

Acacia drops to one knee. "Sire, I did plead with the Veil, but the injuries are of Aodh's fire and evil. Only the power of a king may undo the desecration inflicted by such darkness."

Finn lays the soon-to-be-dead Faerie onto the grass that's replaced the metal floor. He presses a palm to Robber Bright's chest, muttering Fae gibberish. A shroud made of the Veil's prism wavers around the still body.

Ma's iron grip numbs my hand. I gently pull my fingers free and slide my arm around her shoulder, stunned at what I see. Her tears gush along with Finn's. Who is it she's weeping for, the king or a fallen warrior? Ma's strong, but she's got a soft heart for anyone who's hurting. Even so, I don't understand why this man's end cuts her so deeply.

"Fetch his bond-promised to me at once. I need the strength of her devotion to join with mine if we are to keep Robálaí Geal from disappearing into the merciless void of consequence."

"Yes, Majesty."

Acacia isn't gone for three blinks of an eye before she's back in front of the king. I about choke when I see who's with her.

Colleen.

Ma and I call the name in the same breath.

She barely spares us a glance before she drops to the ground next to Robber Bright's shimmery body. Colleen presses her cheek to his still one. "Robálaí. Robálaí. Come back to me, please, oh please, oh please." She reaches to run her hands over him but doesn't seem to know where to touch. "I love you. Don't leave me." Her tears splash against the Veil's sheath. "Wherever you're going, take me with you."

These fucking Faeries sink into new, unforgivable depths of cruelty. Robber Bright enchanted Colleen and stole her away from her life and her world. Now the tormented woman thinks she's losing someone she truly loves. The Fae have less regard for the human heart than they do a crushed twig beneath their dancing shoes.

"Leave them be," Ma says, wrapping herself around me when I try to move toward Colleen.

I've no desire to cause a tussle over the body of a dying man, but I can't let this travesty stand. I'll protect Eala's friend with fists if I must. "Take the enchantment off her. There's no need to put her through such pain for a man she doesn't even know."

Colleen shoots me a potent glare to rival Finnbheara's. "I'm not enchanted, Sion. Robálaí is mine. Shut your mouth and stay out of this."

It's a cold bucket of water over my head, hearing her call him by his Fae name, not Robin Bright.

She does know him.

The second bucket comes when Finnbheara reaches for her hand with a tenderness I didn't think lived in the bastard. "Will you know his essence?"

Colleen nods. "Always."

Finnbheara's voice strains with desperation. "Listen well. You must leave your conscious mind and pierce the mist to find Robalaí's wandering essence. As his bond-promised, do you know what I ask of you?"

Colleen's eyes are wide with hope. "Yes."

"I will go with you, so you are not alone. When you hear the plea of my essence whispering to yours, I beg you to accept it and join with mine. You have my oath, I will forever hold your generosity as a sacred offering and never abuse it. I fear that only together can we return the light to his spirit and call our dearest *Robalaí's* soul home."

Then the damnedest thing happens. Colleen pulls Finnbheara's hand to her lips and kisses it. "Yes, my king, let's bring him home."

My king?

What in the holy hell am I seeing here?

Colleen and Finn kneel on opposite sides of Robber Bright, holding hands over his chest. Their eyes are vacant, staring at nothing and not blinking. Beside me, Ma's breath comes in short little bursts as if she's holding back a grand crying jag. The woman called Acacia stands back, her eyes closed and lips moving without a sound.

I swear I taste sorrow in the air like a bitter drink.

The king's and Colleen's joined hands shake then send a burst of gold skyward that rains down to cover Robber Bright's funeral shroud.

Finnbheara's voice stirs the radiance into a thousand spirals. "I banish the anger I unjustly thrust upon you. I remove every blight I placed upon your skin. I pledge you my eternal, unwavering loyalty, no matter the challenge or circumstance we face. I extinguish the geas my selfish anger inflicted on your heart. I reforge the blood bond between us. I submit these oaths to the ancient gods and goddesses that eternally dwell in my spirit and yours."

Robber Bright's body turns to a pool of liquid diamond and floats just above the grass. Is this how a Faerie leaves their eternal life for what they believe lies beyond? There's beauty and elegance to it that I can't help but admire. It's a miracle Finnbheara allows three humans in the presence of what surely must be a divine passing.

Does the king grieve with such passion for all Folk lost to him?

Ma wobbles in her sorrow. I catch her before she spills onto the grass, still baffled at the intensity of her emotion. Finnbheara and Colleen don't speak, move, or from what I can tell, breathe.

Acacia's eyes glisten with tears as she disappears from the glade. Like before, she's back in an instant with an outline of the Veil's light clinging to her. In her hands is a bright white satin sheet shot through with gold and silver thread. As she unfurls it, I see it's stamped with the gleaming emblem of the leaf Finnbheara's soldiers wear on their breastplates.

Silent as dawn without a breeze, she moves to a spot near where Robber Bright's head once lay. Colleen and Finnbheara, gazes locked on one another, raise their hands, as if reaching to touch something unseen in the air above them. Acacia snaps the cloth. When it stretches to its full size, she guides it down toward the shining puddle.

The fabric doesn't make it to the liquid. Before it reaches the ground, it settles over a familiar shape—the tall, slender, muscled body of Robber Bright.

Finnbheara nods to Colleen, and she peels the edge away from Robber Bright's face. The Faerie's strangely-colored aquamarine eyes are wide open, his gaze riveted on Colleen. He's no longer burnt and ailing, but his eyes don't blink. They may have healed the body, but the spirit they called hasn't come home. It's tragic, a precursor to my own fate.

And then Robber Bright blinks and gasps. The man sits up in a flash as if someone gave him a sharp poke in the arse. The blanket falls from his bare chest as he reaches for Colleen. Long fingers cradle her face, thumbs stroking her cheeks. "I love. I love. I love," he whispers. "There is no geas upon me?"

Finnbheara's face is pure mush. "None, brother. It fills me with shame that I ever bound your heart in such a ruthless chain."

Robber Bright's eyes sparkle in that starry way of Faeries as he continues to gaze into Colleen's eyes. "There is no geas upon me," he says again as if the man can't quite believe it and then presses his lips to hers.

It's not a kiss swimming in Faerie lust, just the reverent brush of two people who each hold the heart of the other.

Robber Bright pulls back, still staring at Colleen. "My love. My love. My love."

"My Faerie. My Faerie. My Faerie," she answers and kisses him without a drop of restraint.

Finnbheara gets in on the party by throwing his arms around the pair of 'em, saying, "Brother, oh my dearest, dearest brother."

Robber Bright kisses Finn on both cheeks and wraps an arm around the king. The three of them hold tight, heads pressed together.

I turn to Ma. "Brother as in my Fae brother, my Folk, right?"

She's beaming with a smile as wide as the three of 'em. "No, *Mac*, brother as in son of my mother, son of my father."

My wits are as close to leaving me as they ever were in the Gem Kissed Forest. "Robber Bright is Finnbheara's brother?" I shake my head as if to clear the dust. "That makes him—"

Acacia drops to one knee, bowing her head. "Blessings, blessings on this happy day, my king, my prince."

Colleen grabs Robber Bright's shoulders. "Prince?" She smiles like a fool. "Does that make me a princess?"

Robber Bright starts to laugh, but it dies clean away as a knife through butter as he pushes his joy aside for a look of utter misery. "Brother," he says, clutching the front of Finnbheara's armor. "We will not invite happiness or praise blessings in the face of the great sorrow I must now impart." Robber Bright's expression turns stony and cold, the look of most Fae, but there's more ice in his. "The quest we pondered but you bade me not attempt, I undertook without your leave. I had hoped the success of my purpose would, for all time, reunite our sundered brotherly hearts. Instead, it is the direst of dark tidings and not the blessed Nuala that I bring you."

He sucks in a loud breath for a fella who was just a puddle.

"Your queen is dead. Aodh stole the life of Nuala of Tír na nÓg."

Finnbheara's face contorts, the angles of his bones jutting out as if they'd break through his skin. There's no weeping now. The king grabs his brother's wrists as he pants like a beast. "You have proof."

"Her silver flame has gone out. The verse of fading left behind in Caisleán Brón, and vile admission from Aodh's own tongue."

Finnbheara stands then continues to grow until he's as tall as an old oak. Each fist is the size of a ram and could fell my cottage with a single blow. I feel the rumble of his voice to the roots of my teeth. The ground shakes so violently, I see Colleen grab for Robber Bright to keep from keeling over. My mind tumbles from all these shockers, trying to make sense of this Faerie family tragedy I watch playing out.

The booming power of Finn's speech stops me from hearing my heartbeat.

"Aodh shall no longer be his name. He is darkness and doom incarnate, and to those fates I condemn him."

The king's arm lengthens until it touches the edge of the glade. He rips his colossal sword from behind the trees. The blade blazes too brightly to keep my eyes on it. He's working himself up for a massive blow. "This day, the silver sails of Tír na nÓg shall cut down the bloody sails of Bráchthine upon the Faerie seas."

Robber Bright braces a hand against the grass to stand. The fella's still on the wobbly side even after that fine bit of Faerie healing. Colleen helps him up. He leans on her for support as he wraps the white sheet around his waist to spare us all the glory of his bare arse.

Finn catches the movement and does his Faerie shrinking trick from tree height until he's Robber Bright's size. Well, punch my gut, looking at the two of them, they could be hatched from the same nest. I never had cause to notice, spending my energy on hating these brothers grim.

Robber Bright clasps his hands behind the king's neck. It strikes me as a thing I've seen brothers do. His next words freeze my bones.

"Eala Duir." His gaze flicks to Colleen then back to Finn. "As you have reforged the blood bond between us, brother, extend that loyalty to my beloved bond-promised by calling truce with the one you name Finnbheara's Treasure."

The king's eyes flash every shade of fire from red to orange to the deep blue found in the middle of a fierce blaze.

Robber Bright switches his grip to Finn's shoulders and shakes. "Tell me she does not sail with Aodh." He turns to Acacia. "I called to her at the end, saying she should not do this. She cannot. She must not."

My guts turn to water. Eala was intent on sailing with Aodh to save me from Finnbheara, giving both kings the spark they needed to go at each other. That spark blazes into an inferno from Finn's rage.

Robber Bright is still in Finn's face. "May the ancients strike us both down for proposing the use of Eala Duir in trade for our queen. Nuala willingly accepted a place in Aodh's kingdom to bring on the peace of ages. If she sails with him, Eala will turn victim to the whims of the Dark Prince without knowing she was a pawn in the rescue of one who was never held against her will. It dishonors the gravity of our noble Queen Nuala's sacrifice."

"You were going to do what?" I bellow, raising my own inferno.

"Allow the shell of your pride to crack, brother." Robber thrusts an arm in my direction. "Cease your ire with the union of the white swan and her fox because you wish to control the fate of Eala Duir entirely. Grant them the rights of your Folk to live as they may."

I'd like to sink my fox teeth into a goddamned Faerie neck. "For fuck's sake, what is going on?"

They ignore me as Faeries tend to do.

Robber Bright gives Finn what for. "Eala Duir is a gift to us all from the *beads of being*. No crown need sit upon her brow to mark this."

The newly resurrected Faerie lays Colleen's hands atop Finn's then adds his own to the stack. "Learn the wisdom I have only recently gained. It is love, not power over another, that surpasses the might of even the boldest blade. See Eala *bán* for the treasure she truly is, not as Finnbheara's Treasure."

Thank heavens, Finnbheara closes those restless and disturbing eyes before I drive a fist between them and damn the consequences.

My grumbling and grunting alert Acacia that I'm poised to devil the royal pair. She plants herself in front of me with crossed arms and the promise of violence on her face.

Robber Bright gives the silent king no rest. "Brother, Eala Duir is not the answer to your longtime lonely and now shattered heart. You have endured Nuala's loss for ages until surely it is a truth accepted by your spirit. We will all mourn this piteous conclusion together and seek vengeance on he who slew her. The time has come to embrace the one who sees your heart as only our beloved queen has before. Why do you not allow yourself to embrace such a blessed gift?"

When Finn opens his eyes, they aim right for Ma.

Every man has his limits, and I hit mine. My mind already screams with fear for Eala, and now this royal bastard is looking at my mother like she's the answer to a question no one should have asked.

When she takes a step toward him, I grab her. "He'll just use you as he did before. Look what the bastard put you through…the Glade of Chimes…ready to push you out his very gates—"

She sets three fingers against my lips. "This isn't your story, Sionnach. It's mine. One you only see from a son's eyes because that's all I've allowed." Slowly, she takes her hand away. "I will tell you my story from start to finish, *Mac*. But not today."

Ma pulls my head down to kiss my forehead then returns to the king. Acacia keeps acting as a Faerie wall. I strain to see around her.

Finnbheara falls into Ma's arms when she reaches for him and then rests his head on her shoulder. "We'll mourn her together, my darling Finn."

Mist that looks to be made of diamonds returns to stream through the glade, casting a soft edge over everything.

I've not a single notion what to do, how to feel, or whom to throttle. I stand as a scribble in the margins of this page, but I can't remain so when my *anamchara* is sailing into the arms of the devil.

"Eala," I holler. "How do we get to Eala?"

That boils their pot.

Finn slides out of Ma's arms to face Robber Bright. "I have seen your threads in Eala *bán's* essence. Awaken them with the warning not to engage with the Dark Prince."

Robber Bright turns his back on us and moves to lean against one of the clear glass trunks with a soft silver flame burning inside it. He holds a hand to his head. I hold my breath.

Colleen comes to me then and rubs my arm. "It's going to be okay, Sion." This may be the first time unenchanted Colleen wanted to do anything but kick me in the balls.

"And speaking of stories…" I nod at Robber Bright.

She shrugs. "Like Martha said…" Colleen turns a puzzled look at Ma. "That is Martha, right?"

I nod, struck as dumb as a fencepost in a sheep field when it hits me that she's never seen the young version of Ma, only Eala's gran.

Colleen clicks her tongue. "Yep, shitload of stories on the way."

Suddenly, Robber Bright wheels around so fast, he has to grip the tree to steady himself. Locking gazes with Finnbheara, he says, "Eala Duir is no longer with me. My essence holds ribbons of Colleen and you alone, brother."

It feels as if a knife cuts a wicked slash across my heart.

Finn jerks his head in surprise, but anything he's about to say is cut off when a man clad in the armor of Tír na nÓg races from between the trees.

"Aodh's sails have reached our western sea."

CHAPTER 37
THE RAGING SEA

EALA

Biddy and I clutch the rail, trying to stay on our feet as the sea rolls beneath the ship. I have nothing close to sea legs or sea stomach. My gut is still shredded from Robber Bright's wretched fall.

We're not doing much more than floating at the moment. I may need to tie myself to the mast to stay on my feet once we get serious. Grace is in her element. She strides up and down the deck, raising her spyglass toward the ship off to our right...our port? Starboard? I can't keep it straight.

We're waiting on confirmation, via lots of flag signaling, that everyone in the fleet munched their croutons.

I touch my head to the damp wood then look up quickly. Will this be the last time I see a blue sky filled with white clouds in layers so densely packed they form a billowy awning of heavenly pearls above our heads? Will I ever fly as a swan through Aodh's kingdom without singeing my wings?

Great plumes of spray shoot into the air as waves crash against the shore of Inishmore. We're near the Serpent's Lair even though I can't see its perfect rectangle, cut into stone by the powers of the earth, not the hand of men.

Grace stands at my right, and Biddy to my left. Together, we watch the world for a few precious moments.

"'Tis confirmed. Faerie potion lies in every belly," says the Pirate Queen.

"Time to call my mist, Eala." Biddy moves to a spot on the rail where she's hidden behind crates and a towering pile of ropes so her magic won't be spotted by any of the O'Malley sailors.

I follow her. Tucked away from sight, she uncorks the bottle and begins to whisper against its glass. A nearly transparent mist of muted cobalt rises from its neck, imperceptible within the thin layer of spray already adding a gray cast to the air. Biddy smacks the side of the bottle, and the mist begins to splutter out the top like a smokestack. It quickly spreads over Grace's ships.

I begin to chant, adding my magic to Biddy's. "Let nothing strike the souls who sail in our company with awe, fear, or question. To every eye, all is accepted." Without premeditation, but from a certainty in my heart, more words stream from my lips. "At battle's end, with my Faerie wind, let these brave souls be carried home."

We watch as the rapidly moving breeze created by the hands of witch and Faerie settles over the fleet. I close my eyes and sway until my Veil sprites incandesce through my spirit. I take their calm heat as assurance that the humans I'm dragging into an otherworldly realm are safely under my influence. This is no time to dissect Fae intuition, so I choose to trust it.

"The cannons?" asks Biddy

She had the brilliant idea of dousing the cannons in Grace's fleet with a fog of the juniper berry elixir to stave off any Faerie enchantments that might try to melt the weapons or roll them into the sea. I pull the decanter from a pouch tied to my belt and ask it to fill. Once uncorked, bubbles overflow its neck and mingle with mist from Biddy's blue bottle. Together, we magically paint our cannons with Faerie potion.

When we're finished, Biddy and I join the Pirate Queen at the helm. Granuaile O'Malley looks me in the eye. "Many ask who controls the sea. Gods? Fate? Fortune?" She grunts. "None of those. The seas govern themselves. Take us off to new horizons, Eala of the Fae."

I fill my lungs with clean sea air then reach out to Aodh. "I, Eala of the Fae, call to the Folk of Bráchthine. Receive us in our mother sea."

True to its name, the likeness of a gigantic snake made of silver smoke rises from the Serpent's Lair and sparkles before us, blotting out the skies over Inishmore. With a hiss sharp enough to crack the granite cliffs before us, terrifying jaws stretch wide, revealing a dazzling channel of crystalline water.

With the White Seahorse leading the charge, the fleet of the Pirate Queen sails beneath a pair of fangs as long as the tallest tree in the human realm and into the Faerie seas.

Any assumption I made about seas in a Fae realm being as clear as glass and as calm as a forest pond on a windless day is immediately shredded when the White Seahorse crashes hard into a trough between two waves nearly as high as the top of the mast. Grace shouts orders to her crew while I look for anything to grab onto that isn't going to slide across the deck and take me with it.

Whining wind and sloshing sea show me how unprepared I was for this rollicking adventure to save Sionnach. Then, in a blink, the waves on both sides of us collapse in a deafening *slap*. With the ease of sliding down a dune, our ship surges forward onto a much tamer stretch of sea.

"I'd rather face the rear end of a kicking mule than live through that again," says Biddy, holding tight to an iron ring on the railing.

I sip in short breaths to try and flatten my panic. "Magic isn't all pixie dust and unicorns, is it?"

Looking to the sides, I see Grace's fleet in a long line. Her signal guy is whipping flags through the air.

I walk as fast as I can on the slick, wobbly deck to get to the Pirate Queen. Gesturing at the flag, I ask, "Is something wrong?"

She shakes her head. "Not yet. Just seeking confirmation that all my ships made it through the gullet of your Faerie snake."

Instead of clouds, the same sparkling silver smoke that formed the serpent swirls in ever-changing patterns above us. I wonder if this is the normal sky of the Faerie seas or an Aodh thing. A Finnbheara thing? There's no one to ask. An answer of sorts comes in the form of thickening air and a shadow seeping over the stern of the White Seahorse. I rush to the rail and lean over to look behind us.

Aodh's navy looks like a painting. The black ships sit on the water as still as if they were trapped in the muck of a low tide. One thing does move. Within each of the countless niches, embedded in black pumice stone-textured hulls, a single red-orange flame flickers. The ships are a line of smoldering fire.

As I study the fleet of Bráchthine, every ship begins to rise. They ride the crest of bubbling black liquid you'd expect to billow over the edge of a witch's cauldron in a fantasy illustration. Crimson sails with Aodh's triple flame sigil on each unfurl and stretch taut. Embers flow from ship to ship, between sails, creating a fiery streak that winds through the Dark Prince's fleet.

A sudden gust of wind sends the White Seahorse listing precariously to one side. As we scramble to stay on our feet, we watch the two ships at the center of the underworld navy's formation part and sail in opposite diagonals as if they're on gate hinges. Through the opening, an obsidian wave wearing a crest of hissing fire rolls out before a gargantuan ship three times the size of any other and made entirely of what looks like red glass. Its sails are black but instead of Aodh's sigil, a giant version of what could be Thor's hammer is drawn in living flames.

Grace's fleet of ships are toy boats in a kid's bathtub compared to this monster. Thank my Faerie soul Aodh's ships keep some distance. My influence should render the sailors immune to the shock of seeing the sea beast sailing behind us. I pray the underworld navy doesn't push my enchantments and our Faerie elixir croutons past their limit.

Grace's assessment is much more tactical. "Let the devil ships come up between us. We'll need the power of their cannons added to ours to take the ship holding your man."

I think of Tír na nÓg with its gentle mists, and the rolling velvet moss and grasses of the Gem Kissed Forest. All things lovely and light. Behind us is fire and the shadow of destruction. How can Finnbheara's navy begin to overpower Aodh's?

I get my answer pretty damn fast. As if responding to the Underworld God's advance, a tempest of slate blue and white clouds, each outlined with silver, explodes from the sea not ten ship lengths in front of us. Emerging from the sudden storm are scores of silver ships that fan out in a phalanx as if the hull of one were welded to the next.

Every mast is a carved silver tree. Every sail is a cloth of spun silver with hints of gold. Gleaming silver and white adornments stretch across every bow in designs of vines, leaves, and flowers.

Finnbheara is here, and he's coming for me.

SIONNACH

It's a fair bet I'll soil my britches before this is over. We're on a collision course with a fucking wall of ships that mean business. The ones belonging to Eala's pirate queen could be swallowed into the bellies of the hell on water, coming up behind them. Will Aodh let Finn chew through the humans before he scoops Eala from the sea and claims her as his prize? I'm sure the devil bastard will blast as many of Finn's ships as he can in the bargain after Grace O'Malley's people cause a few dents in their precious silver hulls.

Eala still believes she's got to stick with Aodh to save my hide.

Boom.

One of Finn's pretty silver cannons goes off not ten feet from where I stand at the bow. My heart goes off just as loud when I see it cut a gulley in the water next to the ship at the forefront of the pirate's advance.

What's the Faerie ass doing? The king isn't supposed to fire on my wife's people. Finn's priority is to get inside Eala's head with their silent Faerie talking ways to let her know he's changed his tune and removed his knife from my throat. Robber Bright's lost his ties to her, but I pray the king hasn't. We've got to get word to my *anamchara* that Finnbheara is not her enemy and Aodh is no ally.

I can make out people scattering all over the lead ship, but I don't see my swan. Her people need to peel off so Tír na nÓg can skin Bráchthine's hide.

Raking my gaze across the deck, I find Finn and nearly plow into him. I shout above the cannons, starting to sing to each other from both sides. "Have you got to her?"

After seeing the king go to mush over Robber Bright, I admit the Faerie does have a heart and seems Eala's got a place in it other than being a little toy he can keep in a cupboard.

Finn grits his teeth. "Stay out of my way, fox."

"I've a right to know, Finnbheara."

His eyes flash the color of blue crystal but almost immediately settle into their natural silver. The man looks a bit punched in the throat. "I can neither find her essence in this melee nor take the Veil to her side. The sacred passage refuses to answer my call so close to the filth of Bráchthine."

Not what a man wants to hear about the chances of saving his wife. It's no use screaming at a fella who's fighting on the same side as you. "What's to do then?"

Finnbheara rolls his lips together until they are as white as the sails of Grace O'Malley's ships. "We fight."

EALA

The spyglass bashes into my face when a cannonball nicks the side of Grace's ship. "Oww," I scream and cup my eye.

Biddy grabs my hand away, peering at the damage. "Blink it away. You're not cut."

The ship is going nuts. The sea is pissed from being bombarded with silver and black cannon balls and not afraid to show it. Waves smack against the sides of Grace's flagship, showering us with stinging water that oddly smells more sugary than briny. Biddy's magic is doing its damnedest to scatter Fae cannon balls, but they come fast and in unpredictable paths. Thankfully, the damage so far hasn't been bad enough to sink any O'Malley ships.

I holler over the noise. "Hold on to me while I try and look again."

Biddy braces herself and grabs me around the waist. I lean the front of my body against the wooden side of the ship and lift the spyglass again. It slips over my wet skin, but finally, I lock it hard enough against my cheekbone to maneuver it. Damn, it's fucking impossible to zero in on anything specific. Churning spray and angry cross currents fill my field of vision.

Biddy yells in my ear. "Higher."

I change the angle, but all I see are smoky silver clouds that roll and crash into each other with as much rage as the sea. Biddy crushes her body to mine and guides my hands until I'm at the right level for the ships. The spyglass still bounces up and down as the deck tips to one side, then the other, but I'm getting the hang of it.

I aim for what I think is the middle and scan the line of Finnbheara's ships to the right. I see armored Fae at cannons spread across the decks, but none of them are Sion or Finnbheara, the two people I'd recognize.

Shit, did the Pevensies have it this rough in Narnia or the Lost Boys when they battled Hook in Neverland?

I tilt up, searching the huge center ship I take to be Tír na nÓg's royal flagship. I'm betting Finnbheara will keep Sion close and visible so the king can manipulate me. His maddening majesty knows my *anamchara* is the only reason I'd enlist both human and Fae navies to sail against him.

My heart takes off running. There, front and center at the bow, stands my love with his head of flaming fox red curls. "Sionnach," I scream as if he can hear me above the riot. "He's there. He's really there," I bluster, brandishing the spyglass more like a cutlass. "Time to go."

The plan is to send out a bunch of smaller rowboats with me in one of them. Biddy will use her bottle's magic to scramble any boats in danger. I'm not deluded to think there won't be casualties. I just pray Sion isn't one of them.

It's a ridiculous ploy in a military sense, but it'll allow Sion to see me and, fate willing, jump into the water to get away from Finnbheara. We'll grab him from the sea and bring him back to the White Seahorse. Grace's navy will get the hell out of the way and let the two Fae kings have at each other. Sion and I can make our way to Aodh's red glass ship and be free of Finnbheara's manipulative and cruel obsession to separate us and destroy my husband.

It's no happily ever after, but it's all we've got.

If our gamble fails, then Aodh and Grace will have to be the victors in this battle, so I can save Sion once Finnbheara is outgunned. I hesitate for a moment. We've technically got a two to one advantage over Tír na nÓg's navy. Maybe we should ditch the rowboat idea. Grace had a point when she cooked it up. It's unpredictable and inconvenient, and not to mention presenting much smaller targets to hit. That alone can give us an edge. I've got to stick with the plan and hope the sea air is too water-logged for flaming arrows.

Oddly enough, I haven't seen a single arrow zipping through the air. I wonder why? Is the distance too great or the wind too volatile for accuracy? It'll get ugly fast if those suckers start flying from the silver ships.

Biddy will come through. Grace will come through. This will work.

Our little flotilla just clears the line of Grace's fleet, when there's shouting and the oarsmen frantically reverse direction back to the ships.

I slap at the closest man. "What are you doing? Keep going."

The sailor in charge of our boat gestures wildly to the sea in front of us. I see a ridge of water rising higher than the restless surface then…oh holy hell. It starts spinning. A giant whirlpool is forming between us and Finnbheara's ships. We'll be sucked down as easily as the scrap of a leaf over a waterfall. Already, I feel the tug of the whirlpool's suction.

We can't get to Sion.

SIONNACH

"She's just there." I yank the silver brace on Finn's arm and point to the line of wee rowboats leaking from between the sailing ships.

He spots her, and his eyes fade to a light pink. "I see Finnbheara's Treasure," he says. "What in the name of the ancients is she doing?"

"Coming for me, you daft prick," I say, frowning at the king, livid the fool sticks to his possessive title for my *anamchara*.

"Eala Duir thinks her power so great she can climb the sides of my vessel and pluck you from my grasp?"

I find Eala in the front of one of the boats, stabbing her fingers at the water. "Plucking me out of the waves is more likely." I glance around the deck, looking for Finn's rowboats. "Have your oarsmen take me to her, and all this rubbish can be set straight. Unless you plan to sprout wings and carry me down to Eala yourself."

He shoots me the *spawn of Loho* glare I'm accustomed to. "I am not a bird."

I shrug. "Thought since Eala can take to the skies, maybe you could too."

"It is her swan essence that allows—" The king's eyes start up their color jig as his anger sparks. He abandons his explanation and calls for a boat.

I wave my arms, hoping Eala sees me, and jab my fingers toward the sea. "I'm coming, love. I'm com—"

The cursed sea gives a great belch, then the wind starts whipping the water round and round between Eala's and Finn's ship.

I turn to the king, spit flying from my mouth. "What're ya doing? Calm the damn sea, man."

Finn looks like he swallowed a burning peat brick and chokes a single word. "Aodh."

EALA

Banshees may be legend, but the volume of my screams could give them a run for their money as I order the rowboats to go around the whirlpool. It's no use. The sailors are hell bent on returning to their ships. Then the damnedest thing happens. As we pull away, the whirlpool fizzles out, and there's only choppy water between us.

I shake fists toward Finnbheara's ships. "Go back. It's gone. Go back."

The oarsmen hesitate for a moment, staring at one another. It's a shitty thing to do, especially after I recently swore to *Crann na Beatha* not to control or endanger others with my magic. I'll ask for forgiveness later, but this is life or death. I belt the rowers with my influence, forcing them to reverse the retreat.

As soon as we start to cut through the current, there's a slurpy roar, and the whirlpool is back. I kill the influence over the sailors and don't argue as they make for the White Seahorse with muscle-popping effort.

I'm so naïve and stupid to think this sea battle would be straightforward or play by any sort of honorable rulebook. I watch Sion's figure growing smaller. How can our ships even touch Finnbheara's with a spinning watery maw open wide to swallow anything that comes near him?

The way is closed.

Rain starts to fall. I glance at the darkening sky to find a lingering patch of silvery blue with feathery white clouds that look like swan wings.

Swan wings.

The sea is closed, but not the sky.

I call to my swan, and she immediately lifts me toward the heavens. Soaring high above the mob of ships, I arc down to Sion but pull up short. If I try to land on the Fae flagship, Finnbheara will have both of us. I veer away from the silver sails, my mind reeling with hopelessness.

This won't work. My swan has no talons to fight Fae warriors or to carry my husband away from Finnbheara. Blood, death, and battle will be the final act of this Faerie epic after all.

I cut a curve beneath the clouds to head back to the ship, when a single rowboat appears on the sea below. Not from Grace's fleet, but just past the bow of Finnbheara's ship.

A single figure mans the oars. One I would know in the fury of any supernatural storm.

My fox.

With blessed speed, I dive, flopping hard onto the boards of the rowboat. My swan hisses in pain, but before it can take hold, I'm a woman in the arms of her husband.

There's no time for kisses or a reunion. I bat at Sion's arms. "Stop rowing —the whirlpool—I'll call the Veil. We'll leave."

"You can't, love. Finn already tried that to get to you. He claims the Veil steers well clear of Aodh's magic."

Sion works the oars so we're heading into the shadow of Finnbheara's ship.

"What are you doing?" I try to stop him, but he's too damn strong. In moments, we're tucked against the silver hull.

"No time to tell all, Swan, but Finnbheara is with us, not against us. You've got to fly back and tell your pirates to pretend to strike at the silver ships. A fine flight of cannon balls should make your intentions clear. That'll have Aodh shutting off his fecking drain. Once it looks like you're close enough to give old Finn a black eye, scatter and let Tír na nÓg run down the devils at your back."

I want badly to believe Sionnach, but this plan reeks of another manipulation of Finnbheara's to get to me and, as a bonus, strike at Aodh.

"We can't trust him, Sionnach."

"Aye, we can, Eala, 'cause it's not just on his word. Robber Bright knows Aodh's mind. The devil bastard means to steal you and enslave all these fine people here on the waves helping you."

I shake from the cold and the depth of my ignorance. "Robber Bright?"

"He's alive. Never did truly turn on ole Finn." He spreads his fingers on the sides of my neck so I can't look away. "If you don't trust them, trust me, *anamchara.*" Then he does kiss me, hard and deep. "Now fly Eala *bán*. Fly for the both of us."

How far can I push my trust before it's completely spent? If I do as Sion asks, Finnbheara will control him. My soulmate will be smack in the middle of a Faerie war, and we'll still be separated.

Every cell in my body, Fae or swan, screams not to leave him, but I find the strength to do as he asks. Beating my wings in time with the crack of the waves beneath me, I let the wind carry me back to the White Seahorse. My heart tells me that if sending Sion out in that rowboat was a trap, Finnbheara had time to spring it.

He didn't.

The king sent Sionnach to warn me.

Aodh isn't just another megalomaniacal Fae king. He is every bit the hellish horror as the nightmare illustration in my childhood book of myths. He was the face of the devil in the rocks of Howth Head. This malicious God of the Underworld rightly spawned every tale of eternal torment credited to his name.

Tír na nÓg must take him down.

Rain lashes in a relentless curtain as if an ancient power attempts to prevent this savage conflict between its children.

Using the bright yellow sleeves beneath Grace's shawl as my guide, I fight my way to where she stands at the wheel of her ship, transforming from swan to Faerie the moment my feet hit the deck.

"Give the command to attack, Finnbheara, but tell your ships to be ready for the signal to break off and let Aodh's black plague finish the job.

The Pirate Queen practically spits blood. "I'll not lead my kin to the bottom of the sea," she bellows, sweeping an arm toward the whirlpool.

"Take this single step with me, Granuaile O'Malley. Give the order. If the whirlpool fails to sink beneath the waves, then call your ships back."

Her mouth bobs open and shut.

I grab the wheel of the ship and thrust my face right into hers. "If not for me, do it for the life of your son, Tibbott ne Long. Serve me, and you serve your mother's heart."

Thank every shiny silver hair on Finnbheara's royal head my reminder of why she agreed to help me in the first place convinces her. Wet flags crack in the wind, and the fleet of Grace O'Malley, the pirate queen, sets off to war.

We split the waves, barreling down on Finnbheara's ships. At my suggestion, cannons fire shots aimed to fall short of silver hulls. Let Aodh believe human sailors bluster before they bite.

SIONNACH

Eala's Irish pirates reach the stretch of sea where the whirlpool stopped howling its hunger and break formation into dozens of pieces like an eggshell shattered against a stone. I keep my stare locked on the ship my swan flew off to.

I waggle a finger at the galley. "Eala's there on the one in front. Keep Aodh's cursed hands from touching it."

"Faith, fox," says Finn without a whit of concern on his face.

If this isn't the end of all things, a Faerie bastard telling me to have faith. Does Finnbheara believe in anything other than himself? My chest about caves in when I see currents turn and turn, trying to raise the circle of the whirlpool. "Look, he's mixing it up again to swallow Eala's people."

The king practically drools, savoring the lightning-fast approach of Aodh's massive red glass ship with its flaming sails. "He will not. The Dark Prince's ships are too close on the tail of the humans to escape the wrath he would awaken in the sea."

For a glorious moment, it seems all is well. The human fleet flees the oncoming clash, and Finnbheara's ships surge forward like a massive silver battering ram. My heart blackens when the devil's own ship turns to start chasing Eala's.

"He's going after her. For the love of your Folk, Eala, your brother, your sons, and my mother, take him now, Finnbheara."

The king licks his already wet lips.

I've loved and lost. The final blow has come. Finnbheara and Aodh are in this together to capture my white swan.

"Faith, fox."

As I watch Eala's ship run from the beast, I see she's headed straight for a wall of spray and driving rain. The moment the bow touches it, the wall crumbles. Waiting on the other side are rows and rows of golden ships stretching to the far horizon.

Finn stretches his arm to the south. "Behold the gilded fleet of Clíodna, the banshee queen of the Munster *sióga*." Then he turns to the north, where another massive cluster of ships weaves around Eala's pirates to get at Aodh. "And there joins King Lubdan of the Ulster Faylinn. His Folk may be small and his boasts large, but they bear magic to best any giant." He laughs. "Aodh is thrice outnumbered. This pinch will deliver a debilitating blow to the Dark Prince."

"Your Fae pals can kill an underworld god?"

Finnbheara gives me a pitying look. "Alas, Aodh cannot be killed, foolish fox, but he can be rendered weak enough to require many ages of the world to pass before even the smallest measure of his potency may be restored."

The crafty son of a bitch was never going to let Aodh lay a scratch on him. Still, I don't like the odds of these wee human matchsticks out among Fae with blood grudges.

"Swear to me these Folk know to not lay a hand on the pirates. I thought all you Faerie royals had it in for each other. How do you know your banshee and Faylinn aren't here to stab you in the back?"

Finnbheara shakes his head as if he's tired of a griping child. "Faith, fox."

The king barely flicks his finger in the direction of Eala's ship and drops of a thousand colors rain down upon the galley, sending first its hull with rows of oars then deck, masts, and finally sails beneath the surface of the Faerie sea.

CHAPTER 38
THE VOWS FULFILLED

EALA

G race grabs a bucket and, along with the rest of us, starts bailing the water flooding the deck. Under the catastrophic weight of a sudden deluge, the ship is sinking.

Biddy stands alone, the blue bottle bubbling and fizzing as liquid sprays from its neck. Wherever her magic droplets touch the seawater, drowning the planks of the ship, the slosh turns to steam. It's not fast enough.

The smaller boats strapped to the sides of the galley were torn away from the sudden killer rain and bobbed off at too great a speed for anyone to swim for them.

I can fly to Finnbheara's ship and save myself, but will there be time for his Folk—my Folk—to save the rest of the crew? Everyone else, including Biddy and Grace, will soon be at the mercy of a Faerie sea that's shown itself to be voracious and deadly.

I plead with the Veil. I sense it nearby, trying to connect, but something blocks it.

The sound of men and women crying prayers to the God I was raised with as well as Irish gods and goddess I know many still believe in, rings out above the sibilant sea.

Impervious to our plight, ships that look as if they were carved with wood then dipped in gold, stream past us. I swear it sounds like the water unzips as they go by. I can't tell if they're after Aodh or Finnbheara.

My body feels heavier, weighed down with the knowledge I've caused this. I lit the fuse between these Fae kings because I loved Sion. If I had known the cost of loving Sion set dark fates in motion for so many others, would I have jumped out of the soulfall tower after him? The less selfish choice would have been to allow his tormented soul to seek the peace he rightly deserved.

Grace shouts my name from less than a foot away. Her bright red hair is alive in the wind. "Have you no Faerie magic to reverse this foul fortune?"

"I'm so—" My apology is cut short when a wave as tall as the ones that carried us through the Serpent's Lair curls above the masts and begins to drop.

I've lost my chance to fly. I duck and cover my head as if it'll do a damn thing to save me.

The wave never hits. A cavity of the Veil, more immense than a football stadium, opens around the ship. We don't sail, we float through spectral fog until, as gently as a mother laying a sleeping child in a cradle, the Veil sets us back upon the sea. Not a swirling, snarling sea, but a morning calm near a familiar island—Inishmore.

I stand along with the rest of the awestruck crew. The decks are dry. Sails slack in a windless sky.

Silence.

Then the grateful shouting of souls pulled from the lion's mouth rises louder than the roar of any sea.

Biddy and Grace stagger toward me like, well, drunken sailors from the popular sea shanty, except not a drop of drink has passed their lips. Both women collide with me, and the three of us hold each other for a moment before we all start laughing. Our glee is not borne of being *in our cups* from whiskey as Grace might term it, but from the astounding joy of cheating death.

"That was a rare bit of magic, Faerie," says Grace, slapping me on the back hard enough to make me start coughing. She pauses and turns to Biddy. "Or was it you I should be thanking, witch?"

"Not me," I say.

Biddy raises her blue bottle and dumps it upside-down. It's empty. Not a single drop of sapphire magic is left inside the silver filigreed glass. "Wasn't my doing," she says.

A sailor hangs from the rigging, pointing toward the bow. "Inishmore," he calls out.

All around us, the sound of creaking wood, raised voices, and very loud singing skirts through the air as the entire fleet of the Pirate Queen fades into view. The signal flags go to town, and before long, Grace reports every ship is accounted for.

"Never underestimate the strength of determined women, my friends," I say, smiling at my companions.

It's then I understand. What Sion said is true. The King of the Connacht Fae is no longer my enemy. For whom but mighty King Finnbheara, my maker, the leader of my Folk, could grant six thousand souls a journey across time and through mystic realms to carry them safely home?

It's my turn now to use my Faerie powers to honor my promises.

"Granuaile O'Malley, great pirate queen of Ireland, this is your time and your home. By nightfall, I promise all those under your leadership will be as they were and won't suffer nightmares or dark memories of our undertaking."

I take her hands in mine. They're as rough and calloused as Sion's. Just as he is of the land, she is of the sea. How wonderful to be blessed with such a connection to the world. "You will meet the queen, and your son, Tibbott ne Long, will be free. Thank you for your bravery and your loyalty in the face of things that are only spoken of around a blazing hearth with whiskey in hand."

She gives her standard curt nod, but her eyes wear the twinkle of someone who might believe in a little bit of magic. "Will I remember you, Eala of the Fae?"

I shrug. "Maybe as a story you once heard, but nothing more." I expect her to look relieved, but instead, there's a hint of sadness in her expression.

"Blessings to you Granuaile O'Malley," says Biddy, kissing Grace's cheek. "Sailing with a grand pirate queen such as yourself is nothing short of a brilliant marvel."

Grace huffs at her.

Then, as an absolute shocker, Biddy hands Grace the blue bottle. "This is a pretty thing. But when you look at it, as when you look at the sea, know there is more just beyond what your eyes tell you." The witch laughs. "Magic is only ever waiting patiently for an invitation, Granuaile O'Malley."

Grace takes the bottle, uncorks it, and sniffs. She seems satisfied there's no noxious Faerie or witch odor coming from it and puts the stopper back in. "It shall be my wishing vessel for skies as blue as this glass." The Pirate Queen's steely stare takes Biddy and I in. "You'll be leaving then, I suspect." It's a statement, not a question.

"Aye," I say, loving the shape of the word on my tongue. It feels right. "This is where you belong. Biddy's home is off and away. Goodbye, Granuaile."

Before I sweep Biddy with me into the Veil, Grace grabs my arm. "I may forget you, but coerced or not, I'll never regret this grand adventure we've taken." She gives me a shake. "If ever again you'll be needing my help, Eala of the Fae, I'll be waiting for you in time."

A Faerie, a witch, and a pirate queen group hug for the last time. Grace takes a step back, watching as Biddy and I slip into the Veil.

Alfie is right where she should be as we travel to the cottage on the outskirts of Feakle, Ireland, where I chased a hare who was a witch. It's here that the famous Biddy Early fed me a bowl of soup and an even bigger helping of hope.

The Veil window circles to reveal Biddy's cottage. Smoke sneaks out of the chimney, and the aroma of soup wafts through it. Biddy wraps her hand around Alfie's stoutest trunk.

"You're home, Biddy. All will be well with you too. I promise you'll walk free from the witch trial. Those vindictive witch hunters will be uncovered as the hateful idiots they are."

She laughs. "Ah, but Eala Duir, are they such idiots? After all, I am a witch."

I could leave now, but the rest of what I promised the wise woman is unfulfilled. "Biddy, you asked me to help you reconnect with those you've lost—"

The witch holds up a hand to stop me. "That I did, but now's not the time for it. There's half a heart waiting for yours to make it whole. You'll come back to me, Faerie girl, I feel it in my bones."

Alfie's bark begins to glow like sparkling candlelight beneath Biddy's touch. Keeping one hand on my *fánaí* tree, she takes mine in the other. The pulsing liquid fire that lives within the veins of the Tree of Life flows from Alfie, through Biddy, and into my essence.

Biddy speaks in reverent singsong. "Here's where you'll find my spirit, among the blessed roots of *Crann na Beatha,* singing my soulsong to the deep magic of the world." She leans in to kiss one of my cheeks and then the other before stepping out of the Veil.

When she reaches her door, she turns and smiles, pleased to see I haven't gone on my merry way. "I've held hands with magic all my life, Eala of the Fae, but never stepped fully into it until you."

I'm itching to ask her why she gave up her blue bottle. Instead, I watch in silence as she opens the door to her cottage and goes home.

The Veil window irises down to a pinpoint, and then beautiful rainbow walls settle into a delicate iridescent bubble and wait to hear the wish of my heart.

I crook my arms around Alfie's trunks, lean against her, and close my eyes. Letting my Faerie essence pulse around me, I whisper words to the Veil that my heart always believed I'd have the chance to speak, even when my mind doubted.

"Take us home."

CHAPTER 39

THE BEADS OF BEING

EALA

I'm no longer a human marveling at the exquisite wonder of the Veil as its sweet music of violin and bells sings me home. I am Eala of the Fae with a spirit made of magic, myth, and mystique. There is so much I'm finally open to exploring, but not yet.

Above all else, I must seek the one who claims my soul, my life, my love. *Anamchara.*

I'm still entwined with Alfie when the tingle of the Veil dissipates. Allowing my eyes to drift open, I expect to see the bright red wooden front door of the Loho cottage thrown wide and Sionnach in jeans and one of his countless football team sweatshirts leaning on the frame.

Instead, I'm nowhere. Alfie is gone. The Veil is gone. Thick white haze surrounds me. I wave my arms but find nothing. Checking every direction, I strain to see what's hiding in the mist, but I'm blind.

Once, I would have fallen to my knees and hidden my face from the world.

That was Ella O'Dwyer, the girl, the woman, from a life before the miracle of Sionnach Loho, Tír na nÓg, the Veil, and a *fánaí* Tree of Life.

I am Eala Duir Loho, made from the essence of swan and oak, summoned to life by King Finnbheara and the *beads of being*. Fate has to dish out more than fog and the unknown to best me.

Yes, once, I would have fallen to my knees and hidden my face from the world. Now, I laugh.

Behind me, a whisper like wind sliding over the feathers of my swan's wings rises. Spinning around, I see the great gates crafted from tubes of glass and all manner of silken gold and silver threads that guard Tír na nÓg. Instead of keeping me out, they open wide. I walk through with no trepidation or anguish, only the peaceful truth in my heart that I belong here.

Standing before me, resplendent in his crown of glass vines, leaves, and flowers, wearing a white metallic tunic of the same motif, is my king. His straight, flawless locks shine as brightly as quicksilver as they fall over his shoulders. Warriors clad in the white-gold armor of Tír na nÓg stand in an unbroken line behind their monarch.

Open gates are a good start, but not enough. Home is the people I love, who'd better be somewhere beyond the mist.

Finnbheara takes a step toward me, and I suppress the urge to take a step back and start demanding to see Sion, Colleen, and Máthair. If this son of a bitch tries to keep me away from them again, I'll melt every bar in his ostentatious gates so he can never shut me out again.

I flick the braid that managed to mostly survive a Faerie sea battle over my shoulder and curl my hands into fists.

You could knock me over with a look when the king of Tír na nÓg drops to his knee and covers my comparative puny fists in long, willowy Fae fingers. "Eala Duir, it is not in my nature to kneel before any being. I do so now before you."

I wait for him to go on. He would never do this without hoping to gain something. It's a performance to set me up for trickery or to restart his campaign to stick a Faerie crown on my head. The *I can be a nice guy* act doesn't fool me.

"Why are you kneeling before me? What do you want, Finnbheara?"

The corner of his lip quirks up. "How very Fae of you to ask."

I squeeze my fists tighter, and the hint of his humor fades.

"I do not seek your forgiveness, for that is not in my nature."

Of course, he doesn't. If he's expecting reverence or even respect from me, he's sadly mistaken. "Since you're not asking me to forgive you for the hell you've put Sion and me through, you're wasting a knee. You have my thanks for saving Grace O'Malley's fleet, but it stops there until I see my husband… and my grandmother…and my dearest friend, Colleen."

"I waste nothing, Eala Duir. In truth, my bended knee is a request."

Here we go.

Finnbheara pins me with those silver eyes. They are damn hard to look away from.

"I wish for a new beginning between us. Believe I have learned much from that which has come to pass since you first returned to my realm."

"The one you shut me out of."

His grip gets even tighter, and I know there's only so far I should push if I want him to stay civil.

"What you perceive as cruelty in my nature is merely a reflection of the hand fate dealt me."

I'm in no mood to get into a discussion about Finnbheara's character flaws. "We can hash all that out later. Where's Sionnach?"

"Then you will consider my request to start anew?"

"Yes, Finnbheara, I will *consider* your request." I punch out *consider* with volume and emphasis.

He rises to his feet, still holding my fists. "Let us begin thusly." He slides strong thumbs over my palms to relax my clenched fingers then tucks my hand through his elbow. The king leads us to the line of Fae soldiers. One of them winks at me, and I startle to see Artos from the Host of a Thousand Wings in the center of the line. Next to him, Acacia slides her gaze to mine before returning it to her resting warrior face. They both step aside to let ole Finn, as Sion not so lovingly calls the king, and me through.

Silver ribbons twist through the air, sweeping away the dreamy mist Finnbheara loves to use in his decorating.

The king looks down at me with a smile more earnest and gentler than I've ever seen on that curvy mouth and says, "*Sé do beheatha 'bhaile go Tír na nÓg, Eala bán.*" With a grand sweep of his royal arm, he gestures to the group of people standing before us. "You are welcome home."

Sionnach, Colleen, and Máthair are on me in an instant. We can't stop touching and kissing and squeezing and crying and saying I love you over and over. They're here, the souls that mark any place as home.

We are together, welcome in Tír na nÓg without bargains or Faerie threats hanging over our heads.

Máthair is the first to peel off. Despite still being tangled with Sion and Colleen, I watch her go to Finnbheara and slide her arm around his waist. When he does the same to her, my breath hitches.

Sion nuzzles my ear. "I'm keeping quiet on that subject for now, but we'll be dredging it up right soon."

My dearest friend is next to leave our cuddle. I cry out when I see who she's headed for. "Robber." I beat Colleen to him, surprising everyone, including myself, when I throw my arms around the Faerie man who I previously vowed to feed to a vicious Fae beast. "You're alive." I start to escape the slightly awkward hug when he draws me back against a chest that feels pretty damn solid, considering the last time I saw him, he was on fire.

"Alive because you had the courage to face the peril of Oweynagat," he says, then releases me.

Sion's arms wrap around me from behind as Colleen captures Robber in hers.

The line of Fae soldiers is gone. The six of us are left together on the silver green grass of Finnbheara's doorstep. With the mist gone, I see we're in a glade filled with glass trees. A gentle silver flame wavering within every trunk and branch bathes us in a delicate glow.

Finnbheara approaches Sion and me. When he offers me his hand, Sion grunts but steps aside. I lay my hand on the king's.

"Eala Duir—"

I interrupt. "Eala Duir Loho."

The king inhales slowly, forcing himself not to react. "Eala," he starts again, and I keep my mouth shut, satisfied with just plain Eala. "Before this gathering, and in the spirit of our new dawn, I have been encouraged..." He glances at Máthair, who raises her eyebrows. "...to clarify myself."

I know that look of my grandmother's well. Based on Sion's *humph*, he's been on the receiving end of it plenty of times. I never should have doubted Martha O'Dwyer Loho could hold her own with a Faerie king.

Finnbheara lifts his chin. "Long has my heart borne the pain of loss. Queen Nuala was my partner in all things. We ruled this kingdom side by side and brought seventeen sons into the light of the Fae." He pauses, keeping still in that freaky Faerie way. "She was also custodian of my arrogance. With her absence, so went my compassion."

He speaks in an almost monotone, but the story moves me. Confessing he became an irredeemable ass once he lost his queen must be tough for a guy who considers himself perfect.

The king pulls a small silver box from his pocket. After gazing at it for a moment, he opens the lid and withdraws a mostly translucent feather with white edges the color of my hair. A hint of silver veining blinks in and out when the light catches it. "On the eve of Nuala forfeiting her freedom to Aodh to end the ceaseless carnage between Tír na nÓg and Bráchthine, she imbued this vessel with her essence so I may never forget all we had shared."

It's getting harder to fight back tears as his story gets sadder. It's obvious Nuala loved him and their people enough to sacrifice herself. Sion and I share a knowing look. How often have one of us been on the brink of sacrificing themselves for the other? Finnbheara dismisses our *anamchara* bond, but his story proves that what he had with his wife was nothing less.

Finnbheara offers me the feather. It feels incredibly wrong to take the last token his wife left him. "Eala, you have been told you were created from the *beads of being* imbued with the essence of swan and oak. This is so. It is also true that royal magic was necessary to bring your Faerie spirit into the light, but it was not my magic."

He lays the feather on my palm.

"Your life is the gift of a queen, not a king."

My mind reels. Once, it had tentatively cast Finnbheara in the role of a father when I'd first learned he was responsible for making me poof into the world. Now, he claims we're not connected in the *beads of being* Faerie biology. Deep inside, there was always a lingering fear that, because I was part of this Fae king, his legacy of cruelty would show up in me. Discovering I'm made of the essence of swan, oak, and a beloved Faerie queen erases that blemish from my soul.

The pangs of longing to connect with my absentee parents shift to this Faerie queen. At least there are those who, through their memories, will help me know her. I raise my finger with the key tattoo that Robber told me was Queen Nuala's key to show Finnbheara. Instead of black, it now shines silver.

The king's eyes widen then his expression softens into one of reverence. "So passes the legacy of a most gracious queen to a most worthy daughter."

Finnbheara returns to Máthair and takes her hand, leaving me with Nuala's feather. "Your lovely swan essence was indeed inspired by my bond-promised, my queen, whom I loved dearly, but you exist, Eala, because I yearned to believe I could love again."

Máthair is as dewy-eyed as the king.

His voice remains gentle. "When this spirit…" He kisses Máthair's hand. "…who possesses all the kindness and charity that I do not, filled my days with light I had not allowed in for an age, hope became my burden." Finnbheara tries to wear an emotionless mask, but the shifting of his eyes between gold and silver gives him away. "My arrogance claimed Martha as mine until she left me for the human realm, and hope turned to malice. But on the day she called to me, not for my sake, but to save her child's soul, I was again touched by the beauty of her spirit that brightened my own, and hope once again began to stir in my ruined heart."

It's Máthair who takes up his story. "Finnbheara gave you to me, my darling Eala, without hesitation." She turns to Sionnach. "Gave you, to us."

It's a very nice, watered-down Faerie tale. I glare at the king as I wave a hand toward my grandmother. "And banished you to the Glade of Chimes for eternity, not to mention crossing a line with me." I wince, remembering the lusty vibes and inappropriate mouth kisses Finnbheara stole on my previous pops into Tír na nÓg. Damn, I even got a little hot and bothered over him.

Realization smacks me hard. "You were influencing me when I was here before, weren't you?"

The king has the audacity not to look chagrined.

Máthair treats him to a *we'll talk about this later* glare then meets my gaze again. "You do have the look of Queen Nuala." She nods at Finnbheara. "So much so, it seems this one lost himself when he first saw you and forgot his manners."

What Máthair says doesn't excuse it, but I suppose it explains it. I guess anyone, even a Faerie king, can lose themselves a bit. I add the unwanted creepy advances to the list of things he should be asking my forgiveness for. I recite the last couplet of the riddle Finnbheara foisted on Sion and me to earn our place here in his kingdom.

"Prepare your hearts, the end you seek,
May end in sorrow, rift, and crown."

I rejoin Sion as I speak. "Sion was right. You were entertaining thoughts about making me your new queen."

"Fleeting ones I now regret." Finnbheara looks annoyed. "But the crown I spoke of was Aodh's, not mine."

Robber Bright clears his throat. "If I may," he says, looking to Finn, who nods. "This business with you and Aodh is a thing I must atone for, Eala. To win back the favor of my brother, the king—"

"You're brothers?" I blurt, whipping my gaze between the two Fae men.

Sion chuckles. "Lovely family, eh?" he whispers in my ear.

"And I'm a princess," chirps Colleen, smiling at Robber.

I need to be alone with Sion and make the world stop spinning like a damn carnival ride. I've got way too much to unpack already.

He senses me starting to flounder. Sion pulls me against his side and rubs circles on my back as he addresses the room...ah, the glade. "You'll each have time enough to clear your Faerie consciences. Let's get on with it, Finnbheara. You said you'd be giving Eala a say in where we go from here. Speak, man."

"What do you mean, 'where we go from here'?" I ask my husband.

"Seems ole Finn..."

Both Finnbheara and Robber Bright grimace at the casual way Sion refers to the king. Hmm. The deadly friction seems to have de-escalated between my husband and Finnbheara if the latter isn't threatening to turn the former into a fox pelt.

"...has offers on the table for you, for us."

Finnbheara opens his mouth to speak, but my brazen husband forges on. "Seems we can take up here in Tír na nÓg now and live as we are for..." He twirls his hands. "...the rest of all time."

The king is offput by Sion's nonchalance at what his highness must consider a gracious and generous offer. Most likely, the one *ole Finn* prefers since we'll stay closely under his control. Even if he is less vindictive and grudgy, he's still a Fae king. There will be moods.

Sion takes both my hands in his. "Or *anamchara*, we can go back to the mortal world—to Loho cottage for as long as we please."

The tickle of oncoming tears makes my eyes twitch. It's a race between getting words out or being silenced by emotion. "And live a simple, normal life?"

"You can return to your professoring if that's in your heart, and I'll settle just fine to working the family land as Da woulda loved me to."

After all Sion and I faced, the offer of this simple resolution breaks me. I wipe my eyes on the shawl I'm still wearing from my short stint as a pirate. "Without the Veil? Alfie? My swan? Cara? My magic?" A hollow place opens in my chest at the thought of stepping away from the fantastic elements in my life that've become vital to who I am.

It's Colleen who chimes in. "Don't be dramatic, La. My brother-in-law says—"

"You are Fae, Eala," Finnbheara says, cutting her off and frowning at Colleen's irreverence.

Here's the king I know. The guy who can't stand not being the loudest voice in the room.

"You keep all Faerie gifts with you in the human world." He narrows his eyes at Colleen then Sion, with the clear message not to interrupt. "The pull of Tír na nÓg does not cease. The day will come when you long to dwell among your Folk. It is the way of things."

Sion kisses my forehead. "We'll come back, *anamchara*, before my human bones are too useless to be of any good." He meets Finn's stare. "Himself says we'll both be welcomed to make a Faerie home here and be as old or young as it pleases us when that time comes. Seems the stories of Tír na nÓg being the land of eternal youth aren't a Fae brag after all."

"You said she can visit us here if they choose to go back to humanland, right, Faerie King?" says Colleen.

Finnbheara's eyes tumble into a deep maroon. He's not used to his new sister-in-law's lack of self-editing or complete disregard for protocol. Robber Bright looks at Colleen as if she's the light of every star in the sky.

"Yes," the king grits out, on the brink of becoming unpleasant.

Anywhere with Sion is my home—here, the cottage, even the moon. I was prepared to live in hell if it meant we could be together. Now with more attractive options open to us, including never losing my best friend or my grandmother, I'm overwhelmed.

"What do you want, Sionnach?"

"Oh, now that's an easy one, Swan. You, only you."

Only you. There it is. Sion and I for eternity, the wish in our hearts from the moment we understood we'd found our *anamchara*, our soulmate in one another. But I believe there's one more bargain to be had with the Fae King.

I asked Robber Bright during our first lesson if Sion and I could conceive a child. At the time, I was relieved the answer was no and that our only possibility of having kids involved the enigmatic *beads of being*.

Here's my opening to press the king on the subject while he seems to be making an effort to be something other than an overbearing narcissist.

I kiss Sion on the soft skin of his ear and whisper, "Don't overreact to what I'm about to do. We can discuss it later and make our own choices. I can't lose this opportunity."

He pulls me close so he can hiss in my ear. "Last time you took that tone, I watched you fly out Finn's gates."

"I'm never leaving you again, *anamchara*." I kiss him long enough to reassure him there will be no flying through the gates of Tír na nÓg, at least not without him.

Finnbheara clears his throat, and I'm filled with self-satisfaction that my husband and I kissing unnerves his royal sensibility.

To goad ole Finn a wee bit more, I drop one last brief kiss on Sion's lovely lips before turning to the king. "You asked that I *consider* a new beginning between us, my king." I congratulate myself on a matter-of-fact but respectful lead-in. Isn't this the way all bargains begin in the folktales? "As a show of your good faith in our endeavor, I humbly request a gift of the *beads of being*."

I've stunned Finnbheara. He didn't see that one coming. I sneak a look at Robber Bright, who, from the slight curl of his mouth, remembers my question to him and knows exactly what I'm going for. His gaze falls to Colleen's auburn hair then drifts to her slightly swollen lips. Sion and I aren't the only ones who've been kissing lately. *The Tale of the New York Irish American Lass and the Faerie Prince* is another one I've yet to unravel. We may not be alone dipping into Finnbheara's *beads of being* stash.

If I ever do return to professoring, as Sion calls it, I'll have a whole new repertoire of stories, penned by me, to spice up my curriculum.

And then the king I know returns. Finnbheara stands with a mischievous gleam in his eye and throws my words back at me.

"Yes, Eala Duir *Loho*..." He can't resist tossing a sneer in Sion's direction. "I will *consider* your request."

CHAPTER 40
THE PEPPERED APPLE

ROBBER BRIGHT

I gently tug the branch of the ash tree, angling it down to the top of my head, then say the words to release the warm healing waters from its core to flow over my hair and skin. Colleen sits on the rock next to the tree behind my cottage—our cottage—and watches me shower. She squeals whenever the spray catches her then sniffs to take in the subtle cleansing aroma from wet bark.

"How many tree showers do Faeries need in one day? You took half a dozen before we went to meet Eala."

I tip my face to catch the last of the gentle stream. "Waters from the heart of the ash tree will rid my flesh of Bráchthine's stench. I shall continue until I can detect no shade of foulness."

The way her gaze travels along my body heats my skin more than the soothing water. "From where I'm sitting, you smell pretty damn good." If she continues her admiration, I will require freshening after much more pleasant activities.

I intend to request such from her as soon as may be managed, but until I am satisfied nothing of the underworld lingers upon my flesh, restraint is preferable.

"Did you ever consider it's your brain holding on to the stink and not your body? I read somewhere that olfactory memory can blindside you."

I flick my hand to send droplets her way. "How scholarly of you."

Now her sniff is indignant, not indulgent. "I'm so sick of people assuming I'm empty-headed because I'm vivacious."

"Your lovely head is anything but empty, my darling bond-promised," I say, stepping out from under the branches into the light of Tír na nÓg's crystal sun.

Colleen dampens her wine-colored pout with a sweep of her blushberry tongue, watching my cock swing as I shake off the last of the ash's dousing.

"Enjoying the view from your perch?" I tease.

"So far," she says, her pale skin pinking with lust. Colleen slides off the rock to pad over to me.

The apple-colored silk sheath she wears flows around her body as gracefully as water from the ash. She chose it from the piles of Faerie garments Folk left in baskets as gifts once they learned of our bond-promise. It complements the alluring auburn streaks in her lustrous hair.

As if I need any additional lures to draw me to this woman.

"Your dress is lovely."

She runs her hands down the fabric. "I'm never wearing black again."

I press my lips together at the memory of the black attire she was forced to don in Bráchthine.

Her gaze continues to capture my form as if she is contemplating which sweet to pluck first from a feast. "Yes, this view, the flowers, the floating bubbles, the magic trees…"

She names the bounty of the Gem Kissed Forest, but it is my flesh where her attention lies.

"…all very pretty. Very, very pretty."

Her hands slide up the newly unmarred skin of my chest. The diagonal scar that split my torso is gone, along with the horrors I bore from Aodh's fire. My brother blessed me with this rebirth of the flesh along with my reborn heart when he vanquished the geas from my spirit.

She attempts to fit her body to mine, slipping delicate hands across the tops of my shoulders. I stall the contact. "Colleen, I am not yet dry. You shall dampen your dress."

My peppered apple thrusts her hips into mine, then reaches around to grab my naked ass and pull me against her. "Honey, that's not the only thing getting damp."

I lift her into my arms. The less than docile doe wraps her legs around my waist as my tongue tastes her wet, rosy lips. My stiffening cock ceases its low swing and jolts upward.

She catches my wandering tongue between her teeth and growls. "Are you going to make me ask, Faerie man?"

"For a kiss, my sweet one? Never." I give her lips a perfunctory smack and put her down. The front of her soaked gown clings to hard, hungry nipples.

I pretend not to be feverishly drawn to her breasts. She cups the ample treats in her palms, tilting those sweet peaks upward as if they have not already demanded my attention. "How's the view from up there?"

I lazily roll my gaze over the forest. "All the flowers here, the floating bubbles, the magic trees are very, very, pretty." My brutish cock reveals the ruse of my nonchalance.

Colleen spins away from me, lifting her skirts then bends to brace herself on the rock where she sat to admire my nakedness. She smacks her smooth, peppered-apple round bottom and wiggles it. "Is this a better view?"

"Careful, my darling one, or you will awaken the true beast you have bonded yourself to." I try to sound light and playful, but raw need already creeps into my voice.

"Same." She swivels her head to look at me over her shoulder and growls.

I ease in behind her and pinch her hips between my fingers. "A dangerous invitation, *Princess* Colleen." When her breathing deepens in pitch, I step away.

"Where…do…you…think…you're…going?" She pants, spinning to face me.

"Just there…" I point to a shady spot under the wide boughs of a silver oak. "…is a lovely bed of star violets. Lying upon their petals will anoint my skin with a pleasing fragrance." I retrieve a small, fluted glass bottle from the base of the ash. "As will this oil of dewshine lily." I yawn. "If I am not too fatigued to…" With a pop, I uncork the mushroom-shaped top and pour a single drop of oil onto my fingertip before replacing the stopper. "…apply it." In a slow, single stroke, I paint the inside of my thigh with the oil.

Colleen's skin flushes a deeper shade as her pupils grow large, darkening her gorgeous dove gray eyes. I watch her throat bob as she swallows. Her tone is low and sultry, a sound I plan to enjoy frequently. "I can help you with that, Prince Robálaí."

I reach a hand to her, and she slides her fingers between mine. As we stroll to the patch of star violets, I am nearly overcome with emotion. I love, and I am loved. My thumb rests on Colleen's wrist above her pulse. Every inch of my skin vibrates with absolute adoration.

It has been a long time since I rejected my royal title and station after the chasm opened between Finnbheara and me. My brother's bitterness over my decision in battle that led to Nuala's descent to Bráchthine is a burden I gladly relinquish. The delight it gives my bond-promised to embrace the prospect of royalty makes me eager to once again acknowledge my birthright and serve my brother as the true king of my heart. There is much to repair between us, but also much has changed. We have changed.

I lie on my stomach as Colleen kneads the oil into the tense muscles of my shoulders and back. "What do you think they'll do?" she asks. "Stay in Ireland or come live here?"

Her tone is wistful. Tír na nÓg is not yet her beloved home, and the absence of Eala Duir will be difficult for her.

I reach back to take her hand. "They will return, my darling one, and through the strength of our bond-promise, your life too will stretch far beyond mortal comprehension."

"Which I'm totally out of my mind happy about, along with the whole princess gig, but I'm still a human in a place that belongs to Faeries." She leans her head close to mine and brushes her hair behind her ear. "See, totally round. Not even a little point."

I drop a kiss on her adorably curved ear. "And lovelier for it."

"I envy their choice, Robálaí."

I roll onto my back and sit. My cock loses patience with this slow dance, but pleasure must wait. Pulling my knees up to add some decency, and hide my aroused state, I stroke Colleen's hair. My bond-promised is clearly in need of reassurance before I drive myself into her with such fervor her scream will crackle the bark of the tree we lie beneath.

"Do you not understand we enjoy the same choice, my darling one?"

Her eyes stretch wide. "We do?"

Tilting my head to the side for a thoughtful moment, I shrug. "We will once I ask it of the king." A huff escapes my lips. "Perhaps we should have Eala Duir make the request. She appears more skilled at negotiating with Finnbheara than I."

Grabbing my hair, she pulls my mouth to hers. She tastes of the lemonseed cake she indulged in at Finnbheara's banquet table.

I cover my hands with dewshine and slip them under her dress to cup her delectable breasts. "There will, of course, be the small inconvenience of royal duties."

She lays her hands upon mine to still their attention to her flesh. "Before we get down to business, I'm going to say something because I can." My bond-promised throws her head back and roars to the forest. "I love you, Robálaí Geal."

With those blessed words spoken freely for all to hear, I am overcome with awe and unshakeable passion for the woman who dares to love me. I claim her with all the zeal my princely body has to offer.

After our pleasures, we lie together in the star violets, allowing our bodies respite as Colleen draws spirals and meandering lines across my chest. "You had so much less yummy hair because of your scar. It's all over these sweet Faerie muscles now and as soft as a baby's butt."

"I am pleased you enjoy it."

She rises to look me in the eye. "The scar didn't matter, you know. I would have loved you if your body were one big scar."

I think back to her lips sliding across my blighted chest and smile. "I know, my darling one, and that is dearer to me than you will ever know."

"You know, Faerie man, you can say you love me anytime because I'm going to say it to you a million times a day." She takes a deep breath and lays her palm on my chest. "I need you to say it to me, Robálaí, over and over. I never want to feel the way I did when the geas took hold and you looked at me with dead eyes."

I gather her to me. "I love you." I kiss her as if this is our only purpose as long as flowers bloom in Tír na nÓg.

"I love you." She smiles. "That's two. Did I say a million times a day? That was low-balling it."

"Where does your belief stand on fate, Colleen?"

She chews on her lip. "I was brought up on faith, not fate, but I think Eala and Sion and you and I are pretty damn clear proof that even as crazy and impossible as it might seem, some things—some people—are meant to be." Colleen lays her ear to my chest. "I believe every heart searches for the one who gives it a reason to sing."

She taps her fingertips in time with my heartbeat, whispering, "My Faerie. My Faerie," with every tap.

"Robálaí."

Acacia's sharp hail startles us both. I am extremely displeased by the interruption, but I will not avoid the one to whom I owe my life. "Over here," I call out.

"He—llo," Colleen hisses at me, nodding at my still half-hard cock. "Maybe this is not the best time for a visit."

I rise to greet my former second, now soon to be commander of the Host of a Thousand Wings and pull Colleen to her feet. "It is nothing she has not seen before."

My bond-promised grabs her dress and throws it over her head. It bears suggestive streaks of dewshine lily oil. "Well, this is certainly the last time she's going to see it, no matter how grateful I am to her."

Acacia snorts as she rounds the corner of the cottage and takes in my nakedness. "Will I find you anywhere but on your back from now on, Robálaí?"

"Only if you interrupt us while he's on top," says Colleen, crossing her arms over the nipples clearly outlined through her oil-soaked gown. "Don't take too long. We have to get ready for your brother's fancy do." She storms past Acacia toward the front of the cottage. "I'm going to get you a pair of pants, *my* prince."

My bond-promised's possessiveness may ready my cock anew before Acacia has a chance to say her peace.

I drop my hands to cover myself in respect for my friend. "You come for pieces of Aillil's nest. Apologies, I have not yet had the heart to disturb its remnants to gift to your drakaina." Acacia and I thought adding leaf and branch bearing her mate's scent to Eachna's nest might provide comfort in her sorrow. "How does your dear *péist síoda* fare?"

"She fares well, Robálaí. I have come to request that you delay dismantling the nest. She will desire to inhabit it soon."

I will not deny Acacia's wishes, but I muse at my bond-promised's reaction to having a former lover's dragon sleeping in our bed chamber. "You believe Aillil's burrow will ease her mourning?"

Acacia's soft smile is a contrast to her usually hard countenance. "Soon, her mourning will be supplanted. An egg ripens in her belly."

"Aillil," I whisper through the knot in my throat.

"Aye," she says. "The sire will live on through his hatchling."

A thousand sparks of brilliant silver joy fill my spirit. One day, I shall bond with this offspring of my beloved dragon, and upon its back, whisk Colleen into the sky among starshine and moonglow.

Acacia stares at the tear running down my cheek. "Commander Robálaí Geal, your bond-promised turns your steel to flower fluff." Her gaze drifts lower to where my hands shield my cock, and she laughs. "Perhaps not all your steel."

CHAPTER 41
THE FOX AND THE SWAN

EALA

Finnbheara does have an official palace after all. Not of the conventional stone and turret sort, but something infinitely more wonderful. There are no walls. Mists, trees, vines, and flowers, both delicate and as tall as one of his Fae warriors, meander through his royal property, shaping rooms to his will. When he calls, nature unfolds to please its king.

In a shocking turn of magnanimous hospitality, Finnbheara allowed Sion and me to take full advantage of a sumptuous guest suite last night.

This morning, Colleen stands beside Máthair and me, wearing a wreath of lilac petals and juniper berries on her head to match the ones she made us. My best friend insisted on dressing my grandmother and me as well in white-gold calf-length satin tunics embossed with the vine, leaf, and flower pattern of Finnbheara and Robálaí Geal's royal house.

The brothers, both clad in Fae armor along with Sionnach, who looks pissy as he shrugs and tugs at his new white-gold breastplate, wait in front of an arch woven with branches of rowan, oak, and yew. At the top of its curve, matching the emblem adorning each man's chest, is a huge leaf carved of brilliant silver. The veins running through it shimmer with the spectral hues of the Veil.

Today's ceremony is the one condition Finnbheara requested, or more precisely...demanded, before he agreed to gift me a skimpy portion of his vast supply of *beads of being*. I understand his fierce protection of this Faerie miracle in his keeping that holds the power to create life where it otherwise could not be. Knowing every realm under the stars would have been threatened if Aodh's obsession to possess the *beads of being* had succeeded is chilling.

If I'm honest, Finnbheara's guilt over the appalling plan to trade me for Queen Nuala is why he's giving me the *beads of being* at all. The king ultimately gives Máthair credit for his redemption in the long and twisted tale. Martha O'Dwyer Loho may possess the greatest magic of us all.

I catch Finnbheara gazing at Máthair as if the rest of us don't exist. I suppose their story is no more twisted than the one in *The Wooing of Étaín* and her Faerie travails. At least my grandmother was never turned into a butterfly and swallowed.

That I know of. She's yet to tell Sion and me the full story of her centuries-long dance with ole Finn.

I kiss Colleen's cheek and then Máthair's. The three of us take hands and go together to greet our men.

Even though Sion and I were technically married by St. Kevin, the Monk at Glendalough, the Fae don't acknowledge the human binding ritual of a wedding. Colleen and Robber Bright took Faerie vows in Bráchthine, but that's not the king's idea of a true union either, since it was done under shaky circumstances. And Finnbheara and Máthair...well, this is a first for them.

I was devastated to hear the full tale of Queen Nuala's sacrifice and her death at Aodh's cruel hand. It was initially Robber Bright's brainchild to dangle me in front of Aodh to free the queen for a chance to earn back Finnbheara's favor. Colleen insists her loving Faerie swore an oath to her that I wouldn't be snatched by the God of the Underworld. I'll believe that on the day I see his testimony notarized on a Faerie scroll. It's going to take time and massive Faerie groveling for me to completely forgive either of the royal brothers, but Robber Bright and Finnbheara both love and are loved by the two women I cherish most dearly in my life. I suppose I need to work on my trust issues.

For a fleeting moment, I reflect on two other women without whose unfailing support, this moment may never have happened. If there were such a thing as bridesmaids involved in a Faerie ritual, I would be honored to have included Biddy and Grace by my side.

I settle in for Finnbheara to start a long-winded Sunday sermon version of the sacred rite of a bond-promise, but the king simply holds his hands out to Máthair. Robber or rather Robálaí that he deserves to be called since he's no longer stealing what doesn't belong to him, and Sionnach follow suit. We all kneel before our beloveds in unison. The three men pull identical daggers from their belts, gifts from the king. The silver handles shine with otherworldly vibrancy, and inside each glass blade, the silver flame of Tír na nÓg radiates Fae magic.

Three points are raised. Three fingers tap their sharpened tips. As three tiny beads of blood well on our fingertips, Máthair, Colleen, and I speak in unison.

I don't hear their voices. I gaze into the perfect green glass eyes with a blazing *fánaí* ring around the iris gracing the glorious face of my *anamchara*. We are the only two spirits in this realm of magic and endless time. We have no tears for each other, just clear-eyed joy because we know now there will never be a goodbye.

"Sionnach Loho, soul that calls to mine. I offer you the essence of my life. Take this gift through body into spirit as my vow of bond-promise."

My fox closes his lips around my finger and accepts my heart's blood.

"Eala Duir, soul that calls to mine, I offer you the essence of my life. Take this gift through body into spirit as my vow of bond-promise."

I slowly bring his finger to my lips and accept the precious drop that begins our eternity of love.

The Veil sprites within me spin faster and faster until they are not many but a single stream of light flowing through my touch into Sionnach. His skin shimmers with a thousand tiny sparkles, the very ones I saw dancing through the trees when my fox first introduced me to his Veil forest. Sion's eyes widen as the sprites now dwell within us both, bestowing their blessing upon our Faerie union of souls. Sionnach Loho is not only my husband and *anamchara* but my true partner in the eyes of the Fae. In the depths of my spirit, I've always known this *fánaí*, this selfless man, possessed his own beautiful magic.

To anyone driving past the Loho cottage, seeing a man in Faerie armor, carrying a woman in a Faerie gown through the red wooden door would probably cause an accident. We are extraordinarily shiny.

Note to self, don't wear my Tír na nÓg clothes to Tesco.

Sion gazes at me, his brilliant, foxy curls so long they cover his shoulders. "I can't remember if I've properly carried you over my threshold."

He doesn't put me down, and I don't ask him to. Sionnach Loho can carry me around for as long as his arms hold out. I pull one of his curls and let it spring back. "Who's keeping track?"

I smooth my hand along the side of his gorgeously ruddy cheek as I brush my lips to his, indulging in their soft fullness. He kisses me back gently as if it's the first time he's dared to try.

I run my fingertip along his bottom lip. "I love this." He smiles, giving me a wider path to travel. I switch to his top lip, stroking the twin curves. "And this." I give him another first-date kiss. "You have perfect lips for kissing, Sionnach Loho."

He chuckles. "I'd return the compliment, but I don't hand those out to just any beautiful woman with a fine round Amerrrrican ass."

We kiss again as chastely as he might have kissed a wife at their wedding back in his day in front of a church full of neighbors.

"What do you think?" I ask, nuzzling my nose against his jaw. "Will I do?"

"Oh, you'll do fine." Our next kiss is not so chaste, and each after that is less and less so. With me still cradled in Sionnach's arms, he walks us into our bedroom...in our Loho cottage...in our home.

It doesn't take long for our shiny Faerie clothing to be in a heap on the floor, except for one small, round gold box stamped with a silver leaf that sits on a shelf next to the bed.

As we lay naked on our mattress of lady's bedstraw, facing each other, I relearn every contour of his muscles sculpted from a life of nurturing rich Irish soil and blessed by the salty breezes rising from the Atlantic over magnificent sea cliffs. "Your chest is broad...cozy...perfection."

My touch trickles through the russet patch of hair on his chest, along the silky trail from his belly down to the tangled thatch between his legs.

He groans when I tickle my way over the coarse fuzz covering his thighs, popping his mouth off the side of my neck. "If it's my chest you were complimenting, I think you've lost your way, Swan."

I kiss the center of his chest but let my hand continue its travels to his more intimate places. "I'll never be lost with you, my fox."

"There's such a thing as not rushing, which you're very welcome not to do, *anamchara*, since we've now got more time than any star in the heavens, but it's another thing to make a man start praying to Faerie gods for permission to get on with loving his wife."

I roll us so I'm lying on top of him and kiss him in a way that most definitely would not be proper in front of a church full of his nineteenth-century neighbors. His hungry eyes tell me my fox will never have his fill of me. I'm every bit as ravenous for him.

His hands slide past my hips to his favorite Amerrrrican bottom.

"I'd like to hear that prayer," I say, nipping his shoulder.

He guides us back onto our sides. We look into each other's eyes.

Sionnach curves a hand around his mouth and then shouts to the roof. "Hello, you fine Faerie gods and goddesses who thought you'd heard every story Tír na nÓg has to tell. You missed one. I'll be sharing it now for your permission to get on with loving this Faerie wife of mine."

He kisses my nose and shifts into his storyteller cadence I so adore. "There once was a fox who wandered the land, living an empty, foolish life until the day a swan made him look to the sky where true magic waited."

Sion lifts a strand of my feathery white-blond hair, letting it flutter through his fingers. "When she spread her glorious wings and the sun kissed her gold-speckled feathers with its radiant light, the fox heard the three notes of his soulsong. He sang their beauteous melody for all to hear."

He kisses me long and slow. The Veil's fragrance of lemongrass and spearmint suffuses the air of the cottage with its gentle, loving peace. "Time itself stopped just long enough to marvel at a love neither Fae nor fate would ever have the power to steal away from the foolish fox and his wondrous swan." He points skyward to the invisible Fae deities. "Surely, that's a tale worthy enough to earn your blessing."

We kiss again with quiet passion. I break the kiss with a slow glide of my lips against his and reach behind me to lift one small iridescent pebble from the gold box. As lovely as the Veil, the small bead shines with every color the world has ever known and some it hasn't yet created. I let the *bead of being* roll around on the open palm I hold between our bodies.

"Sing me your soulsong, my foolish fox."

To the sound of Sionnach's gorgeous voice, we release the essences of our spirits to rise together and invite the magic of this *bead of being* to join our song. As I make love with my *anamchara*, my soulmate, my bond-promised, my husband, every realm under the stars sings with us.

EPILOGUE
THE NEXT WANDERER

SINÉAD

Uncle Bobbo and I pull into the wide paved drive on the side of the Loho family cottage where I grew up. Uncle Dale pulls in right behind us and unloads my suitcases along with a collapsible wagon full of groceries.

"Better shore up your nerve, Sinéad," says Bobbo, resting his hands on what's left of his belly after Uncle Dale forced him on a diet of more veg than curry chips for his ticker's sake. I adore my two white-haired, honorary uncles from Rowan Bend. All my life, they've spent every Christmas with my family, and Bobbo's stories are almost as good as all the folk and Faerie tales my parents know.

I give him a suspicious look that he swears comes straight from Ma. "Why?"

Dale grunts. "We haven't had a chance for a pop-in since your brother, Robin, and his lady used the cottage as a home base for their wandering about this summer."

Och, my wandering brother who'd rather sleep under the stars or in an old cave than stay long in a bed.

I shake my head. "Grand. There's probably congealed milk and Tír na nÓg knows what..." I say, using one of Da's favorite terms, "...growing on the cheese."

Bobbo squints, running an eye over the fields of the Loho farm that Ma and Da pay fellas to keep thriving while my folks are on their grand adventure with Auntie Colleen and Uncle Robin to see the world. It's been going on two years since I felt Da's stubbly kiss on my cheek or had Ma fuss over my unruly red curls. I miss 'em something fierce.

"You'll be fine out here on your own, eh?" asks Uncle Bobbo.

"Emm, apart from the disaster waiting for me inside, I'll be perfect." I nod at the suitcases fit to bursting with books, notes, and whatnot for the dissertation I'm here to write with no distractions.

"Fine, but we'll be expecting you for Sunday dinner," Bobbo says, shaking a finger at me.

Uncle Dale goes on fretting. "If the car gives you any trouble, ring us." He throws his arms around me and rocks us back and forth.

"We should see her inside," says Uncle Bobbo.

"No need," I say, giving my jolly uncle a hug. "I'll spare you from the ruin of Robin Loho and his lady."

"Fine, but we're not driving off until you open the door and give a thumbs up," says Bobbo.

"That I can do." I smile. "See you Sunday."

They pile into Bobbo's car, leaving Dale's for me. My clunker died last month in Galway, and I haven't taken the time to replace it. Part of me is waiting for Da to come home and do the looking and buying for me. I'm a Da's girl to be sure, sealed when my name got the first part of his, Sionny's Sínny he calls me. Ma would bicker that I'd got just as much of her name with our matching 'ea,' but Da would pinch her arse and that would be that.

I navigate the wagon and my smallest suitcase around front and unlock the red door that Robin and I always called a Faerie door when we were kids because it looked quaint and old-fashioned next to our friends' places. Once I push it open so the uncles can see I'm fine to go in, they roll down the road, waving like mad and honking.

I'm relieved there's no notable stink coming from inside. A good sign that.

"You're looking well, Alfie," I say to the white poplar nearly as tall as the thatched roof, whose leaves and branches block the kitchen window. I pat the green triangles covering her bark and wonder why Da never cut her low to let more sunlight into the cottage. My father insists you can't chop a tree with a name.

I peer up at the thatch that looks fresher than my last visit. Ma and Da get a bit from the government to maintain an authentic look to the roof. Being a budding archeologist myself, I appreciate keeping the past alive. I've been accused more than once of speaking like I was born in the wrong century. It's the way Da talks, and I've always loved the sound of it.

"Yeah, fine new thatch," I say and salute the cottage. I can't imagine the home place with any other topping, although pure authenticity is a bit of a muddle with the rooms Da added for Robin and me onto the original house my several times great-grandparents built back in the day.

I try to call Ma again to tell her I'm holing up here for a while since Da is shit at answering his mobile. My attempt goes to message. Seems they've both gotten shit at answering calls since they took off. They did warn Robin and me to think of them as *off the grid* and to rely on the uncles if there was a need. I'm not grand with the separation, but I'm hoping it'll end soon enough.

After hauling everything inside, I flip on the lights. Robin and his lady left the place in order after all.

"Sure feels empty with only one Loho here," I announce to the room. I'll make Sunday after next dinner here for the uncles to add laughter and sparkle to the quiet.

I start to wheel the suitcase through the living room to my bedroom in the back of the cottage. I'd best grab the others inside before the pattering of rain threatening to visit starts up. On my way back to the door, a white envelope propped against the salt and pepper shakers on the kitchen table catches my eye. My name is written across the front in Ma's curvy writing.

"What's this then?" I ask, opening the envelope. A simple silver ring plinks onto the tabletop. I frown and pick it up. The words engraved on the band stop my heart.

Teacht orm.

I know these words like I know my name.

Find me.

"What in the name of Finnbheara's arse…" I say using one of Da's more colorful phrases, "…is Ma's wedding ring doing here?"

Just then, the wind blows the door open. I go to close it and nearly drop

Ma's ring when I'm met with an incredible sight. My brother and I have been raised with stories encouraging us to take a second look at things we might not believe are true at first glance, and that fear should always take a back seat to wonder.

And above all—sometimes stories are not just stories.

That being so, in the fading light of dusk, I walk toward the shimmering wall of rainbow light waiting right outside my red front door.

Thank you for reading! Did you enjoy? Please add your review because nothing helps an author more and encourages readers to take a chance on a book than a review.

And don't miss more from Leslie O'Sullivan with PINK GUITARS AND FALLING STARS. Turn the page for a sneak peek!

Also be sure to sign up for the City Owl Press newsletter to receive notice of all book releases!

SNEAK PEEK OF PINK GUITARS AND FALLING STARS

You only get one parachute. There's no point packing two for a B.A.S.E. jump since you'll be pavement art before the second chute blossoms.

"Justin!"

Startled by a bellow from my jump leader/uncle, Timmer MacKenzie, my toe jerks to a stop half an inch above the trigger pedal of my launcher. Is his gray matter shredded, distracting me during a safety check? There's no chute on my back. One accidental tap on the business end of this launcher, and I'll be eye to eye with the flock of seagulls patrolling the Hollywood skies. I retreat onto the non-ballistic end of my perch. Peering over the edge of the Rampion Records Tower, I analyze the antics of the wind.

"Join us," Unc calls, teeth clenched in a P.R. smile. He hosts a cluster of reporters near the center of the circular roof. "Meet the rising star of the Slinging Seven."

Their faces morph into a collective portrait of panic as I leap more dramatically than necessary from launcher to the terra firma of the rooftop. After a salute to the Hollywood sign, a photo op my uncle will appreciate, I join the party. Pre-jump interviews are not my happy place, but keeping a smile on Timmer's face is essential. He leads our B.A.S.E. jump troop, giving the green light for my carcass to launch off skyscrapers, bridges, and cliffs in a wing suit.

"This Rampion Records Tower may rival Mount Olympus for acceptable jump altitude," Timmer tells the press jam sandwich. "Even so, I believe in enhancing the safety zone for my lads."

I sweep an arm across the roof. "Thus, the launchers."

"Your latest exhibitions of low altitude B.A.S.E. jumps have raised serious concerns," says a fresh-out-of-journalism-school reporter. He rocks a Channel Six pin on the lapel of a blazer clearly tailored for someone else. We get his type all the time: low man on the news roster, usually stuck with covering mudslides or C-list celebrity screw-ups.

I grunt at the question. Timmer's a walking archive of aerodynamics. His B.A.S.E. jump designs adhere to a superhuman canon of safety. Even Unc can't control the wreath of clouds descending on the tower. Humidity makes trickier conditions. My bangs congeal into a sweaty clump. Twenty-three is too young to die when you have plans, and I have plans.

"To you, B.A.S.E. jumping is an extreme sport. To me, it's a science." Timmer slings an arm around my shoulder. "Would I risk my own nephew's life?"

A grandfatherly dude slides square-framed sunglasses to the end of a nose in serious need of a good hair plucking. "Come on, Mr. MacKenzie, that kid can't be eighteen."

I wince at the familiar speculation my youthful image always dredges up. Satan's roadies have prepped a new circle of hell for Timmer's perpetuation of the lie about me being eighteen. My B.A.S.E. jumping talents at twenty-three are PDG – pretty damn great—but a fresh out of high-school dude rocking my moves is prodigy wonder boy territory, great P.R. fodder.

I keep my lip zipped over the deception. I'm not going to lie, it does not suck being a prodigy wonder boy.

Unc spins me to display the product emblems plastered all over my banana-colored wing suit. "Endorsements like these don't come from launching children into the sky. Justin jumps one-hundred percent legally."

The reporter's skepticism settles at the edges of his mouth. Metallic coating on his sunglasses turn my gray eyes silver as I catch my reflection. The gloaming breeze plucks strands of my tawny mane free from the generous layer of product I always apply before a jump. I'll have to retame those suckers to restore my roguishly hot vibe instead of the young and soft look Timmer prefers. I'd give my right nut to have a growth spurt on the spot. Sadly, thanks to MacKenzie short man genes, there probably aren't any in my future.

A gust of wind blows the press a tiptoe closer to the curved edge of the roof. Timmer and I hold our ground with matching "no big thing" expressions.

A babe in a raspberry-colored lady suit pushes toward me, eyes bulging with concern. Twitchy fingers alight on my shoulder. Next to my banana wingsuit, we're a fruit salad. Here comes the *concerned auntie* vibe.

"Justin, why take risks B.A.S.E. jumping with the Slinging Seven Troupe even for someone as enchanting as Zeli?"

I bite back a groan at the mention of the pop queen.

"Is glorifying her platinum record worth your life?"

Truth rumbles in my throat. *Yes, ma'am, B.A.S.E. jumping is worth the moon. It got me to Hollywood, the land of my music dreams. Dreams that will free me from Timmer's whims so I can make my own destiny.*

Timmer's glare scorches a hole in my suit, cueing the trained monkey answer he expects.

I open my arms to the clouds. "Who doesn't want to fly?" Every person on this roof does. I see it in the way their eyes brighten.

My stomach loops into a knot. Unc may piss himself when his prize canary asks to go AWOL. I've jumped off everything Timmer asked of me on our jiggy pathway around the country to make it here. My gaze drifts to the Hollywood Sign as I press toes into the roof of Rampion Records, the touchstone by which all music greatness is measured.

Tonight, this bird will fly off the Rampion Tower. Tomorrow, I dive into the audition for Rampion's annual singing competition, The Summer Number One. It's the U.S. Open of music, amateurs vs. pros, where Rampion Records dangles a chance for nobodies like me to go mic to mic with their current stable of rock stars. According to the Rampion P.R. machine – *Even the little people in this world have a shot at the Summer Number One dream.* This ammie is going to kick some serious pro ass and score a Rampion Records contract. I've got everything I need for the audition: demo tracks, my guitar, ass-hugging black jeans, and a sexy aviator jacket.

For the last five years, in every crappy rent-a-room the Slinging Seven have crashed, I've done dozens of online music courses. I study. I practice. I'm ready.

Unc laughs at one of the reporters he's chatting up, and I see Ma's smile here on the rooftop. Our signature MacKenzie smile packs serious wattage. I should know, I've busted it out often enough to sway, play, and dazzle females of the species.

Once I grab the top spot in the Summer Number One, my pile of gold for winning will be enough to snag my own digs here in L.A., the last place I remember Ma smiling. The cold burn of loneliness flares when I think of her and wonder if she's safe.

Clouds thicken as I watch the sun dip into the Pacific Ocean. I ignore a stitch of concern at the base of my neck as the jump difficulty ticks up a notch and think in my language of future Justin merch.

T-shirt moment: Music Dreams Sucker Punch Death.

Channel Six pushes in front of his colleagues. "Justin, does Zeli have a lock on the top pro spot in the Summer Number One?"

Lady Suit bumps her shoulder into mine. "Is Zeli your dream girl?"

My lips twist into a frown. Zeli is my nightmare.

Timmer digs his fist into my back, my cue to fix my pissy face. I manage to upgrade to a grimace dressed as a smile. By their winks and snickers, the reporters take my tension as embarrassment. I'd like to water cannon them all off the roof. I'm entitled to a dream girl, but it will never be the plastic diva with her bubblegum diluted pop crap. That chickadee is an affront to everything I love about music.

Unc hasn't run out of bluster. "It's an honor for the Slinging Seven to be part of Zeli's platinum record celebration."

My temple throbs. I'm more than half nuts to risk a concrete sandwich for that over-hyped female commodity with a pink guitar.

Don't stop now. Keep reading with your copy of PINK GUITARS AND FALLING STARS

And find more from Leslie O'Sullivan at
www.leslieosullivanwrites.com

Want even more from Leslie O'Sullivan? Read PINK GUITARS AND FALLING STARS and be sure to check out all the details on her website at www.leslieosullivanwrites.com

Zeli's signature pop diva sound and image are nothing short of magical—literally. Her fame comes with hidden costs, a curse that could ruin her voice forever.

Aspiring indie musician, Justin MacKenzie, is determined to kick it to the top of the Rampion Records' Summer Number One professional vs. amateur singing competition.

The favorite to beat in the annual televised contest is none other than the label's smoking hot superstar, Zeli, whose crazy extensions flow the length of a football field. Those ridiculous extensions, coupled with her bubblegum brand of pop, are an affront to everything Justin loves about music until a stolen kiss blazes into a romantic encounter.

Once inside Zeli's world, Justin discovers things are not as they seem. In their quest to allow the real Zeli, to step into the spotlight, the pair must confront the mysterious force behind the dazzle of Rampion's success. If these star-crossed lovers can't rally their own magic to defeat the darkness, they will lose everything—including each other.

Please sign up for the City Owl Press newsletter for chances to win special subscriber-only contests and giveaways as well as receiving information on upcoming releases and special excerpts.

All reviews are **welcome** and **appreciated**. Please consider leaving one on your favorite social media and book buying sites.

For books in the world of romance and speculative fiction that embody Innovation, Creativity, and Affordability, check out City Owl Press at www. cityowlpress.com.

ACKNOWLEDGMENTS

Huge hugs to all the readers whose support, feedback and enthusiasm make writing stories a delight. To the Bookstagrammers, Tiktokkers, Bookthreaders, MTMC tour hosts, Storygram tour hosts, bloggers, and podcasters who've been wonderfully generous with their support in spreading the word of this series.

Super loud shout out to my ARC/Street Team, A Company of Readers, who are ceaseless in their dedication, and to the super Sav, who holds my hand through all things promotion and beyond. You are stardust.

All the gratitude in the world for the magical talents of the artists, Felicity Munroe and Tim Campbell who bring Eala, Sionnach, Robber Bright and the whole cast of the *Fae Destiny* off the page and into the world in the audiobooks. Your artistry, investment, hours and hours of work, and generosity are seen and appreciated. You fill me with awe.

So much appreciation to everyone in the nest at City Owl Press, especially Tina, Yelena, Lisa, the copyeditors that add that dash of polish, MiblArt for those amazing covers, and my fellow authors who never fail to impress. I don't have the words to express my thankfulness for your support and giving my stories a place in this world.

Another helping of "you amaze me" to the character artists who have contributed their gorgeous work to this series: @lulybot, @Shayndyl_art, @artsiidaisy, and @readersleisure

Massive thanks to the wonderful folks I met in Ireland that helped me paint the pictures in this story: Orla, the tour guide of Clew Bay who made Granuaile O'Malley come alive for me. Kate who led me to Humphrey, the expert who took me trekking around Clare Island to see the haunts of the famous pirate queen. Danny and Geraldine for taking pity on a drenched tourist and offering a ride to Westport. The more than gracious guide at

Westport House that allowed me to take a quick peek inside when I showed up minutes before closing. The fascinating Kevin from Bunratty Castle Folk Park for sharing wonderful insights into the O'Sullivan clan and times past. The patient station master who helped me figure out how to unravel a journey via train and bus from Galway to Belfast. The docents at the Ulster Museum who taught me what my name would look like in ancient Ogham script and pointed out some truly scary weaponry. The lifesaving, Peter, who guided this lost soul back to her Belfast hotel. The magnificent flock of swans next to Dunguaire Castle that were a sight of pure inspiration.

Special thanks to the intrepid Lynn and Melissa who allowed me to drag them through castles, caves, and graveyards on research trips to Ireland for this trilogy as well as surviving my "other side of the road" driving.

Boundless love to my family and dear friends, you are my heartstrings: Cameron, Melissa, Rich, John, Pinkie, Elizabeth, Robert, Sidney, Chuck, Heidi, Caity, Ben, Noah, Joe, Sandra, Diane, Flo, Laurie, Lisa, Sarah, Julie, Tina, Janine, Evelyn, Dana, Rob, Tiffany, Gwynneth, Trillian, and the Pub Club.

Let's connect: https://linktr.ee/LeslieOSullivanWrites

ABOUT THE AUTHOR

LESLIE O'SULLIVAN is the award-winning author of *Fae Destiny*, a romantasy series that explores the collision between the real world and the Irish Faerie realm. Her *Rockin' Fairy Tales* romantasy stories shine a new spotlight on favorite fairy tales set against the backdrop of a fictional Hollywood music scene. The completed *Behind the Scenes* contemporary romcom series peeks into the off-camera sizzle of a wildly popular Irish television drama. She's a UCLA Bruin with a BA and MFA from their Department of Theater where she also taught for years on the design faculty. Her tenure in the world of television was

mainly as the assistant art director on "It's Garry Shandling's Show." Leslie is a voracious reader who loves to connect with other book lovers and indulge her fangirl side at cons.

www.leslieosullivanwrites.com

facebook.com/leslie.osullivanauthor

instagram.com/leslieosullivanwrites

tiktok.com/@leslieosullivanwrites

ABOUT THE PUBLISHER

City Owl Press is a cutting edge indie publishing company, bringing the world of romance and speculative fiction to discerning readers.

Escape Your World. Get Lost in Ours!

www.cityowlpress.com

facebook.com/YourCityOwlPress
x.com/cityowlpress
instagram.com/cityowlbooks
pinterest.com/cityowlpress